SOMEONE SOMEWHERE

To Jane
with my best wishes

Dallin B...

SOMEONE
SOMEWHERE

DEBBIE BALDWIN

gatekeeper press
Tampa, Florida

The content associated with this book is the sole work and responsibility of the author. Gatekeeper Press had no involvement in the generation of this content.

SOMEONE SOMEWHERE
Published by **Gatekeeper Press**
7853 Gunn Hwy., Suite 209
Tampa, FL 33626
www.GatekeeperPress.com

The cover design and editorial work for this book are entirely the product of the author. Gatekeeper Press did not participate in and is not responsible for any aspect of these elements.

Library of Congress Control Number: 2024932633

ISBN (hardcover): 9781662947599
ISBN (paperback): 9781662947605
eISBN: 9781662947612

For the adventurous readers.
Thank you for believing.

CAST OF CHARACTERS

Miles Buchanan
Height 6'3"
Hair color: Dark brown
Eye color: Brown

Miles is Tox's twin brother. He works as a fixer, helping the rich and powerful keep their reputations intact. Scarred by a brutal childhood, Miles is emotionally distant and isolated. The only person who can awaken his passion is the impossibly beautiful and daring thief, Clara Gautreau. Read their adventure in Book 6, *Someone Somewhere*.

Clara Gautreau
Height: 5'7"
Hair color: Blonde
Eye color: Mediterranean blue

To most who know her, Clara is a diligent Art History student at Columbia University. Her secret identity is the infamous art thief, The Lynx. Clara has always loved the complicated and distant Miles but knows he will never return her feelings. When she steps into a trap, Clara needs Miles's help to escape the clutches of the ruthless Lucien Kite. Read their adventure in Book 6, *Someone Somewhere*.

Nathan Bishop

Height: 6'2"

Hair color: Chestnut

Eye color: Green

Head of Bishop Security. Former Naval Intelligence Officer. Consumed by the childhood abduction of his neighbor, Emily Webster, Nathan dedicated his life to helping those in need. Read their story in Book 1, *False Front*.

Emily Webster Bishop

Height: 5'6"

Hair color: Honey Blonde

Eye color: Violet

After being abducted as a child, Emily lived under the false identity of Emma Porter but never forgot the kind boy who had lived next door, Nathan Bishop. She rediscovered Nathan as an adult while Nathan helped protect her from a continuing threat. Read their story in book 1, *False Front*.

Miller "Tox" Buchanan

Height: 6'5"

Hair color: Dark brown (buzzed very short)

Eye color: Brown

Tox is Nathan's number two at Bishop Security and a former Navy SEAL. After Emily's friend, reporter Calliope Garland, got in over her head with an investigation, the six-foot, five-inch warrior came to her aid. Read their story in Book 2, *Illicit Intent*.

Calliope Garland Buchanan

Height 5'8"

Hair color: Black

Eye color: Ice blue

Now a Bishop Security operative, Calliope Garland worked as a reporter for The Harlem Sentry. While investigating a sketchy hedge fund manager, Calliope found herself in possession of valuable financial data and a priceless, stolen work of art. Tox protected Calliope from the threat. Read their story in Book 2, *Illicit Intent*.

Camilo Canto

Height: 6'0"

Hair color: Dark brown

Eye color: Gold

Former SEAL and current Bishop Security operator, Cam worked undercover for the CIA. Last year, an old enemy abducted Cam and brought him to Mallorca, where he took on a drug cartel and joined beautiful archaeologist Evangeline Cole on a treasure hunt. Read their story in Book 3, *Buried Beneath*.

Evangeline Cole

Height 5'6"

Hair color: Caramel brown

Eye color: Caramel brown

Evan is an archaeologist who met Cam Canto while on a dig in the caves of Mallorca. She immediately fell for the gorgeous former SEAL. Evan now lives in Beaufort and is continuing her studies. Read their story in book 3, *Buried Beneath*.

Finn McIntyre
Height: 6'2"
Hair: Sandy brown
Eyes: Cobalt blue

After being captured on a SEAL mission, Finn was tortured for three days, leaving the right side of his face terribly scarred. Bitter and isolated, Finn left the Navy and joined the CIA. After burning his bridges with The Agency and alienating his friends, Finn takes off to try to get his life back. Read their haunting love story in Book 4, *Past Purgatory*.

Charlotte "Twitch" Devlin
Height 5'4"
Hair color: Copper red
Eye color: Sky blue

The Bishop Security cyber guru is a tech genius. Nobody knows exactly what happened between Twitch and Finn McIntyre, but it has left both their hearts damaged. Read their haunting love story in Book 4, *Past Purgatory*.

Jonah "Steady" Lockhart
Height: 6'1"
Hair color: Sandy blond
Eye color: Sage green

His SEAL brothers call him Steady because of his unflappable nature. It's not until Twitch's college friend, the pink-haired Very Valentine, moves in next door that Steady finds himself decidedly unsteady. Read their love story in Book 5, *Chemical Capture*.

Verity "Very" Valentine
Height: 5'6"
Hair color: Fuschia
Eye color: Marble gray

Very is Twitch's best friend from college. She recently moved next door to Steady and works as a chemist at a private lab. When she learns of Steady's calm reputation, she can't resist riling him. Read their love story in Book 5, *Chemical Capture*.

Leo "Ren" Jameson
Height 5'11"
Hair color: Dark brown
Eye color: Hazel

The Teamguys call him the Renaissance Man because Ren has an encyclopedic knowledge of topics ranging from Astrophysics to Zoology. For years, Ren has been captivated by Sofria Kirk, a brilliant CIA analyst, but he keeps her at a distance, fearing she is too young.

Sofria Kirk
Height 5'3"
Hair Color: Mahogany brown
Eye color: Dark brown

CIA analyst Sofria Kirk has helped the team out on numerous occasions. The exotic beauty has a rare gift for detecting patterns, and the CIA has put her skills to use. While she is highly effective behind a desk, Sofria dreams of going into the field.

Andrew "Chat" Dunlap
Height: 6'0"
Hair color: Black, shaved bald
Eye color: Dark brown

Chat is one of the original SEAL Team members at Bishop Security. Nicknamed facetiously for his taciturn nature, the quiet African American possesses an almost uncanny sixth sense.

CHAPTER ONE

September 25
The Outskirts of Paris, France

Shrouded in darkness, Clara Gautreau dangled from the rappelling wire fifteen feet above the warehouse's cement floor. The timer on the military watch circling her wrist clicked down the seconds. Above her, the vent cover of the air shaft hung from two screws raining dust over her head. The only noise was the gentle whirr from the zip line as she lowered herself. The men's size ten boots silently touched the ground: the tread and the lifts added three inches to her height. The padding under her clothes added heft. A patch of skin peeked through the intentional tear at the top of her ski mask. These were dangerous people she was robbing. If everything went to plan, they would be looking for a short, bald man.

The art restoration room was a temperature-controlled warehouse monitored with security cameras. Because the pieces were frequently moved and touched, no alarms were connected to individual paintings. Rather, the building itself had been secured with a state-of-the-art system. Even the wide air shafts that ensured proper ventilation had motion and thermal sensors—except for the duct Clara accessed from the roof. She had created a dummy email from the lead art restorer, complaining that a bird had nested in the shaft and was constantly triggering the alarm. The security company agreed to disengage the motion sensors until the problem was resolved.

Entering from the roof also gave Clara access to the building's generator. If necessary, she could cut the power, disabling the electronic locks that sealed the room. She never orchestrated a theft without a backup plan.

When her feet touched the floor, Clara checked the timer. The green glow of the watch dial was the only light: *three minutes, twelve seconds.*

Stolen from a Jewish family by the Nazis during World War II, the painting, Renoir's *Girl with a Sunflower*, had vanished amid rumors of fires and shipwrecks. Then, in 1964, a British diplomat saw it hanging in the dining room of an Argentinian aristocrat and asked about its provenance. A week after the inquiry, the portrait disappeared again, finally resurfacing in a black-market auction where a notorious financier, Lucien Kite, purchased it for forty-three million dollars.

Lucien Kite.

Clara had been taken aback when she saw the name of the buyer. Kite was infamous in financial circles. He was the number two man at a firm caught running one of the biggest Ponzi schemes in Wall Street history. Lucien Kite had turned informant and ratted out his boss. Somehow, Kite's deal with the Feds had landed him with hundreds of millions of dollars and the thanks of grateful law enforcement.

The scandal, however, was not the reason Clara knew Kite. She had robbed him once before. Kite diversified his ill-gotten gains—blood diamonds, looted antiquities, stolen art; he seemed to relish purchasing items that had caused suffering. Clara had been happy to return the favor by stealing a Matisse from his summer home.

Now, she was going to relieve him of his latest acquisition.

The first stop for *Girl with a Sunflower* after eight decades of questionable storage was this unscrupulous French art restorer known for his dubious ethics.

The original owners had been murdered at Auschwitz, but the young subject of the painting had survived and escaped to the U.S. She was ninety-three now. Clara, a graduate student, had heard her speak at a Columbia University art history seminar. This inspiring woman had been robbed of something precious and meaningful. More than a valuable masterpiece, this painting symbolized all that had been taken in the Holocaust.

Luckily, Clara was a thief.

More accurately, she was a *returner*. There was no question as to who legally owned *Girl with a Sunflower*. It was simply a matter of locating the work of art. Her research and investigation led Clara to this restoration facility located in a secluded area north of Paris.

Clara paused for a moment. Standing in the center of the expansive space, she listened. She could hear the muffled conversation of two of the guards. Above her, a plane flew over, beginning its descent into Charles de Gaul. Inside the building, it was silent. Technology could be circumvented; humans were another matter. The guard stationed in this room left once an hour for about seven minutes to have a cigarette with one of the men patrolling outside. Avoiding the exterior guards and breaking into the air shaft to access the restoration room had left her just enough time.

Switching on the headlamp strapped around the ski mask, Clara turned to the center of the darkened space. Three empty easels stood in the center of the room, surrounded by long, paint-stained tables littered with chemicals and tools. A fourth easel held a small painting covered with a linen sheet. Clara's brow furrowed beneath her mask. It was strange that only one piece of art was sitting out. According to her research, at any given time, this criminal enterprise was smuggling, repairing, and even forging dozens of works.

Outside, one of the guard dogs barked.

Clara had one minute and fifty-two seconds to secure *Girl with a Sunflower* and get out of the warehouse. The air in the room charged, and a knot formed in her chest. Something wasn't right. She lifted the sheet, and some of her fear dissipated. The Renoir was perched on the easel, luminous even in the darkness. Her misgivings eased as she imagined returning the masterpiece to its rightful owner.

Clara had just gripped the ornate frame when she heard the heavy, creaking thud of a lever being thrown, and one after the next, the fluorescent ceiling lights illuminated the room.

CHAPTER TWO

September 25
Dordogne, France

The man known simply as Reynard had earned a well-deserved reputation over the years as a procurer of the priceless and unattainable. Unencumbered by legality or judgment, Reynard found pieces for his clients, ranging from valuable paintings and rare jewels to ancient artifacts and obscure collectors' items. If it could be found, purchased, or stolen, Reynard could acquire it. It appeared, however, that there was one thing Reynard could not secure:

Time.

After thanking his doctor for the unsurprising news, he hung up the phone.

Reynard was dying.

He gazed out the window to the expansive grounds beyond. Funny how the precious art decorating the walls gave him less pleasure than the old rope-and-plank swing suspended from the limb of the big oak.

In his long life, Reynard had known great love, and he had known great loss. Four decades ago, the death of his beloved Annette had turned his heart to stone. For years, there was only work; there were only *things*. It had been a satisfactory existence.

Then, one sunny spring day after a meeting with a particularly unsavory black market exporter in Paris, Reynard had rescued a young girl, a street urchin, from the clutches of a goon. He neither wanted nor needed a dependent, but the way the child had clung to him, the way she had so willingly trusted him to help, he had no choice. Reynard would never admit it, but the fiery waif with her Mediterranean-blue eyes and golden-blonde hair instantly captured his heart. He was hardly cut out for fatherhood, but considering the child's alternative, he took her in.

Clara.

Reynard had never been one to believe in fate or forces in the universe—he had cursed God when his wife died. Nevertheless, he couldn't help but wonder if some mystical force had sent Clara to him.

Every day was filled with surprise and delight as he watched the little ruffian blossom. Even as a child, Clara was an exquisite beauty, but far more interesting to Reynard was her penchant for trickery. Many a night, Reynard would come to dinner to find an item from his private safe on his plate. He would examine the rare coin or the watch while Clara sat innocently across from him, prattling on about her dislike of her English tutor or the ducklings she saw in the pond. Reynard had burst out laughing when one of the exterior guards complained Clara had dangled from a tree limb, slipped into the gatehouse, and repositioned all the security cameras to various animal habitats throughout the property.

Concerned for her safety, Reynard had instructed Clara to choose a surname that didn't connect her to him—she hadn't known her original one. She had instantly been drawn to art as a child, and Reynard had taken her to every major museum. Transfixed by the John Singer Sargeant portrait, *Madam X*, Clara had chosen the last name of the painting's subject, Gautreau. She wanted for nothing, but their bond was not cemented by materialism or spoiling. Clara became his daughter, playing chess, taking long walks, and discussing life. She was a charming thief, and Reynard, despite his repeated scoldings, couldn't have been more proud.

She had breathed life into his comatose soul.

Reynard backed the wheelchair up and circled the desk, moving out the French doors to the slate terrace—the pant leg of his amputated limb pinned neatly at his knee. Autumn would soon arrive, bringing a bonfire of scarlet and gold to the property.

Most of the home had been closed off. Reynard had no use for many of the rooms. These days, he confined his existence to his office, the library, his bedroom, and the kitchen. The housekeeper, Mrs. Trovik, lived in the village but had converted an old servant's room into an office to manage household expenses. So, of the eighty-three rooms in the estate, Reynard made use of five.

As a child, Clara ran through the mansion like a feral cat, exploring every nook and cranny. Years after she had left for school, Mrs. Trovik would find stashes of books and trinkets in hidden cubbies. Reynard hadn't even known about a secret room behind a sliding wall panel. Clara had discovered it during one of her scurries.

Clara's antics had evolved over the years. While Reynard openly disapproved of her hobby, he secretly adored it (and if he had a call to invite the world's best safe cracker or foremost expert on high-tech alarms to the estate for a meeting or informal meal, so be it.). He worried as any parent would, but whenever Clara returned a stolen painting or recovered a lost heirloom, Reynard couldn't help but beam with pride.

Despite his influence, regardless of the blood on his hands, Clara was a do-gooder. She was also fearless—except when it came to her own happiness. Perhaps being surrounded by so much need as a child imprinted this calling to help. Whatever the reason, finding joy in making others whole had replaced her own contentment. The true treasure of life was within her grasp, but Clara never reached for it. He wanted to give her that more than he wanted to live. But like any complexity of human nature, the problem wasn't simple.

Reynard knew what he wanted for Clara. He just needed to figure out the how.

CHAPTER THREE

September 25
The Outskirts of Paris, France

Clara slowly turned from the easel. Men in loose-fitting military attire lined the walls, each holding a rifle trained on her. Their faces betrayed nothing, but their stance indicated a readiness to kill.

The heavy door opened with a groan. A man stepped into the room, escorted by more armed guards. Above her, one of the fluorescent tubes was improperly connected or on its last legs; it flickered and hummed. The man stepped forward, his face shifting in the changing light alternating between man and ghoul. Lucien Kite stopped twenty feet in front of her. He was an unattractive man—mid-fifties with wiry black hair and a crooked nose. A custom suit peeked out from beneath his cashmere overcoat. His smile chilled her blood. An image of this man holding a crowbar flashed in her mind. He may have been wearing the right clothes with the facade of civility, but Clara knew from her research Lucien Kite was no gentleman—he was a gangster at heart.

"Ah, the infamous Lynx," Kite said. "It's an apt moniker. You are a man of stealth, agility, and cunning."

Clara blew out a breath, feeling a modicum of relief that Kite didn't know her identity. Or her gender. She stood silently, waiting for him to continue. The soles of his wingtips ground against the sandy cement as he stepped closer—the sound combined with his menace, setting her nerves on edge.

"You've angered a lot of people, some of whom reached out to me. More importantly, fuckhead, you've angered me." Lucien Kite smoothed the velveteen lapels of his topcoat as if to regain his air of courtesy.

"I knew *Girl with a Sunflower* would be too tempting to pass up. I dropped the hints, revealing tidbits of information with all the elements to lure The Lynx."

Clara wanted to scream at her gullibility. The whole thing was a setup. She had become so confident in her abilities, so skilled in her methods, she hadn't done the proper due diligence researching the sale and provenance of the piece.

One thing Clara did do, however, was plan for contingencies. So, she focused on her captor, every movement and every overpronounced syllable indicating a man trying to convey an image that was not his true essence.

Lucien Kite rounded her, brushing her shoulder with his own, forcing Clara to sidestep. She fought the urge to cover her nose as he inspected the painting. Even the most expensive cologne was sickening when overused. The smell was overpowering despite the barrier of her ski mask.

"It's really quite breathtaking—*Girl with a Sunflower*."

If he noticed her lack of response, he didn't show it. Her captor wandered to one of the restoration tables and examined a chemical bottle. "In a world without law enforcement or insurance, people who lose valuables have very little recourse."

Clara nearly spat. He was referring to the Black Market and purchasers of stolen and illegal goods. She resisted the urge to refute his remark and instead scanned the room, exploring her options. Guards stood at every door and under the high windows, their weapons at the ready. She counted mercenaries and measured the distance to the exit.

Kite returned to the easel. "It's the original, as you well know. I couldn't risk The Lynx getting wind of a fake, so I baited the trap with my own expensive cheese."

Clara felt her face heat under the mask.

Kite continued, "God, the waiting was painful. Watching the dark web for the perfect piece. It took months. My people studied you, your methods, your victims, the items you prefer."

Clara nearly scoffed. The people she robbed were the farthest things from victims.

"That's when I saw it—a long lost Renoir, seized by the Nazis. Best of all, the so-called rightful owner was not only alive but also gave lectures about the stolen art of World War II. I knew it was only a matter of time before it caught your eye."

Every word Kite spoke made Clara feel more and more foolish.

In the center of the room, the nearly invisible rappelling wire hung from the ceiling. At the end of the cord, the clip for the carabiner at her waist rested on a pile of rags.

Without looking up from the painting, Kite said, "Envisioning an escape, are we?" He turned to the nearest sentry and jerked his chin to the ceiling. The guard muttered something in German, aimed his rifle, and shot the spool retraction mechanism. Metal pieces rained down atop the crumpled wire. Clara wouldn't be leaving the way she had come.

The man in charge faced her. He nodded to a guard who brought a folding chair and set it beside her. Another minion took out his phone and held it up, ready to record.

"My clients have lost too many valuables to your thievery. They need assurances. So I'll unmask the bandit and kill him slowly. Live stream. Your victims will enjoy hearing you beg for your life." He chuckled. "Or death."

He commanded the guard who had brought the chair. "Search him, then tie him down."

The lieutenant strode confidently to Clara. He squinted at the beam from her headlamp, then pulled it off and crushed it with a heavy boot. She could smell his breath through her mask as he lifted both hands to begin the pat down. It wouldn't take long for him to realize the truth.

She pressed the button on her utility belt. Five, four, three, two…

One.

CHAPTER FOUR

September 25
The Outskirts of Paris, France

Using the remote detonator, Clara blew the transformer, and the restoration room was plunged into darkness. Guards were blindly throwing tables and scrambling to catch Clara in the shadows. Chaos reigned as Clara snatched the small painting from the easel and shoved it into the empty duffle. She dropped to her hands and knees and scrambled under a table. Lucien Kite shouted directives. A gun went off, shattering one of the high transom windows.

Clara dashed out the open door and emerged onto a paved parking area where a row of five black SUVs sat side-by-side. Two men in suits came around the tailgate of the center car, drawn by the commotion inside the building. Clara dropped to the ground and belly-crawled under the nearest vehicle, mindful of the priceless work of art in her bag. She emerged from the tailgate and ran toward the surrounding woods as the two drivers jogged in the opposite direction.

Clara ducked behind a thick oak, formulating a strategy. Men were already pouring out of the building in hot pursuit. A small guardhouse marked the gated entrance, and the lone occupant raced out toward a fenced substation with an emergency generator. Clara dashed to the back of the guard house and pinned herself to the exterior wall. Dogs barked in the distance.

With no time to lose, Clara put a new plan in motion. She had learned to be devious and resourceful at the age of six, escaping the clutches of those who would do her harm. Her skill had only grown.

Ten seconds later, two security team members, guns drawn, appeared at the back of the shed.

Clara stood before them. Naked.

She covered her breasts with one hand and her face with the other as she hurled a string of expletives in German. *You stupid assholes! Get out of here! I surprised my boyfriend at work, and now I am being assaulted by dogs! You are rapists! You are animals! My boyfriend is chasing some thief and leaves me here alone. I will never speak to him again! Get away from me!*

The two men, who couldn't have been older than twenty, stood momentarily transfixed. Then, one of them whipped out his phone and recorded the encounter with a delighted grin while the other finally mustered the courage to shout over her rant, "Where? Which way did he go?"

Removing her hand from her bare breasts, Clara pointed into the woods. The two men paused for an admiring moment, then took off in the direction she indicated. Clara grabbed the duffle with the painting and the pile of clothes at her feet and darted off through the trees in the opposite direction. The moonlight, which had exposed her earlier, now aided her escape. She ran like the wind. Her car was hidden near the access road, two kilometers away. All around her, dogs barked, and men shouted. She heard another gunshot. Clara never stopped to look, never paused to catch her breath. She raced to the blue fiat concealed under low branches, threw her bundle in the back seat, and peeled out.

The access road was a blind alley. She needed to get to the freeway. If her pursuers blocked her in, there would be no escape. She started the car and floored it. The turn-off was just ahead. There was nothing but darkness in her rearview mirror. One hundred yards, fifty, ten. She took the turn aggressively, the little car fishtailing on the empty thoroughfare. In the pre-dawn hours, traffic was light, but a few cars and trucks were out. A logging truck pulled next to her, the driver swerving. The fellow in the passenger seat was grinning like a child at Christmas.

She was still nude.

Clara threw back a saucy smile and sped up. With one hand, she groped for the T-shirt in the pile of clothes. When she felt the soft fabric, she grabbed the garment and pulled it on. That small matter handled, she pressed down on the gas and sped off toward Paris.

In her rearview mirror, a delivery truck was exiting the autoroute. Only a small Citroen puttered in the distance.

Forty minutes later, Clara pulled into a commuter car park, grabbed her belongings, and exited the Fiat. Dawn was just beginning to paint the sky as she walked to the sleek, black Maserati. In under a minute, Clara had disposed of the items from the heist in the trash, popped the trunk of the luxury car, and pulled a chic gray sheath and matching stilettos from one of four matched pieces of Louis Vuitton luggage. Then she slipped *Girl with a Sunflower* in among the remaining clothing. Clara twisted her blonde hair into a chignon and fastened it with a clip. In the considerably more elegant driver's seat, Clara swapped her men's military watch for a diamond Cartier tank and pressed the button to start the car.

Then, with the ease of an heiress, she sped off toward the Four Seasons Georges V. Hopefully, she could relax at the hotel for a bit before she met her father, Reynard, at his favorite Parisian restaurant, La Coupole.

Her father was an inspiring, if unconventional, role model. He had told her long ago that if she insisted on indulging her penchant for thievery, she should use her talents for good, unlike him. She loved Reynard for understanding her and had taken his words to heart. Tomorrow, Clara would fly to the States and return *Girl with a Sunflower* to its rightful owner. There was no more satisfying feeling. She was a Ph.D. candidate at one of the finest academic institutions in the world, but Clara's obsession was tracking down stolen treasures. And her passion was stealing them back.

What had started as a disastrous night had turned into a Broadway musical morning. The sun was up, and Paris had awakened. Clara pulled up to the hotel and waited for the valet to help her out of the car, then stood at the boot as two liveried men unloaded the luggage. On Avenue Georges V, the Citroen she had spotted on the road drove past and turned the corner. The driver, an older man with a bushy mustache, kept his eyes forward.

Smelling money like a bloodhound, the concierge rushed to her side to greet her.

"Madam O'Keefe, we've been expecting you."

Clara had traveled under one of her usual aliases of female artists. This time, it was the American Georgia O'Keeffe. "Thank you…"

"Jean-Pierre."

"Jean-Pierre," Clara purred.

She plucked the smallest bag from the cart, the one holding the Renoir, and preceded her entourage into the lobby, where she instructed the concierge—with a sultry smile and a hundred euros—to store the bag in the hotel vault. The man was only too happy to oblige as well as oversee her check-in and escort her to the suite.

The lobby was bustling as visitors and staff hurried across the gleaming marble floor. In the center of the room, beneath a crystal chandelier the size of a Volkswagen, a golden table held a vase of fuchsia poppies, lilacs, and roses one meter in diameter. The room seemed in constant motion, except for one man who sat still as a statue in a yellow wingback chair behind a paper copy of *Le Monde*. A wisp of steam drifted up from the demitasse on the side table, indicating its recent arrival.

"This way, madam." The concierge guided Clara to the elevators and whisked them to her Eiffel Tower suite, a crisp, modern living space done in yellow, sage, and teal with a sitting room, cozy dining area overlooking the terrace and—her favorite part—an airy bedroom crowned with the most inviting bed and a stunning view of the Paris skyline.

When her coterie had been tipped and dismissed, Clara kicked off her heels and fell onto the bed, landing in a cloud of Siberian down. The sun peeked through the curtains, and Clara's thoughts drifted. She didn't return to Paris often; her painful start to life in Porte Saint-Denis wasn't a memory she liked to relive.

She hadn't known a thing about Reynard on that fateful day. Yet she had sought the safety of his soft overcoat and wrapped her tiny body around his legs—anything to escape the man chasing her. Clara hadn't batted an eye when Reynard shot her pursuer—her definition of morality and justice had been forged in a hotter fire than most. She had climbed into this stranger's car without hesitation.

All those years ago, they had driven away from Saint-Denis in near-silence. Reynard sat close to the door, looking like a spider was on the other seat. He only said one thing. "*Je suis un criminel.*" *I am a criminal.* It was odd, really, that such an ominous confession could cement her certainty that she had made the right choice. But it had.

Her instincts about people had always been spot-on.

With one glaring exception.

A soft knock on the door pulled Clara from what was sure to be an infuriating line of thought, and she padded barefoot to the door.

A uniformed young man stood in the hall with a trolley. Pulling the door open, she stepped back, confused, and said, "*Je n'ai pas commandé cela.*" *I didn't order this.*

The boy shrugged and followed her inside. "*Je ne sais pas, mais il y a une mot.*" *I don't know, but there is a note.* He pointed to the small white envelope tipped against the champagne bucket beside a decadent plate of her favorite sugared strawberries and Alain Ducasse chocolates.

After giving him a generous tip and closing the door, Clara plucked the envelope from the serving cart. She imagined the arrogance and condescension before she slid the card out. The message did not disappoint.

Dearest Bluebird,
Fruits for the fruits of your labor.
Enjoy Paris.
X
P.S. Consider using aliases that are NOT famous artists.
You're making it too easy for me.

Miles Buchanan. She should have known.

Miles had been the man in the turquoise-blue Citroen. What's worse, Clara suspected she had walked right by him on the way to her room, sitting in the lobby sipping espresso and reading *Le Monde*.

The realization didn't dull her appetite. Clara popped the loosened cork on the champagne, poured herself a glass, and brought the plate of treats into the bedroom. As she sank her teeth into a glistening strawberry, she allowed herself to run through the gamut of emotions Miles Buchanan brought to mind. The order varied depending on the circumstance, but anger was always high on the list, along with disappointment and pity. Today, a different feeling fluttered in her chest, something she couldn't quite name.

She had noticed the little blue car early in her escape. Miles had been nearby.

She plucked a dark chocolate rectangle from the purple paper and took a bite, nearly groaning as the coffee liqueur flowed across her tongue. It wasn't the rich flavor warming her heart, however. It was the fact that Miles had been near.

She had been caught, held at gunpoint, and threatened with torture. She dreaded to think what Miles would have done had he known how close she came to being caught. Clara was well aware that any ordinary girl would have prayed for a white knight at that moment. But Clara was far from ordinary. What's more, she hadn't needed help.

She took the champagne flute and stepped out on the balcony. A wrought iron fence ringed a cheerful patio dotted with potted plants, cushioned chairs, and a round table. In the distance, the Eiffel Tower stood watch. Clara never tired of the view, but it wasn't the cathedral spires or landmarks that pulled her to the balcony's edge. It was a little blue car. She peered over the side of the hotel to the street below.

There, leaning over the top of the Citroen with his hands drumming the roof, Miles Buchanan stared back at her, grinning beneath a big fake mustache. He applauded her, and Clara curtsied in kind. He paused for a moment, his face unreadable from this distance. Then, with a small salute, he slipped into the driver's seat and sped away.

The sun was fully up when Clara returned to the bedroom. She hung the *Prière de ne pas déranger* card on the outside doorknob, pulled the blackout shades, and, after slipping into a lovingly worn Columbia T-shirt, climbed into bed. She always seemed to wear the same sad smile when she thought of Miles. Miles Buchanan, the man of many faces, was as comfortable sitting in a CEO's office as he was throwing darts in a biker bar. Unfortunately, as deft as he was at changing his physical appearance, he was equally inept at tapping into his emotions.

Five years ago, Clara would have swooned at this protective gesture. She would have read into it and analyzed what it meant about his feelings for her.

Now, after years of dashed hope and disappointment, she knew. Miles Buchanan didn't have feelings, or if he did, they were buried under a pile of masks and alternate identities too deep to find. Clara had long ago come to terms with the fact that the man of her dreams and the man who had followed her to this hotel were two very different people.

Unfortunately for her, they looked exactly alike.

So, while she couldn't stop the warmth from spreading in her chest, Clara forced her mind to think of other things: fainting goats, lemon gelato, Basquiat's *Warrior*, anything to ignore those inextinguishable glowing embers of hope. Maybe they would finally burn out.

Thirty-six hours later, Clara sat in the rented car in the shade of a coconut palm and watched as Anya Schmidt opened the door of her Palm Springs home. She picked up the brown-paper-wrapped parcel and glanced up and down the quiet street. The woman was ninety-three but moved gracefully as she lifted the package and slipped her finger under the tape as she returned to the air-conditioned house. The plate glass windows of the Spanish-style home gave Clara a view into the main living area where Anya now stood. The brown paper fluttered to the floor. As Anya turned the painting over and realized what she held, one hand went to her mouth. She stood for long minutes and stared. Readjusting her grasp, Anya Schmidt sank into an easy chair. Clara saw her bright eyes move over the canvas, her fingers hovering just above the paint, an aura of memories surrounding her. Then Anya stood and hurried back to the front stoop. She turned the Renoir and held it to the heavens. With damp cheeks, Anya rechecked the street, her eyes pausing on the dark rental. Clara read Anya's lips as she mouthed *God bless you* before disappearing inside.

This feeling never got old. Being a thief was a thrill; it tapped into some ingrained need to flirt with danger and punish bad actors. Part of it was selfish, no doubt. Clara had never experienced anything close to the mounting tension and cathartic release of stealing. But the satisfaction of seeing the rightful owner reunited with their property? That was the lasting sensation. Stealing was the lightning strike, fast and exhilarating, but making things right was the thunder that rolled through her in fulfilling waves.

Clara pulled away from the curb and entered the GPS instructions for the airport.

Her business concluded, Clara had other tasks on her mind. Her eye caught the corner of the thick card peeking from the top of her Goyard tote. It was the note Miles had left at the hotel in Paris. A slow smile spread across her face. When she got back to New York, she would show Miles that she would not be outfoxed.

CHAPTER FIVE

October 7
New Jersey

Miles Buchanan sat in the back of the limousine and scrolled through his phone as the car ventured deeper into New Jersey. He had taken this trip many times, always in the old-school stretch limo with the same silent, suited driver listening to the same sports talk radio. They drove through elite, Manhattan-adjacent suburbs and into the working-class neighborhoods—not that Miles noticed.

Miles was a fixer who operated under the alias Caleb Cain. He had made a lavish living, ensuring the reputations, incomes, and marriages of the rich and powerful remained intact. The people who hired him didn't have skeletons in their closets—they had freshly rotting corpses, secrets which, if exposed, would end life as they knew it.

Miles used the time to check emails, responding to some, ignoring others. He had reached the pinnacle of his career and only chose assignments that piqued his interest—or, in this case, accepted jobs from repeat clients he felt obligated to assist. Miles's twin brother was a former Navy SEAL, but Miles often thought the people he dealt with were far worse than any insurgent his brother had faced.

Case in point: Chester Ugentti, mobster-turned-politician. He started as a city councilman, promising to be tough on crime. Ugentti made a name for himself in central Jersey by cleaning up the Perth Amboy docks. In reality, he had simply taken over the corrupt operation. While the arrests of local mobsters captured headlines, Ugentti filled the void with his own people. He was smart; Miles would give him that. His kickbacks and bribes were secreted away, and Ugentti lived like a man with a successful contracting business and a fierce dedication to his community.

Last year, he had been elected to Congress.

Chester Ugentti was a snake. And never to be underestimated.

It was a dark evening; clouds obscured the moon and stars, and the streets were poorly lit. They may as well have been in a tunnel as the car's headlights pierced the blackness. In the quiet streets of Perth Amboy, the car turned toward the water and pulled up to a cavernous boarded-up building. The driver got out and opened the passenger door for Miles.

From the outside, the dockside warehouse looked exactly like what it was—a place for dirty deeds.

With a nod of thanks, Miles opened the groaning fire door, crossed the cavernous main room, and took the metal stairs to the building's second floor. He followed the wide hallway overlooking the main floor below. Something about this place—or perhaps its occupant—always made Miles shudder. He forced his unease aside. Today, he wasn't Miles Buchanan. He was Caleb Cain, and Caleb Cain had no dark demons.

At the end of the long row of dock worker offices, Miles entered a kitchen. It was dated and barely functioning except for the restaurant-quality espresso maker that took up an entire wall. At the Formica counter, an overly made-up woman with dyed-blonde hair and a too-tight skirt arranged meats and cheeses on a charcuterie board. With a smile and a jerk of her head, she indicated that Miles should proceed.

At the entry to the shabby sitting area, a bodyguard with a slicked pony-tail and facial piercings stopped Miles with a strange command. "Shoes."

Miles slid off his loafers and set them on the low wooden platform just outside the door, then continued in his stocking feet into the one fixed-up room in the building and took a seat in a leather armchair. The blonde from the kitchen bent lower than necessary to set his scotch on the side table at his elbow. Miles took in the offered view of her cleavage—no need to insult a po-tential ally—and thanked her, ostensibly, for the drink.

"The boss man will be right in," she cooed, then sauntered out of the room.

"Caleb Cain, you son of a bitch! It's been too long, old friend." Ugentti boomed from the opposite entry.

Speak of the devil, and he will appear.

At five foot eight and tipping the scales at two hundred and fifty pounds, Ugentti's lifelong nickname "Chug" suited him. What remained of his graying hair was buzzed short. He wore a red tracksuit and habitually fisted his hands on his hips when he spoke; he reminded Miles of a fire hydrant—minus the usefulness.

"Apologies for the shoes. Theresa carpets this fucking room in white. Don't get me wrong, it looks sensational, but now we all gotta take off our shoes whenever we're in here. God forbid there's a fire. Fat Tony would burn to a crisp trying to get his Nikes back on."

Miles swallowed his annoyance with the whiskey.

"You got your scotch? Excellent." Ugentti answered his own question. "Shawna! I'm ready for my drink, doll."

The same woman returned, walking slowly and balancing a martini glass filled with a dark liquid on a small silver tray. Chug was clearly rising to his new station. In past meetings, his beverage of choice was a can of beer and a shot.

Shawna made it to Ugentti with only a slight slosh of the Manhattan. He accepted the drink and plucked the maraschino cherry out by the stem. Dangling it, Ugentti said, "You know, Shawna can tie the stem in a knot with her tongue. When it's in *my mouth*."

"Oh, Chug, stop." Shawna waved him off with a giggle and left.

Chester Ugentti heaved his massive girth onto the matching oxblood couch with a groan and downed half his drink. "How's tricks, Caleb? Everything good with you, my friend?"

The repeated use of the word *friend* had Miles on edge. He and Chug were not friends. The extent of their relationship to date was Miles paying off the strippers and sex workers Chug had carelessly allowed to video their less-than-conventional interactions.

"Everything is fine, Mr. Ugentti."

"Is my fucking father here? What's with the Mr. Ugentti crap? My friends call me Chug. I'd say you've earned that right."

Miles merely nodded.

Ugentti picked up an auction house listing book from the cheap coffee table, fanned the pages, and tossed it aside. "My wife's got me bidding on some Italian marble statue. A fat Venus in some fucking clam shell. She wants to turn it into a fountain. I don't pay any attention, but Theresa, she's got a real eye for the art."

Miles was well-versed at containing his eye roll.

"Me? I'm not big on auctions. I'm more of a take-it-or-leave-it guy."

"Nor am I," Miles agreed.

"Nor am I," Ugentti echoed. "I'm gonna use that. I should hire you as a fucking etiquette coach. Some of these lock-jaw numbnuts on The Hill," Ugentti blew a raspberry. "They're sitting at lunch eating shrimp cocktail and complaining about their golf swing, and I'm counting the tines on the forks like Julia Roberts in fucking *Pretty Woman*."

Miles laughed as was expected. He was certain Ugentti had no concern whatsoever about table manners and had probably picked the shrimp up with his fingers and tossed the tails on the floor. So once again, his skin prickled at Chug's uncharacteristic commentary. Nevertheless, Miles was a patient man. So he sipped his scotch and waited.

"Goddammit." Ugentti crossed one ankle over his knee and touched his bare big toe through the hole in his sock. "Shawna! Tell Theresa I need new socks!"

She called back from the kitchen, "You got it, Chug!"

Ugentti shot out his wrist and checked the time on the Rolex. It was a decent watch—Miles owned two—worth about half the value of the Vacheron Constantin he was currently wearing.

"You got a wife, Cal? Kids?"

Miles was growing weary of this preamble. What's more, he was not in the habit of divulging details about himself, even his fictional self, to clients.

"What can I do for you, Mr. Ugentti?"

Chug absorbed the insult of being redirected, slapped his thighs, and said, "Straight down to it, then."

"If you don't mind."

Ugentti called for Shawna again, and a moment later, she wheeled in a brass serving cart laden with antipasti and Italian desserts. Sausages, pungent cheeses, and olives were artfully arranged on a rustic cutting board, with a loaf of sliced bread in a basket.

Ugentti rubbed his palms together. "My father never conducted business without food. Even if he was going to *terminate* someone." He winked. "He always gave them a nice meal. Salsitza?"

"Thank you, no," Miles replied. "I have a late dinner in The City."

"Suit yourself." Ugentti waddled over to the spread, heaped food onto a plate, then nodded to Shawna, who left the cart where it was and exited. Two beefy bodyguards lurking at the entryway followed in her wake.

Miles waited while Ugentti devoured a handful of olives and spat the pits into his palm before depositing them in an ashtray. He picked up a framed photo on his desk and turned it to his guest.

"Me and Joe Pesci at a golf pro-am this summer. Nice guy."

"You could be brothers," Miles said mildly.

It was always the same: show your power, show your money, then explain how you shat the bed. Chug thought he was special; he wasn't. He was just another in a long line of influential people who got caught. Miles had to admit he was curious to know what exactly Chester Ugentti had gotten himself into this time; his behavior indicated this was not one of his typical transgressions.

The list of forbidden deeds had grown dramatically shorter over the years. These days, public figures could get away with almost anything. However, some acts remained unacceptable—in both the court of law and the court of public opinion.

I have a proposition for you. No, scratch that. Not a proposition, *a retirement plan.*"

Miles could guess what was coming. "Mr. Ugentti—"

"Chug."

"Chug, let me stop you before you continue."

"Hear me out. You see, Caleb Cain, I can do a lot of good in Congress. The people I represent are the hardest-working people in the country. Good people, salt of the earth."

"I don't need your campaign speech, Chug."

"Fine." Chug sat on the coffee table directly in front of Miles. "I can get a lot more done if I have some leverage on these fucks. You, Caleb Cain, know the dark and dirty on half of Washington. I want that information."

Miles set his drink on the coaster. "Out of the question."

"I'll pay you five million dollars."

"Chug, I've been offered far more than that. Many times. And my answer is always the same."

"It was an opening bid." Ugentti leaned onto his forearms with a hungry look in his eyes. "Let's negotiate."

Miles held back the sigh that desperately wanted to escape and stood. "I'm afraid it's nonnegotiable."

"Everything's negotiable." He stood and retrieved the bottle of Macallan from the bar, then refilled Miles's glass. Returning to the couch and his plate of food, Chug scooped the cherry topping from a mini cheesecake with a fat index finger and ate it. Then he smiled, the red gelatinous filling covering his stubby teeth.

"Not this." Miles stood and turned to the door where the two bodyguards now blocked his path.

"Ten million."

With his back to Ugentti, Miles remained silent.

"Fifteen."

Miles had to walk a fine line here. He had systems in place to ensure problems like this didn't pop up, the most obvious threat he held over his clients being exposure. The issue here was that Ugentti was an outlier from Caleb Cain's typical clientele. He paid to have some scandals swept under the rug, but Miles thought it was more for the sake of his marriage than his reputation. Ugentti was a wise guy, and everyone knew it. People voted for him in spite of the fact that he was a criminal, or maybe even because of that fact. The threat of opening Ugentti's closet to reveal his skeletons didn't have nearly the power it would on a squeaky-clean governor or a high-ranking clergy member. Still, Miles held his ground.

"No deal."

"There's not much information out there about you, Caleb Cain." Ugentti drummed his thumb on the arm of the sofa. "But I have your number. You've got that silver spoon look about you. All prep school smooth and country club polish. Did daddy donate a building to get you into some bullshit Ivy League college?"

Miles remained stoic. Ugentti was wrong on every point, but Miles had carefully cultivated Caleb Cain's image. "Mr. Ugentti—"

"My friends call me Chug. Are we friends?"

"No."

Ugentti considered his reply. "No, I don't think we are. I don't make friends with my employees." He sat back and entwined his fingers on his belly. "Well, not the men, anyway. I've befriended a few women over the years."

Miles turned back, picked up his scotch, and, after taking a steadying swallow, pointed to Ugentti with the glass. "A fact that should deter you from continuing this conversation. I know your secrets too, don't forget."

"Ah, ah, ah," Chug wagged a stubby finger at Miles. "Never play the ace in your sleeve when you have a winning hand."

Miles froze. The glass of scotch slid through his fingers and fell.

Ugentti shot up. "Ah shit, Theresa's gonna have kittens. Shawna, bring a towel yesterday!"

The assistant hurried into the room and knelt by the stain on the carpet.

Miles said, "May I use your washroom?"

"Through there." Chug pointed without looking up from where he was helping Shawna dab the scotch.

In the cramped half bath, Miles turned on the tap. Leaning heavily on the sink, he touched his forehead against the mirror.

Never play the ace up your sleeve when you have a winning hand.

He turned off the water as his mind assembled the scattered pieces of an old puzzle. There was nothing to be done right now, but Chug Ugentti was right.

Miles did have an ace up his sleeve.

Miles found Ugentti sitting behind an overly large desk in the adjoining room. Chug had taken a position of power.

Miles stood before him. "As I said, I have another appointment."

"Twenty million dollars."

Miles paused. Not because of the amount. Chug Ugentti had no idea what information Caleb Cain possessed. It was worth billions to the right people. But Caleb Cain had built his business and reputation on his discretion—not to mention the gratitude he received; he could go anywhere, do anything. Despite the exorbitant price tag for his services, Caleb Cain had earned the favor of many, many powerful people.

No, Miles hesitated because he sensed the desperation of a ruthless man. He needed this conversation to end.

Ugentti misconstrued his reaction and smiled. "Now we're getting somewhere."

Miles met Chug's gleeful gaze. "I'll think about it."

Ugentti slapped his hand flat on the desk with a bang, causing the plate with the remaining food to bounce. "This meeting isn't over until we have an agreement."

Miles wasn't blind to what was happening. Ugentti may be a congressman, but he was a mobster through and through. Miles may not possess his twin brother's brute force, but what he lacked in combat skill, he made up for with charm.

"As you said, Chug, let's keep the conversation open-ended. Maybe we can come up with something that suits both our needs."

The congressman broke eye contact and spoke to his muscle. "Show Mr. Cain out. Let's get that 'maybe' to a 'yes.'"

The two guards grabbed Miles and dragged him out of the office. They stopped briefly in the kitchen for Miles to retrieve his shoes. Strangely, the loafers weren't where he had left them but were positioned about three feet over on the low shelf. Once he slipped them on, the men hauled him out.

Miles didn't regain his footing until they were down the stairs and halfway through the warehouse's main room. At the back of the building, one of the goons elbowed open the door to an area for cleaning machinery. Industrial parts littered the floor, and fire hoses hung on the wall. Heavy hooks were hanging from chains, and the space smelled of solvent and rotting fish. None of that captured his attention. Miles was only looking at the round covered drain in the middle of the floor. Above it sat a heavy wooden chair with restraints dangling from the arms.

One of the men chuckled. He was bald with pitted acne scars. They continued walking, heading for a door at the back to the right of a loading bay. Miles couldn't contain his sagging relief. Ugentti assumed that showing him this room would be enough.

He was ten steps from freedom when one of his escorts grabbed Miles's elbows and pinned them behind his back.

CHAPTER SIX

October 7
Napa Valley, California

"By the power vested in me by the state of California, I now pronounce you husband and wife. You may kiss your bride."

Miller "Tox" Buchanan stood with his fellow groomsmen as Camilo "Cam" Canto planted a Hollywood kiss—complete with a dip—on his new wife, Evan. The scene was picture-perfect. They were at Evan's family's vineyard in Napa Valley, the surrounding hillsides abundant with grape vines ready for harvest. Stone and timber outbuildings dotted the landscape. The fifty or so guests sat in rows of white wooden chairs flanking a grass path carpeted in rose petals. An arbor of grapevines woven with poppies and heather framed the couple.

Cam and Evan stood with the priest on the low wooden platform constructed for the event, with their bridesmaids and groomsmen lined up beside them. Cam had opted not to have the men wear their dress whites—he and Evan had both wanted a more laid-back event. His closest friends wore blue blazers and khaki pants with matching orange ties. The women each had on a different yellow dress in a style of their choosing.

In Tox's opinion, no female held a candle to his wife, but he had to admit Evan looked gorgeous. Her hair was pinned up in a fancy bun, and her white dress made her look like a Greek goddess—fitting, he thought, for an archaeologist. Cam was a lucky man. Almost as lucky as Tox. Calliope looked over from across the aisle as if she could read his thoughts, her pale blue eyes twinkling. One hand held a bouquet of wildflowers; the other rested on the swell of her belly.

Tox swallowed thickly, still getting used to this feeling of happiness, of true love. He was a 6'5" former SEAL. He understood loyalty. He knew dedication. But this? Seeing his wife's eyes reflecting his love, growing their child? Tox Buchanan would burn the world to ashes to keep his family safe.

Beside him, Jonah "Steady" Lockhart was pumping a fist in the air with an accompanying wolf whistle, and Tox's boss and friend Nathan Bishop was applauding. He couldn't see the other three men in the row but could hear Leo "Ren" Jameson, Andrew "Chat" Dunlap, and Herc Reynolds joining in on the cheering.

Tox was about to yell out an enthusiastic *Hooyah* when the air around him shifted.

Tox didn't shout or clap. As the happy couple stepped onto the grassy aisle to greet their families, a vaguely familiar and wholly unsettling cloud surrounded him. The sensation was dizzying, and for a moment, he thought he might throw up. A cramp in his stomach faded, and a wave of a headache came and went. He didn't know why, but Tox's first instinct was to check on his wife. Calliope was seven months pregnant and standing directly across from him with the other bridesmaids. He wasn't sure why this feeling had him looking to see if someone else was okay when he was the one feeling sick. Nevertheless, he scanned Calliope from head to toe as she laughed with Nathan's wife, Emily. Tox couldn't pinpoint the problem; it wasn't sickness or sadness—more like his equilibrium was off. Whatever it was, he couldn't shake the notion that something was wrong.

Calliope looked across the arbor as if sensing his disquiet and immediately crossed to her husband. "You're white as a sheet."

Nathan Bishop shifted his attention from the newlyweds and backed Tox out of the fray. "Are you all right?"

Tox rested his hands on his thighs and dropped his head. "Yeah, I got woozy for a second. It's passing."

Calliope rubbed his back. "Just breathe."

Steady appeared with a glass of water and passed it to him. "You okay? We can't have the big sequoia falling on the altar."

The wave ebbed. Tox accepted the water and drank it. "I'm fine. Too much pinot last night. Probably dehydrated."

"You gonna live up to your nickname and re-tox instead of detox?" Steady clapped him on the back.

Tox pulled his wife close and kissed her temple. "Those days are long gone, brother. Late nights and bottles are about to have a whole new meaning." He placed a protective hand on his wife's middle, his big palm completely covering the small swell. Calliope tucked her head against Tox's chest.

Steady took the empty glass and nodded his approval. Six months ago, Steady would have been shoving a shot into Tox's hand. Now, he was in love. Steady and Very Valentine were living together and headed for the place where they were currently standing: the altar.

"Better?" Calliope asked.

"Right as rain. Let's hit the tent." He held his wife for a few dance steps.

"Not so fast, Swayze. Pictures. Evan wants the formal wedding photos taken at sunset."

Emily appeared at Nathan's side. He kissed his wife. "You look beautiful."

Emily Bishop leaned around Tox to catch Calliope's attention. "And they say weddings make women romantic."

Calliope laughed. "If the world only knew a wedding turned these badasses into big puddles of goo."

Steady stepped in front of his brothers. "A little respect, ladies. We are highly trained, elite goo."

Emily Bishop straightened her husband's tie. "Don't forget dashing."

Very Valentine popped into the group, having overheard. "Can you stand for pictures, or are you boys too weak in the knees?"

Without missing a beat, Steady scooped Very into his arms and marched up the empty aisle.

Nathan's soft chuckle had Tox turning around. "I never thought I'd see the day. Jonah Lockhart is a one-woman man."

"People probably said the same about you," Tox said.

Nathan wrapped a protective arm around his wife. "Not the people who knew me."

Tox smiled, happy to be included in that select group. "True."

Calliope tugged on his hand. "We better go. We're losing daylight."

They walked through the meadow, Emily and Calliope in front, the men following. Tox said, "These days, 'ensuring domestic tranquility' is a much more enjoyable activity."

Nathan watched their wives precede them through the grass. "I couldn't agree more."

His boss picked up the pace and slipped his arms through the elbow crooks of the women, helping them maneuver through the terrain to the spot where the photographer was already positioning the wedding party.

Tox stood for a moment, his hands in his pants pockets, and observed. Cam kissed Evan under the pink sky. The photographer snapped away as the groom held his new bride in the cradle of low hills etched with rows of grapevines. Music and laughter drifted from the white tent. Cam's huge Chilean-American family had already started the festivities. There was magic in the air.

A gentle breeze carried the aromas of the vineyard and the hint of tri-tip grilling. With his head tipped to the sky, Tox inhaled the scent of celebration. It was going to be a great night.

And yet, Tox couldn't shake the aura of unease surrounding him. He knew what it was, despite the fact he hadn't experienced the sensation since he was a child. Their mother had called it the *twin thing*. Tox couldn't explain it or really describe it, but this feeling was as real as the grass under his size fifteen shoes. He pulled his phone from his pocket and sent a text.

Something was wrong with Miles.

CHAPTER SEVEN

October 7
New Jersey

Tall security floodlights lined the parking area, casting beams and shadows on the pitted asphalt. Miles sat on the pavement leaning against a low wall of the loading dock and gathered his strength. A trickle of blood ran from his eyebrow to his chin and dripped onto his white dress shirt. A bolt of pain shot through his ribs every time he moved.

Through the darkness and his blurred vision, Miles could see the black limousine idling. Tinted windows obscured the driver, but Miles imagined him scrolling through social media or checking texts, waiting like he would for any other passenger. When you worked for Chug Ugentti, picking up a beaten man and driving him home was par for the course.

Making no effort to hide his distress, Miles staggered to his feet and crossed to the car. The driver remained behind the wheel as Miles eased himself onto the leather seat and looked out at the dingy warehouse. The tires had just begun rolling across the pavement when Miles said, "Stop."

The slight jerk to a halt had Miles's gut aching. He ignored the pain, opened the rear door, and limped back to the loading dock where his leather portfolio had been tossed carelessly onto the ramp. He scooped up his belongings and returned to the limo. At the back car door, he paused and looked over his shoulder. Standing at the open second-floor window, smiling at Miles, was Ugentti.

Chug shouted, "That was a taste of the stick, Mr. Cain. I'm sending a couple of carrots your way. You can decide how you want to proceed."

The rage must have shown on Miles's face because Ugentti retreated and pulled the curtains.

Back in the car, Miles wiped the blood from his face and poured three fingers of scotch into a crystal highball glass. His phone buzzed in the breast pocket of his suit jacket.

Miles stared at the text from his twin. Two letters. There was no reason for it, no explanation, just a simple question:

Miller: *OK?*

He couldn't explain the stinging in his eyes or the thickness in his throat.

When they were young, Miller—or "Tox" as his Navy buddies called him—always knew when Miles needed him. Miles's mouth got him into trouble—a lot. But Miles had a shadow who was a head taller than every bully in school. Unfortunately, Miles hadn't lost his impetuousness when he lost his protector. He had been in more than one situation in his line of work where he had wished, *prayed*, that his twin was by his side. Now, here was Miller, back in Miles's life, offering to help.

Too late. And he didn't just mean tonight.

Miles had spent a decade digging this hole. He was down so deep, his brother's hand would never reach. He'd have to claw his way out on his own. So rather than reply to Miller, Miles brought up his contacts and texted a different recipient.

Enough was enough.

CHAPTER EIGHT

A hint of autumn was in the Connecticut night air; a chill edged the breeze, and a crescent moon hung low in the sky. The beautiful weather did nothing to improve Lucien Kite's mood. He emerged from the back of the Maybach without waiting for his driver and marched up the marble steps to the massive double doors. They opened before Kite broke stride.

The kindest word his neighbors used to describe the house was garish—not that he had many neighbors. The estate, built by an eccentric toy manufacturer a century ago, sat on twenty acres just north of Darien, Connecticut. Kite had purchased the famed Versailles-inspired mansion, then proceeded to gild, extend, overdecorate, and ornament every square foot of the already ornate home. From the gold leaf capitals of the columns lining the front portico to the elaborate hedge maze at the rear of the property, the residence was a tribute to conspicuous consumption.

Lucien Kite was, without exception, the most polarizing man on Wall Street. After spending a decade as the number two man at finance king, Anton Zorba's fund, a now infamous multi-billion dollar Ponzi scheme, Kite was enjoying the fruits of his labors. He hid vast sums of money everywhere from Belize to Singapore, then Kite turned FBI informant. Two years later, Anton Zorba was dead from a self-inflicted gunshot wound, the investors had lost millions, and Lucien Kite was living like a king.

The media was torn on their depiction of Lucien Kite; some called him a crusader, others a criminal. Most people in the know suspected the latter. Some even speculated Kite had a hand in his boss's suspicious suicide.

That didn't stop people from attending his parties.

Kite's autumn masquerade was in two weeks. It was a highlight of his year. Kite always looked forward to shouting his success to the whispered wealth of Old Money.

Today, however, Kite was far from celebratory.

Storming into the house, he strode across the marble tile of the soaring entry and flew up the left side of the split grand staircase. Kite slammed the office double doors behind him and dropped into the desk chair.

Two weeks had passed since the debacle at the restoration facility, and The Lynx had vanished like a rumor. Kite had been outsmarted. He'd had the bastard dead to rights, but The Lynx had a failsafe Kite hadn't anticipated. What's worse, Kite had played his hand; he doubted he'd ever be able to lure The Lynx into another trap. Best-case scenario now was that Kite had forced the thief into early retirement.

Well, Kite hadn't exhausted every option. At this very moment, he had a team of investigators combing the restoration warehouse looking for any clue to The Lynx's identity. Perhaps the man had left something behind in the chaos of his escape.

Tapping the keyboard of his computer, Kite brought up the security footage of their encounter. He watched and rewatched the silent interaction, unable to pinpoint what bothered him. The Lynx obviously understood English, but was he American? At one point, the thief's eyes darted to his right.

Kite remembered one of his guards had said something in his native German before shooting the rappelling line. Kite couldn't remember his exact words, but it was something along the lines of *I'll shoot that fucker next*. Pausing the video, Kite zoomed in on the masked face. The Lynx's eyes had widened, indicating the thief understood what the guard had said. Kite squinted at the screen. The video was black and white, but suddenly, he remembered what had struck him—those eyes. They were a vibrant shade—the electric blue of a Siamese fighting fish. The thief tried to hide it, but Kite saw the fear in those unusual eyes. Kite played the footage on a loop, toggling between camera angles, trying to force the niggling thought in his head to the surface. Something about The Lynx was...*off*. And Lucien Kite was going to figure out what it was.

CHAPTER NINE

Miles instructed the driver to drop him at his Upper East Side address. It was his alias, Caleb Cain's, apartment. He guarded his real identity and residence with his life.

Outside the highrise, he straightened his tie and smoothed back his hair. Miles didn't want anyone asking questions.

When Miles strode into the lobby, Burton, the doorman, flagged him down. The uniformed man at the circular reception desk said, "Mr. Cain, your guests are waiting in the lounge." Burton cocked his head, and Miles looked over his shoulder to see two exceedingly sexy and professionally dressed women sitting placidly on a small sofa. When they saw Miles, they stood in unison.

Ugentti's words came flooding back: *That was a taste of the stick, Mr. Cain. I'm sending a couple of carrots your way.*

Miles smiled at the doorman. "Oh yes, it must have slipped my mind."

Burton leaned across the desk, then tapped his temple. "You're bleeding."

Miles withdrew a linen handkerchief from his inner pocket and pressed it to his head. "Damn. Caught the corner of the car door. Must have broken the skin."

Burton accepted the explanation and cast an admiring glance at the approaching women.

A redhead and a brunette stood side-by-side before Miles. The redhead spoke. "Mr. Ugentti wanted to make sure we finalized the plans for the agreement?" She phrased it like a question.

Miles knew how to play the game. More importantly, he knew how to win it. "Excellent. Why don't we go upstairs, and we can review the paperwork."

A pair of sultry smiles preceded him into the elevator, and they rode in silence to the eleventh floor. The apartment was a sizable, nondescript two-bedroom along a hallway with a dozen similar units. The decor was beige and minimalist—it looked like an IKEA display room.

The women, whose names were "whatever you want them to be," made quick work of transforming from executives to what they were: high-end prostitutes. Miles poured himself a drink, and by the time he turned back around, their clothes were in a pool on the carpet, and the redhead was fondling the brunette.

"Back in a flash." Miles unbuttoned his shirt and walked into the bedroom. When the door was closed, he blew out an anguished breath. His ribs were no doubt bruised, and his gut throbbed. That asshole's parting kick to his kidney ensured he'd probably be pissing blood for a week. Miles shed his clothes at the dresser and pulled a pair of distressed jeans and a gray T-shirt from the drawer. Mussing his hair with one hand, he stepped into battered boots. In the closet, he removed his watch and replaced it with a military G-shock, then grabbed a money clip thick with bills and shoved it in his front pocket.

When he returned to the living room, he didn't wait for the women to process the transformation. Miles crossed to the closet, retrieved his helmet and black leather jacket, and fished out the wad of cash.

The redhead spoke. "Everything's been taken care of." Her words didn't stop her from eyeing the bankroll.

"Consider this a bonus for your cooperation."

Both women appeared cautious but curious.

Miles continued as he peeled hundreds from the stack, "The bar is stocked. There's food in the fridge. I have every streaming service. Stay for two hours." He held out three thousand dollars folded between two fingers. "You could tell Ugentti I left, but that doesn't say much for your powers of seduction."

The brunette stepped forward and took the cash. "Or my financial sense."

Beside her, the redhead handed him a card. "If you need us in the future. For anything."

Miles slipped the card into his back pocket, nodded his thanks, and left. After taking the elevator to the underground garage, he wound his way to the back, staying in the surveillance blind spots, and pulled the tarp off his baby.

Five minutes later, Miles was speeding down the FDR on the Ducati. Every bump jarred his aching ribs, and he could feel his lip swelling beneath the black helmet.

After traveling the remaining distance to Alphabet City on the Lower East Side, Miles entered the converted Nineteenth Century commercial bakery, stowed the bike in an interior room on the ground floor, and took the industrial elevator to his home. His twin owned the building, so when Miller moved to South Carolina with his wife, Miles convinced his brother not to sell. He then spent three months renovating. The apartment was still a classic open loft, but he had walled off the bedroom and bathroom, installed a spiral staircase to the rooftop, and used the existing beams and support pillars to divide the space subtly.

Miles closed the door behind him and doubled over. His head throbbed, his gut ached, and his fury surged. After pouring himself a large whiskey and downing half, he staggered into the bedroom, pausing in the doorway. Some might call him obsessive. Miles preferred *meticulous*. The room was as he had left it. The king bed was made with a slate gray comforter and matching sheets. The bedside tables each held a small lamp; the one on the far side had a charging station. The dresser was bare. Then, the discrepancy caught his eye. He had uncharacteristically left the closet door ajar. After pushing it closed, Miles peeled off his jacket and shirt to assess the damage. He stepped before the standing mirror in the corner, already seeing the bruises blooming on his torso. He took a half-step closer to inspect the damage. A rustling sound had Miles checking the room in the mirror's reflection. Behind him, the door to the walk-in closet flew open.

CHAPTER TEN

October 7
New York City

Clara burst into the room.

"Oh, my God. What happened?"

With a painful spin, Miles faced the perpetual thorn in his side. Clara Gautreau stood in the closet doorway with both hands over her mouth.

Miles stepped away from the mirror and snatched up his shirt. Her striking cerulean eyes were wide with shock, and both hands covered her pouty lips.

Miles wasn't prone to outbursts, but between his privacy being violated and his usual irritation at her presence, he snapped.

"Jesus, Clara! What the hell are you doing here?"

"Sorry. I didn't mean to scare you." A mischievous grin diluted her apology.

"You didn't scare me."

"Yeah, right."

"Why are you in my home?"

"Well, I planned on stealing your underwear, but—just come, sit."

Clara led him to the end of the bed and held his elbow as she eased him to the mattress. Then, she hurried out of the room.

"Where are your Ziplocks?" she called from the kitchen.

Miles leaned back gingerly on his elbows. "Top drawer, by the stove."

Miles heard her bustling about the kitchen. Clara returned with two plastic bags of ice.

"Here." She shook two ibuprofen into his palm.

He pushed her hand away. "In the medicine cabinet, bottom shelf. Tylenol with codeine."

Clara fetched the prescription. Eying the glass of bourbon still in his hand, she said, "Should you be mixing these with alcohol?"

Miles gave her a flat look, shook two tablets straight from the amber bottle into his mouth, and chased it with the drink. "It's fine."

"Now, lie back."

He obeyed, and she set the makeshift ice packs on his body—one on his aching ribs, the other over the bleeding knot on his head. The concern in her eyes had him tensing. Miles couldn't remember the last time anyone had taken care of him. As a teenager, he had once gone a month with an untreated broken wrist. This felt all wrong.

"Thanks. You can go."

Clara ignored his tone. "You need to go to the hospital. Head injuries are no joke."

An image flashed in his brain—a white room, stale air, he and Miller flanking the bed, each twin holding a weak hand: *I hate to leave you.* Miles sat up, fighting a wave of dizziness that had him gagging.

"Clara, go."

"Miles—" she started to protest.

"Get out of my house." His tone brooked no argument.

"Fine. I'll say it now in case you're dead in the morning. You're a stubborn jackass."

Miles sank back on the mattress, his brain sloshing around in his skull. "Noted."

He didn't hear her leave; Miles was adrift on a sea of memories merging and fracturing. Laughter rattled in his head, then faded. A scent of baking bread. Chug Ugentti puffing a cigar. His foster father cracking open a can of beer. He pondered if he was dying. That wouldn't be so bad. The pain would stop—all of it. And besides, death was only hard on the people left behind, and he was so fucking tired of being on that end of the deal. Miles could simply sleep.

CHAPTER ELEVEN

October 8
New York City

A rumbling pulled him from sleep or unconsciousness, and Miles rolled onto his side toward the transom window that took up most of the bedroom wall. Thankfully, it was overcast; the gray eased him awake. The room came into focus. A bottle of Advil and a half-drunk glass of water were on the nightstand. His bare feet hit the carpet, and Miles looked down at his boxer briefs. He didn't recall undressing or getting the water.

He wandered into the loft's main room and scanned the space. Clara was long gone; there was no trace of her presence. Maybe he had imagined her lilac scent as he slept. Perhaps she had never been here at all. Both thoughts angered him, deep beneath his solidly built wall of indifference. With a painful breath and a slow exhale, Miles composed himself and turned to the kitchen.

There was a used pod in the Keurig—vanilla hazelnut—proof the little prowler hadn't been a fever dream. Miles discarded it and popped in his usual Italian roast. When the coffee had brewed, he carried the mug to the couch and sat on the distressed leather with his free hand cradling his bruised ribs.

As he glanced around the room, his annoyance eased. When his twin had lived here, the place was a glorified shithole. He couldn't blame Miller. He was a former SEAL, used to living in far worse accommodations. Like Miles, his twin must have understood that the cozy comfort of their childhood bedroom was, at best, a memory.

Miles had gutted the place, upgrading the wiring and the plumbing. He'd refinished the original peg and plank floors in a rich walnut. He replaced the hotplate and mini fridge his twin had called a kitchen with state-of-the-art appliances, granite counters, and a sleek island with upholstered barstools. In front of the island sat a farmhouse dining table and eight chairs that had never been used. The rest of the furniture was artfully distressed leather, the couches and chairs partitioned by the building's ornate support girders.

Miles had decorated the living space with precision, if not personality. A Gibson guitar that had once belonged to Eric Clapton hung between the two massive windows. Crisp minimalist art in blacks and grays dotted the walls.

Above the newly built fireplace was a painting by an obscure Brazilian artist. It was a twist on a traditional still-life—the classic fruit bowl had fallen to the floor and shattered. Miles had purchased it at an auction last year. Something about the image spoke to him.

The loft was impeccably decorated, every lamp, every vase chosen by Miles with great care. The only notable absence was any shred of evidence from his childhood. The only photo Miles had was a framed image of the twins playing in a leaf pile. They had been about five when it was taken. His brother had left it for him when he moved out. Miles kept it on a shelf in his closet.

Still, as he took in the clean, stark space, he couldn't help feeling it was somehow haunted. Maybe it was the echoes of his twin or the strangely comforting aroma of baking bread that occasionally wafted through the room, reminding Miles of the bakery that had once occupied the building. Try as he might, Miles couldn't seem to exorcize the ghosts.

After a scorching sip, Miles set the coffee on the end table. When the cup wobbled, he glanced over, spying the watch lying flat on the surface. The digital face blinked *0:00*. Miles picked it up and examined the programming. The timer had counted down from three hours.

Clara had followed concussion protocol and checked on him throughout the night.

He replaced the watch, ignoring the stabbing pain in his sternum. Rising too quickly, Miles steadied himself, then strode to the shower. The water was soothing and rejuvenating, but his anger simmered. Fucking Clara and her misplaced concern.

The first time he ever laid eyes on her, he knew. She was a child then—they both were really—cradling an injured bird and creating a makeshift nest with a cloth and a box. In one breath, Reynard had instructed Miles to deliver a bribe to a border guard, and then, in the next, he was barking at his housekeeper to help Clara save the baby bluebird.

Clara was a do-gooder, a believer in miracles. It stood to reason, after all. Clara had been plucked from adversity and danger by Reynard; like a true fairytale princess, she had been swept from darkness into light.

Their lives had followed opposite trajectories.

Miles had experienced the reverse. Clara would learn at some point that the only person worth looking out for was herself.

After toweling off, Miles crossed naked to the walk-in closet and opened the dresser. Despite all the adversity she had faced, Clara was kind. She was beautiful, bright and magically naïve. She was also protected.

Miles recalled a story from years ago: Clara had broken the nose of one of her boarding school teachers, claiming he made advances. The teacher denied it, insisting that Clara was unbalanced and upset about a bad grade. With the he-said-she-said situation, the school administration sided with the teacher. Reynard flew in the following evening, took his daughter to dinner, and left the next morning. By the time his plane touched down in France, the teacher had confessed and resigned. Clara lived in a bubble of safety beyond her own understanding. While he indulged her unconventional and sometimes dangerous pastime, Reynard stopped at nothing to keep Clara safe.

Her father had enlisted Miles in the effort.

Reynard would spend his last dime protecting Clara—not that it would come to that; her father had fortunes upon fortunes. He was one of the world's most powerful men, and very few even knew his name. Miles was one of the privileged few Reynard allowed into his inner circle. And while he had nothing close to Clara's relationship with Reynard, Miles often entertained the notion that his affection for Reynard was filial.

Miles reminded himself he felt no particular attachment or obligation to Clara or Reynard. His life was one of favors asked and granted. He owed Clara—she had recently helped him run a con—so he put her in the mental debt column. That was the extent of it.

He scanned his wardrobe, contemplating who he needed to be that day, thoughts of Clara banished.

And yet, as he stared into the open dresser drawer, he couldn't help but smile.

She had stolen all of his underwear.

Miles put on a pair of sweatpants, resigning himself to a day or two of going commando until he could replace the boxer briefs. But as he slid the drawer closed, his eye caught the old shoe box in the back previously concealed by the missing garments. The lid was askew. Had Clara looked inside? Did she discover his secret?

Racked with pain, minus all his underwear, and troubled by the prospect Clara had peeked in that box, it took him a full minute to notice the hulking man in the bedroom doorway, holding a cage.

CHAPTER TWELVE

October 8
New York City

Miles's twin brother stood like a colossus in the center of the room. Miles was tall, nearly six-three, but Miller—his buddies called him "Tox"—was bigger in height and breadth. He was also a protector by nature. Miles knew Miller must have been an incredible SEAL with his combination of physical strength and penchant for self-sacrifice. Miles didn't let himself think about how much he had missed having his twin by his side.

A hiss, or more accurately, a rasping screech, emanated from the pet carrier in his brother's hand. Miller's mouth tilted into a devilish smirk.

"I guess my new security measures need some tweaking," Miles deadpanned.

They returned to the living room. Miller set the cage on the coffee table and sank onto the couch. "I still have my key," he explained unapologetically.

Miles sat next to his brother and shoved his arm. "Not that I'm not happy to see you, but why are you here, Miller?"

"Bro, I think you need to start calling me Tox. Only Calliope calls me Miller these days. And it's usually in the heat of the moment if you get my drift."

Miles cradled his ribs with one hand and held up the other to stop his brother from elaborating. "Say no more."

A move like that didn't escape his twin's notice. Miller, *Tox*, always had a sixth sense about Miles.

"What happened?"

Miles lifted his chin toward the pet carrier. "Can we discuss the elephant in the room first?"

"Bro, no way an elephant could fit in there."

"Fuck off."

Tox laughed. "I brought you a present."

"Uh-huh."

Tox leaned forward and patted the top of the cage; a black paw swiped out from the front opening, and his brother snatched his hand back reflexively, then covered the move by cracking his knuckles. Tox lifted the latch and opened the small door. "Miles, meet Loco."

A black shadow flashed across the coffee table, darted into the kitchen, up the cabinet shelves to the top of the fridge, and disappeared above the exposed ductwork in the ceiling.

"What the fuck?"

"Nothing to worry about. He's very low-maintenance and great at catching rats."

Miles felt his face morph into a pose from long ago, as if muscle memory had taken over and reverted to the familiar *what the hell do you think you're doing* expression. Tox saw it, too, and pointed at him with a smile.

"Tox."

His brother sighed. "Calliope's doctor thinks Loco shouldn't be around for the pregnancy. Cats, hunters especially, can spread toxoplasmosis."

"Her doctor said this?"

"Yes. I may have researched it online and asked about it, but the doctor agrees that Loco needs to visit Uncle Miles for the time being."

"I don't want a cat."

"That's probably best. He doesn't want a human either."

"Tox."

His brother continued as if Miles hadn't spoken. "The vet in Beaufort banned him, but a guy in The East Village saw Loco once when he ate rat poison. Loco tolerated that guy."

"Because the cat was dying."

"And semi-conscious. I'll leave his number."

"I'm gone all the time. I can't have a fucking cat."

Tox pushed up off the couch and wandered into the kitchen. "So, you gonna tell me who tuned you up Saturday night?"

Miles looked surprised, then narrowed his gaze. "You had that twin thing again, didn't you."

"It hadn't happened in so long, I forgot what it was. Thought I was passing out."

"I had a run-in with a client," Miles said.

Tox stopped halfway to the fridge and turned back, bumping into Miles. "What kind of rich asshole gets physical?"

"The mobster congressman kind."

Tox shook his head. "Why am I not surprised?"

Miles waited for Tox to lead the way, then said, "No shit. The government these days makes the NBA look like a monastery."

"What happened?"

Miles followed his twin and gingerly sat on a barstool at the island. "Misunderstanding."

Tox stood with a pint of blueberries in one hand and a carton of Chinese food in the other. "Seems like an overreaction to go to blows over a misunderstanding."

"Heard of Chug Ugentti?"

"Who hasn't? The Al Capone of Congress." Tox offered Miles the lo mein. Miles reached for it, then changed his mind.

"He didn't take too kindly to being turned down."

Tox opened the blueberries and emptied half the pint into his mouth. He chewed thoughtfully before saying, "He still in construction in Jersey?"

"Whatever you're thinking, stop. I'll handle it. I deal with a lot of people used to getting their way. This was a tantrum. It's over."

It wasn't over, and Miles knew it, but he couldn't have his brother leaping to his defense. For a year as a kid in that house, he had called out in his sleep for his twin. Until The Man told Miles if he woke him up one more time, he'd be sleeping in the garage. Miles slept with a sock in his mouth after that. He'd long ago learned he would have to solve his own problems.

"You know how to reach me." Tox opened the Chinese food and sniffed. Satisfied, he dug through drawers until he found a fork.

"How's your wife?" Miles asked.

Tox held the noodles inches from his mouth with a grin. "Fucking gorgeous. God, I can't wait til she's out to here." He held his hand a foot away from his middle.

Miles picked up a stray blueberry from the counter and ate it. He started to ask another question when a distinctive alarm sounded from his phone in the bedroom.

"Shit." Miles slid from the stool and hurried back to grab the device.

"What is it?"

Miles returned with his eyes on the screen. "Clara."

"Everything okay?"

"Yeah. She's dabbling in online dating. Her father asked me to do some additional vetting of her prospects."

"Sounds simple enough."

His brother's comment barely registered as Miles scrolled the latest guy's profile. "Jesus, you'd think she'd have a more selective screening process. Look at this shithead."

He spun the phone across the counter. Tox chewed as he scrolled through the bio. "I don't know, Mi. He seems decent enough. Maybe a little boring."

"Boring? The guy has creeper written all over him. An entomologist? He's probably like those two psychos in *Silence of the Lambs*."

"They were the good guys, dumbass."

"Whatever."

Miles and his brother were fraternal twins. They didn't look exactly alike, but they did have nearly identical chocolate-brown eyes. Two of which were currently assessing Miles with amused suspicion.

"Oh, fuck off. You know as well as I do, most of these assholes are predators." He gestured to the phone. "Forgive me for being cautious."

Tox accepted his reasoning and said, "You know, Twitch can help you with background checks. That shit is a walk in the park for her."

"Thanks, but I got it." Miles would definitely not share his unique method of ensuring Clara's safety. His brother already had too many crazy notions about his and Clara's nonexistent relationship.

Tox wiped his hands on a napkin and tossed it along with the empty carton into the trash. "You know I'm here if you need me."

The words burned in Miles's chest. He had spent years teaching himself not to need his twin. The benign comment only reminded him never to rely on anyone else. "Thanks." Miles stood, and they both sidestepped in the same direction, continuing to block Tox's path to the door. His brother gave a frustrated half-laugh and stepped around Miles. They were out of sync, and they both knew it.

At the door, Tox stood silent for a beat with his back to the room. Then, without another word, he left.

CHAPTER THIRTEEN

October 9
Lucien Kite Estate

Lucien Kite paced his expansive office, no less enraged than when his men allowed The Lynx to escape the warehouse. *With his painting.* In the past three days, he had executed a rival, fucked three of his whores into oblivion, and watched while his man tortured a guard he suspected was disloyal. Nothing eased the roiling pit of lava within.

He had planned to capture The Lynx red-handed, film his execution, and earn the thanks and respect of colleagues and billionaires worldwide who had been victimized by this self-proclaimed Robin Hood. The thief had outsmarted him and vanished.

In the hallway, two of his guards were standing shoulder to shoulder, watching something on a phone. He returned to his desk and withdrew the lugar from the hidden holster beneath the center drawer. Maybe shooting these two idiots in the head would improve his mood.

Lucien left his office and came up behind the two men who were trying and failing to stifle their laughter. Glancing over their shoulders, Lucien saw what had so captivated them: a video of a naked woman struggling to cover herself with one hand over her face and the other across her breasts while yelling at whoever was filming her.

"She is hot, no?" Lucien murmured.

The guards jumped apart, the one holding the phone quickly pocketing it.

"Is she your girlfriend?" Kite asked.

The other guard, a blond-haired German who couldn't have been older than twenty, responded, "No, Herr Kite. We found her hiding behind an outbuilding at the restoration facility. She was there for one of the other men."

Something inside Lucien itched. Beckoning with a two-fingered motion, he instructed the man to show him the clip. His immediate thought was, *What guard could get a woman like that?* Despite the darkness and her frenetic movements, Kite could tell she was a great beauty. And another thing, why was she hiding her face rather than covering a more private area? "Which man?"

"We don't know."

"Send me the video."

The other guard withdrew the device. "Yes, sir." Then, fearfully added, "The number?"

Lucien shoved the pistol into his pants and snatched the phone away. He forwarded the file and returned to his office. After settling behind the desk, Kite played the video again. This time, he wasn't ogling the girl's partially covered breasts or admiring her long legs. Well, he wasn't *only* doing that. He was squinting at the dimly lit area behind her where dark clothes were piled in a heap. On the ground by her bare feet, Lucien could just make out...

...a ski mask.

Kite shot to his feet. *Of course!* It all made sense—The Lynx's ability to slip in and out of the most secure apartments and enter parties with exclusive guest lists.

The Lynx was a woman.

Kite's rage doubled at the thought. He never held females in particularly high regard, tolerating them at best and only when he had to. The fact that this *woman* more suited to a bed or a beach had outwitted him was unthinkable.

"Clever little bitch." Lucien Kite watched the video ten times, then another five before sending it to his tech analyst. He was now the owner of a precious secret—the most surprising identity of The Lynx. Lucien pondered his next steps, the endless possibilities. He had enemies and colleagues across Europe who would pay dearly for the opportunity to extract information from The Lynx or, at the very least, dole out revenge.

He himself had been the victim of this elusive thief; she had stolen a Matisse from his country home *while he slept*. He watched the clip of the woman again. She looked vaguely familiar. Had she cased his home posing as a decorator or maid? As he squinted at the footage, Kite caught just enough of her features to know she was stunning. Perhaps he would have a go at her first, then auction her to interested parties.

Yes, Lucien Kite very much liked the idea of breaking this girl. Her outward appearance was extraordinary, but it was her mind that held her true allure. She would fight him. Kite smiled at the thought.

There was plenty of time to plan his next move. First, he needed to identify the woman, then find her—no small feat. He certainly wouldn't underestimate her skill. She had outwitted him twice—first when she stole his Matisse, then at the restoration house.

He sent a brief text: *My office, 9 a.m. tomorrow.*

The reply came immediately: *Confirmed.*

CHAPTER FOURTEEN

October 9
New York City

It was a lovely autumn night. Clouds drifted past the crescent moon, and a gentle breeze signaled the coming cooler weather. Pumpkins decorated stoops, and the small trees in the sidewalk beds had just begun to change color. The street was quiet, and light glowed from the windows of the surrounding brownstones.

Clara strolled beside her date, an entomologist named Alfie Simmons, trying to pay attention to the story—his cycling trip in Moldova. No, it was Monaco. The excursion sounded fantastic; she just couldn't seem to focus on the details.

She couldn't shake the eerie feeling that they were being watched.

"We stopped at this little seaside town called Essaouira. Best seafood I've ever eaten in my life. It's funny to think that the Atlantic is their West Coast."

"Hmm?"

"The Atlantic Ocean. It's Morocco's West Coast."

"*Morocco.* Right."

Clara glanced over her shoulder, the action causing her blonde ponytail to brush her date's face. He laughed and followed her gaze. "Everything okay? Did you forget something at the restaurant?"

She stared at the empty street behind them as she reassured him. "No, no, it's fine. I thought I heard something."

"That's New York for you. Never quiet."

Facing her date and walking backward for a few steps, Clara returned her attention to Alfie. "Yes, it's bustling at all hours, that's for sure."

"This is you?" He gestured to the cement stairs leading to the door of her Harlem pre-war building.

"This is me," she confirmed.

"We'll have to save my crazy adventure in Marrakesh for the second date." He said it like a statement, but there was a question in his eyes.

Clara liked him. She did. Alfie was a researcher who, they discovered, coincidentally lived in the same building as her Department Head. He volunteered at a no-kill shelter and enjoyed travel. They shared a love of Indian food and eighties music.

Now, she was about to accept a second date with a handsome, articulate, well-dressed man. He was pretty darn perfect. So what if he didn't give her butterflies? In Clara's experience, the flutter in her belly was a sign of nausea, not love.

"Marrakesh it is," she said.

"Cool." He bent his head, and Clara met him halfway, redirecting his mouth from her cheek to her lips.

The kiss was nice. She imagined Alfie would be a gentle lover. That was her endgame, after all. To have a lover.

"I'll call you. A friend of mine works at a gallery downtown. Maybe we can go check it out next weekend."

"I'd love that." Clara gave Alfie's hand a reassuring squeeze and hurried up the stairs. He waited on the sidewalk until she was safely inside, then waved and walked off. Through the door glass, Clara watched Alfie leave, then, out of habit, scanned the block. Across the street, a man stood in the shadows beside a trendy sports bar. Nothing particularly unusual about that, except that he wasn't smoking or fighting—the typical reasons people were outside the place. He was also staring directly at her building or, more precisely, at her. Safely on the other side of her secure door, she backed away with a strange shiver and retrieved her mail.

Clara took the elevator to the third floor with a smile. She let herself into her cozy two-bedroom and tossed her keys in the dish on the table by the door. Clara loved her apartment. The main room was a hodgepodge of thrift store purchases, cherished items from home, and street art. Cluttered and colorful, it was a luxurious flat for a twenty-something student, but her father insisted she live, as he put it, *above the poverty line.* She hadn't put up much of a fight. Reynard's home, *her home*, was a literal castle. From the age of eight, she had lived like a princess. And not just her brick-and-mortar surroundings; Reynard had made wishes come true that she hadn't even known she had. He hadn't contributed to her DNA, but Reynard was the best father anyone could ever want.

He had saved her life. Then he had charmed it.

Her thoughts returned to her date. Finally, she had landed on a winner. For the past few months, her dating luck had been horrible. Eight first dates, zero second dates. Even the ones who had promised to call hadn't. It was exhausting and disheartening. So, even if she was only mildly enthusiastic about Alfie, she was eager to break this streak. As soon as he followed up on his offer to take her to the gallery, her first-date curse would be broken.

She kicked off her shoes and set the kettle on the stove to boil. Her gaze traveled the room, settling on one of the two large windows that faced the street. Bothered by that loitering man, Clara crossed the room and peeked through the cranberry-colored curtains. Her side of the street was quiet. An old man was walking a dachshund. A woman Clara knew from the neighborhood was picking aluminum cans from the trash. Across the way, business had picked up at the bar. The bouncer was checking IDs, and some guys were getting high near the curb. The man she had seen earlier was thankfully gone. Looking further down the road, Clara caught the silhouette of her date walking around the corner and coming to an abrupt stop.

The tea kettle whistled.

Shaking herself from this unusual foray into paranoia, Clara returned to the kitchen. She would have a soothing mug of chamomile and do her darndest to get excited for her next date. As the tea steeped, her eyes drifted to the window, a curious thought crossing her mind. The lurking man's presence hadn't really frightened her at all.

Miles scratched his chest through the fabric of the cheap shirt, certain the polyester was giving him a rash. He wore a leather jacket over the offending garment, and his hair was slicked back. A heavy gold chain completed the look.

When Reynard first called to ask him to keep an eye on Clara, Miles easily agreed. He owed Reynard; he always would.

However, once he began fulfilling his obligation, something happened. A bizarre possessiveness had overtaken Miles. It started innocently enough. During the summer, he had driven a wedge between Clara and a young man she was seeing by recruiting her to help with a con he was running. Miles had monopolized every minute of her time, and the would-be boyfriend was history.

Truth be told, Miles had been chasing off potential boyfriends for nearly a decade—long before Reynard had requested his help. He had monitored Clara's social media and kept watch on her at boarding school and college. When necessary, Miles had subtly *discouraged* the boys sniffing around Clara. She wasn't some notch on a dorm room bunk.

He wasn't stalking her; he was protecting her.

This summer, however, something shifted. Working every day with Clara had triggered some sort of strange obsession. She had transformed from a girl to a woman, from a prankster to a partner. Seeing Clara in a new light had seized Miles in an irrational grip.

So here he was, dressed like a seventies porn star and giving up his Saturday night to intimidate yet another loser. Yes, Clara's father had asked him to keep an eye on her, but Miles had perhaps over-invested in the assignment. For the past three months, he had chased off every one of Clara's dates. It may have been overkill, but Miles rationalized it by telling himself he was doing what he had been asked.

Besides, he reasoned, Miles was doing these guys a favor. Clara Gautreau was impossible. She was difficult and rude, and, above all, she was a thief.

She was also impossibly beautiful, which made his job that much harder. Guys were falling over themselves to be with her. In twelve weeks, Clara had been on eight first dates. She had actually gone out with a man she met buying cereal at her corner market. What was she thinking? Why was she so desperate to date?

Shaking off his tumbling thoughts, he got to the matter at hand.

He couldn't believe Clara had kissed this scrawny asshole. Miles lingered in the shadows momentarily, a haze of anger surging, then receding. He cut off Clara's date as he rounded the corner onto Broadway to hail a cab.

"Excuse me, Alfred Simmons?" Miles could easily find the names of Clara's companions by accessing her online dating profile.

Clara's date turned away from the open cab door and squinted in the darkness. "Yes. Who are you?"

Miles did his best wise guy impersonation. "Who I am is not important. You just went on a date with my employer's daughter. Maybe you've heard of him?" Miles leaned down and whispered the name of the notorious crime lord.

"Oh." Alfred swallowed. No law-abiding gnat like Alfred would ever catch the eye of the mob. But guys like him had all seen the movies.

Miles didn't elaborate. He was a master of manipulation and knew a person's own mind created the most frightening scenarios. He pulled a toothpick from the inside pocket of his jacket, revealing just the edge of the holster. "My employer would prefer that the one date be the extent of your interaction."

It was always the same—fear masked by bravado, finding a way to save face. A solution dawns. "Yeah, that's not a problem. I wasn't interested anyway."

Yeah right. Miles let Alfie escape with his dignity intact. "Good. Then we have no problem. Her father has people watching, so if you change your mind…" Alfie hurried to the curb as he replied, "I won't."

Miles had never seen a guy dive into a taxi so quickly.

CHAPTER FIFTEEN

October 11
New York City

In Manhattan, there were cop bars and sports bars, pubs for ex-pats, and saloons for wannabe cowboys. Byline was the watering hole for reporters. Set back in a Lower East Side courtyard, Byline had no sign, but journalists flocked to the vintage speakeasy to sit on stools once occupied by Jimmy Breslin and Walter Winchell.

The small space had a central rectangular bar dotted with backless vinyl stools surrounded by a smattering of tables and booths. It was quiet tonight, and Miles spotted Gordon Fine immediately. He was sitting in a back booth nursing a half-full mug of draft and laughing at something on his phone.

Miles slid into the opposite seat. He was overdressed for the establishment in khakis and a wrinkled button-down with the sleeves rolled to the elbows.

"Hey, Gordie."

"Long time, man." Gordon held up his mug to the waiter and pointed to Miles.

After the waiter delivered the beer, Miles asked, "How's the family?"

Gordon shook his head with a laugh. "Preston started walking last week. It's like someone let a chimp loose in the apartment. Ruthie's mom loves it. She keeps taking videos of him destroying shit and posting them. The old lady has eighty thousand followers."

Miles laughed along. Gordon's life was one he neither wanted nor understood. "Crazy."

Gordon leaned on the table, cradling his beer mug. "So, what do you have?"

Miles slid a piece of paper across the scarred wood.

"What's this?"

"Chug Ugentti."

Gordon blew out a breath. "Forget it. The guy's untouchable."

"Come on, Gordie. He can't have every editor and cop in the city in his pocket."

"It's not that." Gordon sat back and took a swig of his drink. "People fucking love the guy. Last year, *during the campaign*, a buddy at *The Post* got ahold of a video of Ugentti kneecapping some guy in an alley. They couldn't run it because they couldn't positively ID Ugentti in the clip, but it was him. It got leaked on social media. People fucking devoured it. Every comment was shit like *do that in Congress, Chug!* His numbers went up in the polls. He's the mobster politician."

Miles spun his mug on the cardboard coaster for a moment. "I'm not trying to get him indicted. I just need to fire a warning shot across his bow." He tapped the slip of paper he had pulled from an old file on a job he had done for Chug.

Gordon picked it up. "Who are they?"

"Interns Ugentti has screwed. A couple of them were teenagers. Legal but young."

Gordie flicked the page, then pocketed it. "It'll piss off his wife if nothing else. I have a buddy at *The Herald* who will love this."

"Thanks."

Gordon chugged the rest of his beer. "For what it's worth, according to my FBI contact, they've been investigating Ugentti for over a decade and always seem to come up empty. Looks like Jersey has another Teflon Don."

"Well, they nailed Gotti eventually. Ugentti will slip up at some point," Miles said.

"Let's just hope 'eventually' is before his presidential inauguration." Gordon stood reaching for his wallet, but Miles waved him off.

"I'll be in touch." With a mock salute, Gordie took off.

As was their habit, they left separately. Miles finished his beer and threw some cash on the table. Outside, he took a moment for his eyes to adjust. Even the evening twilight was brighter than the dark bar. In the enclosed courtyard, a vaguely familiar man sat on a wrought-iron bench, smoking a joint and scrolling through his phone. The guy never looked up, never did anything out of the ordinary. Miles shook off his disquiet and walked out to the sidewalk.

The East Village was bustling as he made his way along 6th Street back to his Bronco. He navigated the crowd of NYU students and bar hoppers as he walked across town.

Outside a corner bodega, a black man with long dreadlocks was playing the bongos. Miles dropped a twenty in the coffee can-turned-tip jar and murmured his request to the musician. The man nodded without looking up, and Miles slipped inside the store. As he wandered the cramped aisles, the bell above the door jangled. Miles browsed the food and contemplated the situation. His ribs still ached from the beating, and he couldn't yet take a full breath. Sensing a presence, Miles glanced up. The short aisle was empty. At the front of the store, the sales clerk was reading a textbook, unbothered. Miles looked the other way, seeing only the selection of chilled drinks in the wall coolers.

After grabbing a bottled water and a packaged muffin, Miles set his purchases on the counter. The cashier removed one earbud and rang him up. The young man briefly glanced over Miles's shoulder as he handed back the change.

Then, his eyes returned to the cash. Miles followed the clerk's gaze, seeing only the empty aisles behind him. There was, however, the faint smell of weed in the air.

Out on the street, Miles set the muffin and the water at the bongo player's feet, then slipped another twenty into the can as the musician confirmed his suspicion. Walking at an unhurried pace, Miles returned to his Bronco and climbed inside. He pressed the ignition, contemplating how Ugentti's man had followed him.

CHAPTER SIXTEEN

October 12
New York City

"Three days and no call. The first date curse continues."

Clara sat at the artfully distressed farmhouse table in her neighbor Tasha's open kitchen. There were only two apartments on each floor of their five-story building, and Tasha and Dave's was twice the size of hers. Tasha was a pediatrician, and her husband was a scout for the Mets. Their daughter, Layla, was in the sixth grade.

"How long has it been?" Tasha sipped her tea.

Clara sighed. "A week. The gallery event he mentioned has come and gone, so I guess that's that."

Tasha was a highly analytical thinker, and Clara always appreciated her insights, as insensitive as they sometimes were. "It's unlikely that outside forces affected every second date. I mean, if it had been one guy or even two or three, we could consider work, travel, illness—that sort of thing. But nine? The common denominator is you."

"I'm aware." Clara snatched a cookie from the plate.

"I think it's safe to say you're not discussing marriage, babies, or exes on these dates."

"Correct. The first two are off-limits first date topics, and I don't have an ex."

"Maybe I should follow you next time? I could sit at a nearby table and eavesdrop. You know how they do it in the movies? I'll pretend to read a newspaper."

A chill ran down Clara's spine. Hit with sudden suspicion, she stood. "I've got to dash. I need to get ready for a meeting with my advisor."

Tasha walked her to the door. "Okay, babe, keep me posted on the next date. I'll get my trench coat ready."

"Ha ha," Clara deadpanned. "I'll see you later."

CHAPTER SEVENTEEN

October 12
Lucien Kite Estate

Lucien Kite's office was the only tastefully decorated room in the house. With dark wood bookshelves and a sizable masculine desk, the space reflected a decorum and gravitas absent in the rest of the residence. Until visitors saw the chair.

It was a Dada-inspired sculpture called *The Throne*. Kite had purchased the piece a year ago and proudly showed it off to any and all guests. Six feet high and three feet across, the chair had wide armrests with two spired hand holds at the edges.

And the entire piece was constructed from stacks of hundred-dollar bills.

It was intended to be a work of art, a scathing social commentary on greed.

Kite used it as his desk chair.

He stood from the pompous seat and shook the hands of his Bratva associates. Kite was no stranger to the mob. His father had been a low-level enforcer for a family in Brooklyn, and Kite's first job was working for a syndicate bookie. While running the Zorba Fund Ponzi scheme, Kite had created an additional lucrative income stream laundering money for organized crime. He had no allegiance to any family or organization; Kite's loyalty was to money. So, like any good entrepreneur, he was branching out.

The House Manager appeared to escort his Russian friends out. This arms deal would net Kite eight figures, yet his mood had not improved. He was obsessed with something far more tantalizing than providing automatic weapons to heroin traffickers. For days, Kite had done nothing but watch that six-second video clip of the woman, over and over and over, an unprecedented concoction of fury and lust infecting his blood. Last night, his phone battery had died midjack off, and Lucien was forced to imagine the naked blonde hurling German profanity.

His best tracker had gotten no closer to discovering the identity of his little thief. She had covered her face and positioned herself in precisely the right way to block the key markers for facial recognition. Lucien couldn't decide which was more arousing: her slyness or the thought of beating that duplicity out of her. He shifted in his seat at the image of this woman kneeling, subservient.

Lucien Kite was not prone to fits of violence, but his inability to locate this Siren had him ready to hurl his highball glass into the fireplace. Not money, sex, violence (or any combination of the three) could quell this need. Torn between smashing his computer screen and rewatching the video, the clearing of a throat stole his attention.

Raphael Garza loomed in the doorway. Standing well over six feet tall, wearing jeans, combat boots, and a plain black T-shirt, Garza was an imposing presence. His signature Wayfarer sunglasses covered the half-moon scar across his right eye. Even with his compromised vision, Garza was the most vicious man Kite knew.

More important to Kite, Raphael Garza could find a golf ball in a blizzard. "Well?"

His best tracker's face revealed nothing, but a kinetic air surrounded him.

Before the man spoke, Lucien knew Garza had found his mysterious art thief.

"Her name is Clara Gautreau. She's an art Ph.D. student at Columbia University." Garza paused to add gravity to his final bit of information. "She is Reynard's daughter."

Kite arched a brow. Reynard was an underworld king—one of five men controlling the black market. Ten years ago, crossing Reynard would have been a death sentence for both Kite's business and his person. But Reynard was old and rumored to be sick—a manageable threat.

The truth of the matter was it made no difference to Kite whether Reynard was in peak form or had one foot in the grave. His compulsion to claim Clara had strayed beyond the rational. The few gray cells still functioning urged him to act carefully.

"Send me everything you've learned."

With a curt nod, Raphael turned and left.

Lucien Kite ran a calloused hand over his beard, then, for the thousandth time, brought up the video of his future captive.

"Hello, Clara."

Raphael Garza strode out of Lucien Kite's home, slipped into the SUV, and drove away. Garza was slender, but he exuded an aura of menace that parted crowds. Usually, when he was working, Raphael traveled in a nondescript sedan, but in this chic part of town, he was probably just as inconspicuous in the white Range Rover. He pulled into a parking spot at the local marina and shut off the engine.

The truth was, Garza had known who The Lynx was for quite some time. He had enjoyed learning of her exploits and cheered her daring. Garza had put off sharing her identity with Kite for as long as possible without garnering suspicion. He wanted to help her, but Raphael Garza had his own skin—and bank account—to think about.

The idea had occurred to him late one night like a bolt of lightning splitting the sky. Many times, Garza had feasted on the carcass of another lion's kill. Clara was a thief. Raphael Garza wanted to steal something. It was so obvious he was shocked he hadn't thought of it earlier. Garza just needed to tie the thread to his puppets and make them dance. If he set the stage carefully, no one would know Garza was pulling their strings.

He withdrew the secure cell phone from the console and placed the call.

Raphael Garza had never met Reynard, but Raphael had always remembered the inadvertent gift he had bestowed. The day Reynard rescued Clara from that squalid alley, he had kept Garza from a grim fate as well. Reynard had killed the man who was a threat to everyone in their impoverished corner of Paris.

Reynard had also demonstrated in vivid technicolor that the key to getting everything in life was money. He had shot a man in cold blood that day. An hour later, the body was gone, and it was as if it had never happened. The police never came, a crime was never investigated. That was Garza's first taste of money and power, and he was instantly addicted.

"Hello?" Reynard's suspicious voice answered after several rings.

"Lucien Kite is aware Clara is the thief known as The Lynx. He intends to take her."

"Who is this?" Reynard asked.

"It's not important. I owe you, so I'm giving you a warning. You won't hear from me again."

"How will I know who to thank?"

Raphael's chest burned. When had he ever been thanked for anything in his life?

"Not necessary. Protect Clara. Kite is coming."

Raphael ended the call, ensured the data automatically erased, and exited the lot in the direction of Manhattan.

CHAPTER EIGHTEEN

October 14
New York City

Date number ten was a bust. Fidel was an architect recently fired after an altercation with his boss. Clara guessed from the way Fidel treated the waiter and the Uber driver that the termination was justified. Regardless, the perceived injustice was still raw, and Fidel had spent the entire meal ranting about his former colleagues. After the main course, Clara had asked for the bill—her offer to pay was met with an unappreciative nod.

Clara had the driver drop Fidel first—she declined his offer to come in for a drink. She was alone when the car pulled up to her apartment. After thanking the driver, she got out and blew a frustrated sigh. With her luck, Fidel would be the guy who called for a second date.

A breeze rustled the small trees at even intervals along the sidewalk. With the wind came the familiar prickle. Clara glanced across the street. Music drifted from the bar. A group of college guys were huddled in a circle, laughing. Frustrated with her recurring paranoia, she climbed the steps and fished her keys from her tote. As she felt around the bottom of the cavernous bag, Clara looked over her shoulder and reexamined the dark street.

That's when she saw him. A broad-shouldered man slipped from the shadows of a darkened entry next to the bar and proceeded down the block at a leisurely pace. He wore a tight gray T-shirt, jeans, and work boots. With a flick of his fingers, he shot a cigarette into the street.

She didn't recognize him, but she knew him. It was the walk. It was the aura of confidence.

Clara scrambled down the steps and ran to the opposite sidewalk. "Hey!"

He was at the corner, and Clara sensed his hesitation. It would be easy for the guy to bolt. But he didn't. With a resigned drop of his shoulder, Miles Buchanan turned to face her.

The lid on her temper was being pelted by the boiling water beneath. She opened her mouth to release a torrent of French curses when Miles held up both hands. "I can explain."

Her closed-mouth scream had the college guys and the bouncer looking over. Before a confrontation could arise, Miles ushered Clara across the street with a hand at the small of her back.

As they climbed the steps to her building, Miles spoke into her ear. "You were about to yell at me in French, weren't you?"

"The words coming out of my mouth shouldn't concern you nearly as much as the knife coming out of my purse."

"Before you start filling me with holes, let me just say it's not what it looks like."

"Really? Because it looks like you're lurking outside my apartment whenever I'm out on a date." Clara's gaze bounced from one chocolate-brown iris to the other. "Oh, my God! You're scaring them off."

Miles quirked a lopsided grin that, in any other situation, would have been devastatingly charming. "Okay, then it's exactly what it looks like."

The string of French curses finally made an appearance.

Miles leaned close and growled in her ear, "Swear at me inside, Bluebird. People are staring."

When she finally pushed him away, it was with the point of the switchblade in her hand. "Interfere again, and I will change the octave of your voice."

He lifted both hands in a surrender gesture. "It was only to protect you."

Clara poked him with the tip of the knife. "Bullshit."

"Put that away, and let me explain."

She folded the blade into the handle. "Start talking."

Shit.

Miles looked beyond her, and Clara turned and followed his gaze. A mother and daughter were approaching, arguing about something, but stopped when they noticed them.

"Clara?"

She poked her head around Miles's back, gripping his T-shirt at the sides. "Hi, Tasha."

The woman scanned Miles from head to toe as he shifted Clara to his side. "Hey, honey. Everything okay?"

The girl, who looked to be about thirteen, stepped forward and said, "Clara, can you please tell my mom that four-inch heels are normal?"

The mother was shaking her head from behind.

Clara smiled. "Totally normal height. But they're so uncomfortable you end up taking them off at a dance or a party, and the whole look fails. If I'm going to be on my feet all night, I go with a super chic kitten heel."

"What's a kitten heel?" she asked with interest.

Miles nearly laughed. Clara had steered the girl so cleverly.

"What size are you?"

"Seven," the girl replied.

"Oh, my God, Layla, come over after school tomorrow. You can shoe-shop in my closet. I have a silver pair that would look so cute on you."

"Yes?" The girl, Layla, gave her mother a pleading look.

"I think that's a great idea." The mother mouthed *thank you*, and Clara winked.

"Well, we are off to bed. Layla has to be at school early tomorrow. Are you coming up?"

The woman may as well have asked Clara to solve a complex equation. They needed to talk, but inviting him up in front of her neighbors and friends had her hesitating.

Miles offered a solution. "I'd be happy to fix that leaky faucet you mentioned."

Clara played along. "Right. Yes, that would be great."

"Well, come on then." The mother ushered them through the door and into the elevator, then pushed the button for their floor.

Miles was a big guy but knew how to appear disarming and unintimidating. He stood in the back of the car with his hands in his pockets. Out of the corner of his eye, he saw Clara's neighbor mouth *date number two* and give a thumbs up. Miles pulled his lips inward and stared at the lit numbers above the door.

On their floor, the woman waved goodbye and steered Layla to the right. Clara pulled Miles to the left.

It appeared the other apartment took up the back two-thirds of the floor while Clara's ran along the front. Miles had never been inside her place. Clara, on the other hand, not only knew where he really lived but had broken in several times to play some childish prank.

She shoved her key in the lock. "Leaky faucet, huh?"

Miles said, "Your neighbor showed amazing restraint, not making a joke about your pipes."

"I'm sure she's saving it for later."

Clara opened the door and walked in, but Miles paused on the threshold, momentarily surprised.

Clara Gautreau was chic and sophisticated—an art lover raised by a man who spared no expense for her happiness. Miles hated to admit how often he had imagined Clara's home as he lay awake at night tormented. He pictured a stylish, decorated flat with obscure but valuable art and elegant furnishings.

This was not that.

If he had been abducted and his kidnapper had pulled the hood from his head, Miles would have thought he was in a country cottage. Even at night, the space seemed sunny. The inviting couch was a yellow floral pattern and sat atop bleached hardwood. The rustic coffee table held school books, a laptop, and— much to his dismay—a cereal bowl with a spoon resting in an inch of old milk.

She had chosen landscapes to decorate the walls, except over the fireplace where an abstract of children's handprints had pride of place. Curious, Miles stepped closer.

"Layla—the girl in the elevator—her class made it in second grade. I saw it in a box of stuff her mom was moving down to their storage unit and asked if I could have it."

Miles huffed at his lack of expertise. She could have told him it was a priceless work by some trending artist, and he would have believed it. He stared at the mish-mash of tiny, brightly colored hands and swallowed the inexplicable lump in his throat. When he turned, Clara was standing at the kitchen island holding two glasses of wine.

She held out one. "Sacrament before confession."

He crossed the room and accepted the offering. Miles wasn't sure what he was going to say, but he was sure he needed a drink.

Clara led him to the living room and indicated he take the sage green easy chair, also known as the hot seat. Before he complied, he set his glass down and picked up the dirty dish she had left on the table.

"You'll get mice," he said as he took the bowl to the kitchen and rinsed it.

"I have a mouse. His name is Oscar." She tilted her head to the corner where a saucer held a cube of cheese and cracker bits.

Miles dropped the dish into the sink with a clank. "That's disgusting."

"No, it's not. He's adorable."

"It's unsanitary."

"Psh. He pops by from time to time for a snack. It's not like he's colonizing the place."

"Yet."

"You're being ridiculous."

"Oh, *I'm* being ridiculous?"

"And you're stalling."

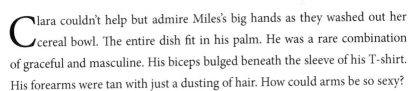

Clara couldn't help but admire Miles's big hands as they washed out her cereal bowl. The entire dish fit in his palm. He was a rare combination of graceful and masculine. His biceps bulged beneath the sleeve of his T-shirt. His forearms were tan with just a dusting of hair. How could arms be so sexy?

She forced her attention to her chardonnay and took a healthy swig. When she looked up from her place on the couch, Miles was in the armchair. He slotted the stem of the glass between his third and fourth fingers and cupped the bowl.

"Have I mentioned that Reynard asked me to look out for you?" he asked.

"It must have slipped your mind."

"When I relocated to New York, your father was happy someone he trusted would be near you. He worries."

"I know." Clara's chest tightened. She didn't want Reynard to lose sleep over her safety, but at the same time, she had to live her life.

"Reynard knew you wouldn't accept a bodyguard, but he couldn't live without protecting you. He thought my presence was a good compromise."

"And how did that work? I can't imagine Papa ordering you to accompany me on dates."

"That wasn't what I was doing. Exactly."

"Oh? And what were you doing? Exactly?"

Miles took a drink, then replied unapologetically, "Scaring them off."

Clara shot to her feet. "Oh, my God. Miles! I've had nine, no, ten first dates and zero second dates. Are you telling me that's because of you?" She ran a hand up and down, gesturing to his body. "You pulled some macho biker bullshit and threatened them."

Something about her outburst seemed to please him, and he sat back and crossed an ankle over his knee. "Not always a biker. Sometimes I'm a wise guy. With that hipster musician, I was your drug dealer ex."

"Miles!"

"Oh," He chuckled. "With the first guy, I was your stalker."

"Method acting, I see."

He set his wine glass on the table and rose to his full height. Even with the coffee table between them, he still dominated her.

"They weren't worthy of you, Clara. That guy tonight? Did you know he trashed his office when they fired him? And the poet two weeks ago? He has a fucking record! Assault, drunk and disorderly; the guy's a criminal."

Clara watched Miles as he spoke. He didn't shout, but this was without question the most animated she had ever seen him. The guy had the emotional range of a tree trunk. Clara was French. She was passionate. Just yesterday, she yelled at a man who refused to give up his subway seat to a pregnant woman. Things *affected* her. Miles, on the other hand, had a distance to his interactions that bordered on callous.

"Not one of them deserved a second date with you."

For so long, she had imagined Miles as this robot—ever since the one word that burned her heart to a cinder when she was a starry-eyed teen.

"I could fall in love with you."

"Don't."

Clara had comforted her tattered heart by picturing gears and wires beneath his skin. But this, this hint of lava beneath the glacier, birthed a dreaded hope. His vehemence was blowing on an ember she thought she had doused.

As if sensing her reaction, Miles stopped speaking, retook his seat, and finished the wine in one gulp.

His cool demeanor restored, he said, "I was simply doing what Reynard asked. If I overstepped, I apologize."

Clara mirrored his movements, sitting and finishing her drink. "Well, you certainly committed to the assignment. How did you ever find the time to stalk me in your busy life of covering up scandals and fucking prostitutes."

Her remark got no reaction. Miles replied, "I managed."

"And will you stop?"

"No."

She didn't bother to analyze why his answer pleased her. Instead, she gathered their empty glasses and took them to the kitchen. "It's late."

Miles stood and walked to the door. He tugged on the safety chain and examined the deadbolt. Clara stood behind him, watching as he inspected her locks. He turned to speak, then seemed to rethink and left without a word.

Clara turned back to her empty apartment. She hated admitting she had wanted *a moment*—some parting words from him to tell her she mattered. She released a frustrated growl. Why, after all this time, was she still clinging to false hope?

Looking up at the handprint painting, Clara realized the hope wasn't for her; it was for Miles. Because as cold and distant as he appeared, she saw the sadness behind his eyes, and that, more than any rejection or disappointment, broke her heart.

After refilling her wine glass, Clara returned to her cozy couch, her body humming like a plucked guitar string. Why was she so consumed by that frustrating, aggravating man? With chardonnay and lust heating her blood, Clara got an idea, a terrible, sensational idea. If Miles was going to prevent her from finding a man, he left her no alternative.

He did owe her a favor, after all.

CHAPTER NINETEEN

Lucien Kite flipped through the paperwork in the folder. He had instruct-ed Raphael Garza to gather information on Clara Gatreau and her father, the infamous Reynard, and his tracker had delivered. Kite paused at an eight-by-ten photo. He withdrew the picture and examined it. "This is the painting Reynard bought?"

Raphael Garza stood at ease, feet shoulder-width apart, hands folded behind him. "Yes, sir."

Kite returned to the file. "I've never heard of the artist. Tavarro."

"He's a lesser-known Spanish artist."

"Two mil seems like a hefty price tag for 'lesser-known.'"

Garza shifted his stance. "There are rumors surrounding that painting."

Kite set the file down. "What kind of rumors?"

"Most reputable sources insist there is no truth to them."

"But."

"In the 1700s, Ferdinand the Sixth, the Spanish King who was widely thought to be insane—he was known as Mad King Ferdinand—became convinced he was going to be assassinated. He planned an escape in the event of a siege and supposedly hid money and jewels along the route. The legend goes that Ferdinand would sneak off during hunts to bury bundles of treasure. After the deaths of Ferdinand and his wife, Queen Barbara, it was discovered that her wedding jewelry was missing. Notably, her ceremonial tiara. The center stone is a rare twenty-carat Kashmir sapphire."

Kite gave a low whistle.

"There was no evidence that any of this was true until the late eighteen-nineties when a father and son were fishing in the river where Ferdinand was known to hunt. The boy was digging for worms and unearthed a pouch filled with antique coins."

"Dating back to Ferdinand the Sixth," Kite surmised.

Garza nodded. "The discovery triggered a massive treasure hunt. The Spanish government had to intervene to stop tourists from digging up an entire river bank."

"The sapphire was never found?" Kite asked.

"As I said, most authorities on the subject have concluded that the jewels were stolen by servants or courtiers. Neither the king nor the queen were in their right minds. It would have been easy for anyone with access to take advantage. But stories persist that Ferdinand hid the items."

"How is the painting connected?"

"Tavarro's village is along the river where King Ferdinand held lavish hunting events. The artist was poor, and Tavarro scraped by selling paintings and teaching. In the nineteen twenties, Tavarro acquired a large, unexplained sum of money. Locals whispered that perhaps Tavarro had discovered one of Ferdinand's treasure troves. Tavarro refused to answer when questioned. He moved to the mountains and became a recluse. He lived alone until his death in 1938. That was his last painting." Garza nodded to the closed file on Kite's desk.

Kite pulled out the photo and read the portrait's title. "*Somewhere.*"

"Do you see the writing along the bottom?"

"Yes. I can't make it out."

"It's a cryptic poem. Conspiracy theorists think it's a map or a code. That, combined with the strange title, *Somewhere*, has treasure hunters believing that painting holds the key to finding the Kashmir sapphire. It's a lot of nonsense."

"Reynard doesn't seem to think so."

"Or he's a smart collector. Tavarro has gained a lot of notoriety over the years—for his talent, not this treasure nonsense." Garza gestured to the photo Kite held.

Kite returned his attention to the paperwork. "The painting was auctioned in Madrid and is being shipped to Reynard in France?"

"It's in transit," Garza confirmed.

"Where is it now?" Kite asked.

"At a customs house in Marseilles."

"Thank you, Garza. You can go."

When the door closed behind his tracker, Lucien Kite placed a call. He was no one's prey. It was time to become the predator.

CHAPTER TWENTY

October 17
New York City

Miles lifted the gate of the industrial elevator, unlocked the steel fire door, and entered his loft. On his way to the bedroom, he caught a hint of Clara's lingering lilac scent. Annoyed by how it soothed him, Miles tugged at the knot in his tie. When he passed the dining table, he saw it—the small T-shirt draped across the kitchen island. Miles was meticulous; he had learned to keep things in their place at a young age. Walking to the open kitchen, he eyed the white fabric. He rubbed the cotton between his fingers and lifted the garment to his nose. His mind echoed her name as he inhaled.

The bedroom was dimly lit by the single lamp on the side table. The gray bamboo curtains were drawn. The expanse of the dark duvet was interrupted by the perfect girl sitting on the end, her bare pink-tipped toes just touching the floor.

Clara's blonde hair was in a loose braid, and the white demi bra did little to conceal apple breasts with pert nipples. Her jeans had holes in the knees and frayed hems. Miles's first thought was to tear the denim from her body— punish those pants for hiding her legs.

He was instantly hard and royally pissed. "What do you think you're doing?"

Clara jutted out her chin and sat up straighter. "I've made a decision."

Miles leaned against the doorway and crossed his arms. "Oh, you have, have you?"

"I have."

"And what have you decided?"

"You owe me a favor, and I'm here to collect."

"Collect how?"

"You're going to take my virginity."

Miles summoned every ounce of composure to keep his feet from staggering back. How was it possible? He hadn't kept an eye on her every minute. Clara had traveled the world, attended boarding school and college. She was the most beautiful girl Miles had ever laid eyes on. Men had to have pursued her like hounds after a fox. With seasoned expertise, he covered his shock and arousal with a chuckle.

"And why have you chosen me for the honor?"

She leaned back on her palms. "I didn't choose you. *You* chose you. If you're going to chase off any man I try to date, you'll have to be the one to do it. Simple as that."

"Reynard..."

"Please, don't mention Papa. It's my business. I've decided."

Damn, the little witch. Miles had seen Clara in nearly every conceivable attire, from ball gowns to bikinis. Her body was the stuff of wet dreams. There had been times in the shower or late at night when he actively had to force the vision of her from his head as he wrapped a hand around his erection. He would run through the saved mental images of models and actresses desperately trying to replace a memory of Clara eating a strawberry or bending down to pick up a book.

She had arrived at the worst possible time. Between his troubles with Chug Ugentti and the career change he was finally considering, everything was coming to a head. The last thing he needed or wanted was for Clara to pay the price of his own emotional turmoil.

One thing he knew, Clara was single-minded. The more he tried to bully her into relenting, the more she would dig in her heels. *Dig in her heels.* The thought produced a picture of those bare feet around his back. Shaking the idea loose, he came to the inevitable conclusion that there was only one way to get Clara to reconsider.

In three long strides, Miles was towering over her. With a flick of his fingers, he popped the front clasp on Clara's bra, and the fabric fell away. With a feather-light touch, he ran the back of his index finger over the swell of her breast. Goose bumps rose on her flesh, and her nipple hardened beneath his touch.

"*You've* decided?" he said.

"Y-yes."

"Let me make one thing clear, Clara. In this room, you don't make decisions. I do."

Those Mediterranean blue eyes widened in shock. Was she surprised he had agreed? Or was she afraid of what was to come? Both, probably.

"This is what you want? An emotionless deflowering?"

"Well, not emotionless. I hate you."

His response was stoic as he continued his gentle strokes. "I see."

"And I assume you feel the same," she whispered.

"Why would you assume that?"

"You've never been kind or friendly. When I was a child—" She stopped herself. "You don't have to worry about romantic entanglements. You owe me a favor, and I'm collecting."

It was true. He did owe Clara. She had helped him run a con over the summer, bringing down a corrupt pharmaceutical company CEO. This was the last way he had ever imagined repaying.

Slowly, intentionally, Miles removed his suit jacket, folded it, and laid it across the back of the reading chair by the windows. Deep inside him, the demons were growling in their cages.

"Lie back on the bed."

Clara undid the button on her jeans and reached for the zipper. "Do what I tell you, Clara. Nothing more."

"Can I... can I ask a question?"

Unbuttoning his dress shirt, he replied, "Yes."

"Does it take... I know it hurts, but is it quick? Does it last long?"

"The pain or the fucking?"

If she was shocked by his choice of words, she didn't show it. "The fucking."

Miles leaned forward on one arm. Hovering over her, he replied, "All night."

With his free hand, he unzipped her pants tooth by tooth. He stepped back, pulling the jeans with him, leaving Clara in her unclasped bra and matching white thong. Suddenly, Miles wasn't sure of his plan. Would she relent? Could he hold back? He breathed in her scent, consumed by the primal urge to mate. Still, the evolved man within held back. She didn't comprehend the magnitude of this gift. She didn't know how undeserving he was. He had intended to show her what a poor choice she had made, to make her lose her nerve. Now, it all felt out of his control, as if some magnetic field between their bodies was pulling them together. Miles needed to stop this before they both did something they would regret.

"Clara—"

She shot to her knees with fierce agility. "Oh, no, you don't. I don't know what's going on in your head, if I'm not your type, or if you're having second thoughts, but you can check your brain at the door. We've walked to the cliff's edge, and, Miles Buchanan, we are going to jump."

In a flash, Miles had Clara on her back, pinned beneath him. He ground his hips between her legs, and she lifted to meet him. He took her earlobe between his teeth and pulled, then he whispered. "Bluebird, you don't know the first thing about being on the edge of a cliff."

"That's not true, and you know it."

"I'm about to show you how wrong you are. I'm about to make you beg."

The feel of her body beneath his was too much. He was only a man. Still, Miles drew on the last of his self-control and executed his plan. "Now, who would you like to do the honors?"

"What do you mean?"

"I'm a man of many faces, Clara." He pushed off of her, stood, and crossed to the closet. Waving her to his side, Miles opened the door, revealing a room-sized space divided into sections. Miles faced her like a salesman displaying his wares. "There's the fixer, Caleb Cain. He's a bit cold—all about efficiency. He goes fast and rough." He stepped to another rack. "Then there's Jake, the biker. I'll warn you. Jake has some kinks—into bondage and toys. He throws in some breath play now and then." Miles wrapped a hand around her throat and whispered, "I don't think you're ready for Jake." Miles moved to the next section of clothes. "Ah, how 'bout the busker, Paco. He plays guitar in the subway. He might be perfect for a deflowering. Paco is gentle; he makes love."

"Miles—"

He pressed a finger to Clara's lips to shush her. "You'd never survive Zander. He's a dom. No backtalk. Disobedience would earn you a spanking. With your attitude, you wouldn't be able to sit down for a week."

Miles was supposed to be freaking her out, sending this misguided virgin fleeing the loft. Nevertheless, he couldn't stop himself from making a mental inventory of the things he mentioned that had Clara's pupils dilating, her cheeks pinking, and her pebbled breasts leaning into his body. She was aggravated by his performance, but she was also curious. Leave it to his perfect little witch to get turned on by the thought of a spanking. Undeterred and half-hard, he pressed on.

"There's Henry, the Duke of Pembroke-on-Trent. Bit of an exhibitionist, that guy. He likes to be watched. Would you like to pop your cherry against the window, Clara? Maybe let the neighbors see the big event?" Without waiting for an answer, Miles pulled a vibrant silk shirt from its hanger. "Oh, wait. Of course. Francois, the French art collector. He's perfect—gentle but creative and a bit of a dirty talker." When he turned around, Clara was sitting on the bed, shimmying into her jeans.

"Stop. Just stop."

"Where are you going?" Miles feigned surprise.

"Fuck you. I know what you're doing."

"What's that?"

"You charm and manipulate every minute of every day. I guess a moment with the real you was too much to ask."

"You hate me, Clara. I thought I could give you someone you might like."

"If this is how you see the situation, I think you must hate me, too."

"I don't hate you."

"I'm not sure I believe you."

"I don't have any feelings for you at all."

"What?"

"I stopped having feelings one way or the other years ago. I don't hate anyone."

"And you don't love anyone? Your twin brother?"

"I think it's time to call it a night." Miles ducked into the kitchen and grabbed the T-shirt she had left as bait. Returning to the bedroom, he tossed it to her.

She shrugged it on, and with a deep sadness in her voice, she asked, "What happened to you?"

Miles ignored the question. He wasn't about to bare his soul. "If you change your mind about the fucking, you know where to find me."

"Only if Miles Buchanan is available. I may hate him, but I trust him. I'm not interested in one of your characters. I only want Miles."

She turned and left.

Miles watched the industrial elevator disappear and turned to the bar. Grabbing a full bottle of bourbon, he headed up to the roof.

Clara didn't understand.

There was no Miles Buchanan. That boy had vanished like steam from a tea kettle years ago.

CHAPTER TWENTY-ONE

October 18
Dordogne, France

It was a spectacular fall morning in Dordogne. Reynard briefly glanced past the two uniformed customs officials standing in his office to admire the stunning show Mother Nature was staging on the property outside. The orchards and woods beyond were flames of red and gold. He'd always loved this estate, but as he neared the end of his life, Reynard found himself savoring these moments.

One of the men cleared his throat, regaining Reynard's attention. "The surveillance feed was cut, so nothing inside the facility was recorded. But," He held up a finger. "We captured the truck pulling up and the men getting out. Perhaps some information can be gained from that."

Last night, armed mercenaries broke into the Marseilles Customs House and stole *one thing*.

The other official chimed in. "As usual, your purchases were stored in a secure room. The thieves gained entry by blowing the door off its hinges!"

Reynard stifled a laugh at the man's classically French outrage at a perceived affront. In his mind, he had finished this conversation an hour ago. He knew who had stolen the painting, and he knew why. Reynard was onto the more critical stage of what to do about it.

The first man shifted on his feet and took half a step closer to the desk. "Monsieur, one thing we know. We are completely confident no customs employees were complicit in the crime. This was not, how they say, an inside job."

Reynard put them out of their misery. "I'm sure you are correct, Gil."

Gil blew out a relieved breath and returned to his spot beside his cohort.

The other man offered, "We can have what video we did recover forwarded to you. Perhaps your..." he hesitated. "Expertise in... Well, perhaps you will notice something."

"That won't be necessary. I know all I need to know."

Reynard wheeled back from the desk and led the two customs officials to the door, where his man stood in a dark suit.

"Your response to this event has been excellent, gentleman. You can't be expected to fend off an army. I'm relieved no one was injured."

"Of course, sir, and rest assured, the other items in your shipment have been fast-tracked and are on their way to you now."

"I'm grateful for your diligence." Reynard nodded to his guard, who handed each man a thick envelope. Gil and his associate each pocketed the item without examining the contents.

"Thank you, sir. We will keep you apprised of any news from the authorities."

"Very good. Ahmed, show them out, please."

When the office was vacated, Reynard returned to his desk. Opening a lower drawer, he retrieved the file on the painting. It was for Clara, something to convey all she meant to him. The art hadn't been outrageously expensive, but it was incredibly valuable—something he hoped would lead his daughter to the ultimate happiness. Perhaps she felt undeserving of life's most precious gift. Maybe selflessness was in her DNA. Whatever the reason, Reynard wanted

Clara to have something for herself. He loved her more than life, and his dying wish was that she never want.

He couldn't give her that true joy, but he could set her on a path. That painting was the first step. And now Lucien Kite had stolen it.

What a wonderful saint of a man.

Reynard released a laugh so hearty his wheelchair rolled. That little weasel had unintentionally provided him with the perfect way to bestow his gift upon Clara. What better way to give his daughter a present than to ask her to steal it?

With a devilish grin, Reynard dialed Clara's number.

CHAPTER TWENTY-TWO

October 18
New York City

Thunder rumbled in the distance, and the mid-morning sky was dark. Standing on a ladder in worn 501s, a gray T-shirt, and blue suede Adidas, Miles tightened the nuts on the new section of pipe. Twice, he had nearly driven the tool into his hand, so distracted by his encounter with Clara. The cavalcade of thoughts galloped through his head relentlessly. *She was a virgin. She wanted to get laid. She was trolling dating apps for a man to do the job.* It was only a matter of time before Clara gave the nod to some jackass investment banker or pencil-dick art collector. Miles nearly ripped the pipe from the bracket, imagining some coked-up corporate lawyer undressing her.

Over my dead body.

"Sugar, what's going on up there? You look like you're about to murder that pipe with a screwdriver." Foxy Amour stood with her hands on her hips at the base of the ladder, wearing a fuschia turban and a tropical-patterned mumu.

The first floor of the building was Foxy's domain. Miles's twin brother had offered her the dilapidated space a few years ago when Foxy was a struggling sex worker and needed a safe place to crash. Since then, Foxy had tapped into her entrepreneurial spirit, changed careers, and converted the ground level of the building into what Foxy described as a Psychic Spa.

Unlike the nickel-and-dime fortune-telling establishments peppered throughout Manhattan, this place was a welcoming hybrid of a coffee shop, seance venue, and Victorian parlor. Foxy employed seven people, all former sex workers, as psychics, baristas, and servers. That was just in the front room—the back of the building housed an under-the-radar gambling hall.

"All set," Miles replied, regaining his composure.

"Make sure it's tight, baby. That leak ruined two silk roll pillows."

"Maybe I'll keep it loose then," he deadpanned.

Miles hated clutter. He had spent most of his teen years being invisible, and possessions made that difficult. So, he had few belongings, and they were never out of place. In Foxy's domain, there wasn't an inch of space undecorated by trinkets, tassels, and beads.

Ignoring him, she added, "And clean the rust off that old pipe."

"You know you can always get up here and fix it yourself. I'm not a fucking plumber."

"First off, I can't climb a ladder in six-inch heels. Second, you *are* a plumber. And an electrician. And an appliance repairman."

"And a landlord in the mood for an eviction."

"Hardy har. Now get down here and have a cup of tea."

Miles stepped down the rungs. "No, thank you, *Madame* Foxy. I hate tea, and the last time you tried to predict my future, you had me working as a cop and dating a man. I had Village People songs running through my head for a week."

Foxy chuckled. "No, cher, the tea leaves foretold you would fight for justice and become very close to one man."

Miles rubbed at the familiar tightness in his chest, thinking of his twin. "Neither of which happened."

"The future is ever unfolding."

"Is that the fake psychic motto? Do you place your hand on a crystal ball and say that at the meetings?"

"Sugar, I spent four years in Baton Rouge hiding from bullies in the back of a shop run by a Hoodoo priestess. You don't get a better occult education than that."

Outside, the first drops of rain pelted the storefront window.

Foxy led him over to the coffee counter and prepared her tea. "When I told the priestess I liked to dress in costumes, you know what she said? She pointed at my trousers and button-up shirt and said, '*This* is the costume.'"

"Which, I'm guessing, came as no surprise to you," Miles said.

"I think it was the validation that was surprising. To hear my truth spoken from another mouth. That was a good feeling." Foxy's smile was warm, painted lips against ebony skin.

She poured Miles a black coffee and pointed with the mug to the round wooden table covered with a purple cloth and a lace overlay. "Come. I'm in a tarot mood."

"Foxy, no. I can't take the mumbo jumbo today. I've got a lot on my mind." Despite his protest, he followed.

A warm breeze swept through from an unknown source, and Miles swore he smelled the familiar scent of bread baking.

Foxy set her tea on the table, waved a silk scarf theatrically over her head, and withdrew the battered cards from a hidden drawer. Taking the chair facing the street, she tapped the deck firmly on the table.

"Tarot is not about spirits or goblins, cher. It's not about the outside world coming in; it's about the inside world coming out."

Miles sat opposite her. He picked up the top card and flipped it over. "How have they never made a horror movie where the Tarot characters come to life and eat your brain."

Foxy smacked his hand and shuffled. "I'll give you that. It would be a terrifying movie."

Miles reclaimed the deck and fanned the cards. "How does anyone get a tarot reading and not leave petrified?" He slipped a card out. "Look at this."

"The Hanged Man," Foxy said. "It doesn't mean—" She didn't finish her sentence before Miles set another card beside it.

"And this maniac, what the hell?"

"The Magician," Foxy watched intently as Miles examined the splayed cards.

"And here." He picked out a third card, an ominous stone structure, and placed it in the row. "Those first two psychopaths can bring their victims here."

"Ah, The Tower. Stop there."

Miles pushed the fanned deck aside and waited. Behind him, he could hear the rain pounding the pavement.

Foxy straightened each card in the line. "The Tower is your past. It represents upheaval."

"Shocking." Miles crossed his arms over his chest, knowing his twin brother had told Foxy about their parents' death and the twins' subsequent separation.

"The people that fostered you, they were unkind."

"Unkindness would have required effort," he said.

"Neglect is a form of cruelty."

"It's in the past." Miles shifted in the tiny chair.

"The tower casts a long shadow, cher."

Miles rested his elbows on the table. "Not my tower. Someone blew it up."

"Care to share?"

Miles didn't talk about his childhood, and he had no intention of doing so now, but somehow, the words spilled out. "The couple that took me—they told me they adopted me, but that was a lie—they were running from the mob. The man stole a bunch of money, ratted out the guy he robbed, and ran. Part of their plan was adopting a kid; they thought they could escape because the mobsters wouldn't be looking for a family."

Foxy mirrored his pose. "But someone did find you."

Miles sat back again. "About two years later. Blew the house and the couple to kingdom come. It was reported as a gas leak."

"Where were you?"

"The public library. As usual. I was home as little as possible. I was sort of like a stray cat. The Woman would leave a plate of food on the counter; I'd come in, eat, and leave again. I slept there, but that was basically it."

Foxy pushed the Tower Card back and forth with her fingertips, thinking. "That's strange, don't you think?"

"Foxy, there's a ton of strange in my luggage. Which part?"

"If these mobsters caught up with you, I'd assume they'd watch the house for a minute. Learn the routine of the occupants."

As usual, Foxy saw more than she should. Miles didn't want to pull on those threads. There was more to the story of that house explosion, and Miles wanted it buried with the occupants.

He tapped the center card. "Who's this mutant?"

Foxy had to know Miles was redirecting her, but she complied. Foxy had plenty of her own secrets and knew better than most when she danced too close to the flame.

"The Magician. In this position, the card represents your Present."

"Sounds about right."

"The cards rarely mean what you think. It's not a literal thing. The Magician symbolizes desire."

An image of Clara flashed in his mind. He was quick to shoo it away.

"I was in love once," she said.

Miles didn't reply. Love was an emotion he hadn't allowed himself to feel for nearly two decades. And romantic love would never factor into his life.

Despite his disinterest, Foxy continued, "She lived up the street."

"She?"

Foxy laughed. "I've always loved the girls, cher, even when I was little Darnell. My poor parents, so thrilled to think I was a straight boy only to discover—and banish—this glorious gay woman."

Miles had no words. Yes, his childhood had been rough, but he had no doubt Foxy's had been infinitely worse. He rested his hand over hers above The Magician.

She waved him off. "As you said, it's in the past."

"And as you said, The Tower casts a long shadow."

"We are both magicians then, sugar. Turning pain into profit."

He waggled a finger. "You said it wasn't literal."

Foxy bowed her head in agreement. "Creation, illusion, desire."

Ignoring the accuracy, Miles pushed the third card an inch in her direction. "I'm afraid to ask."

"The Hanged Man. He stands for sacrifice."

Another given. "Do people seriously pay for this?"

Foxy tsked, "This is The Future, my precious Miles. Something not yet known will demand a sacrifice."

"The pinpoint vagueness of tarot never ceases to amaze."

"The cards are open-ended because the answers come from within."

Miles scooped up all the cards and pushed to his feet, ending this ridiculous reading. "As always, the hocus pocus has been delightful, but I have somewhere I need to be." He tossed the tarot deck onto the table, sending the cards scattering.

Behind Foxy, the beaded curtains separating the fortune-telling space from the back room parted. One of Foxy's employees hurried through, holding an inside-out umbrella and drying her face with a hand towel.

"Sorry, I'm late. The subway just stopped! We sat on the tracks for twenty minutes. I got off a stop early and got drenched."

Foxy straightened the tarot deck and replaced it in the drawer. "The bakery boxes are on the table in the corner. Get the pastries in the case and check the coffee supplies."

"Yes, ma'am," the girl replied, hurrying around the space.

"And don't call me ma'am," Foxy shouted after the girl as she disappeared into the back.

Miles knocked on the tabletop. "Text me if that pipe leaks again. I'll perform some more magic."

Foxy waved him off. "If it leaks again, you've run out of tricks."

He pulled open the gate, stepped into the industrial elevator, and tipped an imaginary top hat as he pressed the button for his loft.

Foxy smiled at Georgia as she hurried back to the espresso machine with a stack of to-go cups and cardboard sleeves. Foxy had hired the sixteen-year-old a month ago after finding her sleeping in Madison Square Park. She had run away from her home in rural Macon, hence her new name. Her entire left arm was scarred from what Foxy guessed was a chemical burn. Foxy didn't ask questions; the girls spoke in their own time.

"You missed one." Georgia pointed to the floor.

Foxy picked up the fallen tarot card and turned it over. The card revealed a robed skeleton holding a scythe and a scepter.

Georgia appeared at her shoulder. "Creepy."

"They're just pictures, cher. The scary stuff is in here." Foxy tapped her temple.

Above them, she heard the heavy sound of the elevator lurching to a stop. A moment later, Georgia jumped back with a shriek. The reclusive black cat

Foxy thought had moved to South Carolina with Tox leapt from the overhead ductwork and landed on the table. With an arched back and bared teeth, he spat at both of them and darted off.

Foxy recoiled, with the hand holding the tarot card at her chest. When the cat was gone, she looked down at the shrouded figure.

Death.

Georgia peered over her shoulder. "What's it mean?"

"It means change is coming."

CHAPTER TWENTY-THREE

October 18
New York City

Clara slammed the door to her apartment and flopped onto her couch. A full day later, she was still fuming. Her Modern Masters seminar had been canceled, so she had nothing to distract her from the infuriating, humiliating encounter with Miles. Or whoever the hell that was in his apartment. Or *they* were. Jesus, the guy carried around a cast of characters like a Broadway road show. She muffled a frustrated growl between clenched teeth.

Regardless of her methods, Clara had asked Miles for something deeply personal. She had exposed a vulnerability, and he had all but laughed in her face—that insensitive, insufferable, unfeeling jerk.

To make matters worse, despite her rage and embarrassment, her mind couldn't stop the highlight reel of the different sexual scenarios Miles had described. Did she want to get deflowered against a window with the neighbors watching? *Yes*. Did she want to experiment with toys? Did she want to be tied up? Did she want a man whispering vulgarities in her ear as he fucked her? *Yes, yes, yes*.

The fantasies didn't numb the wound of his insult. The encounter forced the long-buried memory to the surface.

(She had rehearsed for weeks. Clara knew Miles would wander out to the orchard to say hello and ask his usual questions about her schoolwork and travels. When the movie moment came, Clara gripped her blonde braid and jutted out a hip like she'd practiced.

"Miles?"

"Yes, Bluebird?

"Have you ever been in love?"

"No. And I promise you this: I never will."

"What? Why?"

"Because love is the heel that will crush you."

He didn't say it with any particular malice—more a casual observation.

Undeterred, she continued, "I could fall in love with you."

He reached out his big, strong hand and ran his thumb along her jawline. She welcomed his touch as if someone were brushing satin on her cheek.

"Don't."

Then, as if nothing had ever passed between them, he reached into the inner pocket of his suit jacket and withdrew a small wrapped package.

"I saw this in the airport in New York. It reminded me of you. Happy Birthday, Bluebird."

He didn't even wait for her to open it.

*Clara stood among the swirling autumn leaves, holding the gift, and watched as he strode away. Miles never paused, never looked back. She tore the paper away, foolishly imagining some romantic gesture. Clara stared down at the paperback book—*1001 Practical Jokes*—sank to the grass and cried.)*

In the corner, she spied the bag overflowing with gray boxer briefs she had stolen earlier, mitigating her anger only slightly.

Clara snatched up the tote bag and walked across the open living area to the windows along the front wall. She raised the nearest one and tossed a fistful of underwear. They fluttered down to the sidewalk, one pair landing on her front stoop, another dangling from a tree limb. As she cocked her arm to launch another bunch, her skin prickled. Stopping mid-throw, Clara scanned the street for the source of her unease. Nothing seemed out of the ordinary.

Nevertheless, Clara abandoned her underwear ejection, grabbed a Pellegrino from the fridge, and returned to the couch. Staring at the now half-empty bag of boxer briefs, her mind returned to the man she was trying desperately to hate.

Her father, Reynard, had shared some of Miles's troubled childhood. Clara knew Miles's parents had died tragically within months of each other—his mother from a brain tumor, his father in a car accident. She also knew that at some point after that, the twins had been separated, and Miles had been put in a bad situation. Then, there was the house fire that killed his adoptive parents. Her mind drifted to the shoebox she had found in Miles's dresser. She decided to put the thought out of her mind. Clara knew she would never mention it to Miles, so there was no point in pondering the meaning of the items in the battered box in his drawer.

Instead, she decided to focus on something she could control. Payback. Miles was arrogant and cold, but one thing did seem to get a reaction—Clara's dating life. She didn't know why Miles was out to destroy her happiness. When Clara played pranks, her aim had only ever been to inconvenience and amuse him. Her father had asked Miles to watch out for her, but he was taking the request too far. He seemed to want to ruin any chance she had for love.

Well, maybe it was time for his little power trip to backfire.

Clara pulled her phone from her purse and opened the dating app, quickly retrieving the saved profiles.

"Okay, boys. Let's see who's game."

She started to tap out the message when a noise at her front door drew her attention. Generally, at this time of day, she would be in class. Clara glanced up to see the latch of the deadbolt rotating.

"Tasha?" she called her neighbor's name.

The rattling stopped.

She tiptoed over and checked the peephole. With the safety chain latched, she cracked open the door and looked out at the empty hallway. At her feet was a tacky, Halloween-themed flower arrangement—orange roses and sunflowers tucked among dancing skeletons and mini plastic pumpkins. Puzzled and amused, Clara retrieved the gift and set it on the kitchen island. She plucked the small envelope from the bunch and withdrew the card—then stopped breathing.

No words were written; it was simply a pen and ink drawing.

It was of a lynx.

CHAPTER TWENTY-FOUR

October 18
New York City

Molloy's gym was only a block from Equinox, the premium place where Caleb Cain worked out, but it may as well have been on another planet. The blood-stained boxing ring with tattered ropes was surrounded by speed bags, training equipment, and a smattering of folding chairs where would-bes and washed-ups traded war stories and advice.

Here, Miles was Jake Cutter, a construction worker who made a little cash on the side as an underground fighter. Jake didn't talk much, and the guys here respected that. He'd listen to Marty tell his story about being a towel man for Evander Holyfield and cheer on the kid Marty believed had a real shot, but mostly, Miles took out his frustrations. He could hit the heavy bag until his knuckles bled, and no one would look twice.

Ever since his encounter with Clara, Miles felt like a high-tension wire had been strung inside his chest. Every heartbeat seemed to crank it tighter and tighter. Sweat poured from his bare torso, every muscle tense and powerful as he moved. The pain focused him and, more importantly, kept his mind from returning to the woman who plagued his thoughts.

Today, Jake was in the ring, going a few rounds with Pavel, a guy twice his size and half his speed. Jake was pummeling him. Pavel wiped the blood from his eyebrow and spat on the canvas.

"What's gotten into you today, bruh?"

"Sorry, man. Just working some shit out." Miles stepped to the corner and grabbed a towel.

"Well, quit working it out on my face. If I come home all pounded, my girl is going to step in the ring with you, and you do not want that."

Miles chuckled despite his frustration.

"You gotta girl?" Pavel asked.

"No."

Pavel shook his head. "When I first met Kitty—that's my girl—she refused to go out with me. I used to come in here and flatten guys on the regular."

"What's your point?"

"I think you know, brother."

"She's not my gi—" Miles stopped himself too late. Pavel pointed at him in a *gotcha* gesture.

Climbing between the ropes, Miles hopped down and squirted water from the plastic bottle into his mouth. In his open bag, his cell phone lit with a notification. He snatched it up and tapped on Clara's dating app. His outburst was uncontrolled. "Goddammit!"

Pavel's booming laugh echoed in the cavernous space.

Inside Miles's chest, the wire snapped.

CHAPTER TWENTY-FIVE

October 18
Lucien Kite Estate

Lucien Kite sat on the wildly uncomfortable money throne and greeted two visitors. He double-checked their names on the small writing pad. Abner Fitch was the scruffy historian—average height, average looks. One of the arms of the horned-rimmed glasses he wore had a safety pin protruding from the hinge. The other man, Winston Frobisher, didn't have a job title. Kite understood; there wasn't exactly a major in college for what Frobisher did. Cryptographer wasn't quite right, nor was treasure hunter. The closest job title Kite could come up with was solver of riddles.

"Gentleman, please take a seat."

The men complied, looking ill at ease.

"What have you discovered?"

Abner Fitch spoke for both of them. "It will come as no surprise that this will take some time. Almost a century has passed. There have been shifts in both landscape and language."

"I'm not interested in what you haven't discovered, Fitch. I want to know what progress you've made."

"Of course." Fitch stood and crossed to the painting.

It was a portrait of a woman in profile. The model sat nude on a riverbank, her waist-length dark hair cascading around her. She was wet from her swim—her skin dewy with droplets. Staring to her right, her hand reached out to something beyond the bounds of the canvas, her longing palpable.

Lucien Kite neither knew nor cared about art. This sad painting was no exception.

Fitch spoke like he was giving a lecture. "Painted in 1928 by the famed Spanish painter Francisco Tavarro, the painting is of an unnamed woman. Historians believe the subject is a young British aristocrat named Anne Covington. In 1926, Anne and her family moved to the Spanish coastal village where Tavarro lived, hoping the sea air would help Anne's brother recover from tuberculosis.

"Tavarro was forty at the time and instantly developed an obsession with nineteen-year-old Anne. The Covington family encouraged the modeling work and art lessons the already famous painter offered, and soon, Tavarro and Anne were caught up in a torrid love affair. The family left the town in the spring of 1927, ending the affair and breaking Tavarro's heart. Tavarro lived for ten years after Anne left, before jumping from a cliff to his death, and in all that time, he only painted one painting." Fitch swung his arm to the artwork.

"Tavarro's murals and landscapes hang in museums and civic venues worldwide. This piece is his only portrait. Measuring two feet by three, it is his smallest work, appropriately titled *En Algún Lugar. Somewhere.*"

Finch continued, "The work is a declaration of everlasting love to a woman he would never see again."

Lucien Kite wasn't interested in the painting for the love story. He wasn't interested in its two million dollar price tag. It was bait.

"Note the poem the artist painted in the grass along the bottom.

Kite stepped closer and read it.

away from the world beneath the arching cliffs
in the blood-red sage beside the river
I find the riches all men seek but rarely find
beneath the laden vines, I am a king

Abner Finch pointed to the words. "Historians believe, I among them, that the artist was simply writing thoughts as they occurred to him while he painted his lover. That explains why the words are in English. Anne was British."

Frobisher interrupted with a lift of his finger. "While I have no doubt that is correct, I find it noteworthy that Tavarro was a genius. After analyzing the words and structure, I'm convinced this is a carefully worded guide."

"To where?" Kite asked, dubious.

Frobisher chuckled. "That is the question. I'm taking it apart by phrase, word, and letter." He stood and joined his colleague at the painting. "There are the subtle references: the river, the arching cliffs, even the mention of the blood-red sage. Then there are more obvious hints—the words 'seek' and 'riches.' These are all clues."

Kite could smell a swindle a mile away. If this guy was soaking him, it'd be the last job Frobisher ever pulled. Popping two aspirins, he made a *get-on-with-it* motion with his free hand.

"I am convinced that for centuries." He paused for effect.

Kite half expected to hear a drumroll.

"People have been looking for the sapphire in the wrong place."

"Really?"

"I'm still attempting to map Tavarro's words."

"Get me something by next week."

Frobisher's lips tipped in a condescending smirk. "If it were easy, Mr. Kite. Someone would have already done it."

Kite ran a hand down his face. "Frobisher, I may not be in my limo, but I know when I'm being taken for a ride. If you think I'm a difficult client now, you should see me angry."

Frobisher took an involuntary step back. "I'll let you know when I have something actionable."

Kite stood. "In the meantime, I'll have it reframed. It's not a bad-looking thing. At least she's not one of those heifers from the old days."

Fitch stepped in front of Frobisher and said, "No, don't reframe it. You were lucky the painting was still in the original frame." He ran his hand over the splintered wood along the left edge. "This damage could be significant. See how it's mainly here and here." Frobisher pointed to the top, then the bottom. "As if the painting had been hinged." Then he added meaningfully, "Perhaps it was concealing a safe at some point."

Kite stepped closer and examined the area Frobisher indicated. He was right. The intricately carved frame did indeed appear as though it had been connected to something else and then ripped away, splitting the wood.

"Is it possible Tavarro found the jewel? Had it in a safe and was robbed?"

"I think it's improbable. News would have spread. Someone would have heard something."

Kite blew out a relieved breath. "Yes, that's true."

Fitch said, "Let us keep investigating. The area's topography has changed over the last century—cliffs have crumbled, the river has shifted. I'm confident with our combined knowledge base, we can solve the mystery."

Kite led the men to the door. "Then get to it. If I wanted to pay someone to stand in my office and look pretty, I'd get a woman."

Frobisher laughed awkwardly despite the fact that Kite wasn't joking, and the two men left.

Kite stared at the painting long after their departure. Like the woman reaching out, beckoning her lover, Kite, too, desperately wanted something, or, more accurately, someone.

It was time to show The Lynx his latest acquisition.

CHAPTER TWENTY-SIX

October 18
New York City

Clara was just settling in at her desk to review a chapter of her dissertation when, again, the noises of someone fiddling with her door had her looking up. She watched as the deadbolt latch rotated, then scrambled to the kitchen and grabbed a carving knife from the block.

The door flew open.

Miles Buchanan stood in the doorway like an avenging angel. He was still sweaty from a workout, wearing trainers, a gray T-shirt, and loose-fitting sweatpants. The needle on her emotional spectrum swung from fear to relief and finally settled on fury.

Clara started to unleash her wrath, but Miles beat her to it.

"What the hell do you think you're doing?" he barked.

She set the knife on the island and snapped, "How did you get in? Do you have a key to my apartment?"

Miles strode in like he owned the place. "Oh, please. You come and go at will at my place. Are you really going to throw some hypocritical outrage in my face?"

With a calming breath, Clara said, "Fine. I would like to know how you got a key."

"I copied yours. Lifted it from your bag when we ran that con over the summer."

Clara rolled her eyes and walked into the kitchen. "Whatever."

Miles held up his phone, showing Clara's dating app profile. "I thought we settled this."

As she suspected, he had accessed her account. "We did settle it. You're going to stop interfering in my personal life, and I will stop making your life miserable."

"No, Clara. We agreed you would stop dating strangers you meet online, *and* you will stop making my life miserable."

Clara walked to the kitchen and examined the drink options in the fridge, settling on an Orangina. "We seem to have reached an impasse."

"What are you playing at?"

She gave the bottle a shake and twisted off the cap. "Nothing, Miles. In addition to my fulfilling work and friends, I am trying to have a sex life. I asked for your help. You refused, so I'm doing what every normal, single, red-blood-ed woman does." She tipped her head to the open dating app on his screen. "You are the one who is playing, not me."

"This," Miles shook the phone. "Is not safe."

"Millions of people do it. I have six requests out to perfectly respectable, law-abiding men."

"Don't test me, Clara."

She brushed by him on her way to the living area, ticking off her options on her fingers. "Dante is a football coach at a junior college. Mario is a waiter. Jamie is unemployed but has an engineering degree. David—"

Clara was cut off by a hand over her mouth. Miles spun her around and lifted her over his shoulder with no effort. Then he leveled a fierce smack on her ass, eliciting a yelp. Clara had never been spanked in her life. Her response was… unexpected.

Masking her excitement, Clara barked, "What the hell, Miles? Put me down!"

Miles didn't reply until he dumped her unceremoniously on the bed with a bounce. Clara stared up at him, wide-eyed and speechless.

"You want to get fucked?"

She blanched at the term, a wonderful combination of panic and arousal running through her veins. Clara tried to muster some bravado, but her voice sounded timid and vulnerable. "What are we going to do?"

"Answer my question."

Clara gave a jerky nod.

"With words, Clara."

She finally found her backbone and propped herself up on her elbows. "Yes, I want to get fucked."

His expression didn't change, but his eyes flashed at her defiance. "Then let me be clear. In this room, I give the orders. The only words I want to hear from you for the next two hours are 'Yes, Miles' or 'No, Miles.'" He stepped closer, towering over Clara at the foot of the bed. "Do you understand?"

Two hours? "Yes, Miles."

His half-smirk seemed to say, *You don't know what you're in for.* And she didn't, but this was Miles. She might hate him, but she trusted him.

"Good," he said, pulling off his T-shirt by the back of the neck. "Then let's begin."

CHAPTER TWENTY-SEVEN

October 18
New York City

Once, Clara had broken into the vault of a Russian oligarch to retrieve a stolen Seurat and stepped on a newly installed pressure plate. She had ten seconds to disable the backup alarm. Now, lying on her comforter, she felt the same cocktail of adrenaline and apprehension—this time with another element: arousal.

His body could have been cut from marble. The afternoon sun cast his body in a soft light, and despite her nerves, Clara couldn't help but admire Miles's lean, muscular frame.

He wants me to use his real name.

She would never admit it, even to herself, but Miles had been the star of Clara's late-night fantasies for years. In this very bedroom, she had slipped a determined hand into her panties and imagined Miles coming over her, entering her. Sometimes, he was gentle and loving, other times, reckless and rough.

She had neither the experience nor the creativity to picture him like this.

Still fully clothed except for the T-shirt in his fist, Miles stepped to the side of the bed and secured her wrists with the garment. Then he lifted her arms over her head and guided her fingers to the base of the headboard. "Hold on to this. Don't let go."

Clara wanted to stop time, to spend hours, days living in this moment. The way Miles was looking at her, the barely leashed restraint in his eyes, it was intoxicating.

He sat beside her on the bed and pulled a lock of her hair between his fingers. "Clara, this is a transaction. Nothing more. I'm repaying a debt. It won't happen again. Are we clear?"

"Yes, Miles."

His eyes flared at her obedience.

"I'll make it as pleasurable as possible, but the first time rarely lives up to the hype. There will be no intimacy. You won't touch me, and I won't kiss you."

"Yes, Miles."

"Well, on the mouth." He leaned forward, biting her earlobe before whispering, "Do you still hate me?"

"Yes, Miles."

"Good."

In one swift motion, Miles yanked her cutoffs and panties down her legs and discarded them. Then he bent her knees and spread her legs as if she were a doll. A darkness deep inside her loved the image of lying there as his toy.

When she was in the position he wanted, Miles rubbed his fingertips with his thumb. With his eyes lasered to the apex of her thighs, he toed off his sneakers. The thud of the shoes as he kicked them away, her own staccato breaths, every sound was amplified.

Miles pulled a condom from his wallet and dropped it on the bed. Then his sweatpants hit the floor. He was commando—of course, he was. She had stolen his underwear. Clara grinned, and Miles shook his head.

"Let's wipe that smile off your face, shall we?'

His journey up her legs was like a lesson in erogenous zones. He bit the arch of her foot, sending shock waves through her. Then he kissed his way up her calf, caressing the back of one ankle while he nipped the inside of the opposite thigh. Gripping the headboard and awash in desire, Clara couldn't help but think he was learning her. Miles paused at the nook of her knee when she shivered and repeated biting at the flesh of her thigh at her soft moan. It was an overload of sensation, and Miles hadn't even reached her drenched center. Clara fell back, squirmed, and whimpered.

Miles lifted his head at her wordless protests.

"Please, Miles," she begged.

With a growl, Miles threw her legs over his shoulders and dove at her core. No man had ever touched her there, much less put his mouth on her. The sensation was otherworldly. Miles was devouring her, body and soul. He was feasting on her sanity. Disobeying his directive, Clara's tethered hands flew down to his thick, dark hair, urging him on. When he pushed two long fingers inside her and wrapped his tongue around her delicate bud, Clara felt as though all the molecules in the room had rushed into her, then burst in a flash of light and color. Her body wasn't her own; it was his.

Before she'd had a chance to recover, Miles flipped her over and pushed her knees beneath her. Clara's cheek rested against the comforter. Her bound hands were jammed awkwardly beneath her body. She couldn't process what was happening. She'd barely recovered from the earth-shattering orgasm he'd just delivered.

Miles sheathed himself and gripped her hips. She felt his probing erection. Suddenly, everything felt wrong.

"Miles, wait. No."

He retreated immediately. "What's wrong?"

"Not like this. I don't want this position."

Miles released a frustrated grunt. "This isn't… We aren't…"

"*I know.* But, please, not like this."

With his hands still cradling her hips, Miles spun Clara to her back. He hooked a finger in the T-shirt binding her wrists and returned her hands to the headboard. "Keep them there this time, or you'll have my palm print on your ass."

Clara knew Miles detected the spark of interest at his threat. The thought of a firm swat sent a spike of arousal through her. He smirked, then moved between her legs, aligning their bodies.

"The first spring swim you take at the lake on the estate, do you wade in from the shore or dive right into the cold water?"

She stared up at his beautiful face, his chocolate gaze fixed on the landscape painting hanging on the wall above her head. "You know the answer to that."

Without another word, Miles drove forward, filling her completely. Clara gasped as his girth stretched her. Her legs flew up and locked around Miles's hips. Whether to prevent further intrusion or keep him connected to her, she wasn't sure.

Yes, she was.

As the pain faded, the ache inside her was replaced by a different sensation—a feeling of need, *of want*. She tilted her hips experimentally. When Clara glanced up at Miles, his face was squeezed as if in pain, his head turned toward the window.

She moved beneath him again, and Miles groaned. Whatever internal battle he was fighting ended with a growled, "Fuck it."

With a surge of his hips, Miles pushed deeper. *Oh my God.* Clara didn't think there was any room left inside her as he continued to fill her body. Still looking to the side, he bit out, "Ready?"

"Yes, Miles."

He withdrew to the tip, then surged again. Clara had never experienced such a sense of bliss. She had never felt so complete, as if this long-awaited missing piece of her had finally slotted into place. She joined him in perfect rhythm, meeting his thrusts with her welcoming body.

Her hands slipped off the headboard of their own accord, and she lassoed his neck with her bound wrists. Miles looked at her then. His eyes were unguarded, his expression raw and vulnerable. Clara surged up and kissed his sternum, then fell back to drown in euphoria.

He looked away. "Clara."

"Miles."

The tension was building again. Miles played her body like an instrument. Reaching behind him, he unclasped her ankles and hooked one leg over his shoulder, sending him impossibly deeper.

"Say it again."

"*Miles.*"

He unleashed—slamming into her as if he could stop the world from spinning. Propping himself on one bulging arm, he reached beneath their bodies and squeezed the globe of her ass in a vice grip.

"Give me what I want, Clara."

His words ripped the orgasm from her body, and she screamed his name, her release triggering his. Clara writhed and gasped as Miles throbbed within her. Still in the throes, Miles used his grip on her ass to pull them over until Clara sat astride his taut form. His body was a work of art.

Miles unhooked her tied wrists from his neck, tugged the knot free with his teeth, and pulled Clara to his chest. She lifted herself from his thick erection and settled beside him. Resting her head on his broad chest, she sighed contentedly.

She knew the moment wouldn't last, knew one word from Miles would shatter this dream state. In exhausted bliss, she drifted, imagining the man beside her whole and at peace. She had given him her virginity, and he had returned the gift ten thousand times with unimaginable pleasure. But as she surrendered to sleep, her thoughts were not of her own happiness but his.

It was dusk when Clara woke to an empty bed, her body deliciously sore. She lifted her head, taking in her bedroom. It was the same cozy nest it had always been, but different. The painting she had done years ago of the row of little houses lining the river near her home looked cheerier. The lavender comforter covering her naked body was brighter. The honks and grumbles of the Harlem traffic outside sounded harmonious.

Clara didn't care that Miles was gone; she'd expected it. Whenever a situation got...*emotional*, Miles either vanished into one of his alter egos or disappeared altogether. His absence merely confirmed that what they shared had mattered. It more than *mattered* to Clara. The sex had been mind-blowing. And while admittedly, she had nothing to compare it to, instinctually, she knew what had passed between them had changed everything.

And while Miles's disappearing act was to be expected, she had to admit, some acknowledgment of the event, some small act of kindness would have meant the world. Clara scanned the spot where Miles had collapsed beside her, checked the nightstand, and ran her hand beneath the pillow, hoping to find a note, but there was nothing.

Disheartened, Clara slipped on her white terrycloth robe and padded into the main room. The only indication Miles had ever been in her apartment was the half-drunk mug of tea she had left on the end table was now upside down in her dish rack.

With a resigned sigh, Clara returned to her bedroom, shed the robe, and entered the bathroom. She started the shower, but before she stepped in, Clara caught the image of her naked body in the full-length mirror mounted on the door.

Their encounter had been no dream. Her body bore the wonderful, filthy evidence. A hickey seared her neck; her nipples were red from his torture, and when she turned, she spotted the five fingerprint bruises dotting her ass cheek. God, Clara wanted to tattoo the small circles onto her body, a permanent reminder of what she and Miles had shared.

Standing under the warm spray, Clara replayed every moment of their lovemaking—*fucking*, she corrected herself—in a photo burst of images: his muscled torso and eight-pack abs, the vee of his hips and…*lower*. Her usual ten-minute shower took half an hour as she fantasized and explored her awakened body.

Back in the bedroom, wrapped in a fluffy towel, Clara couldn't help but glance once more at the nightstand and the floor beside it. Miles could have at least left one of his quippy, condescending notes. He had warned her, but still. There was romance, and there was kindness. She had hoped he would at least be kind.

Enough. Clara had things to do. She was late to deliver a new section of her dissertation to her advisor, and she desperately needed to do laundry and get groceries. Resolved to shake the image of Miles from her mind, Clara dropped the towel and pulled open the top drawer of her dresser.

A second of confusion passed as she stared at the meager contents. A tidal wave of joy obliterated her frustration.

Miles had stolen all of her bras.

CHAPTER TWENTY-EIGHT

October 19
New York City

Miles refilled his coffee mug and returned to his workspace in the loft. He scanned the emails on his laptop, responding to a few, deleting others, and ignoring the vaguely worded message from Chug Ugentti's personal assistant requesting an update. Scanning the desktop, Miles searched for a reason for his disquiet. The blotter was aligned with the edge of the desk. His Monte Blanc pen sat perpendicular on his right. A thin semicircular coffee stain ringed the base of his mug on the coaster. That must be it. Miles wiped away the spot and dried the cup with a tissue before returning it to its place.

Who was he kidding? The coffee was not the reason he couldn't concentrate. Miles closed his eyes, each beat of his heart triggering a picture in his mind. Thump: Clara naked and on the bed, submissive and needy: *yes, Miles*. Thump: a bead of sweat dripping from his face to her cleavage. Thump: those sea-blue eyes staring up at him in wonder. Thump: his thick erection ripping through her virginity. Thump, thump, thump.

For years, Miles had denied himself the privilege of touching Clara, of even entertaining the idea that she could be his. He had been content kissing her with pranks, holding her with sharp remarks, and protecting her by chasing off any man who had the slightest notion of the forbidden acts that ran through his own head on a loop. But now his axis had tipped. Everything had changed.

He had known not to look at her; one glance into those fathomless eyes would be like plunging into the miraculous depths of the ocean—he would never want to resurface, happy to drown in her gaze. Nevertheless, he chanced a glance. That was his big mistake. Well, one of many. Her face, it was incandescent. The mere thought that he had brought her such pleasure—the feeling was indescribable. He wanted that look on her face every minute of every day, and he wanted to be the one to put it there. The only one.

Miles adjusted himself. Jesus, his dick hadn't settled down yet despite thoroughly fucking Clara and two subsequent showers. *Thoroughly fucking Clara.* That was a bell he could never unring. *Congratulations, Jackass. You're officially standing knee-deep in worms from the barrel-sized can you just opened.*

Rustling at his feet had Miles looking down. Loco, the psychotic cat, was weaving around his legs in a figure-eight.

He nudged the animal away. "Fuck off."

He hoped Clara knew that that was the end of it—a one-off. Miles wasn't capable of more. Whatever the fuck *more* even meant. Clara needed to realize that one night was all they would ever share.

Miles needed to realize it.

As much as he tried to tell himself that he was repaying a debt, that he was attempting to prevent Clara from finding some random hook-up for the sole purpose of deflowering her, that he was fucking her into submission, Miles knew it was a big fat lie.

He wanted her.

For years, Miles had slammed the drawbridge in his brain, refusing to acknowledge, beyond dispassionate observation, Clara's allure. She was captivating and wild. But that wasn't what pulled Miles into her orbit.

He was drawn to her soul.

Yes, their lives had followed very different paths, but Miles firmly believed Clara wasn't the woman she was because good things had happened to her. Good things had happened because she was the woman she was. She was kind and generous and trusting. And now he knew her body, her taste, her scent...

Enough. Never in his life had he allowed a woman to occupy his thoughts, and he wasn't about to start now. Determined to get the vixen out of his mind, Miles returned to his work.

His phone buzzed in the stand, set at a forty-five-degree angle beside his laptop.

The first message was a text from Clara: *I think your prank backfired.*

The second was a photo.

It took him a moment to process the picture in the text thread. Once he realized what he was looking at, Miles slammed the phone on the desk with such force that a spiderweb crack shattered the screen.

Without thought or hesitation, he flew out the door.

Clara emerged from the Art History building and paused at the top of the stone stairs. It was a warm day, and the autumn sun was rejuvenating. She tipped her head to the sky to soak it in. Continuing across the quad, Clara waved to some of her undergraduate students sitting on a blanket in the grass. Columbia was in the middle of one of the largest metropolitan areas on Earth, but it was a world unto itself—a serene, sheltered enclave amidst the chaos. Even during breaks, it was a bustling, vibrant place. She loved it here.

A presence keeping stride had Clara slowing her pace. She didn't need to look up to know who it was. Miles had an aura of composure and command that she sensed. She did notice the group of women pause their tai chi routine to glance his way.

Hiking her book-laden tote higher on her shoulder, she grumbled, "What do you want?"

"I'm still deciding." With a graceful move, Miles took the bookbag from her shoulder and slipped it over his own.

"Perhaps there are some lingering effects from that untreated head injury. I'm Clara, by the way," she deadpanned.

Miles huffed. "As if I could forget you."

Clara made a sound of disbelief.

"Glad to see you wore a sweater. I was concerned your classmates would have trouble focusing on the lecture."

Clara looked away to hide her delight. After texting him that his prank had backfired, she'd added a photo of just her chest, braless in a tiny, white T-shirt.

"I'm not an idiot, Miles." Clara crossed her arms over her chest, concealing her body's response to his inspection.

He replied sincerely, "I know that."

"Good. Maybe you and Reynard will finally learn your lesson. I don't need a chaperone."

"A father will never stop worrying about his little girl, Clara."

They exited the campus and continued on 116th Street. Clara sighed, "I know. What's your excuse."

Ever the gentleman, Miles shifted her to his left side, away from the street. "Your sparkling personality?" he replied.

"Could be. Or maybe you don't like the idea of another man touching me."

"I thought we settled that *issue.*"

"Or maybe you just showed me what I've been missing."

Miles pulled her to his chest and out of the flow of pedestrians. He growled into her ear. "Careful, Bluebird. I wouldn't kick the hornet's nest if I were you. Bad girls get punished."

Oh. My. God. Clara nearly gasped. Miles's breath on her neck, his clean scent surrounding her—her body remembered him. And responded.

"If I reached between your legs right now, what would I find, Bluebird?"

God, the arrogance. Clara wished it didn't add to his intoxicating dominance. She shoved him back to cover her arousal.

"I'll deal with my personal life. You, on the other hand, need to *get a life.*" She was about to resume her rant when Miles stared over her head, his eyes wide. Behind her, she heard the gunning engine. Before she knew what was happening, Miles wrapped her in his arms and pulled her behind the traffic light pole. Just then, a dark van hopped the curb with skidding tires, coming so close it brushed the side of Miles's body. They staggered closer to the storefronts. Miles kept her cocooned until the van was long gone. She heard him mutter, "Fucking Ugentti."

Clara stayed in the safety of his embrace longer than she should have. Miles, too, seemed reluctant to let her go.

"Are you all right?" he asked.

She stared up into his concerned brown eyes. "You're the one who was hit. Are you?"

"Fine."

"Who's Ugentti?"

"Hmm?"

"Just now. You said 'fucking Ugentti.'"

"It's nothing."

"Miles," she scolded. "You were almost flattened."

He turned her forward and resumed walking. "I have a client who is dissatisfied."

"So he's trying to kill you?"

"Warn me, most likely."

They paused at the base of her stoop, and Clara faced him again. "Miles, if your clients are expressing their dissatisfaction by running you down, it might be time for a career change. Maybe a job where people who don't like your service post a Yelp review."

Miles brushed her cheek with his thumb; against her will, Clara leaned into his touch. He bent down, and for the briefest moment, Clara thought he was going to kiss her. She froze as his lips touched her forehead.

"See you later, Bluebird." Miles slipped her messenger bag from his shoulder and gently hung it across her body.

"Where are you going?"

"I think you're right," he said. "It's time for a career change."

Clara stood on the sidewalk for a full five minutes, watching until Miles hailed a cab on the corner. Shaking her head at her foolishness, she retrieved her keys and turned to her building. As was her habit, Clara checked her surroundings before opening the front door. The sidewalk had the usual foot traffic—a dog walker with a handful of leashes, a mother pushing a stroller, a mail carrier. Across the street, a man sat in an older model sedan. He wouldn't have caught Clara's attention, but for the fact he was looking right at her. When she met his gaze, the guy looked away. Unconcerned—Clara received plenty of unwanted attention on the streets of New York—she opened the door and went inside.

Miles spoke on the phone as he stepped into the elevator of his Upper East Side apartment building.

"It's a good fit for you, Miles. I can't think of a better man for the job."

"I'm excited. It's time for a change."

"And I need someone running Bishop Security in New York. It's long overdue."

"I appreciate your patience, Nathan."

On the other end of the line, Nathan Bishop had a smile in his voice. "I knew you'd come around. We'll fly you down here next week, and we can iron out the details."

"Look forward to it."

"The team will be happy to know you've finally agreed," Nathan said.

"When will you tell them?"

There was a brief pause. Then Nathan replied, "You can tell them yourself."

Puzzled, Miles replied, "Okay."

"Have a good night." Nathan ended the call as the doors parted.

In the eleventh-floor hallway, Miles was already shedding his suit jacket. The entire drive there, he was consumed with how Ugentti had managed to track him to Harlem. As he slipped the key into the lock, his phone vibrated in his pocket.

After checking the caller, he swiped accept and said, "Give me some good news, Gordie."

The reporter chuckled. "As I predicted, my buddy at *The Herald* was all over it. He lapped up the story of Ugentti screwing his interns. That shit never gets old. He's finishing up the article and fact-checking tomorrow. It'll be in the online edition and the morning paper—front page below the fold—the day after. "

"I owe you, Gordie."

"And I'll collect." Gordie grew serious. "Be careful with this guy, my friend."

"Always."

Miles ended the call and entered his apartment, returning his attention to the task at hand.

The only article of clothing he was wearing that he had also worn to the Ugentti meet was the pair of John Lobb loafers. After sitting at his desk in the small study, Miles slipped off the shoes. Opening a desk drawer, he withdrew a scanner. Slowly, he ran the device over the shoes and watched as the red light on the small screen filled the bar.

Sitting back in the chair, Miles looked out the window at the clear autumn sky. On that busy Harlem street, he had hoped the incident with the van had simply been an accident—a deliveryman running late or distracted by their phone.

Now, as he walked in his socks to the bedroom, Miles knew that the driver had been aiming for him.

Miles placed the shoes with the tracker on their assigned shelf in his closet. They would come in handy when the time was right. He grabbed the battered biker boots.

Ugentti thought he was smart.

Miles was smarter.

CHAPTER TWENTY-NINE

New York City
October 19

Ten minutes later, the Ducati was flying down Second Avenue.

When he reached his block in Alphabet City, Miles walked the bike onto the sidewalk and down the alley that abutted his building. After punching the security code into the keypad by the service door, Miles pushed the bike into the storage room. When he entered the back gaming area, the scene stopped him dead in his tracks.

Three former Navy SEALs and two trans former-sex workers were sitting around a poker table playing Texas Holdem. Now Miles understood why Nathan had been so cagey on the phone.

Andrew "Chat" Dunlap nodded a greeting while contemplating his hand.

Jonah "Steady" Lockhart, the laid-back southern charmer, spoke around an unlit cigar. "Foxy, there better be a queen swimming in that river."

"Sugar, you got two queens sitting across from you." Foxy set three cards face up in the center of the table.

Foxy ran the fortune-telling business. The other player at the table, Veronique, handled the gambling. "Foxy, love, these men want a *cis*-ter, not a sister."

Tox smirked. "Well, there was that little mix-up in Bangkok. Remember that, Steady?"

Chat's booming laugh echoed in the room.

Steady leaned forward and spoke around Foxy. "What part of *'take it to the grave'* was unclear to you?"

Foxy patted Steady's shoulder. "Easy, big guy. Haven't you heard? There's no *opposite* sex anymore. There's just sex."

"It wasn't sex," Steady grumbled.

"A little more of this." Veronique tapped the cards. "And a little less of this." She mimicked talking with a hand gesture. "I have money to win."

"Tox, it's to you," Foxy said.

Miles's fraternal twin brother sat on Foxy's left. "Call." Tox didn't turn around, just kicked out the empty chair on his other side.

Miles couldn't stop his lips from creeping up as he strode to the table and sat. "Watch out for these ladies, bro. They cheat."

Veronique shot Miles an indignant look. "No need to cheat, Hun. These boys play like a bunch of toddlers. Except for this fine Denzel." She rubbed a hand over Chat's bald head. "He knows what he's doin'."

"Toddler, my ass." Steady pushed a stack of chips into the pot.

Chat shook his head and muttered, "She's playing you, Steady."

Miles watched Veronique take the pot, then said, "Deal me in."

Steady eyed Miles's leather jacket and ripped jeans, pointing with the cigar. "This is a new look for you."

"Took the bike out."

"What do you have?" Steady asked with interest.

"Ducati Streetfighter."

"Nice. I may need to take that for a spin."

"Mind telling me what you're doing here?" Miles eyeballed the guys.

"Funny you should ask." Steady slid the new cards into a stack. "Our ladies planned a little girls' weekend baby shower for Calliope. Your brother's leash only reaches so far when it comes to his knocked-up wife, so Very offered up our beach house to host a testicle-free weekend with cucumber sandwiches and diaper genies."

"Do you even know what a diaper genie is?" Tox asked.

"Nope, and don't tell me. I'm sure the real thing isn't half as cool as what I'm picturing." Steady popped the cigar back in his mouth. "Chat has a meeting with some suit at Kinghtsgrove-Bishop—that's basically our parent company— and I thought to myself, *self*, when's the last time you had a decent New York slice?"

Miles raised a skeptical brow at his twin. "Uh-huh."

Tox gave his brother a shove. "I missed you."

Miles was momentarily taken aback. His twin had always worn his heart on his sleeve, but Tox's ability to voice his feelings so effortlessly after everything they had been through as children, well, it amazed him. Miles didn't think he'd expressed an honest emotion in the last twenty years. His *thank you* was unspoken, but, like always, his brother heard it.

Tox tilted his head and pierced his twin with an all too familiar look. "Something's different."

Miles attempted to redirect his twin and gestured to the room. "You mean the thrift-store Moulin Rouge?"

"Hey!" Foxy protested.

"You know what I mean," his brother said pointedly.

Chat leaned in. "He means something about you, my friend. Anything you'd like to talk about?"

Chat was the man in their group who always saw beneath the surface, but in Miles's case, that person had always been his twin. So Chat may have been thinking it, but Tox voiced the thought. "You did something stupid, didn't you?"

Yes, he had. He had slept with Clara and awakened this dormant beast within. On top of that, instead of being a mature, thoughtful man, instead of waking Clara and kissing her goodbye like he had wanted, instead of making sure she was okay after what had to be a milestone in her life, he had acted like a twelve-year-old and stolen her bras.

The encounter had shaken him to his very core. As Miles claimed Clara, *melded with her*, something shifted. Inside him, the scattered pieces of the person he had once been had started to reassemble. Being with her was like coming home. And the sensation was wholly and utterly terrifying.

Miles shifted in his seat. He'd just had the most mind-bending sex of his life with a woman he shouldn't even be fantasizing about, much less touching. And now, even as he sat in this room with friends and family and countless distractions, Miles couldn't stop his mind from reliving the encounter, of touching Clara's mile-long legs, of the innocence and trust in those fathomless eyes, of taking what no man had. So yes, something had changed.

"Nothing's changed."

Miles braced himself as Steady joined the perusal. "Yes, it has. You have that satisfied, exasperated look about you that can only be caused by a woman."

"It's not a woman," Miles snapped too quickly.

"Well, that confirms it," Steady said.

"Fuck off, Steady. There is no woman."

Steady bracketed his chips with his forearms and pinned Miles with a look. "You know what Granny June would say?"

Chat muttered into his beer, "Oh, here we go."

Steady waved off the comment. "You can put cowpies in the oven, but that don't make 'em biscuits. Now start talkin'."

Before Miles even looked at Tox, he knew he would see his twin's brows raised in silent agreement. He wasn't ready to talk about Clara. Hell, he wasn't prepared to face the situation himself. So, Miles volunteered the one plausible excuse for his agitated state. If his twin didn't buy it, at least it would distract him. "Remember I was telling you about Chug Ugentti?"

"The wise guy who got elected to Congress?" Steady asked.

When Tox nodded, Miles said, "I'm pretty sure he had a guy try to run me down this afternoon."

Tox crumpled the paper napkin in his hand. "What?"

"I was walking in Harlem with Clara when a van came right at us. Hopped the curb, then sped off." He tugged up the leather jacket sleeve to reveal the large bruise on his forearm. "Clipped me as I was moving Clara out of the way."

Tox was a gentle giant, but Miles saw the bear inside his brother when he said, "Maybe I need to pay this prick a visit."

Chat rolled the bottle of Stella between his palms. "You're sure it was intentional? Lots of crazy drivers in this city."

Miles sighed and ran a hand through his dark brown hair. "Yeah, I found a tracker in my shoe. He slipped it in at our last meeting."

Chat asked, "What does he want? What's the goal of the intimidation tactic?"

Tox placed a protective arm around the back of his brother's chair. "Ugentti wants Miles to feed him dirt on his new Congressional colleagues."

Miles shook the ice in his glass. "Ugentti may be a gangster, but he's not stupid. He knows I have information on half the politicians in D.C."

Chat added, "If he knows his colleagues' secrets, he controls them."

Steady refilled his mug from the pitcher. "Hold on. Killing you doesn't get him what he wants."

Chat said, "But warning you does."

Tox pulled out his phone. "I'm letting Calliope know I'm staying in New York for a few days. You need protection."

Miles looked at his brother, a painful warmth forming in his chest. Tox had always been his bodyguard—until he wasn't. He rubbed his sternum, trying to alleviate the ache. "You don't need to do that. Your wife is pregnant. She needs you home."

Tox looked up from his phone. "Nah, she's sick of my hovering. I came home from work last week, and she was up on a ladder changing a lightbulb."

Miles glanced around the table, noting the amused looks on Tox's buddies' faces. "I don't understand. Did you make her get down?"

"Like she was a jumper on a ledge," Steady said.

"Then I hid the ladder. I mean, what the fuck? Crazy, right?" Tox looked for confirmation of his wife's recklessness.

Steady replied, "Yep. Crazy. Definitely crazy."

Chat chuckled and said, "Miles, take him. Please."

Steady added. "I don't know. Calliope might try to assemble the crib or knit booties. Those needles can be dangerous."

Tox paused, no doubt envisioning a freak knitting needle accident. He reached for his phone.

Steady plucked the device from his friend's grip. "Dude, no."

Tox huffed, "So you're giving relationship advice now? Two months with Very Valentine, and you're the love doctor."

"I'm not giving relationship advice. I'm giving *survival* advice. I know dick about marriage, but I know a shit load about how not to get killed." He took a swig of beer, then added, "I do like the nickname The Love Doctor, though. I may take that for a spin."

A poker chip hit Steady in the face.

Miles watched as Tox considered his options. "We're crashing at Calliope's parents' place. We could extend for a day or two."

Chat eased his worry. "She'll be fine, big man."

Miles reached for his cards when a commotion overhead had the table looking up. The metal ductwork thundered, and a black shadow dropped from the ceiling onto the table, knocking the stacks of chips askew.

Loco crouched and hissed.

Steady scooted back. "Jesus, I have nightmares that cat is trying to kill me in my sleep."

Chat inspected his cards. "Could be true, brother. That creature is out hunting at all hours. Easy enough to slip in your room, claws sharp, teeth bared."

"Cut the shit." Steady stood and tried to look casual as he meandered to the bar.

Foxy and Veronique laughed, then stopped abruptly when Loco straightened and padded to Miles. He didn't nuzzle or purr; he simply sat on his lap like an Egyptian statue and placidly took in the room.

Tox stared in disbelief. "What the fuck?"

"Don't ask me." Miles ignored Loco and accepted the beer Steady set on the table at arm's length. When the cat rotated his head, Steady snatched back his hand.

Tox was indignant. "I fed and housed that fucker for three years. The closest he ever came to me was weaving around my feet. Then, when I tried to pet him, he ran off."

Miles tossed his ante into the pot. "He's probably just hungry and knows who fills his bowl."

Chat sat back and crossed his arms over his broad chest. "Or he senses a kindred spirit."

Steady frowned at his pair of cards, then turned to Miles. "It's true you deal with a lot of rats."

Foxy chimed in, "And you disappear for long stretches."

Veronique added, "And you're prickly." She jutted her thumb toward Miles. "Not a hugger, this one."

"You eat fast and kind of guard your food." Steady wrapped his arm around his chips to demonstrate.

That habit had developed out of necessity. Miles's eyes shot to his twin. Tox furrowed his brow, clearly bothered by Steady's observation. Damn his brother and his stupid *twinstinct*.

Miles held up both hands. "Enough, okay? Jesus." He brushed Loco off his lap, and the cat padded off, unphased. "I don't know why I don't invite you guys over more often," he deadpanned.

Steady looked sheepish. "You know we love that cat, right? He's an awesome, prickly asshole."

Foxy tapped the deck on the table. "Subtle as a trainwreck, Steady. Now, are we playing cards, or should we all put on our shorty robes and give each other pedicures?"

Veronique sipped her mimosa. "She's asking sincerely, boys."

With that, the Bishop Security men tossed their chips in the pot and enthusiastically returned their attention to the game.

When the hand was finished, and Foxy won the pot again, she stood and said, "I have a client, and Veronique needs to stock the bar for tonight. Tox, sweetie, anything you need, you just whistle." She smiled at her benefactor and disappeared through a beaded curtain.

Miles stood. "Let's get going. The last thing you guys need is to get caught up in a police raid."

Tox joined his brother. "Have the cops raided this place?"

Miles shrugged. "Not yet." He ticked off the violations on his fingers. "Illegal gambling, no liquor license, and *additional* recreational activities. It's inevitable."

Foxy called from the front room, "Two detectives from the Seventh play Caribbean Stud twice a week, and a lieutenant from the Ninth gets her tarot cards read once a month. You worry about you, Sweet Cheeks."

When the guys had gone, Miles returned to the loft to shower. In his bedroom, he shed his clothes and grabbed a towel from the folded stack. His cell phone vibrated on the dresser as he opened the bathroom door.

Miles glanced at the notification with suspicion. Clara had added a dinner to her calendar. He quickly checked her dating app and found nothing. That didn't mean she hadn't met some pervert on the subway or lurking on campus. His blood boiled as he imagined it. Bottling his frustration, he strode into the bathroom and started the shower. He would know what she was up to soon enough.

CHAPTER THIRTY

New York City
October 19

Tosca was Reynard's favorite restaurant, a locals-only bistro tucked away in a quiet corner of Little Italy. Tony Bennett crooned over the antiquated sound system as waiters squeezed by one another in the narrow alley between tables, delivering exquisite plates of pasta. Framed autographed photos of New York sports legends, politicians, and a movie star or two covered the entry walls. A mouth-watering aroma filled the air, flowing around laughter and lively conversation.

The boisterous host cupped Clara's cheeks so forcefully that her lips pursed. "Your father is in town for ten minutes, and I hear from him. He calls me before he gets in the car at the airport. You live in this city, and I haven't seen this pretty face for months."

Clara circled Tony's wrists and extricated herself from his grasp. "I know, Tony. School keeps me busy, but I'm so happy to see you."

"Not half as happy as me. A gorgeous girl is good for business." He winked, then tipped his head to the back. "Usual table, Bellissima."

"Thanks, Tony."

Clara spotted her father sitting in the two-person booth tucked into an alcove. As she walked in his direction, a heavy-set man approached, returning to his table from the restroom. Rather than step out of the way, he took Clara in a dance hold and spun her as Sinatra's "Fly Me to the Moon" drifted from the speakers. With a laugh, she continued the short distance.

Reynard looked up from the large laminated menu. "Ah, *mon raton laveur* has arrived."

As a child, Clara pickpocketed a chocolate bar from one of the guards patrolling Reynard's estate. When he discovered her crime—by spotting her sitting in a tree and eating it—the guard complained, *She's like a raccoon! A tiny bandit!* Reynard had loved the endearment.

"Hi, Papa. How was the flight?"

"*Rien.* I worked, slept. I'm much more interested in you. How is school?"

She and Reynard each spoke seven languages; he had decided early on that English would be their chosen method of communication. Nevertheless, Clara couldn't stop herself from a preamble of muttered French. "The dissertation is going much more slowly than I had hoped. I have to rethink an entire section on emotional symbology."

"Ah, yes, your theory that artists hide love notes in their work."

Clara laughed. "That's oversimplifying a bit."

The waiter, a wiry man with a hook nose and broad smile, presented her father's favorite Barolo with a flourish.

"Thank you, Matty. You may pour."

Reynard had no need to test the wine. It was expertly handled and stored and his usual choice at Tosca.

After filling their glasses, Matty picked up both menus. "With your permission, Signore, the chef has a special meal planned."

Clara spun the wine in her goblet. Reynard was a valued customer. It was also clear from his gaunt frame and pallor that he was unwell.

"Wonderful." Reynard toasted Matty and took a generous sip from his glass.

"What time is your appointment tomorrow?" Clara asked.

"Pfft." Reynard hushed her as if she had uttered a hex. "No talk of doctors or hospitals. Tonight, I want to enjoy a delicious meal with my daughter."

Clara reached across the table and took her father's hand. "Of course."

The first course arrived, chilled roasted beets with chevre and endive, and they ate with gusto.

"I have a favor to ask of you, darling girl. One that I think you will find rather pleasant."

Clara lifted her brow. "I'm listening."

"I assume you have heard of Francesco Tavarro."

"A bit. His work isn't really my period of interest. Obviously, the Madrid auction made headlines."

"What do you know?"

"Reclusive Spanish painter, primarily a muralist. The majority of his work is from the early Twentieth Century."

"I've followed Tavarro's career for many years. His work has always piqued my interest. You know the painting above the fireplace in the library? Irises and Lilies? That's a Tavarro."

"Oh yes. I'd forgotten. That's a beautiful piece."

"I bought it on holiday in Chamonix when you were a teenager. Do you remember?"

"Now I do. You said the blue of the flowers was the same color as my eyes."

"A fortunate purchase, as it turns out. I think I paid what would be about three thousand euros for it."

"You've always had a good eye, Papa."

The waiter cleared the salad plates and presented a chilled bottle of Pinot Bianco for the next course. After the standard ritual, he poured each of them a glass. The second course was three seared diver scallops with brown butter and an apple puree.

Reynard set his hands on the weathered table and traced a scar in the wood. "For years, I've been trying to locate a work of Tavarro's. His only portrait."

Clara bit into a divine scallop. "Go on."

He continued, "It's a painting of an unknown woman. Unfortunately, rumors about a hidden message in the painting made it harder to acquire."

"What type of hidden message?"

Reynard chuckled. "No doubt a rumor started by some dealer to escalate the value. It has no bearing on my interest in the piece. There is talk that a poem painted along the bottom and other symbols in the background map the way to a missing royal jewel."

Reynard passed his phone to Clara. It was difficult to see the canvas on the small screen, but that didn't stop her sharp intake of breath. The painting was of a woman, nude but for a diaphanous piece of fabric that swirled around her body. She was reaching out for something—her lover perhaps. Her face was a mask of pain and longing. The bright foreground was balanced by a dark, almost ominous depiction of trees and storm clouds in the distance. It was arresting.

She scrolled down to look at the description. Painted in 1928, the work was titled *Somewhere*.

"This is the painting from the Madrid auction?"

"Yes. I purchased it," Reynard replied.

"I'd love to see it up close."

"That may be a problem. The painting was stolen in transit."

"The Marseilles Customs House theft." Clara had seen the story on the news. A heavily armed tactical team of mercenaries had broken into the building and stolen a painting in broad daylight."

"Why?"

"Lucien Kite."

Clara had told Reynard about her narrow escape with the Renoir. "Oh, no."

Clara sat back in shock. The move was perfectly timed as the waiter set down the plate of veal medallions, roasted heirloom carrots, and herbed risotto. It looked delicious, but her appetite had vanished.

Reynard nodded his thanks and picked up his fork. "I believe this is payback."

"He discovered my identity." Clara thought of those creepily comical Halloween flowers and that ominous card. She wouldn't worry her father with that added concern. Clara already had her hands full with one overprotective man.

"I received a phone call from a man in Kite's organization confirming it. I'm afraid The Lynx is being forced into early retirement." Reynard savored a bite of veal. "Lucien Kite will need to be handled."

Clara buried her face in her hands. "This is terrible."

Reynard smiled. "This is life. Little bumps in the road, small setbacks. Nothing that can't be solved with a little lateral thinking."

Encouraged by her father's words, more so by the twinkle in his eye, Clara tucked into her meal. "Please tell me you want me to steal that painting."

When the waiter cleared and then doused scoops of vanilla gelato with hot espresso for their affogato, Reynard nodded his thanks, then returned his attention to Clara.

"I want you to steal that painting." Reynard wiped the corner of his mouth with the napkin. "But this is a task that will require more than your skill, *ma fille.* Lucien Kite is an ambitious man without a conscience. In my experience, nothing is more dangerous."

Clara wanted to reassure her father. She was happy to do it with the truth. "I have protection and help if I need it, Papa."

Her father cupped the snifter of his preferred brandy and took a fortifying sip when something drew Reynard's attention to the front of the restaurant. Clara followed his gaze over her shoulder; nothing caught her eye. She turned back to her father, who was innocently swirling the liquor.

"What did you see?" she asked.

"Hmm?"

"Did someone come in?"

"I don't think so, dear."

"Why do you have that look on your face?"

"What look is that?"

Clara leaned forward, squinting. "I'm not sure."

Reynard finished his digestif and signaled for the bill. "Let's get you home. Busy day tomorrow."

CHAPTER THIRTY-ONE

New York City
October 19

She was having dinner with her father. Reynard had spotted him—the old man missed nothing—but Miles had no misgivings. Reynard was the one who had requested Miles keep an eye on Clara, and he was taking the task seriously. In his profession, Miles had a front-row seat to the depravity that lived in plain sight.

None of that explained the red mist clouding his vision as he tailed Clara to the restaurant, his thoughts pinging through images of Clara on a romantic date. *Where had she met him? Who the fuck was he? Was he touching the small of her back? Kissing her hello?* Rationality flew out the window of the Lyft as the demons within pounded their chests.

The minute Miles saw Reynard's gaunt face, he pivoted and left the restaurant. His relief that Clara wasn't on a date was eclipsed by Miles's shock at his mentor's appearance. He had known Reynard was unwell, but seeing the man Miles had always thought of as invincible, so frail and gray, it was a punch in the gut.

Fifteen years ago, Fate had put Miles in Reynard's path. In the blink of an eye, he had gone from teenage pickpocket to errand boy for a kingpin. Anything Reynard needed, Miles did with honesty and loyalty, and a month to the day after he had "bumped" into Reynard, Miles was living in a Paris apartment and earning heaps. Once a month, he would take the short flight to the estate in Dordogne, where he would spend the week studying with a tutor to finish his high school coursework (Reynard insisted) and reviewing job assignments. Miles may have only been sixteen, but he was a businessman through and through. Reynard had seen his potential and nurtured it.

Meanwhile, Clara had been a ten-year-old menace. If she wasn't putting frogs in his bed, she was forcing him to help her build a catapult or rig a trap for the goblin who lived in the woods. Miles had hated doing these childish things—and if a small part of him enjoyed it, he certainly would never admit it—but Clara had been impossible to refuse, even then. If anything, his need to indulge her had only gotten worse.

On the quaint Little Italy side street, he took a moment to recalibrate. These feelings of frustration and obsession were nothing new when it came to Clara. Fucking her, taking her virginity had somehow upped the ante. Suddenly, he didn't simply want to scare off men who sniffed around her; he wanted to rip them limb from limb. What was happening to him?

Rounding the corner, Miles scanned the street until he spotted the pub. He stopped at the bodega to buy a copy of the paper, then headed to the bar. A few patrons sat at sidewalk tables as a waiter delivered beer and food. Knowing right where to look when he entered the dark bar, Miles spotted his twin at the back. Tox and his SEAL buddies always sat where they had the best vantage point.

Tox stood when he spotted his brother and came around the table to embrace him. "Twice in one week, bro. Before long, we'll have you moving to Beaufort."

The other three men at the table, Steady, Chat, and Ren, stood and greeted him. Leo "Ren" Jameson had arrived this morning. Miles knew Ren the least, but his intelligence and keen perspective were impressive.

"Welcome to the team." Ren shook his hand.

"News travels fast," Miles replied with a smile.

Steady shook him by the shoulders. "Ready to join the good guys?"

Chat grabbed a chair from an empty table and spun it around. "Let the guy order a drink, would you?"

Steady scooted his chair over. Chat flagged the waiter, and Miles pointed to Steady's mug.

Tox must have sensed Miles's apprehension. His twin faced him fully with an angry growl. "What now?"

Miles placed the newspaper in front of his brother. The headline, in *The Herald's* signature style, read: *Ugentti Underage Undulations.* Then, below it: *Will anything put this guy in jail?*

Tox nodded his approval. "You?"

"I was pissed about the... you know." Yes, Miles was angry Chug's men had attacked him, but that wasn't the actual impetus for his actions. Miles was sick of corrupt politicians. God knows he had enough dirt on the D.C. power brokers to grind the wheels of government to a halt. Inside the Beltway, information was the gold standard, and Miles was the richest man in town.

Tox heard Miles's unspoken words. "Good work, brother."

"Felt good. But Ugentti's not going to let this go unanswered."

Steady tapped his chin and deadpanned, "If only we knew a highly trained team of security experts who could protect you."

Tox rested a hand on his brother's shoulder. "Why don't you come down to Beaufort for a while? Calliope and the gang would love to see you, and you can have a little vacation while things simmer down."

Miles held up a hand. "Let's not jump the gun. The guy is in Congress now. It's not like he can send a hitman to shoot me on the street."

Miles was content to watch these guys rib one another. He was here to have drinks with his new coworkers, not discuss threats and drive-bys. He and Tox had been separated for over twenty years, but it seemed some things were ingrained or maybe coded into their DNA. As children, he and Tox had developed a perfect synergy. Tox was the cameraman; Miles was the actor. Tox was the quiet one; Miles was the spokesman. And just like old times, his twin once again aimed the spotlight his way.

"So, Mi, where's Clara tonight?"

"Having dinner with her father in Little Italy. Why?"

The words were still hanging in the air when Miles realized his brother's intention. Tox had killed terrorists with his bare hands. He had carried a teammate on his back for ten kilometers to get to safety. He had jumped out of planes into the most dangerous places on Earth. But his twin was, and always had been, a true romantic. After everything they had been through, Tox's heart had only grown. Miles's had shriveled and died like an unwatered plant.

"No reason." His brother shot Miles a familiar side-eye.

"What will it take to get that idea out of your head?" Miles asked.

"A wrecking ball."

CHAPTER THIRTY-TWO

New York City
October 20

Miles watched the time on his phone change from 4:47 a.m. to 4:48 a.m. Giving up on sleep, he made a mug of coffee and wandered up the spiral staircase to the trellised pavilion of the rooftop garden. Miles may have hated his insomnia, but he loved this time of day—dark with the promise of morning, the sounds of the city reduced to the white noise of traffic and distant rumblings.

His father liked to drink his morning coffee outside, even in winter. His dad had been a surgeon; he was Miles's hero. Six months after their mother died from a brain tumor, their dad was T-boned by a drunk driver and killed instantly. The twins' perfect world crumbled to ash.

In the predawn darkness, he rolled the mug between his palms. Usually, on the rare occasion when Miles thought about the past, it was with a malignant bitterness and cursing his fate. But this morning, the crisp fall air and his father's familiar ritual brought comforting images of their dad. He showed his sons how to bait a hook and make pancakes shaped like mouse faces. He taught them to be kind.

The comforting smell of warm bread wafted around him, and Miles wondered if there was a new bakery in the neighborhood.

How disappointed his parents must be. Miles prayed for guidance in those early days, but heaven had turned a deaf ear. So Miles closed himself off to everyone. No one would ever leave him again because no one would ever get close.

After all those early lessons, all that parental effort, Miles had grown into a miscreant. He made sure that the rich and powerful escaped retribution. He silenced whistleblowers, paid off cops, and controlled the media. In many ways, Miles was worse than the offenders he protected. He lived his life alone to keep the stench from spreading.

Movement caught his eye, and Miles glanced over to see his brother's cat slink out from behind the HVAC unit and hop onto the low brick wall surrounding the roof. With his head and tail held high, Loco patrolled the perimeter like a sentry. Woe betide the pigeon who landed here.

When the animal seemed satisfied that his domain was secure, he hopped down and padded over to the sitting area. Miles sipped his coffee and stared at the dark sky. The gentle push against his calf pulled his attention, and Miles looked down to see Loco moving beneath his dangling hand, letting his fingers run the length of the cat's shiny black fur. Then, Loco hopped into Miles's lap. After kneading his sweatpants with sharp claws, the cat curled up and rested his head on crossed paws.

Miles scratched Loco behind the ears. It seemed nobody wanted to be alone on this desolate morning.

A few minutes later, Loco turned a placid green-eyed face to Miles, then hopped down and sauntered away.

After finishing his coffee, Miles set the mug at his feet. He thought of Clara. Ever since he held her in his arms, bathed in her scent, lost himself in her body, she was never far. At this moment, however, his typical obsession, anger, and worry were replaced by an unfamiliar peace. Last night, Clara had been with her father. Tonight, she was home working on her dissertation. Not only was she safe, but she was happy.

Knowing he could never be the source of Clara's contentment, it was a relief that she could find joy in life. She adored her father; school was fulfilling, and her *little hobby* brought obvious pleasure. Pleasure. An image flashed in his mind of fucking Clara in the middle of one of her heists—the adrenaline, the eroticism—Miles nearly passed out from the loss of blood to his brain.

Miles needed to purge Clara from his thoughts. Maybe he was doing the wrong thing, chasing off her dates. If she found someone, got married…

Out of habit, he logged in to Clara's dating app.

Miles's blood was already simmering with imagined jealousy. It boiled when he brought up Clara's account. "Hondo" was an aspiring professional bodybuilder and fitness model. The oiled, fake-tanned photo showed this roided-out asshole sporting a speedo in a Mr. Universe pose.

If it was a joke, Miles was too blinded by jealousy to see it. "Goddammit!"

He was angry with himself for letting this woman provoke him. Miles didn't get provoked. Only Clara had the ability to bring out this unhinged side. He wasn't keen on self-reflection and didn't do it now as he stormed to the shower.

His little Bluebird needed another lesson.

CHAPTER THIRTY-THREE

New York City
October 20

Clara had just finished her classes for the day and bought a snack at her corner market when she spotted Miles emerging from the subway, looking fit to be tied. She tucked her purchases, apple juice and a granola bar, into her book bag. She grinned. Looked like someone had been snooping on her dating app.

"Miles?" she asked innocently.

When he spotted her, his eyes flamed. Miles strode the short distance to the front of the corner store and caught her by the elbow. "Just the person I was looking for."

"Why were you looking for me?" She batted her lashes.

"You know why."

"Where are we going?"

"Your place. You need a reminder about how to conduct your social life."

"It was a joke, Miles."

"It wasn't funny, Clara. I have more important things to do than make sure you aren't assaulted by some online predator."

"So *you're* going to assault me instead."

He pulled her to face him on the sidewalk. "Exactly."

"Say the words, Clara."

Miles had her right where he wanted her. Naked and begging. For an hour, he had tormented her with his fingers and mouth. She was trembling and desperate, her hands gripping the sheets.

"Please, Miles."

"Not those words."

"I will delete my online dating profile," she panted.

"Continue."

"I will not put myself in dangerous situations with strangers."

He nestled his hips at the apex of her thighs and reached for the condom beside him. "And?"

Clara glared at him.

"*And?*"

She spoke through clenched teeth. "And I will let you vet any man I want to date."

Miles ripped the foil with his teeth.

Clara looked up at him and said, "I'm on the pill."

"I've never not used a condom, Clara. And I've been tested."

"I trust you, Miles."

Those words had more impact than any foreplay. He pushed into her, devouring her sounds of pleasure. God, her body was heaven. Miles gave no reprieve as he fucked her relentlessly. Like the fearless, gorgeous thing she was, Clara welcomed him into her body, returning his strokes with a tilt of her hips and a squeeze of her inner walls. She wanted everything he gave.

Miles bent forward, his mouth drawn to hers, but redirected. He had told Clara this wasn't about intimacy—there would be no kissing. Her pink lips parted, inviting, but he settled for closing his eyes and touching his forehead to hers.

She was a devil. And at that moment, Miles wanted to sell his soul.

She released the sheets when her orgasm hit and gripped his back. He lifted his head and met her gaze. They tumbled together, spiraling down, intertwined. It had been so long since he'd been held that way, since he had *connected*. He should look away. He should roll out of bed and leave. He should...

Just one more minute.

It was dark when Miles awoke, entwined with a sleeping Clara. She nuzzled his neck. Fortunately, sanity had returned, and he pulled away. Miles was determined to distance himself, but apparently, his body hadn't gotten the memo. His erection was heavy between his legs as he stepped into his pants.

"Where are you going?"

Away from you. Nowhere.

Somewhere.

He had never hesitated to snipe at Clara, to go tit for tat when she goaded him.

This was different.

She was naked on the bed, foggy with sleep and unashamed. Those vivid blue eyes were guileless and vulnerable. Miles blew out a breath and searched for some justification to do what he was about to do. *You like her.* That was true enough. The greater truth was that he needed to get Clara out of his life before he destroyed her.

Miles picked up a half-full mug of tea and rinsed it in the sink. After drying his hands, he stepped on the pedal to lift the trash can lid and toss the paper towel. Leaning closer, he spotted the dead arrangement at the bottom of the bin. Without guilt or hesitation, Miles took the card from among the dried leaves and opened it. As he stood in her kitchen, something burned hot in his chest. He stared at the door with the deadbolt thrown and the safety chain latched—even in their rush to the bedroom, Clara had secured the door. He thought back to how she had scanned the street and checked over her shoulder as they had rushed inside. Now, this disturbing card with a drawing of a lynx. Consumed by his obsession with her and preoccupied with Ugentti, something vital had escaped his notice.

Clara was afraid.

Miles couldn't leave her now. He wouldn't. He needed to know what was going on.

"That depends. What's in your fridge?"

"Mustard."

"And?"

"Maybe beer?"

"Then, to answer your question, I'm going to get us food."

Miles climbed onto the bed and straddled her. Running his nose along her cheek, he whispered, "If you've learned your lesson properly, you'll be rewarded. Have you learned your lesson, Bluebird?"

"Yes, Miles."

"Good girl."

Her nipples brushed his bare chest as Clara arched her back. Miles pulled away and stood. "Get dressed. Let's grab some Thai food from the place on the corner."

"Yes, Miles."

"Smartass."

Ten minutes later, they were walking side-by-side down the street. Miles had to resist the urge to wrap an arm around her shoulder or rest his hand at the small of her back. He wanted her close.

The buzzing of his cell phone pulled him from the maddening posses-siveness that seemed to be overtaking him.

The text from Chug Ugentti jolted him back to reality. Miles fumed at the not-so-veiled threat. After finding the contact information he was looking for, Miles sent another text. The reply came promptly.

Miles placed a call. "Giselle? Set up table forty. Four people." He checked his watch. "About an hour, thanks."

"What's all that about?" Clara asked.

"Change of plan." He took Clara's hand and pulled her to the curb as he hailed a taxi.

"Where are we going?"

He helped her into the back seat. "First, my place on the East Side. I need to change shoes."

The loafers with the tracker were about to come in handy. It was time to turn the tables on Chug Ugentti.

CHAPTER THIRTY-FOUR

New York City
October 20

Clara was still in the dark as they rode in the town car back uptown. He had dragged her to a nondescript apartment in a sterile highrise and done exactly as he had said: he changed shoes. Clara's imagination ran amok in this personality-less place; it was one step up from a hotel room. She could only think of one thing Miles did in this hideaway—fuck women. She had no right to the jealousy that clouded her vision, but it roared inside her nonetheless.

After their task was completed, Miles instructed the driver to pull over and helped Clara out of the car. "Let's walk a few blocks. It's a nice night."

This part of Harlem was a far cry from the crime-infested neighborhood from decades past. Renovated brownstones with stunning architectural details lined the street. Chic cafés and designer shops added to the vibe. The busier streets, Broadway and 112th Street, were still haunted by the ghosts of older Harlem: check cashing stores, unhoused people in alleys and on church steps, urban decay, but a block away, politicians and movie stars had created an enclave. While they waited on a corner for the light, Miles removed his tie, released the top two buttons of his dress shirt, and ran a hand through his hair. He seemed to change before her eyes. It wasn't the subtle wardrobe alteration; it was his demeanor. His posture eased, his center shifted. She couldn't exactly pinpoint it, but she found herself caught in his gravitational pull. With his necktie still in his hand, Miles retook hers and led her across the street and halfway down the next block. They stopped in front of an unmarked building between a French bakery and a cozy bookstore.

"In here."

As he released her hand, the tie caught on her wrist. Clara lifted her arm so Miles could untangle her, but the look that flared in his eyes had her wishing he would loop it around again. Tightly. Forcing her face to neutral, she lifted the silk over her hand and turned to face the building. Then recognition hit.

"Clef?"

"You know it?"

"My advisor Jeffrey and his husband Hassan ate here last spring."

"And what did he think?" Miles asked.

"They sat next to Damien Lewis and Idris Elba, and Damien told him he'd been trying to get a reservation for six months. Jeffrey also said there weren't enough Michelin stars to accurately rate the meal, and the music was even better than the food."

"Good to know. Come on."

"Miles, are you nuts? You can't just walk into Clef."

"We need someplace private and safe."

"I agree, but we also need someplace that's not going to ask security to escort us out."

"Let's just take a peek. Maybe they had a last-minute cancellation."

Without listening to further protest, Miles tugged Clara through the inconspicuous double doors through an entry alcove and into a wide art deco-inspired hallway. The walls were bronze with a design of gold branches. Sconces shaped like half-open hand fans lined the walls at even intervals. A gorgeous woman stood at a dais at the base of a wide staircase. She was easily as tall as Miles with an elaborate knot of blonde hair pierced with two chopsticks, adding another four inches. She looked up with a pleasantly bored expression before her eyes widened. The woman transformed right in front of them. Her lids dipped, and her lips pursed. In a whisper, the guardian of the gate became a seductress. A rather obvious and cheap seductress if you asked Clara, but some men went for that.

"Good evening, Mr. Cain. I didn't know we were expecting you."

"Last minute thing, Giselle. I assume you're completely booked."

Clara had never seen a lusty nod before—how a simple tip of the head could be so sultry, Clara would never know. Giselle licked her lips, ignoring Clara, and leaned forward on the podium, spotlighting her ample cleavage. Clara told herself it was the presumptuousness of the woman that caused her blood to simmer. She glanced down at her short floral dress and gray cardigan. Compared to the goddess in the strapless silk number, Clara felt like a little girl. Nevertheless, she sidled closer to Miles and tucked her arm through the crook of his elbow. Miles cocked a brow at her action but otherwise made no comment.

"Have my guests arrived?" Miles asked.

"About ten minutes ago. Are you dining tonight?"

"Yes. Set up a table in the nook."

"Of course." Giselle turned and tapped the unobtrusive headset. When she had finished issuing instructions, Miles leaned across the dais, dislodging Clara's arm, and spoke under his breath. Giselle nodded and made a note on her tablet screen.

Clara was sure her nails were leaving half-moon marks in her palms.

Miles rested his hand against the small of Clara's back. The dominant move sent a shiver through her as they moved past Giselle and up the stairs.

Clara whispered, "Anything you'd care to share, *Mr. Cain*?"

Miles simply smirked and continued on.

"What first name do you use here? I'd hate to call you Miles when the staff knows you at Brock or Lance."

"Do you really see me as a Brock or a Lance?"

"No. But I never saw you as a Caleb or a Jake either."

"So, what do you see me as?"

"Miles."

His fingertips pressed into her skin as they reached the top of the stairs. "Miles is fine. Just don't let anyone hear you."

They rounded the banister with a brass finial in the shape of a flapper in a long gown, her pearled headdress patinated from the many hands touching it, coming and going.

Clara had abbreviated her advisor's description of his experience at the legendary supper club. Jeffrey had gone on and on about every phase of the experience. The songs chosen specifically for the food, the tasting menu designed to crescendo and fade, each course building to the next. An atmosphere that, as he put it, "simultaneously evoked thoughts of royal courts and raunchy sex."

As a lilting female voice singing Bruce Springsteen's *Fire* floated down the hall, Clara was already anticipating the experience. She slowed, enjoying the press of Miles's hand from the momentum shift. "Care to explain the VIP service? Do you have a deep, dark secret about the owner?"

Miles turned to Clara and cupped her face with his big hands. "Many." Then he leaned down and raked her earlobe between his teeth before whispering, "I'm the owner." He strode down the hall, leaving Clara standing beneath a portrait of F. Scott and Zelda Fitzgerald with her jaw on the lavender carpet. Miles disappeared through a wide archway, and she hurried after him, feeling woefully underdressed for what she suspected would be a memorable evening.

He was waiting for her just inside, reclaiming her hand and leading her around the perimeter to an alcove shielded by a single velvet curtain held to the wall by a tasseled rope. Miles ushered Clara into the intimate space and released the knot, shielding them from the room of patrons who had shifted their gazes from the chanteuse to watch them.

Miles pulled out the heavy chair for her, then seated himself as a waiter ducked into the room. He placed a small plate and a flute of champagne in front of each of them.

Clara glanced at the tempting morsel. The colors were enticing—pink and black, green and white. It was a glimmering sculpture on the plate.

"Watermelon with Pule, lucque olives, and micro greens. The champagne is your usual, sir—the Veuve Clicquot."

"Thank you, Wayne."

The waiter didn't attempt to hide his pleasure that Miles knew his name. He delivered a crisp nod before adding, "Your Montrachet is chilling," and exiting.

Clara lifted her salad fork and ran the tines along the wedge of Pule. The Balkan cheese famously made from donkey's milk was unique and wonderful. She opened her mouth to encourage Miles to taste it when her gaze landed on his empty plate. He was dabbing his mouth with a napkin and looking at Clara expectantly. With a shake of her head, she returned to the amuse-bouche.

"I'm not the only one here with deep, dark secrets, Clara."

The delicious bite clogged her throat as she said, "I know."

"Now, my little Bluebird, I'm going to feed you and ply you with alcohol. And you will tell me exactly what I want to know."

Clara pierced the tiny quail egg with her fork and stared as the yolk fell like lava over the lardons and broad beans. The food was exquisite. Despite her apprehension about the ensuing conversation, she relished every bite.

She worked alone, solved her own problems. If anyone could relate to that, it was Miles. It was perhaps the only thing they had in common. He must have sensed this similarity because he sat patiently sipping the buttery wine and listening to a jazz quartet play Peggy Lee's *Fever*. Clara couldn't help but sink into the music and the food. While the snare drum whispered and the bass pulsed, the singer rasped the sexy lyrics about a woman who gets a fever when her man puts his arms around her.

Clara didn't pretend not to know what Miles meant. He was too percep- tive not to pick up on her unease. "You remember Paris."

He smirked, no doubt remembering the little gift he had sent to her room at the George V.

"It got a little messy."

Miles didn't like the sound of that. He set down the goblet and leaned forward. "Messy, how?"

"It was a setup. The painting, a Renoir, was part of the Nazi stash. It be- longed to a Jewish family and was stolen in World War II. The subject of the painting is in her nineties now and lives in California. A sketchy financier bought it illegally on the black market and sent it to the restoration house in Paris to be refurbished. All that is true."

"But?"

"But, that sketchy financier I mentioned? He was out for revenge. I stole a painting from him the year before. He wanted to set a trap to catch me."

"Clara," Miles prodded. He twirled the wine glass by its stem, waiting for the full story.

"He wanted to catch me and record killing me to show all his criminal cronies he had managed to eliminate The Lynx."

"Jesus, Clara. I was half a mile away while some lunatic was attacking you."

Clara entwined their fingers. "I escaped."

Miles ran a frustrated hand through his hair. "How?"

"Blew the lights and slipped out in the chaos. You know I always have a backup plan."

The corners of his mouth tipped ever so slightly. "That's my girl." He cupped her face and leaned closer, and Clara couldn't stop the surge of warmth within.

On the stage, the singer belted out, "Fevah!"

Indeed.

The moment broke, and Miles leaned back with a sigh. Clara sipped her wine as she continued, equally excited and fearful for his reaction to the rest of the story. "It wasn't a clean getaway. Two guards found me. I stripped and pretended I was the girlfriend of one of the men. The perverts videoed it on their phones. That must be how he figured out who I am."

"You were naked."

It wasn't a question, but Clara answered anyway. "Yes, Miles."

"And they recorded you."

"Yes, Miles." She repeated in a traitorously breathy voice.

Her reply seemed to elicit the same response in Miles. His eyes took on that fiery intensity she remembered. His free hand pressed into the tablecloth, leaving small indentations in the fabric.

"Who is he?"

"Lucien Kite."

The stem of the wine glass snapped in Miles's hand.

"Lucien Kite is pure evil."

"Seriously? Of all the vermin you deal with on a daily basis, you're singling out a scummy Wall Street player? Gaming the system is the norm these days."

"Clara, do you know Kite's history? 'Wall Street Player' isn't even on his resume, and he stole nearly a billion dollars!"

"I know he worked for Anton Zorba. Kite discovered Zorba was running a Ponzi scheme and went to the feds."

Miles rolled his hands as he added, "Zorba killed himself before his trial, and Kite helped the government-appointed attorney recover the stolen funds."

"Yes, I know all that."

"Clara, Kite engineered the whole thing."

"How do you know that?" she asked.

Miles replied. "You don't want to know."

"So, what? You're saying Kite was complicit in the Ponzi scheme? I think everyone thinks that."

"No. I'm saying Lucien Kite was the mastermind behind it, and Zorba was the shill." He moved his plate aside and leaned across the table. "Kite set Zorba up, then murdered him and made it look like a suicide. Kite worked for the Zorba Fund for six years. I think he spent most of that time setting up the dominoes so when they fell, he could walk away with a fortune and a pat on the back from law enforcement."

"How is that even possible?"

"We ran a con this summer, Bluebird. What's the first rule I taught you?"

Clara's eyes widened. "The key is making sure the mark can't come for you."

"Exactly." Miles leaned closer. "They blame someone else."

"Anton Zorba."

"Who is conveniently dead."

Clara felt the blood drain from her face.

Miles slid his chair nearer. He took Clara's face and ran his thumbs along her jawline. Leaning close, he murmured, "I'm with you, Clara. I won't let anyone hurt you *ever*. I'll call in every favor I am owed, threaten to expose anyone. Whatever it takes."

The intensity of his vow was so erotic Clara needed to feel his mouth on hers. He still hadn't kissed her despite their newfound intimacy and his poetic words. She mirrored his hands and stretched for his lips just as the curtains shielding their table parted, and the woman who had greeted them at the door peeked her head past the heavy fabric and gave Miles a dispassionate nod. Before she left, the hostess hooked the curtain on the wall-mounted holder, providing them a view of both the crowded dining room and the musicians on the low stage.

"What now?" Clara blew a lock of hair from her forehead.

"Now, we have some fun. Follow my lead."

She couldn't help the way her body responded to Miles's command. As she opened her mouth to ask another question, a shadow darkened their table, and a man in a suit as ugly as it was expensive stood before them, grinning.

Miles feigned concern as Chug Ugentti took in the romantic setting with one hand in his pants pocket and the other holding a toothpick. Clara was not frightened but taken aback. Miles soothed her with his palm on the back of her hand. Miles had deliberately worn the alligator loafers. He hadn't mapped out an exact plan when it came to Chug, but he needed to make Ugentti *think* he still had the upper hand. So Miles had worn the shoes with the tracker. He had instructed his hostess to treat Ugentti like an honored guest and set a table for him where Miles would be in his sightline. He told Giselle to treat Chug's arrival as a welcome surprise, and he had no doubt she had played her part. Seeing Ugentti's smug face confirmed it.

"Well, if it isn't my old friend Caleb Cain."

Miles wiped his mouth and slid his chair back into its original position. "What a coincidence."

Ugentti popped the toothpick between his teeth and spoke around it. "It is. It is. I seem to have a knack for being in the right place at the right time."

The waiter moved deftly past the two thick bodyguards, replaced the broken wine glass with a fresh one, and filled it. Miles lifted his hand. "Bring me a single malt, neat. Make it a double."

Ugentti revealed a line of yellow teeth. "Need something a little stiffer?" Then he leered at Clara. "Although, I don't think *stiffer* is a problem with this lady at the table. And who might you be?"

Clara's Mediterranean-blue eyes widened as she wordlessly asked Miles: *yes, who might I be?*

"This is Collette. She's an associate of the two *carrots* you sent to my apartment after our first meeting. I'm surprised you two haven't already met. Although, she's a decade too old for you, Chug."

That did the trick. Ugentti swung his attention back to Miles. "Careful."

Miles accepted the scotch and downed half. "Don't let me keep you from a delicious meal."

"I'd never let you keep me from anything, Mr. Cain." He directed the comment to Clara, then returned his gaze to Miles. "Since we're both here, coincidentally, have you made any progress with my case?"

Ugentti sensed his guards moving aside. He turned to see what the issue was and immediately straightened. "Don Barzetti, this is a pleasant surprise."

Miles nearly laughed at how quickly Chug flipped from king to court jester. Vincent Barzetti was a kingpin in every circumstance, the head of East Coast organized crime.

Tall and fit with a full head of silver hair, Barzetti was an imposing presence. Even Clara looked a little star-struck by the notorious crime boss.

"Chug," Barzetti greeted Ugentti. "How's everything in The Garden State?"

"I'm holding down the fort. And, of course, I'm headed to Washington in a few weeks."

"I'm aware."

Of course, Barzetti was aware. He probably knew Chug would get elected before he ran for office.

Ugentti pulled the toothpick from his mouth and pocketed it. "Yeah, excited to do a lot of good."

Barzetti smirked. "I have no doubt. Now, if you'll excuse me, I was hoping to have a drink with my friend."

"Sure thing. I was just leaving." Ugentti turned to Miles. "We'll talk soon, Cain."

"Of course. I'll be in touch with an update tomorrow."

Ugentti tugged his pants over his fat gut. "Excellent. Looking forward to hearing your progress."

"Enjoy your dinner, Congressman."

"Unfortunately, I can't stay. I have a prior engagement. But I'll have to give this place a try." Ugentti eyed Clara and licked his lips. "Everything on the menu looks delicious."

Clara batted her eyes and delivered a sultry smile. Miles nearly broke another wine glass.

Chug snapped his stubby fingers, and his guards fell in behind him as he wandered to the exit, stopping at a few tables to greet diners.

Barzetti flashed a pearly smile. "How was that?"

Miles stood and shook the crime boss's hand. "Perfect, Vincent. Thank you."

"A meal at Clef for coming over and saying hello? I think I'm the one who should be thanking you. Again."

"Well, I appreciate it just the same."

"Don't mention it. Now, I think I'll get back to my exceptional dinner."

When Barzetti was once again seated at the best table in the house, Clara raised a questioning brow.

"One of his daughters got caught up in a scandal at Harvard. I smoothed things over."

"He has college-aged kids? The guy has to be pushing eighty."

"He's seventy-six. Nine kids with two wives. Well, eight kids now. His oldest daughter was killed years ago."

"And Ugentti? How did he know how to find you?"

"I arranged it."

His manager appeared beside the curtain. "Was that all right?"

Miles nearly smiled at the way Clara stiffened. He was battling his own unfamiliar possessive streak. Nice to know he wasn't alone. "Perfect. Thank you, Giselle."

Clara stared daggers at Giselle's back as she walked away as a string quartet finished playing a classical version of the Doors hit *Light My Fire*.

The waiter set the key lime sorbet palate cleanser before them, and Miles scooped a bite with the tiny spoon. "There's a tracker in my shoe."

Clara's eyes danced as she tasted the frozen treat. "You lured him here?"

"Not *lured* per se, but there's an advantage to letting Ugentti think he has the upper hand."

"What does that creep want with you?"

A man in a black suit stood a few feet from the table and cleared his throat, interrupting them. Miles set his spoon down and finished the scotch. "Hold that thought."

Clara sat alone at the small table, worried and confused. She had eaten her Mississippi Mud tart in one bite and then polished off the one at the empty place across from her. Where had Miles gone? No sooner had she silently asked the question than the stage lights dimmed, and Miles strode to the standing mic in the center. Behind him, in the shadows, musicians were ghosting about.

"Good evening. I'm honored you were able to join us tonight. I'm not here as often as I'd like, but I can only go so long before the craving for Chef Serena's food is overwhelming." Miles paused for effect. "When I am here, the gang and I have a tradition. So I hope you'll permit this little indulgence."

Clara saw the nods of approval and the raised glasses.

"For the final course of the night, the waiters are placing a plate of four miniature truffles before you. As you know, the theme for this evening is fire. Like this evening's music, each chocolate gets progressively hotter. The fourth truffle has a hint of Savina Habanero. So proceed with caution."

Clara glanced at the narrow rectangular plate the waiter had set down. The first truffle was dusted in cocoa powder, the second dotted with ruby chocolate, the third streaked with white chocolate, and the innocent-looking fourth was dipped in a shimmering glaze.

She picked up the first little ball and popped it in her mouth as the music started. The guitar and the base played as the drummer joined in. When Clara glanced up again, her heart slammed into her chest. Miles was still standing center stage. He had removed his jacket and rolled up his sleeves, revealing muscled forearms. With both hands wrapped around the mic, Miles leaned close, eyes locked with Clara's. Then he started to sing.

Clara knew the song—Kings of Leon, *Sex on Fire*. But she had never heard anything like what she was listening to. Miles rasped out the opening lyrics, a man ordering a woman to stay lying where she was and not make a sound. It was sensation overload—the chocolate on her tongue, the sexy-as-sin man in front of her. She didn't know Miles could sing, much less sing like this.

Clara was reasonably sure she would slide down her chair into a molten puddle on the floor by the time he got to the chorus.

Miles tore his gaze away from her and sang to the room. Clara's advisor had also mentioned that, depending on the wine selection, patrons paid upwards of five thousand dollars to dine at Clef. Miles was wise to make his audience feel a part of the performance. That, and Miles was a natural showman. He may want to serenade Clara with a steamy song, but the star in him demanded he spread the magic.

Miles returned the microphone to the stand and gave a humble bow as gentle applause filled the dining room. He navigated tables as a few patrons stood to shake his hand and introduce themselves. He wasn't in the mood for pleasantries. He was in the mood for Clara.

He stood at the nook staring into the empty space in confusion. Then a hand slipped down his forearm and slid into his. He turned to find lusty blue eyes staring at him. Clara held up a small, glossy white bag.

"I got the truffles to go."

"Did you, now?"

"I thought we could eat them back at my place and see how spicy they really are."

Miles grabbed her ass cheek and pulled Clara to his body, his erection pressing against her side. He bent down and raked his teeth across her neck—then felt her knees buckle as he growled exactly what he planned to do with those truffles in explicit detail.

"Lead the way, Bluebird."

Miles handed the bag containing the shoes with the tracker to the Uber driver with instructions to give it to the doorman at his decoy apartment. He was now wearing a pair of white leather sneakers he had stashed in his office at the restaurant that somehow looked even more stylish with his suit than the loafers.

They strolled casually in the crisp night, but inside, Clara was anything but calm. The heat from Miles's proximity was melting her. She wondered if Miles had the same filthy thoughts running through his mind. Miles had his hands in his pants pockets, and Clara hooked her arm through his. He was relaxed as he chatted about this and that. It was funny how this innocent moment made her feel more like one-half of a couple than anything they had done in her bedroom.

Outside her building, Miles paused, bringing Clara to a stop beside him. In her happy haze, she hadn't paid much attention to her surroundings. Miles was staring at an Escalade parked across the street. The windows were tinted, but Clara could see the driver through the windshield, his face illuminated by his phone screen as he texted.

"What is it?" she asked.

"It's sitting lower than a regular SUV. It's armored." He withdrew his phone and hit a preprogrammed number.

"It's Miles."

He chuckled at something whoever he was talking to said, then replied. "Fuck you. Listen, can you send a squad car to this address? A friend of mine has some unwanted visitors. Black Escalade parked out front."

He listened for a second again, then pinned his location. "Thanks, man. I owe you."

Miles ended the call and guided Clara back to the corner, where a taxi was waiting at the light. Miles ushered her into the back.

"Who did you call?"

"The Chief of Police."

"You think those are Kite's men?"

"I'm sure of it." Miles held her thigh in a firm grip. "Nothing to do about it tonight."

The adrenaline and fear had only fueled her arousal; she was desperate for him.

"Where to?" the driver asked.

"*Yes, Miles.* Where to?"

His brown eyes flared at her wording. Miles delivered the address of his loft downtown as his hand plunged beneath her skirt.

CHAPTER THIRTY-FIVE

New York City
October 21

Chug Ugentti slammed the newspaper onto his desk with a thwack. "I'm going to bust some kneecaps."

His chief of staff, Garrett, was a pin-thin man with a neatly trimmed beard and a Harvard MBA. He was a late hire, brought on to polish the rough edges of the mobster's tattered image. "Relax, Chug. Stories like this are forgotten by the next news cycle. There's no news, only propaganda. Readers assume these hatchet jobs are agenda-driven. I have a social media service planting rumors and conspiracy theories about both the writer and the girls quoted in the article. Make a casual comment to the press. Something to the tune of you won't be distracted by false accusations intended to undermine your work for the people of New Jersey."

Ugentti considered Garrett's words. "That's not bad."

Garrett leaned forward with his palms flat on the desk. "I'm not reinventing the wheel."

It took every ounce of self-control Chug Ugentti had to stop himself from picking up the letter opener and pinning this pencil pusher's hand to the wood. Instead, he offered up his newly minted politician's smile and, with a hand on Garrett's shoulder, steered him toward the door.

"Yes, I know, but you're earning your paycheck just reminding me to let cooler heads prevail. I can't walk around the House floor with a baseball bat."

Garrett chuckled. "Maybe for a publicity stunt." He held up a hand. "That being said, no one needs to end up in the hospital—or the East River—over a news story. The media is subjective and agenda-driven and, therefore, easily refuted."

Chug clapped Garrett on the shoulder and nudged him out the door. "As always, your words of wisdom save the day."

Garrett blushed at the compliment. "Just doing my job, sir."

"And doing a bang-up one at that. You meet with the PR team—make sure everyone is on the same page. I'm going to get back to this healthcare bill."

His Chief of Staff delivered an enthusiastic "Will do" as the door closed, and Chug turned to the three men lingering in the seating area.

Mikey, his best enforcer from the good old days, pulled at his collar. "Please tell me we're going to knock some heads."

"Like coconuts, Mikey."

His words were met with grunts of agreement. "But," Chug continued. "Pencil Neck has a point. We need an added level of *discretion*."

"What does that mean?" Mikey asked.

"It means I have a solid alibi. It means no witnesses. And make it look like a mugging or a robbery."

"You got it, boss." The other man was also named Michael. For clarity and because of his size, he went by Big Mike.

"And don't kill him. Caleb Cain has dirt on every player in town."

"Not yet, anyway." Big Mike cracked his knuckles.

Chug grinned. "Deliver a message. Let's make it clear how I feel about the little story, and in a few days, I'll have another meeting with Pretty Boy—Jersey-style."

The Mikes approved.

"Caleb Cain is going to be sharing secrets like a preteen girl at a slumber party."

CHAPTER THIRTY-SIX

New York City
October 22

Miles sat on the little bench in front of the closed bakery and tracked Clara's movements on his phone. The night was chilly, and Harlem was active as New Yorkers headed to the bars and restaurants that lined the street. None of that distracted him from the pulsing dot on his screen.

Clara would be coming around the corner right about… now.

He looked up, and there she was, laughing and giving her companion a little shove. Miles couldn't explain why he was here tonight. The man with her was her friend, Richie, another Art History TA at Columbia who lived with his husband and their daughter. This wasn't a date. Additionally, Richie was a karate black belt who taught self-defense. Clara was safe with him.

Still, something compelled him to take his Ducati a hundred blocks to check on her. When it came to Clara, there was a demon inside him, a little, evil thing that punched and kicked at his gut until Miles did what it demanded. Once he saw her, the tiny devil calmed.

There wasn't a doubt in his mind Lucien Kite had unmasked The Lynx, and the men in that armored SUV in front of her apartment were watching her. *That* was his reason for his watch-keeping. Had he known she had been tangling with Lucien Kite when she was at that warehouse in France, Miles would have handcuffed her to his wrist.

Clara pointed to the sky, and Richie followed her motion, as did Miles. The moon was full and orange; clouds swept past at nearly time-lapse speed. Clara was an art lover, an art connoisseur, an art thief. Every facet of her life was colored with beauty. Her world had a gilded frame.

Miles stood as Clara and her friend stopped at her stoop to say good-night. He was annoyed with his irrational need to watch her, to know that she was safe.

Suddenly, an SUV pulled around the corner in front of him and made a screeching U-turn. It was the same Escalade that had been parked in front of Clara's apartment. All four doors opened at once. Richie put up a good fight but was no match for what looked like trained mercenaries. Two of the men subdued him, knocking him out cold. The other two grabbed Clara and tossed her in the back seat while she screamed and clawed like a wild cat. She scratched one guy in the eye, and he reared back, covering the injury with one hand and backhanding her with the other. A feral rage filled Miles as he ran to her aid—and quite possibly to kill the man who had hit her. He was two steps into the street when the driver floored it as the final door slammed shut.

The entire event took half a minute. When the Escalade sped away, and he could see a neighbor calling nine-one-one to help Clara's friend, Miles jumped on his Ducati and followed.

CHAPTER THIRTY-SEVEN

New York City
October 22

Clara sat in the back seat of the SUV. Her fight or flight instinct was always pointed to fight—it was the residual effect from her childhood. She'd still be kicking and punching if it weren't for the vicious-looking knife the man on her right held to her throat. The guy on her left was the one she poked in the eye. His face was impassive, but tears leaked down his cheek from the injury. Good. She hoped she blinded him.

They drove for an hour. The knife never shifted; the passengers never spoke. Clara made note of the route and location, but her abductors seemed unconcerned with her knowledge of their destination. As they ventured deeper into the Connecticut suburbs, traffic was sparse, and the streets were quiet. The only sound she heard was the high-pitched *ngggg* of a revving motorcycle in the distance.

Eventually, they pulled into a gated drive and stopped in the cobblestone circle surrounding an abstract gold sculpture Clara could only describe as *phallic*.

The men escorted her up the stone steps to the front door. The heavy knocker was a cast of the head of Poseidon, the handle his beard. One of her guards banged twice, and the door opened to a smartly dressed man with a warm smile.

Her host dismissed her captors with a disapproving sweep of his fingers, then turned his attention to Clara. "I apologize for the rude treatment, Miss Gautreau."

"Who are you?"

"My name is Willoughby. I'm the house manager. Mr. Kite would like a word." He extended an arm toward the grand staircase. "Through the double doors at the top."

Clara took the steps alone. Halfway up, she glanced back to see the house manager walk over to a woman half-hidden in the next room. She was wearing a nightgown. Willoughby joined her but stopped to study a stain on the carpet.

Clara climbed the stairs, angry and apprehensive. One of the heavy maple doors was ajar. Clara pushed it open the remaining distance. The office was lovely. There was a subtle elegance to it. On her right, bookshelves lined the walls of a tasteful seating area. Her eyes widened when she saw the painting stolen from her father hanging on the opposite wall. And straight ahead, Lucien Kite sat behind a kingly desk, smiling. Was he sitting on a chair made of money?

Kite spoke first. "I have a celebrity in my midst. The infamous Lynx."

Clara didn't pretend. She knew her little ruse at the warehouse would be discovered eventually. "What do you want?"

"Two things. First, since you will never possess it, I thought you might like to see my latest acquisition."

"That you stole," she spat.

"Oh, that's rich coming from you."

Clara entered the room fully and crossed to the portrait. The depiction drew her in, the woman so desperate, reaching out for someone. An aura surrounded the image so poignant that Clara felt the despair in her soul.

"I'm not particularly impressed with it." Kite interrupted her perusal. "But I know the painting's secret and why your father wants it."

Clara knew the rumors. Something about the portrait told her that Reynard wanted it for its beauty, not some inane treasure hunt. Lucien Kite's tastes were determined by price tag and not quality. Reynard purchased art that affected him. She kept those thoughts to herself.

Instead, she said, "You're a brave man stealing from Reynard. He has many friends."

Clara returned her attention to the painting. This time, she examined the mounting and the frame, checking for motion sensors and alarms.

Kite replied, "Your father is the Old Guard. He is respected but no longer feared."

A thud against the window behind Lucien Kite stole their attention. In the dim exterior lighting, Clara could see a bird had flown into the floor-to-ceiling plate glass and landed dazed on the balcony. After flopping on the flagstone for a moment, it flew into the darkness.

Kite grumbled. "There's a nest of great grey owls on the balcony. Some loony birdwatcher reported it to the bird police. They're protected, so as much as I'd like to tip the whole fucking lot of them right off the edge, the last thing I need is a swarm of nature cops arresting me. Can you picture it? Al Capone went to jail for tax evasion. Lucien Kite gets pinched for animal abuse."

"Yes, that would be comical."

He joined her at the fireplace and regarded the portrait. "Ever done any modeling? Been lured to a photographer's studio after one too many mojitos?"

"No," she replied flatly.

Kite shrugged. "Still, I can see why he painted her. Unlike those chubs in the Louvre, this gal is sexy." He fingered a strand of Clara's hair.

She stepped away. "What else?"

"Hmm?"

"You said you brought me here for two things."

"Ah, yes." Lucien Kite picked up a thick envelope with a wax seal and extended his hand. "For you. I'm hosting a costume party next weekend. I realize it's short notice, but I wanted to invite you. You see, Clara, I have studied The Lynx for quite some time. I know how you think. I know how you steal. So I thought I'd save you the trouble of sneaking into my home and open my doors for you. Give it your best shot." Kite stood and came around the desk. "Oh, and feel free to use your ruse of requesting a tour of the house and my art collection for research on your Ph.D. My house manager can schedule it any time."

"I'll bear that in mind."

"Why you want it is beyond me; it's not what I would steal if I robbed this house." His expression conveyed Kite had a valuable secret hidden here.

When Clara said nothing, he walked her to the office entry, pulling both doors open with bravado. "Willoughby can show you out. One of my men will return you to The City."

A persistent banging on the front door had them both turning their heads. A muffled shout came through the wood. "Open the goddamned door!"

Clara couldn't hide her smile. "Thanks, I have a ride. Oh, and Lucien?"

"Yes?"

"I'm going to steal that painting right out from under your nose." She turned and descended the stairs. "See you at the party."

She started for the front door, but a tsking sound had her looking over her shoulder. Willoughby was where she had last seen him. Only now, he was staring at a water stain on the ceiling. A drop fell and landed at his feet. Clara tracked the water damage up to what must be a bathroom next to Kite's office.

Remembering his duty, the house manager hurried to her side and opened the door, still vibrating from the incessant pounding.

Miles stood on the threshold like a warrior god. Dressed in jeans, boots, and a plain gray T-shirt, he looked young. And angry. Clara felt her face heat and her nipples harden beneath her bra. Without a word to her escort, Miles grabbed her hand and yanked her out of the house. She had to jog to keep up with his strides as he pulled her toward a motorcycle.

Holy shit, he's the hottest man I've ever seen. The thought ran through her mind unbidden as Miles grabbed the spare helmet and placed it on her head. Then he secured his own, lifted Clara onto the seat, and mounted the bike.

She instinctively reached around his body. He smelled like ocean air and clean laundry. Clara wanted to press her face between his shoulder blades and inhale the scent. With a Herculean effort, she resisted, reminding herself that she hated Miles Buchanan. A voice in her head seemed to say *oh, who the hell are you kidding?*

With a rev of the motor and a spray of gravel, they shot away from the mansion.

CHAPTER THIRTY-EIGHT

Lucien Kite Estate
October 22

Lucien Kite looked out the soaring Palladian window above the front door as Clara Gautreau climbed on the back of the motorcycle. The guy was a surprise—a biker in ripped jeans and a T-shirt. Kite would have thought Clara was more of an Armani suit type. The helmet obscured his face, but Lucian pictured a bearded tough guy who fancied himself a player. Still, the man had been clever enough to follow Kite's guards or track Clara's phone. Perhaps Reynard had hired a bodyguard for his princess.

It hardly mattered. Reynard could hire an army; it wouldn't stop Lucien Kite from getting what he wanted. Or, in this case, keeping what he wanted. Clara Gautreau had fucked with the wrong man. Putting an end to her little Robin Hood act would not only curry favor with some very influential people—many of whom would be in attendance at his soiree—it would give Lucien the satisfaction of knowing he had been the one to outsmart the uncatchable Lynx. He had already unmasked her. Now, he was going to catch her in the act in front of hundreds of gossiping witnesses.

His mind danced with fantasies of what he would do to her then. Killing her seemed like such a waste. Maybe he would keep her caged in his bedroom or chained in the stables. Kite knew he wanted to ruin that pretty face; beauty was the ultimate privilege—one he could not buy despite his best efforts. Kite would destroy her body and soul.

Or perhaps auction that privilege to the highest bidder.

His ego had gotten the better of him today, but he couldn't resist taunting Clara. What had she done? She had returned his bravado in equal measure. *I'm going to steal that painting right out from under your nose.*

Unfortunately for Clara, Lucien Kite was not some unsuspecting art lover content with a good alarm and a deadbolt. He turned back to the office, finding his house manager waiting by the double doors.

Willoughby followed him into the room and stood between the two guest chairs opposite the desk while Kite took his usual seat.

"How are the preparations coming?"

"Like clockwork, sir. The event will exceed your guests' expectations, as it does every year."

"No one comes into this house without being vetted. No cater waiter, no maintenance person, no delivery man, no one."

"Of course."

"One of those goddamned birds cracked the window. Have the pane replaced."

"I'll add it to my list," Willoughby said.

"And have the security company check the alarm on the new glass. I want this office locked up tight for the party. There will be a thief in attendance."

"Your guest list always includes colorful characters. Part of what makes this party so memorable."

"This particular thief plans to steal that painting." Kite gestured to *Somewhere.*

Willoughby smirked. "I wish him luck. The security in this room is impenetrable."

"Her. The thief is a woman."

His house manager merely shrugged. Kite had information in his bedroom safe worth infinitely more than this annoying work of art. Part of him wished Clara would steal the damn thing. It would be an excellent test of his security measures.

"I want two guards at the door at all times during the party."

"Understood. Do you really think she'll try to steal the painting?"

"I'm absolutely sure of it."

"Should make for an interesting evening, sir."

"Indeed."

CHAPTER THIRTY-NINE

Hutchinson River Parkway, Connecticut
October 22

Clara gripped Miles around the waist as the bike flew down the expressway toward Manhattan. When the motorcycle was well away from Lucien Kite and prying eyes, Miles pulled to the side of the road. He removed her helmet and tossed it into the grass, then did the same with his. Before she could formulate a thought, Miles hauled Clara from the seat and dragged her into the woods. At the first secluded tree, he backed her up against the bark.

"When did you get a motorcycle?" she asked.

Miles didn't answer. He was breathing hard, and she had never seen the look in his eyes before. Miles was always so coolheaded, so distant. At this moment, he looked like he might kill someone.

"Miles?"

He responded with a kiss.

It was the kiss Clara had waited for all her life. The kiss she had dreamed of long before she knew the man who would deliver it. The magnetic eruption exceeded her wildest dreams. Clara's head banged against the tree at the force of it. Miles was devouring her. One of his big arms circled her lower back. His other hand gripped her nape. He was in complete control, and she loved it. The feeling of being so possessed, it was intoxicating.

"You kissed me."

Miles rested his forehead against hers, breathing hard. "I don't know how I managed to hold out as long as I did."

Clara wound her arms around his neck and ran her tongue along the seam of his lips. He responded with a growl and another ferocious kiss.

Breaking away, he bit out, "I need to be inside you."

With no further words, Miles hauled her up and guided her legs around his body. With a rough tug, he ripped her drenched thong from her body and drove inside of her. Miles fucked her like a man possessed, like a man *possessing*.

Clara arched her back as she adjusted to his size, then matched his passion stroke for stroke. She felt like a ticking time bomb.

"I need you with me, Clara," Miles rasped. She cried out as the orgasm mounted. Miles's control unraveled, and they exploded together.

Miles buried his face in the valley of her neck. "I don't like this feeling, Clara."

She cupped his face in her palms and urged Miles to look at her. "What feeling?"

"Caring."

"You care about things."

"Not like this." He took a step back and scanned her from head to toe. His fingers traced Clara's jawline. "You're okay?"

"I'm perfect." She stepped forward to return to his orbit. Mirroring his earlier gesture, she tucked her face in the hollow of his throat. Miles responded by wrapping Clara in his arms. She could feel his breath in her hair.

"I think I might be starting to hate you, Bluebird." He tightened his hold.

She laughed into his neck. "I hate you too, Miles Buchanan."

"Good."

When she stepped back, Miles was more composed. She didn't think there was anything hotter than Miles in a suit, but this badass biker look was buckling her knees. She switched gears before she tackled him into the leaves.

"Lucien Kite has my father's painting. He brought me there to show me."

Miles narrowed his gaze. "I don't like where this is going."

"Reynard asked me to get it back. Papa is sick; he may be dying, and for some reason, that painting is important to him."

Miles gripped the back of his neck. "You're not doing this alone."

Before Clara could ask or even ponder what he meant, Miles looked past her shoulder. She turned to watch a dark SUV with tinted windows pull to a stop behind the Ducati.

CHAPTER FORTY

Hutchinson River Parkway, Connecticut
October 22

All four doors of the SUV opened simultaneously. Miles shielded Clara with his body despite knowing who was in the car. Eight booted feet hit the gravel on the shoulder, one pair particularly large and familiar. His twin brother, Tox, emerged from the front passenger door. Andrew "Chat" Dunlop and Leo "Ren" Jameson appeared from the back seat, and Jonah "Steady" Lockhart looked across the car from the driver's side.

Miles knew Clara had briefly met the Bishop Security men on a few occasions over the past two years. Nevertheless, battle-ready and serious, they were an intimidating bunch. Miles felt a surge of pleasure at the thought of joining the team, of being one of the good guys. He had waded in the muck for so long that the idea of swimming in clean water was suddenly very compelling. Miles hadn't anticipated the lure of doing good.

"Hope we're not interrupting," Tox said with an unapologetic grin.

Miles took Clara's hand and led her back to the road. "You didn't need to come. I sent a follow-up text that I had her, and everything was okay."

Steady joined them. "Miles, you're dealing with a bunch of knucklehead former sailors. We don't handle downtime well. Ren's got girl trouble, so it was either get drunk and give him shitty advice or saddle up."

Tox added, "So I ignored the all-clear and tracked you."

Miles embraced his brother with his usual distantly affectionate hug and said, "I'm glad you did."

Tox laughed. "Doesn't look like it to me. Hello Clara."

Miles pulled Clara to his side. There was no point in hiding his attachment from his twin. Tox always knew what Miles was thinking and feeling. Miles hadn't underestimated his brother's intuition. Tox's nearly imperceptible nod spoke volumes.

A pickup drove by, laying on the horn. Chat said, "We should move off this shoulder."

Miles retrieved both helmets. "Meet us back at the place. I need your help."

"Oh, hell no." Steady snatched one of the helmets from Miles's grasp. "You two ride in the back. I've got a date with this fine lady."

Miles had no sooner tossed Steady the fob than the Ducati shot off. Miles put his hands on his hips. "If he puts so much as a scratch on it, I'll wring his neck."

Ren clapped Miles on the shoulder as he headed around the car to the driver's seat. "No worries there. The guy could fly an F-18 through the Lincoln Tunnel."

As they pulled into traffic, Tox said, "Tell Clara your troubles, Ren. Might help to have a woman's perspective."

Miles saw the muscle in Ren's jaw flex, causing the arm of his wire-framed glasses to bob.

Ren changed the subject. "I think there are more pressing issues at the moment."

Tox blew a raspberry. "Fine. Sitrep?"

Miles deferred to Clara, and she told the team about her complicated history with Lucien Kite.

Tox texted Twitch, their cyber security expert, no doubt getting background info on Kite.

Tox's voice was lethal. "What happened at the house just now?"

Clara explained, "He stole a painting from my father. Well, he stole it from the Marseilles Customs House, but it belongs to Papa. Kite wanted to show me."

"What painting?" Miles asked.

"It's a portrait by a fairly obscure artist. *Somewhere* by Francisco Tavarro. Reynard bought it as a gift for me. It has sentimental value. I think Kite found out who I am and wanted to show me his reach. Then he invited me to a party."

"What party?" Miles demanded.

Clara pulled the invitation from her crossbody bag and passed it to him.

Miles took the card, then pulled a red leaf from her golden hair.

"I also may have told him I was going to steal the painting back."

"May have?" Miles prodded.

"I think my exact words were, 'I'm going to steal that painting right out from under your nose.'"

"What's this party he mentioned?" Tox asked.

Miles read the invitation. "It's a masquerade party—a return to Versailles."

Ren shook his head. "The guy has no shame."

Miles kept his eyes on the card. "You can send your regrets."

Clara snatched it out of his hand. "Maybe I'll go."

He gripped the back of Clara's neck, sending a shiver down her spine. "Over my dead body."

"It's my decision, Miles," she replied, annoyed with the sudden breathiness of her voice.

Miles growled in her ear, "Then, I hope Kite's expecting a plus one."

Ren stepped on the gas. "The game is afoot."

Clara sat in the middle between the twins. She leaned forward and spoke to Ren. "No more than usual, really. I need to steal a painting from a crook. I won't apologize or make excuses."

Tox rested a hand on her knee. "You don't have to justify your actions to us, Clara. We understand doing the right thing isn't always black and white."

Miles stared straight ahead. "This time is different. He knows you're coming, and, what's more, he knows your methods."

Tox pointed to the exit for Ren and said. "Miles is right. Might be time to shuffle the playlist."

Clara chewed on her lip. "Maybe."

Tox pointed at the invitation with his chin. "When's the shindig."

Miles checked. "Next Saturday."

"That's not enough time," Clara said.

Steady's voice came over the speakers. "You've got a team now, Sugar. We've deposed dictators in less than a week."

"Steady?"

"Bluetooth in the helmet is a nice touch, bro. I've been muting when I holler. Goddamn, this bike is sweet. The only thing missing is Very on the back wrapped around me like a python."

Tox disconnected the call with a chuckle. "It's a frosty day in hell. Steady's in love."

Clara saw Ren's fingers tense on the steering wheel and remembered Steady's comment earlier about woman trouble. "So, what's going on with you, Ren?"

Ren released a weary sigh but didn't speak.

Tox got the ball rolling. "Ren's been ass over tea kettle for a CIA analyst named Sofria Kirk. He's had a crush on her for years. He finally grew a pair and asked her out a few months ago."

Chat spun around to face the trio in the back. "I think his expectations were too high. His buddies were all thunderstruck by love, and he pictured the same thing happening to him."

Clara's voice grew sympathetic. "And it didn't?"

Ren finally spoke for himself. "It did. That's the thing." He checked the mirror and changed lanes. "Every time I saw her before we got together, I felt that... What does Cam's dad call it?"

Tox and Chat replied simultaneously, "The zing."

"Yes, the zing. I felt it. Sofria is gorgeous and brilliant. There's nothing about her I don't like."

Clara asked the obvious question. "So, what's the problem?"

"I don't know!" Ren hit the steering wheel with the heel of his hand, then composed himself. "Maybe she's too naive or too innocent. Maybe she's just not that passionate. She can talk about physics or the theater or poetry, but I never sense her fire."

"She's a CIA analyst, you say?" Clara asked.

"Yes," Ren confirmed.

"It's hard to imagine someone doing that job who wasn't passionate. Working long hours for low pay all to serve your country."

Ren thought about Clara's remark. "I agree, but if something gets her heart racing, I have yet to see it."

"You could be right," Clara replied.

"Or?" Ren pushed.

"She's hiding something."

The Suburban swerved as Ren overcorrected, then righted the SUV. "What makes you say that?"

"Personal experience." Clara flopped back between the twins. "I'm a thief. Most people don't know that, so I'm sure a lot of my acquaintances think I'm distant or don't have passion. Because I'm hiding it."

Chat looked out the passenger window as they crossed the 59th Street Bridge into Manhattan. "Clara makes an interesting point."

Ren waved him off. "Come on. It's not like she's doing Finn's old job or Cam's."

Miles knew both Bishop Security operatives had worked undercover for the CIA.

Ren continued. "Sofria's an analyst for Chrissake. She just left for her first field assignment, an embassy job. I almost wish she had some deep, dark secret. At least then there'd be something there."

Chat held up his hand. "Hold that thought. Ren?"

Ren glanced in the rearview mirror. "I see him."

"What's going on?' Clara looked behind her.

Miles looked back, too. A dark sedan was doing a poor job remaining hidden in traffic as it swerved around cars following them.

"We picked up a tail," he said.

"How?" Clara asked.

"Kite must have had men hanging back," Chat said. "Probably curious about your white knight."

Tox held the phone to his ear. "No worries bro. I'm about to make Steady's day."

Ren maneuvered the car through Manhattan traffic, stopping at a red light.

Steady said over the speaker, "I'm coming in from the east."

Tox replied, "It's a blue BMW, three cars back."

"Good copy."

When the light turned green, Ren drove forward at an average speed. Three vehicles back, the sedan jerked to a halt as a motorcycle ran the red at the cross street, popped the front tire, and slammed to a stop, propped on the car's hood.

Clara swore she saw Steady's grin through the tinted helmet shield.

Miles grabbed his brother's shoulder in a firm grip. Tox understood. "Let's swing by both your places. You have a go-bag?"

Miles said, "We both do."

"How do you—" Clara narrowed her eyes at him but held her tongue. He had obviously poked around while she slept. She couldn't very well call him out for snooping. Clara knew every inch of Miles's home.

They drove downtown in silence. As they neared Alphabet City, Tox said, "Clara, ever been to South Carolina?"

CHAPTER FORTY-ONE

New York City
October 23

Miles wanted to kill Lucien Kite. His brother had convinced him that laying low was the safer option. So, while Ren took Clara to Harlem to get her things, Miles sat in the passenger seat of the Suburban as he and Tox drove to the Upper East Side. They were mid-discussion about the Broncos' offensive line when Miles spotted an open space and directed his twin to park.

Tox leaned forward and eyed the highrise through the windshield. "So this is what? A vacation apartment?"

"It's Caleb Cain's apartment. I don't want clients knowing where I live. I just need to grab a few things, then I'm never coming back."

Tox placed a big hand on his shoulder. "I'm really glad you're taking Nathan's offer."

"Honestly, I don't know if I'm cut out to be a team player. I've been a solo act for a long time."

"We used to be a pretty good team," Tox said.

Miles held out his fist. Tox bumped it twice with exploding fingers like they did when they were kids. They were getting some of their mojo back. It felt good.

Miles opened the passenger door. "Come on, I'll give you the tour."

On the sidewalk, a man was leaning against the building, eating a hotdog. Miles waved to Burton, the uniformed doorman who ushered them into the lobby and onto the elevator. The twins walked down the hall on the eleventh floor—beige carpet, taupe walls, generic wall sconces.

"This place is charming. In an airport motel kind of way," Tox said.

Miles jiggled his keys. "Wait'll you see the luxury six grand a month buys on the Upper East Side."

Tox stopped him with a hand to his brother's chest and a tip of his head to the open door. "Expecting anyone?"

"No, but Ugentti's people have a habit of showing up."

Tox tsked, "I hate the pop-in. Fucking call if you want to come over."

"It's only polite," Miles agreed.

Through the cracked door, they spied a man bent over with his head in the fridge. He was as big as the appliance.

Tox whispered, "You ever learn how to fight beyond delivering a scathing insult?"

Miles chuckled. "Fuck off. I train bare knuckle. I can throw a punch."

"He's got a buddy in the bedroom."

"How do you know?" Miles asked.

"They always do."

Something bloomed inside Miles—like a time-lapse image of a tree in spring. He turned to his twin with a core memory burning bright.

Tox's eyes lit. "Mrs. Conroy's banana cake?"

Miles rechecked the room. "The cage match version. I'll distract. You sneak attack."

"I'd rather be stealing banana cake."

"Just get this fucker." Miles scolded.

"Go."

Miles entered the apartment and tossed his keys on the side table by the door as though nothing were amiss.

The behemoth at the fridge jumped to attention and grabbed him by the collar.

"What the hell? Who are you?" Miles asked.

"Mr. Ugentti wanted to make sure you were gathering the information he requested and remind you that he doesn't like delays or *publicity*." He shoved Miles forcefully against the wall.

Miles stalled, waiting for an opportunity to strike. "Look, asshole, tell your boss I'm working on it. And I don't *appreciate* the interruptions." A sound from behind them distracted his captor, and Miles delivered an uppercut to the guy's nose that had him staggering back a step. The big man sneered as blood ran down his yellow teeth. He was big but slow, and Miles dodged the first punch easily as the guy's fist smashed into the drywall.

"Mr. Ugentti says you have one week to deliver." The goon cocked his meaty fist but never threw the punch.

Tox stood behind him, gripping the man's hand in his huge palm.

Miles said, "Tell Mr. Ugentti our business is concluded."

The hulk spun out of his brother's hold and moved to the coffee table where he'd left his Beretta.

"Looking for this?" Tox trained the weapon on their assailant. The goon immediately raised both hands.

Miles looked over his brother's shoulder. "What about the other guy in the bedroom?"

"Nobody there."

"But you said there's always another guy."

"There always is."

They both heard the elevator bing its arrival.

Miles remembered the man leaning against the building when they arrived. "Hotdog guy?" Miles asked.

Tox nodded. "He was wearing military boots."

The twins moved in sync. Tox held the gun on the first intruder while Miles moved to the wall beside the front door. The man from the sidewalk came through the entrance and jabbed his gun into Tox's back. "Drop it."

Tox let the weapon fall to his feet as Miles leveled a punch to the second man's temple, dropping him to the floor unconscious.

"Nice punch, Miles." Tox nodded his approval.

"Told you I've been training." Miles turned to the first guy. "Out on the balcony."

"Oh, come on. I wasn't gonna kill you."

Tox turned to Miles. "He has a point. He didn't seem murderous."

"I realize that, but he came into my home and attacked me."

Tox retrieved the beretta and dismantled it without looking. "Bro, one punch, and he didn't even land it. I've punched you harder."

"When have you punched me harder?" Miles asked.

"Uh, third-grade play when you made fart noises before my line."

"Oh yeah." Miles laughed. "I actually saw stars."

"Fellas?" Ugentti's man interrupted.

"Balcony." The twins said in unison. Miles added, "When sleeping beauty wakes up, he can let you out. Tell Chug—you know what? I'll talk to Chug myself."

"What about my gun?"

"It's not a gun," Tox said.

Miles grinned. "It's Mrs. Conroy's banana cake."

When the guy was locked on the balcony, Tox said, "Grab what you need, and let's go."

Miles threw his suits and a few items of clothing he kept there into a duffle—he definitely needed the boxer briefs. "One last thing." Taking the pair of loafers from the closet, Miles peeled back the insole and removed the tracker.

"Do I want to know?" Tox asked.

"More horse shit," Miles replied.

"Here. I'll crush it."

"Nah, I have a better idea." Miles dropped the shoes in the bag and zipped it closed.

"Ready?"

"Ready. I'm done with this place."

"Good." Tox said as he stepped over the unconscious man, "I don't like the vibe in here."

Miles said, "Let's meet up with Clara and the boys and get going."

At the car, Tox popped the locks and tossed the duffle in the back.

Miles scanned the street. "Hang on a sec." In front of the neighboring building, a Lyft driver was loading a suitcase into the trunk as a passenger climbed in the back seat. Miles walked over, tossed the tracker into the trunk, and jogged back to his brother, who clearly enjoyed Miles's little move.

Tox started the SUV. "Is there a bakery around here? I'm suddenly craving banana cake."

Miles shoved his brother, both men stifling their laughter.

CHAPTER FORTY-TWO

Dordogne, France
October 23

Reynard was through with hospitals. His primary bedroom had everything he needed. The four-poster bed he had shared with his wife was comfortable. Logs crackled in the great stone fireplace. The framed photos of Annette and childhood pictures of Clara by the bedside warmed his heart. Outside, a full October moon hung in the sky like a beacon. Reynard had been a very lucky man.

At the moment, he was watching the pulsing red dot on his laptop screen with an amused gleam in his eye as Clara's shared location signal slowly blinked south down the eastern seaboard. Doctor Chu and his hulk of a nurse, Gerome, buzzed around, monitoring the immunotherapy IV treatment and checking his vitals. Gerome adjusted the pillow under Reynard's one remaining leg.

Reynard winced. "Easy, Gerome. Are you trying to lop that one off, too?"

The nurse's laugh was rich and deep. "Naw, Mr. Reynard. You're gonna need it for when we enter the three-legged race at the annual hospital picnic next spring."

Even the stoic Dr. Chu chuckled as he scanned the real-time data on his tablet. "You're responding as expected, Luka. I'm encouraged."

The use of his Croatian given name made Reynard feel as though Dr. Chu was speaking of someone else. Luka Kovac was a scrawny, helpless street rat. Reynard was a rich and powerful man. Now, as he lay in bed, weak but determined, he supposed he was both those things.

Dr. Chu and hyperbole had never been acquainted. So the word *encouraged* had Reynard sitting up. "How encouraged?"

The doctor took the chair beside the bed and held the tablet so they both could see the screen. "We'll take it week by week."

"Yes, of course," Reynard replied. At this late stage, Dr. Chu was trying to extend Reynard's life by weeks, not years.

"You've beaten the odds so far—partly by sheer force of will.

When the doctor and Gerome had departed, Reynard settled in for the night. As was his habit, he ran a frail finger down his wedding photo. *Soon, Annette.* He glanced at a picture of a bundled-up ten-year-old Clara sitting on a sled in the snow. Her beaming smile reminded him that heaven or hell didn't matter at the moment; he still had business on the corporeal plane.

CHAPTER FORTY-THREE

Beaufort, South Carolina
October 24

Clara took in the landscape as Tox pulled the Suburban into the gravel driveway. Marshland gave way to water as low-flying shore birds swooped along the wetlands for food. Farther from the shore, dark forest, rich with pines and autumn trees shrouded them. They had all agreed that staying in this anonymous rental was the safest option for Miles and Clara. Clara noticed Tox's wife, Calliope, hadn't put up too much of an argument when Miles suggested the housing arrangement. Calliope and her best friend, Emily Bishop, were playing Cupid. Little did they know how hopeless their attempt would be. Clara had been shooting suction cup arrows at a fortress for a long enough time to see the wall was impenetrable.

The stilted low country cottage was white with black shutters and an inviting front porch. Miles and his twin had been silent and vigilant on the drive here. Twitch had provided a laptop with security features, and her college bestie, Very Valentine, had sent along what she called "survival provisions:" wine, chocolate, junk food, a jigsaw puzzle, and a zipped cosmetics bag that Clara assumed contained female essentials.

Tox skipped all three front porch steps in one stride with their packed duffles. Miles carried the groceries. Clara followed the men inside, marveling at the synchronicity of the twins. They had spent most of their lives apart. Tox was unguarded and, well, happy. In contrast, Miles was distant and serious. And yet, as they moved wordlessly through the house, checking rooms and putting away food, Clara saw that neonatal connection. It was as if they knew the other's movements before they made them. Tox ducked his head as Miles opened a cupboard. Miles sidestepped the freezer door when Tox turned with a pint of ice cream. As she watched this magical dance, Clara imagined them as boys, so connected, so reliant. The separation must have been devastating.

Clara took in the space. The cottage belonged to a friend of Nathan's aunt and uncle. The woman was retired and rented out the house for extra income. The owner was all too happy to accept double the rent in cash and keep the whole exchange off the books.

Clara had been all over the world. Reynard had taken her to see the salt farms of Malta and pearl divers in the Philippines. She had been scuba diving in Kiribati and hiked in Nepal. Standing at the bay window and looking past the front porch into the woods and wetlands beyond, Clara could honestly say she had never been to a place so charming and so haunted. Half a world hid in this shadowed, mysterious biome. Good and evil. Predator and prey. A venomous snake entwined on a blossoming orchid. Poisonous berries growing beside a nest of bunnies.

A sound from the kitchen interrupted Clara's dark thoughts, familiar yet foreign. She turned to the brothers, who were side by side at the kitchen island. Tox was holding a jar of peanut butter, and Miles was…laughing.

Clara hadn't realized it until that moment, but she had never actually heard Miles laugh. Surely, that couldn't be right. She had known him for twelve years. Not every day, of course, but they had certainly spent enough time together that she would have heard him laugh at least once. But no. She hadn't.

She knew she hadn't because the sound was so wonderful, a rich, clear baritone from deep in his chest; if she had heard it before, she certainly would have remembered. Clara had to know what prompted this jovial first.

She walked past the chintz-covered living room furniture and into the open kitchen. "What's got you so broken up?"

Miles was still laughing. Tox held up the Jif with a huge grin. "When we were kids, we had this dog, a beagle named Leonard. He was the best fucking dog. He used to—"

"Follow us to school," Miles cut in.

"And he'd sit by the window in the afternoon waiting for us to get home," Tox finished.

"But," Miles started chuckling again. "He wouldn't let you trim his nails."

"Mom bought this dog nail trimmer thing from the vet, and if you even opened the drawer she kept it in—"

"Leonard would disappear under a bed."

Back to Tox. "So one day, Miles decides we can do it if we can create a distraction for the dog."

"*Rig*," Miles corrected. "Rig a distraction. Clara, I'm telling you, it was a stroke of genius."

"He takes a bath towel and cuts four holes in it."

"Sounds like a bad start," Clara said.

Tox held up a hand. "Oh, the punishments will pile up as the story continues."

Miles defended, "The idea was sound. We may have had some glitches in the execution."

"Miles fits Leonard's legs through each of the holes in the towel. The theory being—"

"That if he couldn't see his paws, he wouldn't be scared," Miles finished.

"But that was only part one," Tox said.

"Part two," Miles started laughing again. "For part two, we put the dog in the empty bathtub and taped the edges of the towel to the side of the tub."

"Now, bear in mind that Leonard is not on board with any part of this plan. The dog hates water even more than getting his nails cut."

Miles took over. "But there's no water in the tub, so he's not freaking out."

Clara leaned her forearms on the kitchen island and asked, "How old are you at this point?"

Miles looked at Tox. "Seven?"

Tox corrected, "Eight."

"That's right. Eight. So Tox sneaks the clippers into his pocket, and I grab the peanut butter. And I just sink my whole hand into the jar and start smearing it on the side of the tub."

"Leonard loved peanut butter. Miles passes me the jar, and I do the same." Tox starts laughing again and can barely get the words out. "We are finger painting the entire tub. And we are covered in it. Miles runs his hand down my face, and I'm smearing it in his hair—"

"And Leonard is now fully on board with the plan, and he starts squirming against this towel hammock we've rigged."

Miles rested his hand over the back of Clara's and slipped his fingers between hers. Clara didn't react. It was as if a squirrel had come over beside her and was eating a nut from her palm. She didn't want to startle the creature.

"But now the tape is coming loose, and Leonard is rubbing the sides of the tub and getting peanut butter all over his fur."

"Tox starts clipping his back paws, and it's working."

"But the clippers keep slipping out of my hand because I'm covered in peanut butter."

"Meanwhile, I'm trying to resecure the tape, and I fall in the tub."

Both men say simultaneously, "And that's when our mom walks in."

"Oh my God, how much trouble were you in?"

"She tried so hard not to laugh." Miles squeezed Clara's hand.

Tox said, "She took the clippers and finished the job. Then she started the water in the tub."

Again, the brothers spoke in sync. "Nobody leaves this bathroom until you're clean." Tox wagged his finger in a parental gesture.

"Oh shit, Mi, we were a handful," Tox said.

"Mom was a saint. That's for sure."

And just like that, the moment was gone, painted over with grief.

Tox slapped both hands on the granite. "I'll let you two get settled—dinner at our place at seven. Calliope is craving Portuguese food, so she's making this rice and duck thing she ate as a child. I was skeptical first time I tried it, but it's insanely good. She has to make two now because I eat an entire casserole myself."

"You would eat shoe leather if it had gravy on top. We know the dish." Miles turned to Clara. "Arroz de Pato. I bet Calliope is a great cook."

Clara explained to Tox, "Our old cook in Dordogne was Portuguese. That's one of my favorite meals."

"Righty-Oh. Mi, the homeowner, said the old pickup in the back runs great. Keys are on the rack in the mud room. See you tonight." With a slap on the back to his twin and a wave to Clara, Tox left.

Miles returned to unpacking the remaining groceries. She couldn't read him, which meant the walls were back up. He had returned to the impassive professional. Still, against her better judgment, that brief moment of pure joy between the twins had ignited a glimmer of hope.

Miles held up a box of cereal with a questioning look.

"Pantry?" Clara suggested, pointing to the door behind him. Miles turned and disappeared behind the doorway while she finished putting away the eggs and milk in the fridge. Clara folded the reusable bags and put them in a drawer. When Miles still hadn't returned, she followed his path.

Clara opened the door and saw Miles's broad frame standing in the middle of a small mud room. He still held the box of cereal. "Did you get lost?"

When he didn't respond, Clara came around and faced him. Miles was pale as a ghost, staring at the wall. Nothing was inherently disturbing about the room—a pantry on the right and the back door leading to a raised deck on the left. Miles was staring at a row of cubbies holding waders, boots, and some fishing gear. He wasn't staring at it, Clara corrected. He was staring through it, lost in some memory.

"Miles?" Clara murmured. No response.

She pulled the cereal box from his clenched fists and set it aside, then led Miles out of the alcove back into the kitchen. He followed robotically as she clasped his hand and walked him to the living room. By the time she helped him sit on the cheery floral sofa, he snapped out of it.

"Shit, sorry, Clara." He ran a hand down his face, clasping his jaw. "That's never happened before."

"And what would you say was 'that?'"

"Not sure. Low blood sugar?"

"Miles—"

"I'm fine, Clara. It's nothing."

More little arrows flying toward solid stone. "Yes, Miles. You're fine." She stood and crossed the living space, heading for the bedroom in the back. At the doorway, she turned to him. "You know, I had a dream about you the other night. We were on the Titanic. I was barefoot in my pajamas, standing in one of those wooden lifeboats hitched to the side of the ship. You were wandering the deck, oblivious to the people around you. The porters started lowering my lifeboat, and I frantically waved for you to get in."

A piercing screech had both of them turning to the open window. Some small creature had fallen prey to an owl or other predator.

Miles returned his attention to Clara. "So what happened?"

Clara shook her head with a self-deprecating laugh. "You picked up a violin."

CHAPTER FORTY-FOUR

Beaufort, South Carolina
October 26

Two days passed. They had all agreed that Miles and Clara would stay isolated while the Bishop Security team scouted the area and checked for chatter to ensure no one had tracked them. Clara imagined Emily, Calliope, Very, and Twitch agreeing to this plan with twinkling eyes. Little did they know.

Miles was cordial and attentive. He was his normal self. Clara had just never realized before how detached his normal self was. After seeing the fire in his eyes, the glimpses of vulnerability, going back to this arm's length detente was depressing.

They hadn't had sex since Miles pinned her to the tree in the woods outside Lucien Kite's house. They didn't even share the bed. Miles stayed up late, watching their surroundings and reading. She guessed he eventually drifted off on the living room couch, where she would find him in the morning.

She was desperate to know what had triggered Miles's reaction in the mud room, but Clara knew the surest way to get him to retreat further was to press. So she mirrored his distant civility and busied herself plotting the art heist.

Clara was sitting at the distressed farm table off the kitchen, poring over an aerial map of Lucien Kite's property, when Miles appeared holding two highball glasses filled with a drink the color of sunrise. He was barefoot, wearing battered jeans and a white T-shirt, and Clara nearly melted into a puddle.

"Aperol spritz on the porch?"

It was the sincerity that got her. Something in his soft tone said *sorry, I've been a colossal ass for the past two days.*

"Where did you find Aperol?"

"In the liquor cabinet. There are postcards on the fridge from Lake Como and Florence, and the print in the bedroom is the Bridge of Sighs in Venice. I think the owner is an Italophile."

Clara accepted the drink and took a sip. "Lucky us."

"Indeed." Miles winked. My God, he was the hottest man Clara had ever seen. His sheer masculine beauty, coupled with his relief that she had accepted his peace offering, prompted a heated response. Clara shifted in her seat.

If Miles noticed her reaction, he didn't show it. He simply turned and walked to the front door, holding it open so she could pass through.

Clara sat on the white wicker porch swing, cradling her drink in both hands. Miles parked next to her. The supporting chains creaked gently as he slowly rocked the swing with his feet. After a healthy swig of the cocktail, he said, "Do you ever think about your childhood? Before you went to live with Reynard?"

"Sure. Sometimes."

"Do you mind if I ask you about it?"

"Of course not. We've known each other long enough. I think I assumed you knew. That maybe Reynard had told you."

Some emotion colored his cheeks. "I never bothered to ask."

"What do you want to know?"

"Everything. What was your life like? Did you go to school? Did you have a home?"

"The answer to both is sometimes. My mother was a prostitute. She died when I was five. I don't remember her. The landlord found her body when he came to collect the rent. He was creepy. I hid, then I ran. It was easy to disappear in that part of Paris. The streets were lined with tents where immigrants and refugees lived. There was a family from Armenia who lived in the basement apartment of our building. I mostly stayed with them.

In the woods beyond the lawn, a white-tailed doe and her yearling munched leaves. The mother's ears twitched, aware of their presence but unthreatened.

Clara sipped her drink, and Miles spread his arm along the back of the bench. He was so close to comforting her, she could feel his heat. Clara knew opening herself up like this was tipping an already uneven playing field, but she didn't care. She wasn't ashamed of her wretched start in life; she was proud.

"Saint-Denis is where I learned to judge people. It's also where I learned to steal."

"I don't imagine there was much worth stealing in that neighborhood," he said.

She laughed at that. "I used to sneak onto the metro. In the Fifth and the Sixth, the police would chase me off even if I was just poking through trash cans. Then, one day, I was wandering in the Jardin du Luxembourg, and a nanny was watching two children. The little girl left her coat on a bench—bright blue wool with a black velvet collar. It was the fanciest thing I had ever seen. Life got a lot easier with that coat."

Mile's hand brushed her nape as he toyed with her ponytail. "I bet."

"I could pickpocket anyone. I would say I couldn't find my mother or that my puppy got loose, and as they scanned the crowd, I helped myself."

"You were a regular Oliver Twist."

"Except my Fagen was not how Dickens portrayed. There was a man in Saint-Denis. All the children knew to stay away. We called him *Le Chasseur*."

"The Hunter."

A chill ran down her spine. Miles sensed it and wrapped his hand around the back of her neck. The feeling of that big, protective palm was instantly soothing.

"One day, I stole money from him. He passed out in a lawn chair in front of his building. The black bag, stuffed with euros, open at his feet. It was like he was showing all these starving people how much he had and daring someone to take it."

Against her better judgment, she relaxed into the warmth of Miles's side. "I snatched the money and ran down the row of tents, throwing cash and coins into the openings. People were cheering and shouting."

"Even as a child, you couldn't stand inequity."

She snorted. "I couldn't stand hunger."

"But you still shared the bounty."

"Then we heard The Hunter roar."

Miles stiffened beside her.

"I ran like a rat, slipping into all the little hidey holes and spaces between walls. Le Chasseur was like a wrecking ball, storming through allies, ripping down shanties. He was yelling *Je vais te vendre au pire des hommes que je connaisse*."

"He was going to traffic you."

Miles slid his arm from the back of the swing and circled her shoulders as if he could protect her from the memory.

"I ran like my legs were on fire. I aimed for the warehouses across the road. There were a million places to hide in those huge buildings. I paused for just a second to check the traffic. The Hunter grabbed me."

"Oh, Clara."

"Now comes the best part. A sleek black car pulled out from the dock entrance. It was expensive. No one good drove cars like that in Saint-Denis. It came to a stop right in front of me. I was scratching and clawing to escape. The back door of the car opened, and a man in a black wool coat stepped out. His driver came around beside him. I was still kicking and struggling. The man lifted his hand and told The Hunter to release me. *Libérer l'enfant.*"

"Reynard." Miles relaxed his hold. He knew how the story ended.

"The Hunter refused, but I squirmed free and ran and hid in the folds of Reynard's coat. I was filthy. I'm sure I ruined it, but Reynard didn't care. He stood and listened as The Hunter ranted that I was a thief and he was going to kill me or sell me. Then, as calmly as he would reach for a handkerchief, Reynard pulled a gun and shot The Hunter dead. Reynard handed his driver the weapon; then, he lifted the flap of his coat. He didn't touch me or speak. He just looked at me."

Clara looked up at Miles and blinked the moisture from her eyes. "I can't explain his expression. All I remember was one word popped into my head. *Famille.*"

"Family," Miles echoed in English.

"I didn't ask permission. I just scrambled into the back of the car. He followed me in, and we drove away."

"Did he say anything?"

"Just one thing. *Je suis un criminel.*"

"That couldn't have been comforting."

"It was everything." His words were honest, apologetic. They were a warning and a promise. She had known instantly Reynard was worthy of her trust. And he had never disappointed her.

"Those first days in Dordogne must have been a shock."

"First few *months*. I spent weeks stealing food and hiding it in my room. The drawers of my dresser looked like a larder. One day, cook knocked on the door and asked if I had any jam. She had run out."

Miles chuckled. "I imagine it was strange."

"Not the house. I know it's funny, but to me, it felt like my old block in Paris, just all covered with a roof. Lots of hidden rooms with old furniture and back passageways. Quiet, peculiar people wandering about. To me, the magic was outside. I had never seen so much green. I can remember so clearly plucking an apple from a tree in the orchard and eating it. Then another. Then another. Reynard never crowded me in those early days; he let me do anything I wanted, but that day, he came out from his study. He laughed so hard. Imagine the sight—this scrawny child standing among a sea of apple cores. Reynard scolded me, told me I would get sick, and then he stood there as I filled my shirt with apples and trotted off to the house."

Miles squeezed her thigh. "Reynard was always kind to me, too. He has a fatherly way about him."

"He barely spoke to me the first month I lived there. We ate dinner every night in virtual silence, seated at opposite ends of a formal table. He bought boxes and boxes of gifts: clothes, books, electronics. The housekeeper, Mrs. Trovik, showed me how to take a bath—my first bath ever. I would swim in the tub until I looked like a raisin. I had awful head lice, so Mrs. Trovik and I cut off all my hair."

Miles wrapped a hand around her long ponytail. "I'm glad it grew back."

"Finally, I got fed up with Reynard. I picked up my dinner plate, marched to his end of the table, and sat. I said, '*Je n'ai pas peur de toi.*'"

"I'm not afraid of you." Miles translated.

"He had a morsel of duck on the end of his fork, stopped halfway between the plate and his mouth. He set it down and said, '*Ma chérie, j'ai peur de toi.*'"

Miles laughed. "I bet he was afraid of you—a widower with no children in his fifties. Reynard wouldn't know the first thing about raising a child. What did you say?"

"*Je vous apprendrai.*" I will teach you. "Reynard said, '*Bien.*'"

"The next day, he took me into town. I was a little tour guide blabbering about everything. Look at that tree. Look at that bird. Look at that bug. Every time I pointed something out, Reynard would follow my direction and smile. He was always so patient."

The feel of Miles's big hand on her neck grounded Clara once again as she continued the story.

"We stopped at a dress shop. In the window was a child-sized mannequin wearing a bright blue coat with a black velvet color. It looked nearly identical to the one I had taken in Paris. Reynard saw my expression and walked into the store. The only time I had ever been in shops like this was to steal, so I huddled near his legs. The salespeople swirled around him like butterflies. One of the ladies came toward me with a measuring tape, and I was terrified. Reynard stopped her. He told her to bring a coat to try on to determine my size."

"He didn't want anyone touching you or frightening you."

"I like to pretend nothing scares me, but Reynard always knew."

"Did you get the coat?" he asked.

"In red, gray, and blue. I used to wear the blue one around the house like a robe. I hated taking it off."

Miles's arm stretched around Clara and pulled her close.

"Reynard would read me bedtime stories in a big chair upholstered with butterflies, and I would sit against the headboard in my pajamas wearing one of the coats."

"What was your favorite story?"

"At first, it was *Eloise at the Plaza*. A little girl roaming free in that big hotel. It felt like my life. Then, when I was a little older, Reynard chose a book that..." Clara searched for the words. "*Cela a parlé à mon âme.*"

"It spoke to your soul," Miles translated.

"Lupin," Clara said.

"Ah, the gentleman thief."

"Fighting to avenge his father and bring the evil-doer to justice."

"It does have a familiar ring to it," Miles added.

"In my mind, I imagined the Louvre. I had never even been inside, but the very idea of sneaking in and wandering about all that priceless art." She sighed. "One day, I'm going to do it."

"I have no doubt."

"I feel like the luckiest girl in the world, sometimes."

"Even with your rough start?"

"Especially because of that. Reynard gave me safety. He gave me purpose. But if I had nothing to compare it to, I wouldn't appreciate it."

Miles kissed Clara gently on her temple. "Thank you for telling me."

She looked at him expectantly. Clara had followed him out to the porch, hoping to hear his story, not share her own. Why had he turned to stone in that mud room? What had made him the way he was? Even now, with the added quid pro quo, Miles was locked up tight. With his palms on his thighs, he pushed to his feet and walked to the edge of the porch. Examining the sky, he said, "Looks like rain." Then he turned and walked into the house.

Clara stayed on the porch swing for a long while, processing yet another disappointment. In the woods beyond, the doe rotated her head and looked blankly at Clara as if to say *What did you expect?*

Eventually, the smell of garlic and roasting chicken lured her back inside. Clara prepared herself for another evening of polite chit-chat and planning the heist. Her quiver was empty. She had shot her useless arrows at the Miles Buchanan fortress, and the walls still stood. With sad resolve and a fake smile, she set the table.

CHAPTER FORTY-FIVE

Beaufort, South Carolina
October 26

Miles glanced around Steady's living room at the Bishop Security team. Cam was still on his honeymoon with his new bride, Evan, but the rest of the group was there. Miles had helped them out on several occasions—most recently running a con that brought Steady together with his feisty neighbor, Very Valentine. They were deeply in love and, by the look of the beach house, living together.

Nathan's wife, Emily Bishop, was sitting with Ren, looking at blueprints of Lucien Kite's house. Emily wasn't a Bishop Security employee, but she was skilled and smart. She had escaped the clutches of a powerful arms dealer all on her own, so she knew a thing or two. Ren pointed to something on the floor plan. Emily nodded in agreement and marked it with a tab.

Steady and Nathan were bent over the kitchen island, reviewing drone footage of the exterior. Steady's laid-back grin was in place as he listened to his boss. Occasionally, his eyes would wander to his pink-haired paramour sitting with Calliope, Tox's wife. They were researching Lucien Kite.

Twitch, the team's cyber security expert, was sitting on the floor, her laptop resting on the coffee table. Behind her, Finn McIntyre sat on the couch holding their son, Trevor. The baby looked fit to be tied, kicking his little legs and spitting out the pacifier Finn was trying to stick in his mouth.

"He wants the real thing, angel," Finn said.

"What time do we need to pick up Auggie?" Finn and Twitch were in the process of adopting an eight-year-old.

"Ben's dad texted from the game. Auggie's sleeping over." Then he leaned down and whispered something in Twitch's ear that had her face turning as red as her hair.

She pushed to her feet and handed Finn her computer. "Take over." She took the baby, then placed her hand on Finn's scarred cheek. "Be right back."

Emily called from her spot on the opposite couch, "You can nurse him in here, sweetie."

Twitch blushed again and tipped her head toward the deck. "I like looking at the waves."

Finn left the laptop where it was, opened the sliding glass doors, and settled next to his love on the outdoor couch. The moon was full and low in the sky, and a salty breeze wafted in from the beach.

Clara sat beside Miles at the end of the kitchen table. "Do you want kids?"

Miles looked at her in disbelief. "What?"

"Kids? The smaller version of us? Do you want them?"

His insides suddenly felt like a shaken soda bottle. "Clara, I don't want adults, much less kids."

"Hmm."

"What was that?" he demanded.

"What?"

"That 'hmm'?"

Clara set down the information on Lucien Kite's alarm system and stared across the room. His brother was delivering a plate of food to his pregnant wife. Calliope scooped up the pizza slice and leaned back to thank him with a kiss.

"Tox is so into impending fatherhood. I guess I'm just surprised you're so different from your twin."

Miles shoved back his chair and stood. "Nature versus nurture, I guess."

"Do you want to know if I want them?"

"What? Children?"

"No jalapeno poppers. Of course, kids."

"Sure." Miles ran a hand over the scruff on his jaw, willing the conversation to end.

"I do. I'd like to have a baby, but also adopt. Papa saved me. I'd love to do that for a child."

Miles was stone-faced. "You should. Things always seem to work out for you, Clara. I have no doubt one day you'll be living in the suburbs with your doting husband and a house full of filthy, happy brats."

He ignored the misting of her bright blue eyes. Clara cleared her throat. She opened her mouth to speak, then closed it. Finally, she said, "Yes, maybe."

Miles swallowed the ball of lead in his throat. He had never seen Clara lose her spirit. Her fire was unquenchable, yet he had somehow managed to douse it. The guilt angered him—he wasn't responsible for Clara's happiness. How could he be when he couldn't even manage his own?

"I need some air."

That was enough of that. They were here to plan a heist, not discuss family planning. Miles walked out the front door to avoid disturbing Twitch and Finn on the deck. He cut across the driveway and rounded the side of the house to the beach.

When he was out of sight, Miles sank to the sand and rested his head in his hands. The ground was shifting beneath his feet, sending cracks up walls he had spent years constructing. Stones were toppling, and Miles was powerless to stop it.

His twin's broad form cast a shadow over him in the moonlight. Tox sat beside him, and together, they listened to the waves lapping rhythmically on the shore.

"Do you remember that time we found the box of old bedsheets in the attic, and you hatched that cockamamie plan to knot them together, climb out the dormer, and swing over to the tree house?"

Miles huffed a laugh. "Even for third-graders, that was dumb."

"It took us until you were six feet down the sheet to realize exactly how dumb," Tox said.

"After Dad hauled me in through the bedroom window, he couldn't decide whether to hug me or strangle me."

"You were trying to act so brave. Then you got out the window, and the fear took over."

"Yeah."

"You kept repeating, *don't let go*. Looking right at me and saying, *don't let go*. I could feel how scared you were. Inside. I could feel it in my gut. I didn't care if my wrist snapped; nothing was going to make me drop that sheet."

"I know."

"Do you?" Tox asked.

"Nothing good has ever happened when things changed."

Tox sighed, "Yeah, I know. Do you want to tell me about it? What happened with that family?"

"It wasn't a family. *We* were a fucking family."

"And if you let those people take that away, they win."

"I don't know how to come back from that, Miller. I only know how to keep it from happening again."

"By shutting everyone out?" Tox asked.

"It's worked so far."

"Has it?"

Miles shook his head with a sad laugh. "Fuck you."

Tox mirrored Miles's position, locking his hands around his bent knees. "I got to know Foxy when I left the SEALs and bought that building. You can't imagine her life growing up—a gay, trans, black, skinny kid in Louisiana. I've seen horrible shit, and I know you have too, but that?" Tox shook his head. "And still she helps, keeps an eye out, gives money she doesn't have to feed others. I asked her once how she could be so caring after everything that had happened in her life."

"What'd she say?"

"That people who hate, hate themselves. So as long as she can love, life is good."

"She's something," Miles said.

"Like Yoda in a glitter tube dress and six-inch heels."

"Hey, Tox?"

"Yeah?"

"Why did you buy that building in Alphabet City?" Miles asked.

Tox shrugged. "I had some money saved up. It was a good investment." He paused, staring up at the night sky. "I liked that it was an old bakery. Made me think of home. Remember how mom used to bake bread?"

A memory flashed in Miles's mind—he and Tox standing on kitchen chairs, kneading dough. "I'd forgotten that."

"I guess I thought the building had good vibes." Tox chuckled. "Bad plumbing but good vibes."

"Thanks for coming out."

"Any time, Mi."

"You know, I think I could have survived anything if I'd had you with me."

Tox picked up a rock and tossed it into the ocean. "I'm still holding onto that sheet rope, brother. Just so you know." With that, he got up, shoved both hands in his pockets, and walked back toward the house.

CHAPTER FORTY-SIX

Beaufort, South Carolina
October 27

Clara was familiar with Bishop Security. She had helped them, at least peripherally, twice before. Once, when Tox's wife, Calliope, had discovered a stolen Degas, and again this summer when Miles roped her into an elaborate con he ran on a corrupt pharmaceutical company CEO. Clara had met most of the team, but even Tox was no more than an acquaintance.

This morning, five women were crammed into a booth for four at a kitschy local diner. The table was already loaded with coffee, baskets of biscuits, and juice glasses, and they hadn't even ordered. Clara sat between Very Valentine, the chemist, and Twitch, while Emily Bishop and Calliope sat across. Very and Twitch had been best friends since their college days at the University of Virginia, and Emily and Calliope had been close since their reporter days at *The Harlem Sentry*. With their shared history and obvious love for one another, Clara should have felt excluded. She was surprised to discover it was quite the opposite.

Despite the different circumstances and locations of their upbringings, Clara felt an unfamiliar kinship with these women. They each had struggles and had not only survived but thrived. Emily Bishop had been abducted as a child and then stalked by her kidnapper until she and Nathan killed the lunatic. Calliope and her single mom struggled for years before her mother married the Prime Minister of Portugal. Very Valentine had spent most of her adult life avenging her mother's murder. Even Twitch, with her silver-spoon upbringing and celebrity parents, faced hardships. Clara hadn't met Evan yet; she was still on her Chilean honeymoon with her new husband, Cam, but she warmed at how fondly the group spoke of her.

Clara had always been popular and well-liked. She'd had friends and roommates over the years, girls she still kept in touch with and genuinely liked. Today, however, something was different. These women knew her secret; they knew she was a thief, and, what's more, they didn't care. Very Valentine, the pink-haired firecracker to her right, seemed downright delighted.

Twitch held the giant menu in her lap and asked, "Clara, are you a sweet or savory breakfast person? Very and I are obsessed with the waffles here. Emily and Calliope always go for eggs."

Emily peeked over her menu. "The omelets are unreal. You'll love them, very Parisian—thin with not a touch of color."

"Done." Clara looked up at the waitress, who had materialized with pen in hand. "With ham and swiss and a short stack on the side with jam instead of syrup, please."

Passing her menu across the table, Very said, "Waffles for me."

"Me too." Twitch did the same.

Emily looked at Calliope. "Your usual spicy huevos?"

Calliope looked exhausted. Clara had seen the exotic beauty several times over the past two years. Today, she appeared drained and a bit green.

"Just some yogurt and fruit, please. I must've eaten too much pizza last night. I'm a little queasy."

"Don't tell Tox." Very grabbed a biscuit from the wicker basket and split it with her fingers. "He'll have you at the E.R."

Calliope agreed, "I don't need my O.B. to tell me I need a ginger ale and a nap."

Emily turned to the waitress. "May we have a ginger ale, too, please?"

"Back in a flash." The waitress darted away.

"So," Calliope leaned forward with a twinkle in her tired eyes. "Clara, I know you don't know us well, but Miles is family, and that makes you, by extension, family too. We want to help."

Clara warmed her hands on her mug. Speaking unfiltered about her *sideline* was a foreign sensation, and Clara discovered it felt wonderful. "Thank you. The thing I'm caught up on is my stupid threat. Lucien Kite knows I intend to steal *Somewhere*. I've lost the element of surprise. I'm thinking there are two ways to regain the advantage—"

When Clara looked up, the women were staring at her in confusion. "What?"

Twitch patted Clara's hand. "The painting is definitely a problem. It is not, however, the problem Calliope meant."

"What do you mean?" Clara asked.

Very Valentine stole her attention. "She means, what is going on with you and Miles? I could have sparked kindling from the sexual tension in the room last night."

Twitch's laugh had Clara looking left. "Normally, I cringe at her bluntness, but in this case, she's right."

Emily scooted closer to Calliope. "Twitch, come over here. If we're going to grill the poor girl, we can do it without spraining her neck."

Calliope tapped Emily on the shoulder. "Give me the aisle seat. Just in case."

When the women had scooted out and back in, the waitress appeared with a packed tray and expertly delivered the proper meal to each of them despite the seating rearrangement. The delay gave Clara some much-needed time to consider her answer. And yet, she didn't quite know how to respond.

Emily sensed her strife and leaned forward over her omelet. "That was too forward of us. It's okay if you don't want to talk about it."

That small act of kindness had the cork popping out of the shaken champagne bottle of her emotions, and Clara started talking. And she kept talking.

She told them everything. Clara started with her teenage crush and Miles's cruel rejection. While they all agreed that, as a twenty-year-old man, he was right to refuse a fourteen-year-old girl, they also echoed Clara's sentiment that he could have been gentler.

Mostly, the women listened. Clara was twenty-six and had had one sexual partner, yet the saga of Miles seemed to go on and on. She shared about Miles's frequent visits to their estate in Dordogne and how, despite the fact that Papa clearly had affection for him, Miles always seemed to hold people at arm's length.

She heard how back and forth she sounded. Clara could have been reading a pros and cons list about this mercurial man. Pro: he was charming and thoughtful. Con: he could ice over like frost on a tree branch. Pro: they could talk about anything. Con: he did bad things for terrible people.

"We started this crazy habit of playing pranks on each other. I'd break into his house, or Miles would show up at my college disguised as a guest professor and deliver an actual lecture before taking me to lunch."

Clara blushed fiercely at the next "pro" that crossed her mind.

Very Valentine didn't miss it. "Well, that answers my next question." When Clara didn't respond, Very continued, "That good, eh?"

Calliope held up a hand. "Stop. Brother-in-law."

"What? I'm not asking for erotica deets. I just asked if it was good."

Emily sipped her coffee. "And we got our answer. You love him."

There was no use denying it. Clara had lied to herself for too long. "I think I always have."

Calliope sipped her ginger ale. "For what it's worth, Tox thinks he loves you, too."

"But?" Clara asked.

"When they were little, Tox said they were inseparable."

"Like in that creepy twin way?" Very shivered.

"Hey!" Emily defended. "It's sweet."

"Sorry, sorry. *Your* twins are adorable. My mind just goes straight to *The Shining*. That book ruined twins for me."

Twitch speared a blueberry. "You know you just jinxed yourself, Ver."

Very gulped and redirected. "Calliope, what were you saying?"

"Ever since Tox and Miles have reconnected, things are different." She held up a hand. "I know they're older and siblings drift apart, but Tox says it's more than that. He thinks, and I agree, that Miles has a lot of scars from their childhood, and he has deliberately cut himself off."

"You think he's dead inside," Clara replied.

"Not dead." Calliope cast a warm glance at Emily and Twitch beside her. "Emotionally frozen, maybe."

Emily agreed, "Exactly. He just needs to thaw."

Clara poked at her food. "It would be so much easier if he was just a jerk. But sometimes, he'll look at me, and I see it, you know? Like he'd kill anyone who hurt me. Like he'll die if he can't touch me."

Very sighed. "I love that feeling."

"But then, in the blink of an eye, he's back to being this, this unfeeling asshole. It has me—"

"Questioning your sanity?" Twitch offered.

"Wondering if you made it all up in your head?" Very added.

"Thinking you're fooling yourself?" Calliope suggested.

"Yes! Maybe I want him to feel something so badly that I'm projecting."

"You're not. At least, I don't think you are." Calliope squeezed Clara's hand. "Miles may be fighting it, but he feels something for you. Last summer, Tox and I had dinner with him while you were helping him run that con. Your name came up. Miles said your father asked him to keep an eye on you."

Clara rolled her eyes. "Lord save me from overprotective men."

Calliope continued, "Miles took that to mean break up the relationship with that man you were seeing."

"What?" Clara expressed outrage, but the truth was she hadn't been attracted to the guy. She'd never admit it, but Miles had done her a favor.

Calliope raised both hands in a calming gesture. "The point I'm trying to make is that even if Miles doesn't realize it, he's acting like your man."

"Or keeping anyone else from doing it," Clara grumbled.

Emily smiled. "My guess is that's not an entirely unwelcome side effect."

These women saw everything, Clara conceded. There was no point in lying to them or herself. She only wanted Miles.

"So what do I do?"

"Fortunately, we have some experience in that department." Emily looked at Very. "Is it too early for mimosas?"

Clara laughed as Very Valentine flagged down the waitress before Emily finished the question.

An hour and a round of cocktails later, the women left the restaurant. Clara took in the warm sunlight and waved goodbye to her new friends. Outside, Finn McIntyre was waiting for Twitch. Their ten-month-old Trevor was in the stroller, throwing anything he could get his little hands on at passersby while their older son, Auggie, dodged projectiles and laughed. Twitch kissed them all, and they headed off down the sidewalk. Nathan and Tox pulled up in Tox's old Defender. Nathan hopped out of the car and kissed Calliope on the cheek before taking his wife's hand.

"Where are the kids?" Emily asked.

"The boys are fishing with Uncle Charlie, and Aunt Maggie is watching Charlotte." Nathan kissed her temple.

Emily looked at Tox's battered utility vehicle. "Time for a baby-friendly car, you two."

Calliope tucked into Tox's side. "We bought one. The big man's just having a little trouble letting go."

"I looked into making the Defender baby safe—added roll bar, side impact protection. The problem is the tech—GPS, Bluetooth, satellite. I'd practically have to replace the engine. Then it just gets ridiculous."

"*Then* it gets ridiculous?" Nathan drawled.

Tox relented. "I know. I know. Once little MB junior arrives, I'm taking the old girl to the office and leaving her there as a backup vehicle. The guards can use it to patrol the property off-road."

Nathan patted his arm. "I'm sure the Defender will love it there. Plenty of open space to roam and lots of other cars around for her to play with."

Calliope pulled him toward the vehicle in question. "Come on. Baby furniture awaits."

Clara waved goodbye, forcing down the pang of envy that reared its head. Maybe she was a fool for hoping Miles would one day look at her the way Nathan looked at Emily, or he would be a devoted father like Finn. Miles already had his twin's overprotective streak, but would it ever be more? Clara was pulled from her thoughts by an arm hooking through hers. Very Valentine pulled her along up the street.

"Where's Steady?"

"He's flying. I was going to walk around town, maybe do a little shopping if you want to join me?"

"I'd love to." Clara gave her pink-haired companion a warm smile. Standing here, slightly tipsy, it felt like friendship at first sight.

Very interrupted her musings. "I also wanted to thank you."

"For what?" Clara asked.

"Over the summer, that con you ran? It was for me."

"When Miles ropes me into things, I always pretend to be put out, but secretly, I love pulling his little capers. Now that I know it was helping you, I'm doubly happy I did it."

Very pointed at an antique store ahead and then to the small movie theater across the street. "Retail therapy or Chris Hemsworth?"

Clara tugged Very's arm. "There is only ever one right answer to that question."

"I'll get the tickets. You get the popcorn."

They dashed across the street, and Very continued to the ticket window. Clara paused on the broad sidewalk and scanned the road. Nothing was out of the ordinary; two young girls were taking pictures of each other with their phones. People were window shopping and strolling by. In the green space at the end of the block, a woman was gathering osage oranges in a basket. A man in a feed cap was reading beneath a shady magnolia. It was a warm fall day in a quaint southern town.

Everything was fine.

Miles sat on the bench in a feed cap and jeans, pretending to read the spy novel he had purchased as a prop. There was nothing to worry about in their safe haven. He and Clara were surrounded by some of the most highly trained, elite fighting men in the world. Miles couldn't imagine a more secure place. And it was that same sense of well-being that had him realizing that everything felt wrong.

The Bishop Security guys were friends. Well, as close to friends as Miles allowed himself to get. Then, there was his twin, a man who had been the other half of his being for the first decade of Miles's life. Now, he was an acquaintance, a guy he liked but would probably never get to know beyond the occasional dinner or holiday visit.

Clara had slipped seamlessly into this group, but they were not "Miles and Clara." He would never be Miles and anyone. If she wanted to be friends with them, fantastic, but Clara needed to realize they wouldn't be wandering hand-in-hand over to Tox and Calliope's for a cookout. He pictured the scene even as he denied it. She wouldn't be wearing a pale yellow sundress with her hair falling across her bare shoulders, laughing at something his brother said. Clara would never sink onto his lap while their kids played in the treehouse, and Loco, the cat, chased his brother's rottweiler.

Taken aback by the specificity of the image he had conjured, Miles set the novel on the bench and stood. Fuck this cozy storybook town. Fuck his twin, and fuck Clara. He had spent years carving out exactly this life. Miles was making millions and enjoying every minute. If anyone in his orbit died, Miles could deliver a cursory, *what a shame* or *I'm sorry for your loss*, and continue with his day. Everything was exactly how he wanted it.

And yet, as he wandered back to the borrowed pickup, he couldn't seem to shake the fantasy of Clara in that yellow sundress.

CHAPTER FORTY-SEVEN

Oceanside, New Jersey
October 27

The crowd on the Atlantic City Boardwalk and the seaside noise did little to drown out Chester Ugentti's rant.

"I don't just want him dead, Mikey. I want every vertebra crushed. I want every fingernail and toenail extracted. Take this motherfucker apart bit by bit. After I get the information I need from Caleb Cain, I want his body to fit in a bowling bag." Chug Ugentti was irate. Nobody got the drop on him, and Caleb Cain had done it twice.

Mikey had done his best to downplay the run-in at Caleb Cain's apartment, but he couldn't hide the butterfly bandage across the bridge of his nose and the black eye.

Chug cleared his throat and spat, then pivoted toward a saltwater taffy stand. "Tell me you found something in his apartment before he delivered this beat down."

"*They*," Mikey corrected. "There were two of them. I'm pretty sure they were brothers. The other guy was bigger, but they looked alike."

"You're sure?" Ugentti skirted a lost, crying child. "The information I dug up says Caleb Cain is an only child."

Mikey snapped his fingers. "Oh, and that was another thing. The other guy called him Miles."

Chug stopped walking. "Repeat that."

"The guy you know, Caleb Cain—the other guy with him called him Miles."

Of course, he did. *Of course,* Caleb Cain was a fake identity. Ugentti wanted to kick his own ass for not realizing it earlier.

"Mikey, go back to that apartment. Take Joey B. Tell him to get prints, DNA, anything he can find. I want to know who Caleb Cain really is. And then I'm gonna give him a taste of his own medicine."

Mikey nodded. "You got it, Boss."

"And toss the place. See what you can find." He browsed the salt water taffy selection. After choosing a large bag of assorted flavors, Chug handed a hundred to the teenage salesgirl with a wink. "That's for you, Princess, from your favorite Congressman, Chug Ugentti."

"Wow, thanks."

Chug turned to Mikey. "I want all his electronics, paperwork, everything." Then, he smiled at the girl. "You old enough to vote?"

"Not yet." She rang up the taffy purchase and pocketed the tip.

Chug withdrew a business card from a silver case. "Call my office. Ask for Jared. Tell him Chug said he may have a job for you."

"Um, I'm in tenth grade."

The congressman leaned in and tapped her plastic name tag. "We have a fantastic internship program for high schoolers, Penny. Jared will ask you for a code word so he knows you're legit. Tell him 'peaches.'"

She blushed and accepted the business card. "Okay, cool."

"Cool." Chug took his taffy bag and returned to the boardwalk.

Chug took a deep breath of salt air and wrapped a chubby arm around his underling. "You know what the air is filled with, Mikey?" He swept the hand holding the bag of taffy around the boardwalk. "Potential."

CHAPTER FORTY-EIGHT

Beaufort, South Carolina
October 27

When Clara found Miles waiting on the sidewalk outside the movie theater, she said goodbye to Very, who was quick to disappear, and greeted him with a cautious smile.

"I thought we could walk around a bit," he said.

After popping into a local cafe for a caffeine fix, Clara and Miles strolled through the quaint town, window shopping and sipping their coffees—Clara's with cream and cinnamon, Miles's black.

"I love Calliope and the other women, too." Clara inhaled the fresh air. "It's nice here."

"Yeah, Tox did well."

"He's a trip. I can see how you two are twins," she said.

"Really? Sure, there's the resemblance, but we're so different."

"Yes, but it's easy to see how you fit together. You're the performer; Tox is the audience. But most of all, you're the risk-taker, and Tox is the guardian." The feeling of Miles's hand at the small of her back reminded her Tox wasn't the only brother who was a protector.

Miles guided her across the way to the park, and they settled on a bench looking out at the water. "When we were kids, I got us into all kinds of crazy shit, but he always had my back."

"How old were you when you were separated?"

"Twelve. When we were eight, our parents died. We lived with our grandmother, but she passed away, and when we were twelve, we went into the system. Tox had a foster mom near where we grew up. I was adopted."

Clara turned to look at him. Miles's face was calm, but she sensed his pain beneath the surface.

"Papa told me about your adoptive family," she said.

"Family," he scoffed.

Miles ran a hand down his face. "It was just a fucked up situation. The couple didn't want a kid. They *needed* a kid. The man got in trouble with some local mobsters and ratted them out to the feds to save his own skin. They were slated to go into Witness Protection, but The Man knew there was a mole in the Marshal's office. So he and his wife escaped on their own."

Clara guessed the rest. "And they figured no one would be looking for a couple with a child."

"Exactly. The Man gave the Feds enough to get the guys who were after him indicted and then escaped to Europe."

"You keep calling him 'The Man.'"

"That's all I ever called him. He certainly wasn't a father. I don't think he ever learned my name. He called me 'The Kid.'"

"Oh, Miles."

"It wasn't so bad as long as I avoided him. I learned to be invisible. Just another part to play."

"And if you didn't avoid him?"

Miles tapped the scar over his right eye. "You want to know something crazy? When I found Tox two years ago, one of the first things I noticed was his scar. He has almost the same one over his left eye from a shrapnel injury in the SEALs."

"Mirror images."

"His is worse."

"Our scars are our own Miles. It's not about seeing whose is worse; it's about healing."

"What about you, Clara? Have your scars healed?"

"My childhood was the only reality I knew. Looking back, it was hard, but at the time, it was just life. Looking through trash was a treasure hunt. Begging was performance art. That's just how it was."

"I unfortunately had something to compare my situation to," Miles said.

"I'll listen if you want to tell me."

Miles pulled her to her feet, and they continued walking, pausing at storefronts and pondering random purchases. He looked like he had a ten-ton steamer trunk weighing him down. He asked Clara if she thought Nathan's twins were too young for bikes and if Steady would use a kayak. She began to think he wasn't going to open up when, in the same bored tone, he said, "We moved constantly. The Man couldn't keep his mouth shut. Wherever we went, he sought out the local wise guys, bragging about his connections, trying to insert himself, and, soon enough, we were running again. We ended up in Detroit."

"That must have been hard, all that moving."

"It wasn't the moving. It was the silence. I was a prop. After a couple of years, I had outlived my usefulness; I'm sure word got back to the people after us that The Man was with a woman and a kid. If he thought he could have gotten away with it, he would have killed me."

"Oh, Miles."

"It was really bad in the beginning. I was a smart aleck with a big mouth. That first month, we lived in a village outside Milan. I was in the kitchen practicing Italian. The Man walked in, picked up a pan, and hit me in the back of the head. He stood over me and said, 'Lesson one: shut the fuck up.' If lesson one was not to be heard, lesson two was not to be seen. So I lived like a ghost, sneaking around, never leaving a trace."

Clara thought back to all the times Miles straightened up after himself, the times she wondered if he'd actually even been in her apartment.

"But even with all my stealth, I couldn't control my sleep."

"What do you mean?"

"I would talk in my sleep. Calling for Miller or just crying out. I tried sleeping with a sock in my mouth, but I ended up spitting it out. One night, The Man hauled me out of bed, dragged me down the stairs, and shoved me in this mud room off the kitchen. That's where I basically lived."

No wonder he had responded so strangely to the mud room in their rental. Clara wanted to take Miles in her arms, comfort him, somehow convey that that neglected child was safe now; there were people in his life who loved him. But she didn't want to risk it. Miles was talking, and she wanted him to expel this poison from his childhood.

Miles stopped walking. "You know the rest. The house blew up because of a faulty gas line. Really, his mob associates finally caught up with The Man and his wife. The police didn't have the budget or desire to investigate—or they were paid off. So, when no one could find me, they assumed I was in the house as well. And just like that, I was free."

Clara remembered the old shoe box in Miles's dresser and the puzzling contents—the newspaper clippings, the gun. Her stomach roiled as she imagined what it all meant. She opted not to mention it. Miles was talking; that was enough for now.

"Where did you go?"

"I used to hang out at the local library. The best way to be invisible was not to be at the house. So, I'd bike over there after school and do my homework and fuck around on the computers until it closed. The Man's wife, Angelina, would put a plate out for me every night at seven. The food had to be eaten and the dish washed and put away by seven-fifteen. So that was my routine: school, library, home, hide."

"But you weren't at home the night of the fire."

Miles stopped walking, visibly tensing. He stared blindly through a pharmacy window. Clara thought he was deciding how much to share. When he turned to face her, Clara could tell by his guarded expression that she wouldn't get the whole truth.

"Anita, the librarian, took me under her wing. I guess a teenage boy loitering in a library every day for four hours sent up a red flag."

"Anita helped you," Clara confirmed.

Miles guided Clara across a cobblestone street. "She became kind of a surrogate mother. I was at her house the night of the fire. Anita knew what was up with The Man—his real name was Paulie Marcone. I hid in her basement for two weeks while Anita gathered money and clothes for me. She didn't want me to go, but I was determined. She drove me to a roadside bus stop a few towns away, and off I went."

Clara took his hand. It was the wrong thing to do. The small act of intimacy jarred him from his confession.

"Hey, do you think Calliope would like a foot massager?"

Clara wanted to take Miles by the shoulders and shake him. She had looked in that box in his dresser; she knew there was more to the story. But she also knew that Miles Buchanan wasn't going to share anything else today. He had told her more than he had ever shared before, and that was enough for now. Ever the optimist, Clara decided that was a step forward.

"I think she would love a foot massager."

"Come." Miles pulled her into the store.

Clara stopped him at the threshold. "When did you meet Papa?"

"You're determined to get the whole saga, eh, Bluebird?"

"Quite determined."

"About a year later." Miles flagged down a salesperson. "I picked his pocket."

"How did I not know this?" Clara laughed.

He leaned down and whispered in her ear, "I am a riddle wrapped in a mystery."

She took his hand as he pulled away. "Just so you know. It doesn't make me hate you any less."

His smile was warm and genuine. "That's my girl."

Clara was surprised Miles continued the story. "I lifted Reynard's wallet in Grand Central Station. As you can imagine, it was fat. I was about sixteen at the time. Young and dumb. I went straight into the terminal cafe and ordered half the menu. Two bites into my cheeseburger, Reynard slides into the booth."

"What did you do?" Clara pulled a boxed foot massager from the shelf.

"I gave him back the wallet."

They continued to browse as Miles talked. "Reynard pulled out three hundred dollar bills and set them on the table. Then he put his card on top of them. I picked it up and said, 'What the fuck am I supposed to do with this?' He said, 'If you can't figure that out, then I have no use for you.' And he left."

They set their purchase on the counter, and the salesgirl rang them up.

"I started working for him the next day."

"Doing what?"

"Whatever he wanted. That's when I started developing characters. I didn't want any of the sketchy fucks Reynard had me contacting to recognize me. So sometimes I was a kid in a hoodie. Sometimes, I was a low-level dealer. Sometimes, I wore a suit. It was a dream job for me. I could disappear into any role."

Clara made a contemplative sound somewhere between a *hmm* and a scoff.

"What?"

"You know it's funny to me that you think of all these personas you play as other people."

"They are other people," Miles said.

"Miles, they are all you. Sure, you may not be a mobster or a duke or a subway musician, or the heir to a diamond mine, but you are brave and sophisticated and talented. Roll them all together, and it's you, Miles."

"I didn't realize your doctorate was in psychology, Bluebird."

"I'm not a shrink, Miles. I just know you. I see you."

"Glad it all makes sense."

"Almost everything." It was the perfect time to ask about the shoe box in his dresser, but when he wrapped an arm around her shoulders and kissed her temple, Clara couldn't bring herself to shatter the moment.

The little white house was quiet as Clara set their purchases on the kitchen table and put the kettle on. Miles moved beside her and turned off the burner.

"I know you looked in the box."

Clara slid over and allowed him to cage her against the counter.

"Yes, I looked."

"What did you see?"

"There were newspaper clippings about the house fire."

Miles pinned her with his chocolate gaze. "And?"

"I saw an old handheld camcorder."

He stepped closer and cupped her cheek. "And?"

She blew out a breath and whispered, "And a gun."

Miles bent forward and murmured into her ear, "Ask me, Clara."

"Did you kill those people who adopted you?"

When he wrapped her in his arms, she knew the answer didn't matter.

"No, Bluebird. I didn't kill them."

Clara nodded into his chest, not wanting to leave the comfort of his embrace.

"But I saw who did."

Miles didn't know what had compelled him to tell Clara, but now she knew. He had laid himself bare, and while part of him felt relieved, the overwhelming part was shaken by his uncharacteristic behavior—so Miles did what came naturally: he withdrew. He straightened the kitchen and busied himself doing nothing.

Clara stood on the periphery, rearranging the refrigerator magnets, shifting from one foot to the other like an impatient child.

"Oh, for fuck sake, just ask," he said.

"It's not about the house fire."

"Good."

"It's about Tox."

Miles stiffened, but Clara continued. "You thought he was dead."

He didn't respond.

"Why?"

"Anita, the librarian, told me Miller had died. She gave up a child for adoption years earlier and spent years trying to unseal the records but was never able to find the child. I think in her mind she was sparing me that heart-ache—helping me get a fresh start." Miles turned to the window to hide his shame. "The fact is, I could have easily discovered the truth. I always thought if Miller had died, I would know." He tapped his chest. "Inside. He wasn't hiding, wasn't using a different name. Hell, he was a college football star. I could have found him."

"Why didn't you?" she asked.

"Because I wasn't me anymore, Clara. How could I have my brother when there was no me? We wouldn't fit. There couldn't be an us. I didn't want to see that." He pinched his eyes closed in pain. "It happened anyway."

"What?"

This was a confession he dreaded more than the revelation about his past. It was the most soul-wrenching part of his childhood. "You don't see it. His friends don't see it, but I see it, and I sure as hell know Tox feels it. We aren't connected. Every once in a while, that old connection appears, and it's just a painful reminder of how much we've lost. I can't find my way back, Clara. I'm trying."

She surprised him when she said, "Well, stop."

"What do you mean?"

"It'll come, Miles. Let trust build. Let your mind remember what it was like to have people who care and love you."

Miles pulled her close and kissed Clara until his body was on fire for her.

"Does that include you?" he asked, running his nose up her neck.

"Of course," she answered in a breathy voice. "We've always trusted each other. Not the love part, though, because, you know, I hate you."

That's my girl. He smiled and kissed her again. "I hate you too, Bluebird."

Miles scooped her up, carried Clara to the bedroom, and laid her on the quilt. Standing above her warm, welcoming body with those ocean-blue eyes filled with mischief and hope, Miles felt every ounce of resolve drain from his body, every brick in the wall crumble in a heap at his feet. He had no defenses against her. How could he? Clara was the water that filled the well inside him. He would die without her.

Peeling Clara's jeans and panties down her mile-long legs, Miles didn't waste another second and set to work showing Clara Gautreau that she was his.

The minute Miles's eyes found hers, Clara knew this was different. He drove into her with the same force, fucked her with the same passion, but he was present. He was Miles.

And he was making love to her.

As her orgasm hovered on the brink, Clara prayed she wasn't imagining it. She lifted her hips to meet his rhythm as he continued to move. Faster, harder.

"Miles."

"I'm here, Clara." Miles ran his nose up and down the length of hers. Then he took her mouth, his lips matching the ferocity of his strokes. They came together, connected in every way.

When Miles fell to his back and pulled her into the nook under his arm, Clara didn't speak. As earth-shattering as that had been for her, she knew it was a monumental shift for Miles. So she did the only thing she could and wrapped an arm around his waist and held him close. After several long minutes, Clara glanced up.

Miles Buchanan was asleep.

CHAPTER FORTY-NINE

Beaufort, South Carolina
October 28

Three days until the heist.

The Bishop Security conference room was depressingly silent. Clara had to admit, stealing this painting was impossible. In the past, her greatest weapon was the element of surprise. Her targets were entitled, unsuspecting fatcats. Sure, they had security, often elaborate systems, but alone, and with time, she could defeat even the most sophisticated alarm. Clara had openly thrown down the gauntlet and told Lucien Kite her intentions. Staring blankly at the floor plan of his Connecticut mansion, she couldn't see a way to back up her bold words.

Steady Lockhart, the most laid-back one in the group, rolled his chair to the corner and crossed his booted feet. On his lap were aerial photos of the property. He was subtle about it, but every so often, he would glance past whatever he was working on to check on Very. And if she caught him, her expression would soften. It was a subtle thing, a moment between the two, but it conveyed so much love it made Clara's heart hurt. What would it be like to feel so...complete?

Steady interrupted her thoughts. "You'd have to be nuttier than squirrel shit to try to rob this guy. Short of building an exact duplicate of the house, drugging him, and putting him and all his people in it while you rob the real one, it ain't happening."

Finn, the scarred one, agreed. "Even with the interior alarms turned off for the party prep and the event, Kite has almost as many guards as guests. Twitch sent a dummy email to several of the guards. One of them opened the malware link so we can access their internal communication. Two men are stationed outside of Kite's office at all times unless Kite's in there. And these guys know the consequences if the painting is stolen on their watch."

Clara's stomach dropped. It had never occurred to her that others might pay the price for her actions. The people she stole from were thieves themselves; they deserved to be stripped of their ill-gotten gains. But the unsuspecting doormen she slipped past and the security guards she duped?

Miles read her thoughts. "Clara, these people understand how things work. You're not responsible for their life choices."

Emily tugged on Miles's sleeve. "Look at this." She nodded in the direction of her twin sons, Jack and Charlie. "This is how I picture you and Tox at this age. Watch what they do."

Miles peered discreetly over his laptop screen as Charlie inched over to a sideboard that held a carafe of ice water and a bowl of cut fruit. He pulled the tablecloth toward him with a tug, toppling the food and drink to the floor with a crash. The child then began to wail.

Miles stood to assist, but Emily stopped him and cocked her head to Charlie's brother. With the stealth of a seasoned spy, Jack slid to the plate of cookies on the opposite side of the room and filled his pockets.

"Those brilliant little deviants." Miles shook his head, laughing. "And yes, that's exactly the sort of thing Miller and I would do."

Finn kissed Twitch on the cheek. "I'll run these two down to the daycare room. They can entertain Trev and Charlotte."

Emily mouthed *thank you* as Finn took the boys' hands and led them out.

Clara's small hand gripped his forearm, and Miles turned to face her. "That's how we steal the painting."

"Kite will surely be expecting a distraction."

"But what if we make him think the painting is the distraction?"

"You mean lead Lucien Kite to believe we are really trying to steal something else?"

"He said himself that he doesn't understand the allure of the painting. Kite said the treasure hunt was a myth and the painting was ugly. It wouldn't be a huge leap to convince him we're not trying to steal it at all."

"The question then becomes, what does Lucien Kite have in that house that we might be after?"

"I think I can help with that." Nathan stood in the doorway of the conference room. Behind him was a well-built man, an inch or two shorter than Nathan's 6'2" frame, with a brutal-looking crescent-shaped scar visible above and below his black sunglasses.

Miles's curiosity quickly turned to inexplicable hatred for the mystery guest when Clara leapt to her feet and threw herself into his arms. Their rapid-fire French was so overlapping and intimate that Miles, despite being fluent, couldn't make out what they were saying. That and the low-grade siren sounding in his ears as a red haze descended over him. Before he knew what he was doing, Miles was on his feet, preparing to pry the pair apart. A hand on his shoulder stayed him.

"Easy tiger." Emily soothed. "She's greeting an old friend."

Miles hated the man instantly.

Clara turned to the group. "Everyone, this is Raphael Garza. We're from the same neighborhood in Paris."

"Born on the trash heap of Saint-Denis," Garza said.

Clara's English was accented, an indication that she was emotional. "I lived with Raphael's family. We'd wait together in alleys for the cooks to dump the trash. Oh! Remember begging in the Gare de Leon?"

"I remember stealing in the Gare de Leon."

They fell back into French, chattering away as if they had a happy, normal childhood.

"*De la misére á la richesse*. Rags to riches as you say," Garza said as they laughed.

Miles looked past the intruder to see Finn standing in the doorway just behind where Clara was fawning over Garza. The pair was in profile. Finn took one look at Garza and, with the grace of the seasoned spy that he was, continued down the hall.

Twitch glanced at her vibrating phone a moment later, read a text, then tapped something on her keyboard as she rotated her laptop in Garza's direction.

Nathan cleared his throat. "Clara's father, Reynard, arranged this meeting. Mr. Garza does some freelance work for Lucien Kite."

Miles pinned Garza with a stare. "What kind of freelance work?"

Garza was unphased. "Tracking, mostly." He shrugged. "Hunting down people or objects."

"Hunting people?" Miles pressed.

Garza fired back, "I don't shoot them and mount them on a wall, but yes, I locate people. After he discovered the video of Clara from the restoration house, Kite hired me to find The Lynx."

"You saw the video?" Miles asked as the demons inside him rattled their cages.

Garza smirked, "If it's any consolation, it's very low quality. You can barely see her."

This asshole had seen the video of Clara. Naked. It took every ounce of self-restraint Miles possessed not to dive across the table and choke the life out of Garza. *Miles* was the only person who got to see her naked.

Miles balled his fists. "It's not."

"Not what?"

"Any consolation."

Garza turned to Clara. "Judging from his reaction, I'd guess someone caught the live show."

Clara socked her friend playfully in the arm.

Miles shot to his feet.

Calliope did the same. "Miles, walk me to the kitchen. I need some tea."

His sister-in-law continued to drag him until they were halfway up the stairs leading to the third-floor kitchen.

"That arm is attached."

She released him. "I needed to get those people clear of the blast radius."

"I'm fine," he grumbled.

They walked into the kitchen, and Calliope filled the kettle. "You looked like you were about to throw an innocent man through a plate glass window."

Miles fetched a mug from the cupboard. "It's fine. It's just I've known Clara most of my life, and I've never even heard of this joker."

"Clearly, he's a friend. I mean, you know Clara has great instincts. She certainly wouldn't have greeted someone she didn't trust with so much enthusiasm."

He turned away.

"Did you just growl?" she asked.

"What? No."

"Yes, you did. Your brother makes the same sound when another man looks at me."

"I'm fine, okay? Seeing an unfamiliar person with her like that threw me off for a second."

"You do realize you've used the word *fine* three times in the last thirty seconds."

"Leave it, Calliope. I'm fi—" Miles stopped himself before he added another "fine" to her tally. "I'm just… This whole situation has got me on edge." He was preparing to unburden himself and ask her advice, but when Miles turned back, Calliope was clutching the counter, her face pinched.

"Are you okay?"

Miles hurried to her side and pried one hand free, taking it in his.

"Yes." She blew out a breath. "I called my O.B. about it last week." She squeezed his hand. "It's Braxton-Hicks. These pseudo contractions that feel really fucking real." Straightening as if nothing had happened, Calliope returned to preparing her tea. "Last time it happened, Tox was ready to call an ambulance."

"I know he's overprotective, but I think I might have done the same."

With the steaming mug in her hand, his sister-in-law gave him a warm smile. "It's nice having you around, Miles."

He looked at Calliope for a moment—tall and lean with a basketball-sized bump. Her black hair fell over her shoulders, and her pale blue eyes sparkled. She looked like a portrait, one Miles would title *Contentment*.

Unbidden, a thought flashed; Miles wondered what Clara would look like, full with his child. An image of Clara smiling and round sent a strange sensation down his spine.

"Thanks," he replied.

"And for the record, that man? Garza? He's just a friend."

Miles took the mug to carry it back to the conference room for her. "How can you tell?"

Calliope slipped her arm through the crook of his elbow. "She has striking blue eyes."

"I'm aware."

She stared straight ahead with a smirk and said, "And they are always looking at you."

Back in the conference room, Raphael Garza had taken the chair next to Clara. Sensing his resurfacing jealousy, Calliope squeezed Miles's hand and led him to the seat beside his brother. Clearly, the group had filled this complete stranger in on the plan.

"The distraction plan is definitely your best bet. There is something in that house you might want to get your hands on."

"What?" Clara asked.

Miles scanned the room, his gaze settling on Nathan Bishop, who listened intently. Finn McIntyre still hadn't returned.

Garza continued, "As you know, Kite cut a deal with the feds in exchange for his damning testimony exposing the Zorba Fund Ponzi scheme. As a result, the head of Zorba Fund killed himself, and the government was able to recover ninety percent of the money and reimburse investors."

Ren seemed to guess where this was going. "The fund was valued at forty-eight billion dollars. Ninety percent of forty-eight billion dollars is about forty-three billion."

"Forty-three point two, give or take," Garza corrected.

Tox blew out a breath. "Hard to imagine two hundred million dollars after the decimal point."

Steady agreed, "I was thinking the same thing."

Garza continued, "The Feds estimated, with Kite's help, that Zorba himself had blown through two billion over the ten years of the fund's existence. Then, there were salaries, undocumented bonuses, and business expenses. At the end of the day, the government was more than happy with the result. They didn't put their star witness under a microscope. But if they had, they would have seen that Lucien Kite had been skimming money from day one. Kite's estimates of Zorba's personal spending and the firm's expenses were grossly overestimated. What the government assumed was about two hundred million in unaccounted-for cash—that they think Zorba hid in some offshore account—is actually three times that amount siphoned off by Kite."

"Someone had to have been on the take. Even the most incompetent bean counter would have to notice the numbers didn't add up."

"Possibly. But remember, Kite started out as a bookie in the Bronx, running numbers for the local mob. The guy cut his teeth laundering money and cooking books, and the most important lesson he learned was not to leave a paper trail. Or to update, not to leave an electronic footprint. Every transaction Kite made was in person, every deposit in cash. No crypto, no emails, no wire transfers. He keeps handwritten records of every account in a little black book in his bedroom wall safe."

"That's pretty genius," Tox said.

"How the fuck do you know all this?" Miles leaned forward in challenge.

Garza shrugged. "Some of it I dug up on my own, but that was just to confirm."

"Confirm what?"

"What Kite told me."

"He told you?"

"Not just me. Kite can't resist spouting off. He thinks he's untouchable."

Miles tapped the table. "We need to reshuffle our playlist."

Nathan pointed at him in agreement. "If the painting is the distraction?"

Miles leaned forward and laced his fingers on the table. "Then Clara can steal the little black book."

After saying goodbye to Raphael and promising to keep in touch, Garza left, and Clara wandered out to the hallway. She was frustrated at the pivot their plan had taken. She loved her dear friend, but Raphael Garza had upended everything with the information about Kite's secret accounts.

Miles hovered in the doorway. "Where's your friend?"

"Don't, Miles. I'm not in the mood for you right now."

"What's wrong?"

"What's wrong? I don't care about Kite's money. I care about that painting. Papa is sick, Miles. I don't know how long he has, and he asked me to retrieve *Somewhere*. I don't see how that's going to happen."

"Clara—"

"I get it. I do. Bringing down Kite is the right thing to do. It's the greater good."

"But?" he asked.

"Reynard has never asked me for anything, Miles. Oh sure, occasionally, he'll have me track down a painting or create a forgery, but this? This means something to him."

"Clara—"

"You should have heard him, Miles. This painting is important to him. I don't know why, but I want to return it."

Miles walked over and enveloped Clara in his arms. Shocked by the display of affection and lost in his clean scent, she nearly forgot her distress.

"Bluebird?"

"Yes?"

"We're stealing that painting."

Nathan and Steady joined them, and Miles moved away.

Steady gave Miles a good-natured shove and spoke to her. "You didn't think we were gonna forget the skills of The Lynx, did you?"

Clara blushed. "Well, you all seem determined to get Kite's book."

Nathan said, "Clara, we want to bring Kite down, but as Miles said, we're going to help you reacquire *Somewhere*. If anything, Garza's information makes the job easier. The key here is keeping Kite off balance."

Steady gave her shoulder a pat. "The painting is the ice cream, sweetheart. The little black book is the cherry on top."

Clara blew out a relieved breath, and Miles couldn't stop himself from resting his hands on her shoulders. "We just need a plan."

Nathan waved them back into the conference room. "Now, Clara, tell us everything you remember from when you were in Kite's house."

Clara recounted everything, from the placement of security cameras to alarm panels and guard positions. She detailed Kite's office and the position of the painting.

"Kite knew my tactic of casing locations by requesting a tour for my doctoral research. He's so convinced I can't pull it off, or so confident in his security, he actually suggested I do that."

Nathan said, "Then do. The more information you can gather, the better."

Miles placed a hand on her thigh. "Anything out of the ordinary? Workers doing repairs? Outside maintenance people on the property?"

Her eyes widened at the memory. "Oh, there was a leak."

"In the roof?" Finn asked. He had returned to the room shortly after Garza departed.

"No. Internal. I think it was a recurring issue with an upstairs pipe. As I was leaving, I noticed the house manager staring at a water stain on the ceiling. He said something that made me think it wasn't the first time. I think it was coming from the bathroom next to Kite's office."

"Is there a connecting door?" Miles asked. "Can we get into the office that way?"

"No bathroom door," Chat said. "And the main door is a bear: electronic locks, biometric scanners, and we know there are two guards stationed outside."

Steady tipped back on two chair legs. "Windows? Ducts? Can she slide down the chimney like Santa?"

Clara had stopped listening halfway through Chat's description of the door security, an idea forming in her mind. She ran a finger over the rim of her water glass. "Actually, I have a thought."

Six hours later, the plan was in place. Half con, half heist; it was the perfect combination of Miles and Clara. She would do what she did best; he would provide the smoke and mirrors. Twitch would work her magic with the security cameras and tech, and the rest of the team would be hidden in plain sight, keeping watch and providing backup.

Before he left, Raphael Garza agreed to help. As part of Lucien Kite's inner circle, Garza could come and go unquestioned. Miles hated to admit it, but Garza was essential to pulling this off. Miles scanned the room, taking in the laughter and high-fives as they all agreed they had come up with a particularly devious and elegant way to separate Lucien Kite from his possessions. Tomorrow, they would head to New York.

This collaborative energy was a foreign feeling for Miles. He had gone into it with trepidation, not because he thought he couldn't work with a team but because he knew he would love it. He and Tox had built on each other's suggestions. Clara had finished his sentences. It was an incredible feeling that filled him with dread.

He'd had that love and security once, and it was ripped away. That fact left Miles waiting for the other shoe to drop.

The sun was setting as Miles helped Clara into the borrowed pickup in the Bishop Security lot. He was coming around the tailgate when Finn McIntyre stopped him.

"Hey, where'd you disappear to?" Miles asked.

"I need to talk to you. About Garza."

Miles couldn't help but be pleased someone else seemed to dislike Clara's *friend*. "What's up?"

"Not here. Can you meet me for a beer tonight?"

"Sure."

"Come to The Sand Bar at nine," Finn said.

"Okay."

Finn jogged off, and Miles climbed in the driver's seat.

"What did Finn want?" Clara asked.

"Oh, nothing. He just wanted to see if I could grab a beer later."

"Calliope told me Finn used to be a real jerk. Hard to believe. He's so warm and friendly."

Miles had the feeling Finn's past was extremely complicated. And he was eager to hear what the former CIA officer had to say about Raphael Garza.

CHAPTER FIFTY

Beaufort, South Carolina
October 28

Inside the dark bar, Halloween had arrived early. A local band played Monster Mash as costumed partiers sang along. The crowd had spilled out onto the deck, and on the beach, three guys all dressed as Michael Myers were chasing people with rubber knives.

Miles spotted his brother and Finn sitting away from the commotion at a corner table decorated with a fake jack-o-lantern. He greeted the men and sat.

"So, Garza." Miles couldn't be bothered with small talk tonight.

Tox pulled a beer from the ice bucket and passed it over. Without looking away from Finn, Miles took the beer and twisted off the cap.

"Yeah," Finn sighed.

"What's on the back of this guy's baseball card?" Tox asked.

"Garza's a utility player. He'll work for anyone if the price is right."

"Doing what?" Miles took a swig.

"Locating targets, live drops, recon, kidnapping. If there's a paycheck in it Garza will do it. I met him once—in Odessa. Garza was facilitating a payoff for an arms dealer to a corrupt government official to use the ports. Someone tipped off the local bratva, who didn't take too kindly to their turf being invaded. The short version is that by the end of the night, five people were dead, and two million dollars in Bitcoin had vanished."

Finn shelled a peanut from the bowl on the table and ate it.

"He has a solid reputation in his world. Reliable, effective. Flies under the radar. After Odessa, I had my CIA handler look into him. More than once, Garza has been on the outskirts when a deal went FUBAR and money vanished. He's good at covering his tracks."

Miles ran a hand over his stubbled jaw. "You think he's pulling something with this Lucien Kite heist?"

"I think we'd be wise to watch our six with this guy."

Tox slapped the table. "Let's kick Garza to the curb. We can't work with someone we don't trust."

Miles rested a hand on his brother's shoulder. "Or we make sure we're one step ahead."

CHAPTER FIFTY-ONE

Beaufort, South Carolina
October 28

It was midnight when Miles pulled the pickup into the driveway. He was immediately on alert when he spotted the Volvo parked in front of the house. He hopped out of the truck, entered the cottage, and followed the voices to the spare bedroom.

Very Valentine was holding a caddy of paints and standing beside an easel with a blank canvas. "It acts like regular oil paint. You can create the forgery like you normally would. But," Very pulled a small aerosol can from her pocket. "When you spray this on the painting, the fun starts."

"How does it work?" Clara asked as she took the item.

Very wiggled her fingers and said in her best spooky voice, "Science."

Clara laughed. "Got it. Thanks so much, Very."

"Are you kidding? Chemistry and payback? This was the most fun favor ever. Hey, Miles."

He stepped fully into the room and stood beside Clara.

"Hi, Very. Where's Steady?"

"If everything is as it should be, he's curled up on a deck chair having a snoring contest with Tilly."

Miles laughed at the image of Steady Lockhart snuggling with his deaf yellow lab. "Well, tell him 'hello.'"

"Will do. Clara, call me if you have any questions or if the paint isn't right."

"Thanks again, Very. I don't know how you do it."

Miles watched Very watch him. Then, she said, "I'm a chemist. I know *chemistry*." With a wink and a wave, Very Valentine left.

"You two have a little girls' night?"

"Sort of. She was dropping off the special paint for the forgery."

"It works?" Miles asked.

"Very says it will work. Should be a fun little surprise for Lucien Kite."

Miles pulled Clara into his arms.

"How was your visit with Finn?" she asked.

"Good. He and Tox are tight, and I can see why. Finn's smart and intuitive."

"And what intuition did he share with you?"

Miles squeezed Clara tighter. He had no intention of sharing what Finn had told him about Raphael Garza. For one thing, he already looked like a jealous asshole. For another, he didn't want to shatter Clara's image of her childhood friend. If, as Miles suspected, Garza wanted Kite's banking records for himself, he would have to take additional precautions.

He turned her to the side and, with an arm wrapped around her shoulders, guided Clara out of the spare room. "The subtle differences in the flavor and quality of the local microbrews."

"Were you okay to drive?"

"One beer, Bluebird."

"Are you tired?" she asked.

"Clara, when your body is pressed up against mine, the last thing I'm thinking about is sleep."

She gave him a nip on his lower lip. "Then let's go to bed."

Miles growled into her neck, "Go get naked. I'll lock up."

When Clara disappeared into the bedroom, Miles stepped onto the porch and scanned the woods. The forest was silent and alive. Some strange plant emitted an iridescent green light, giving the scene an otherworldly glow. Not a creature was stirring.

And that was the most unsettling aspect of all.

CHAPTER FIFTY-TWO

Lucien Kite Estate
October 29

Lucien Kite stood before *Somewhere* with his hands on his hips. The alarm was armed, the painting secure. Nevertheless, he refused to be outsmarted. Staring at the ceiling, Kite's lips spread into an evil grin. He withdrew his phone from his pants pocket and placed a call.

When his man at the security company answered, Kite said, "I have a special order, a rush job."

The man listened as Kite explained, "Can you install a pressure plate that releases a cargo net when activated?"

The associate readily agreed—for a hefty sum.

"And keep this between us. I don't want anyone knowing it's there."

Kite ended the call and returned to his desk. He had been beaten by The Lynx twice. It wouldn't happen a third time.

CHAPTER FIFTY-THREE

New York City
October 29

Miles surveyed the vast space from the open fire door at the front of the room. In six hours, the team had converted the empty floor below Miles's loft into a makeshift HQ. Bishop Security had a New York office, an office Miles would soon be running, but this op was off the books, so the team did what they did best and adapted.

Twitch and Chat had taken over a corner cordoned off with thick construction plastic and created a state-of-the-art cyber security center. Long temporary tables were scattered throughout. Ren and Finn stood at one, unloading equipment and organizing it.

Despite the efficiency with which they worked and the confidence Miles had in the plan, he was feeling out of sorts. Maybe it was the sudden influx of people in his private space. He couldn't put his finger on it.

"Hey, man." Steady brushed by Miles with a cardboard box filled with packaged air mattresses tucked under one arm. He handed Miles a black garment bag with the logo of the masks of comedy and tragedy above the words "Crupp's Costumes."

"Any problems?" Miles asked.

"Nah, I handed your list to Maury like you told me. He took care of everything. Nice guy."

Miles unzipped the bag, nodding his approval at the contents. "Thanks, Steady."

"Any time, bro."

A golden blonde head appeared beside him.

"I'm going to enjoy seeing you like this," Clara said, peering at the costume shop purchases.

Everything burning and swirling inside Miles settled. It was like a warm blanket wrapping around shivering shoulders. He clasped Clara's nape and turned her to face him. "Maybe I'll hang onto it."

Clara stood on her tiptoes and whispered in his ear. "And maybe I'll buy a costume of my own."

With a hand on her ass, Miles pulled her flush with his body. "Go upstairs, get undressed, and sit on the end of my bed."

Miles felt Clara's body soften and shiver. She leaned back, those hypnotic blue eyes of hers reflecting her arousal. "Yes, Miles."

When Miles was satisfied everyone was occupied, he slipped out, hot on Clara's heels.

CHAPTER FIFTY-FOUR

Lucien Kite Estate
October 30

Lucien Kite's house manager, Willoughby Daniels, stood at the entry to the catering kitchen wearing his usual uniform of perfectly pressed khaki pants and a blue blazer. At the rear door, his wife, Gretchen, the frantic cook, was barking at the hired party staff and stabbing at the alarm panel.

"Access the second-floor balcony bar from the yard! You're setting off the motion sensors using the inside stairs."

Just as she silenced the alert, another quadrant flashed. "Who is in an upstairs bathroom?" she bellowed, trying and failing to silence the system. She turned desperate eyes to Willoughby, who smoothed his yellow tie and strode forward.

"Do you need another lesson?" he asked as he deftly silenced the alarm.

"No, I need a house manager to oversee these idiots so I can get back to managing the prep cooks—the job I am paid to do."

Willoughby chuckled. "It's off, Gretch. Go back to wrapping figs in bacon and baking mini quiches. I'll walk around upstairs until they leave—make sure none of the minions decide to pocket the family jewels."

Appeased, Gretchen smoothed down his lapels. "I'll set aside some lamb chops and those caviar potatoes you like."

"Bring them to the guest house. I'll snag a bottle of Chianti, and we can have a pre-party of our own before tomorrow's chaos."

"It's a date. Now get out of my kitchen."

The black door opened, and a heavy-set man wearing baggy jeans, work boots, and a sweatshirt with "Perfect Pipes Plumbing" printed across the front stuck his head in. He had a handlebar mustache that reached his ears. "Gretchen?"

The housekeeper eyed the unfamiliar plumber. "Where's Bodie?"

The man stepped fully into the room, and Willoughby slid closer to Gretchen. He didn't like the way this guy was eyeballing his wife. "He's got the flu." The guy winked. "I'm his much better-looking younger brother, Butch." The plumber scanned the space and whistled. "I haven't been here before. Nice digs. I bet the pipes give you hell, though."

Gretchen flirted back, "Like you wouldn't believe."

Willoughby stepped in front of his wife. "It's a leaking pipe in one of the upstairs bathrooms. I'll show you."

Butch pointed his toolbox at Willoughby. "Ah, the man of the house. All righty, let's get to it. Looks like you're throwing a shindig."

Willougby didn't bother correcting the plumber. If the man thought he was the homeowner, all the better. "This way."

The two men walked through the house so Willoughby could point out the water spot in the ceiling. After taking him upstairs, he showed Butch the offending pipe.

"You've had a problem with this before?"

"Yes. Your brother repaired it six months ago."

The plumber smoothed over his mustache in thought and said, "I'll know more once I get in there. These old houses don't have access panels. I'm guessing I'll have to replace a fitting. These old copper pipes can survive anything. Trouble is, someone back in the day used PVC or galvanized steel to redo the bathroom." He pulled a wrench from his toolbox and shook it at the shower wall. "That shit don't last. Now—"

Before the idiot could continue this mind-numbing plumbing lecture, Willoughby said, "We're hosting a large party tomorrow, so I need this fixed today."

"Not a problem, boss." The plumber tapped the plaster with the wrench. "I'll grab some tarps from my truck and get to it. I should have the parts I need—"

Thankfully, the doorbell gave Willoughby a convenient excuse to leave. "I'll check in on you in a bit."

"Copy that." The plumber saluted with the tool, and Willoughby hurried down the stairs to greet the expected visitor.

He opened the door with a flourish. "Miss Gautreau, right on time."

"Thank you, Willoughby. Nice to see you under better circumstances."

"Indeed. Mr. Kite is out for the day, but he's instructed me to give you the full tour. The only place to avoid is the kitchen. My wife may take a cleaver to an unwelcome visitor."

Clara chuckled. "I understand completely. I'm looking forward to the party. The preparations must be elaborate."

Willoughby led Clara to the right side of the split grand staircase. "You have no idea. Shall we?"

Her striking blue eyes scanned the art in the main foyer. "Could we start on the first floor and work our way up? That's normally how I do it; that way, I can keep my tour notes consistent."

Noticing the plumber carrying a load of canvas tarps down the open upstairs hall, Willoughby saw the wisdom of her suggestion. He didn't want the noise and clutter distracting him. Lucien Kite had been very specific about this visit. He was to stick to Clara Gautreau like glue. His exact words were *She doesn't take a piss without you standing in front of her.* "Of course. May I call you Clara?"

"Yes, please do."

"Then, Clara, let's start in the solarium."

"That sounds perfect."

Willoughby had to admit the tour was a refreshing change of pace. The century-old home had over sixty rooms and numerous nooks and back hallways. He hadn't been in some of them in over a year. Clara had adored the sixteenth-century fainting couch in the parlor and gushed over the Gaugin in the formal dining room. Other objects were less impressive. Kite's commissioned portrait, which depicted him as a Hun, hung at the top of the stairs. Clara's expression upon seeing it was one of a person who had just smelled bad cheese. Willoughby had to fight back his chuckle. The painting was absurd.

An hour after Clara's arrival, they were standing in the sitting room of Kite's suite. This wing of the house also held the primary bedroom, a pool room with a bar, and a small study.

Clara took diligent notes as she admired the furnishings and architecture. "Is the bedroom ceiling vaulted?"

"Shall we take a look?" Willoughby asked.

"Oh, I just assumed—"

"Mr. Kite insists you see any room you like. Including his private chambers."

She wrinkled her nose at that but followed him into the expansive space. Clara was particularly drawn to the Edward Hopper hanging opposite the bed. It was Willoughby's favorite painting in the house. It was also the artwork that concealed the wall safe. Of course, Clara would have no way of knowing that. In awe, she examined the depiction of a row of storefronts along a dirt road. Clara stepped to the right to see it from another angle, then to the left.

"The oriel window in the sitting area is particularly interesting. The carvings were done by a famed woodworker."

Willoughby watched as Clara followed his extended hand, but as he turned, a looming shadow in the doorway halted him.

The plumber was staring unabashedly at Clara's ass. Willoughby side-stepped and blocked his view.

Butch scratched his chest. "Good as new. Took a little hunting, but I found the corroded joint. Don't use that shower for forty-eight hours. The plaster under the tile needs to dry."

"Very good. Leave the bill with Gretchen and see yourself out."

"Will do. I just need to grab my tarps and tools, and you'll never know I was here."

"God willing."

Willoughby stood behind Clara at the ornate bay window and watched as the beastly plumber loaded his van and drove away. Clara turned to him with a bright smile. "And the pièce de résistance?"

"Right this way."

They walked side-by-side down the hall, stopping at the double doors to Lucien Kite's office. The two suited guards who had been instructed to remain there for the duration of Ms. Gautreau's visit stepped away, and Willoughby entered the code on the keypad. Then, he pushed open both doors. His gaze went immediately to the spot above the fireplace where *Somewhere* hung.

Clara stepped to the mantel without hesitation and gazed up at the painting Kite had stolen from her father. Willoughby joined her.

"I know Mr. Kite doesn't think much of it, but it is quite lovely."

Clara sighed. "It's even more beautiful than the first time I saw it."

"Well, this concludes the tour, my dear."

"Oh, I wanted to ask, is there really a spiral slide?"

Willoughby grinned. "Would you like to see it?"

"Definitely," she replied.

Willoughby led her down the long hall in the opposite direction. At a nondescript closet door, he whispered conspiratorially, "The morning after last year's party, I found two guests passed out at the foot of it—*in flagrante delicto*."

"That must have been quite a shock."

"To say the least." He pulled open the door, revealing the swirling metal structure. "The home's original owner was a toy manufacturer. He had this built for his grandchildren. I think we had better take the stairs."

Clara stepped back into the hall. "Please extend my thanks to Mr. Kite. The visit was very illuminating."

Willoughby nodded and led Clara down the stairs. The entire experience was bizarre. He guided Clara through the house as if they didn't all know she was casing it. He pointed out architectural features like a museum docent, and she took notes like an avid student. One thing was certain; he never for an instant let Clara Gautreau out of his sight.

As he watched her drive away, Willoughby couldn't help but think if anyone could steal *Somewhere* out of Lucien Kite's Fort Knox of a study, it would be her.

CHAPTER FIFTY-FIVE

Lucien Kite Estate
October 31

The party was a tribute to excess. Lucien Kite had never attempted to assimilate with the subtle wealth of his neighbors. The fountain in the middle of the circular drive featured a Jenga tower of gold bars with arcs of Krugerrands mimicking the spray of water.

The mansion was illuminated with ground lights, throwing massive beams up the white stone facade.

The theme was The Court of Louis XVI. Guests were greeted by valets at the gatehouse and transferred to vintage horse-drawn carriages for the long trek up the drive to the main house.

Clara was dressed as a young page in a brocade tunic with puffed sleeves cinched at the elbow and wrist. Her blonde mane was tucked under a brown wig tied in a short ponytail, and a simple mask covered her face. After the team dropped her near the entrance, Clara loitered near the hedge row, waiting for an opportunity to blend in. It didn't take long.

A Bentley rolled to a stop, and a couple emerged from the front in a cloud of satin and tulle as the costumed valet ran over. The driver adjusted his white wig and stepped out of the way. "Am I the only asshole who drove himself?" He called across the car to his wife. "Who knew not having a chauffeur put you below the fucking poverty line?"

His wife laughed and set a crown on top of her mile-high hair. "Save the jokes for inside. You want them as clients, you better charm their asses off."

These two were perfect—outsiders and attention seekers. When the Bentley pulled away, Clara slipped into the space between them and hooked her arms through theirs. "May I share your carriage?"

The woman's scarlet gown was adorned with a collar of ostrich feathers that brushed Clara's face. "Oh, Chet," she cooed. "Isn't this fun."

Ten yards up the driveway, security stopped them, checked their invitations, and directed the trio to the line of waiting carriages.

"Are we early? I hope we're not early," the man grumbled.

"Early is good. You don't want to wait until people are too drunk to have a conversation. I've heard Kite's parties turn into complete orgies," his wife replied with veiled excitement.

"I'm sure people are exaggerating, but who knows? Maybe we can show the boys those magnificent tits."

"Chet," she scolded halfheartedly.

Clara cleared her throat and dropped the pitch of her voice. "You're not too early. Lots of guests have arrived." She gestured to the group of people waiting to enter at the main doorway.

"Well, that's good," Chet said.

A costumed footman was waiting to assist them at the carriage. The sun had set, but there was enough light in this staging area to host an NFL game. After a moment of awkwardness with the cumbersome costumes, the three of them settled in the single seat of the open-air conveyance.

The plumed horses had just begun clopping their way up the cobblestones when a sleek black Astin Martin Volante glided to a stop beside the coach. Clara wasn't particularly impressed by cars, but she had to admit that car may have been the sexiest thing she had ever seen.

Until the door opened, and two black riding boots hit the pavement.

White britches, gold-trimmed, navy-blue military tailcoat—a simple black mask rested over his eyes beneath neatly styled dark brown hair.

Clara lost her breath. Miles Buchanan was a work of art.

And to top it off, he was dressed as the revolutionary Lafayette. He came with his own private joke, and Clara knew Miles was letting her in on it. God, she loved that.

"Have you got room for one more?" Miles asked in a crisp British accent with a panty-melting smile.

The husband began to decline the request when his wife spoke over him. "Of course! It's a short trip. We'll squeeze in."

Miles joined the group in two long strides and leaned against the backrest of the coachman's seat. He extended his hand to Chet, "Henry Rutledge."

"Chet Neill."

Clara saw the signet ring on Miles's pinky and knew her role. If there was one party in all the world where a royal would be welcomed without question, it was this one. She stood and balanced herself using the armrest.

"Apologies, your grace. Would you take my seat?"

"Thank you, *young man*. You can sit at my feet," he said—his words paired with a smoldering gaze.

"Oh, ah…"

"I insist."

Clara had much more to lose in this little battle of wills. So, in an artless dance step, they switched positions, and Clara sank to her knees at Miles's feet. The couple didn't seem to notice the overt sexuality of the position. Clara rather enjoyed it and used a convenient bump on the cobblestones to steady herself by leaning on his thigh just below the outline of his growing erection. She kept her hand where it was.

Chet's wife leaned forward. "Joanne Neill." She tipped her head to Clara. "Did he say 'your grace?'"

Miles looked suitably abashed.

Clara said, "His Grace is the Duke of Pembroke-on-Trent. His picture was on Page Six this week."

Miles rested his hand on the side of Clara's neck and pulled her slightly forward. "No need for formalities, young man. In The States, Henry will do just fine." Then he grabbed the traditional tricorn hat from his head and rested it on his lap. When Clara moved to withdraw, Miles snaked his hand under the hat and placed her fingers around his erection. He squeezed, and she, in turn, gripped him.

Miles turned his attention to Joanne Neill. "Let's keep that information between us if you don't mind. I'd prefer to be a regular party-goer tonight. It'll be our little secret."

Clara couldn't stop the eye roll. Joanne Neill all but swooned at Miles's attention. She tightened her grip, and Miles made a sound in his throat, a sort of moaning grunt. Clara didn't know if it was their secret touching, the jostle of the wheels over the cobblestones, or the man at whose feet she knelt, but her body felt like a cracking dam about to give way.

Clara wished this carriage ride would go on forever. She lost sight of why she was there, forgot about the couple a hair's breadth away. All that mattered was this man, this strange kismet between them.

The carriage rolled to a stop under a portico draped with garlands of roses and lilies, and they climbed down. Chet was overly casual as he clapped Miles on the back. "Looking forward to talking more inside." Clara had to hold her hand over her mouth to stop the laugh from escaping when Joanne bobbed up and down in what appeared to be a curtsy.

Clara handed Miles his hat. "Your Grace."

Miles grabbed her by the arm and hauled her behind the carriage. With a bite of her ear lobe, he whispered, "If you didn't have a job to do, I'd put you back on your knees between my legs in that carriage and have the driver go until I was satisfied." She started to pull away when he added, "And Clara, I wouldn't be satisfied until we switched places."

Her knees gave out, and Clara stumbled back.

Miles smirked, "You okay there, *young man*?"

She ran her hands down the front of her brocade tunic and shot back, "I'd be a lot better if you stopped talking and started doing."

He strode toward her in measured steps, unconcerned by the clip-clopping of hooves indicating another carriage was approaching. Miles was too close when he slipped his hand under her tunic and traced between her legs. She could feel his breath on her lips as he spoke. "After we do this, the real action starts. Now, tell me the word."

Clara spoke with her lips touching his. "Valkyrie."

"Good girl." He dropped the tiny device into her palm. "If anyone says Valkyrie over comms, we abort immediately."

She leaned back, and those hypnotic blue eyes met his. "What if I say it?"

"I'll find you. No matter what."

With a decisive tug on the short front of his tailcoat, Miles inserted the earpiece, brushed by her, and entered the party.

In the center of the grand foyer, a liveried attendant stood beside a large wooden panel with what appeared to be the handles of at least fifty knives protruding at even intervals. The attendant gestured to the makeshift wall. "Choose your seat assignment for dinner, please."

Miles withdrew a dagger. "*Table Eight*" was printed on the blade.

Clara did the same. "Table seventeen," she said.

"Very good. Dinner will be served at nine. Enjoy your evening."

"Well, buddy, the good news is if you fall in the pool, there's no shortage of flotation devices."

Steady's running commentary over the comm in his ear had Miles fighting to contain his smile. It was true; he had never seen so many corsetted breasts in his life. Miles was living out some thirteen-year-old boy's masturbation fantasy and had no one to blame but himself. After informing Joanne Neill in the carriage that he was a Duke, he had uttered the magic words to her: *let's keep this between us*. Miles had all but handed her a bullhorn. Husbands had been lurking, and wives had pounced. He checked the time on an extravagant grandfather clock: 8:30 p.m. Clara had disappeared twenty minutes ago. It came as no surprise to him that in this ocean of ripe breasts and eager hands, she was the only woman that interested him.

She was the only woman who ever had.

She was the only woman who ever would.

Miles was shaken from his epiphany by a new pair of breasts nudging his bicep. "Tell me, Henry, how long are you staying in town?"

Miles leaned back to escape the press of her cleavage. "Leaving tomorrow, sadly. Duty calls."

"Well, I'd love to help make this a *memorable* visit for you. Lucien is a close friend. I know all the secret spots in the house."

A master at the art of cocktail party extraction, Miles said, "How kind. Excuse me for a moment."

A bony hand gripped his forearm as he made his way through the crowd. Miles turned to find a woman in a high-necked black gown, holding her mask by the end of a stick and giving him a thin smile.

"Good evening, madam. I'm in search of a libation."

"Pembroke-on-Trent, you say, *your grace*."

Uh oh. Miles cleared his throat.

The lady continued, "It must be a very small dukedom."

Miles removed her hand and gave it a gentle pat. "Very."

"Funny, I thought I knew them all." She arched a penciled brow.

"As you said, it's quite small," Miles replied.

"I assume your reasons for attending this gaudy fete are rooted in pleasure, not ill will. My son, Lionel, lost most of his assets in crypto; he's here scouting out investment opportunities for his next *sure thing*. He'll learn eventually. I just hope he has two nickels to rub together when he does. My point is, I would hate to think there are people here who would take advantage of his naïveté."

Leaning closer, Miles replied, "There are many people here who would take advantage. I am not one of them. My interests this evening are purely hedonistic."

The woman patted his hand. "Spoken like a true royal."

Miles laughed. "Indeed."

The lady examined his costume with dancing eyes. "A commoner, pretending to be a Duke, costumed as a revolutionary—I wish we had time to get to know one another. Enjoy your evening."

His crisp bow had the old woman chuckling as Miles left the ballroom. The expansive front hall was equally bustling as guests continued to arrive. A wide corridor at the back was punctuated by paned double doors, which led to a vast terrace where dinner would take place. Round tables with white cloths and massive floral arrangements dotted the flagstone.

In the foyer, the split curved staircase was roped off, but that didn't stop people from coming and going to the second floor.

The attendant with the daggers still stood at the ready, but now only half a dozen knives remained. Miles guessed the blade was removed from the board as each table was filled. The pearl-encrusted handle he had chosen still protruded from the wood. The distinctive curved handle Clara had selected was gone. Miles felt a pique of irritation imagining Clara surrounded by lascivious old men pawing at her.

A servant rang a handheld gong announcing dinner, and a group of costumed courtiers brushed by him, heading to their tables. He surveyed the crowd, looking for Clara with no luck. He stifled his unease. Clara didn't come to be the best thief in the world without incredible agility, timing, and skill. Nevertheless, Miles would keep an eye on her. He always did.

A hand on his shoulder stopped him, and Miles turned to face their host. Lucien Kite was a pompous fool aptly dressed as Louis XVI.

"You must be Henry Rutledge." Kite held out a hand.

It didn't much matter to Miles if Kite knew he was a poser or not. He had a play either way. He was either a corrupt royal interested in partnering with Kite or a con man out to bilk would-be investors. Kite would welcome both versions of his backstory. Either way, Miles was exactly what he was supposed to be: a distraction.

"Lucien Kite."

"Mr. Kite, a pleasure." Miles shook Kite's offered hand.

"Please, call me Lucien. I was intrigued when your people called to secure an invitation to my little shindig. But then, I did a little research."

Miles withdrew a silver case from his breast pocket, took out a cigarette, and tapped it on the closed lid before slipping it between his lips. "And what did you discover?"

Kite withdrew a lighter and held the flame up to Miles. "That your family's shipping business and ties to the Turkish government are being underutilized."

Once again, Twitch's cyber skills have proven unmatched.

Miles let a hint of pleasure show—just enough for Kite to detect it—before masking his emotions. "I'm interested in hearing your thoughts on the matter, Lucien. I've recently inherited control of the company, and I'd like to employ some creative expansion strategies."

"I may have a few ideas. Have your office set up a meeting. No shop talk tonight. Enjoy yourself." Kite leaned closer. "Have a taste of what life is like when you're in business with Lucien Kite."

"Looking forward to it."

Kite straightened his powdered wig with a bejeweled hand, then traded his empty rocks glass for the cocktail from the waiter. "It's whiskey. I can't stomach the bubbly. Cheers to an eventful evening."

Glancing past Kite's bejeweled grandeur, Miles followed the server as he navigated the crowd and saw a small gloved hand pluck the empty glass from the tray. Miles toasted King Louis as he and his entourage departed, Kite's parting words tipping his lips. Eventful, indeed.

Miles dropped the unsmoked cigarette in a half-full champagne flute, strode out to the terrace, and chose the seat at his table with the most direct line of sight to Clara's. After swiping Kite's glass for the needed fingerprint, she would rendezvous with Calliope to change. Her dinner companions were primarily men, and Miles once again bristled at the thought of her surrounded by the letches attending this function. Where was she? How long could it possibly take to change costumes?

The brakes slammed on his thoughts as he followed the turning heads. Miles hadn't even realized he was standing as he shifted to improve his view. He had to have imagined the collective gasp. The band finished a song. Conversation dimmed. Miles could hear the silence. Even his thoughts stopped racing. It was as if all the little demons chattering in his brain, for once, just shut the fuck up. And stared.

She stood at the threshold of the french doors, bathed in the glow of the house lights. Blonde hair cascaded over one shoulder, falling across a sapphire-blue brocade bodice. The bare skin of her chest glowed, and her lips were stained berry red. The gown's skirt was comprised entirely of peacock feathers—the blue and green catching the light and the fronds fluttering in the gentle breeze. Across her eyes was a matching mask, and though her face was hidden, there was no mistaking that vivid blue.

Clara Gautreau was magnificent.

Music and talking resumed, and Miles's brain rebooted as Clara floated across the terrace. She stood by her table while three men fought to hold her chair.

The woman next to Miles asked, "Did you just growl?"

"I beg your pardon?" Miles replied, affronted.

"I could have sworn… Oh, never mind. What brings you across the pond, Henry?"

Miles wanted to snap the woman's head like a twig, but he had a part to play. So, he took his seat and resumed the idle chitchat, most of the time staring over the head of his dinner partner at the vision across the room.

Dinner was torture. Between the blowhards bragging about their race-horses and the women popping up at his shoulder to proposition him, Miles could barely monitor Clara. Every man at the party seemed to be stopping by her table to introduce themselves. Her dinner partner attempted to feed her. Miles watched as she reared back and held up a hand to stay him. *Good girl.*

As planned, Clara excused herself from the table during dessert. Kite's parties were known to devolve into debauchery after dinner. Guests would be tipsy if not drunk and distracted by impending festivities. He watched from his seat as she wandered past the pool. A man dressed as a French soldier plucked two flutes from a passing tray and offered Clara one. She accepted and wound her free arm through his as they continued down the wide stone stairs to the elaborate hedge maze—the entrance bracketed by two immense topiary gargoyles. Miles was calm as the towering man led her into the labyrinth. He glanced around the perimeter and noticed Lucien Kite's guards making the same observation. Fifteen minutes later, the couple reemerged, ascended the steps to the pool, and meandered to the dance floor. The orchestra had gone on break, and a notorious Vegas DJ was now spinning tunes. Colored lights flashed, and Miles watched as the pair danced to Nikki Minaj's latest track.

Checking the time, Miles tapped a booted foot impatiently. Emily Bishop, in Clara's peacock dress, and his brother continued their distraction on the dance floor, and, if all went according to plan, Clara had just entered Lucien Kite's office.

After removing the peacock gown and giving it to Emily Bishop, Clara exited the hedge maze in the back. She skirted the edge of the property wearing the specially made gray gown. She glanced up at the party and spotted Emily and Tox on the dance floor, twirling and jumping to the thumping beat. When Clara had expressed concern about their ability to get into the party the guys had laughed. *Clara, we once infiltrated the compound of a Congolese warlord. I think we can handle it.*

Silent as a shadow, Clara wound through the formal rose garden at the side of the house and entered through an open patio door.

The second floor of Kite's home was a labyrinth of hallways and alcoves. Memorizing the floor plan had been a complicated feat. There were stairways that led to hidden nooks, secret passageways, and even that spiral slide that descended to the kitchen.

Four guards were patrolling the upper floors—Kite had instructed them to be deferential to his guests and not interfere with partiers seeking out a private space to canoodle. Two stood sentry at Kite's office. Clara passed them with a sultry smile as she slipped into the guest bath.

Once inside, she detached the specially constructed skirt of her costume— the four large pleated panels held everything she needed. Wearing the bodice and black leggings, Clara removed the small tool kit and the forgery from the lining.

After donning the latex gloves and setting her watch, she removed the access panel Miles had installed at the back of the tub when he posed as the plumber. Clara slipped through the small opening and stepped into Kite's office. *Somewhere* was hanging above the fireplace.

With the penlight between her teeth, Clara stepped forward, then stopped. It was the smell of cut wood that struck her. Glancing at her feet, she noticed the altered floorboards. Kite was pulling out all the stops. He'd installed a pressure plate. Clara avoided Kite's trap and disconnected the alarm. After removing the painting and replacing it with the forgery, she withdrew the small aerosol can that Very Valentine had given her and sprayed the surface of the copy. She gathered her supplies and stuffed everything into the nylon duffle also hidden in the voluminous skirt. She would lower the painting and the bag down to Ren, disguised as a caterer, waiting on the lawn with a serving trolly. Once again, Twitch had worked her magic to create Ren's airtight employment background.

Thirty seconds to reroute the balcony door alarm, pick the lock, and be gone without a trace. Clara slipped onto the balcony and readied the wire. Just as she was about to attach the painting, a hissing scream and a pair of yellow eyes sent her flailing.

Miles choked down what he was sure was a delicious meal as he made small talk. He rechecked the time, convinced the tricked-out watch the Bishop Security team had given him was broken. How could seconds tick so slowly? Twitch had rigged a two-minute delay on the security feed. If all was going to plan, Clara would be finished in Kite's office, as the video showed her climbing the stairs.

Miles laughed along with the table at a joke he hadn't heard when he spotted Lucien Kite and a phalanx of security storming toward the house. That was his cue. The Duke stood and delivered a half-bow to the table. He started to turn away when a tug on his tailcoat halted him. The hand restraining him belonged to the drunken companion of the woman who had been dry-humping him all through dinner.

"Wallet or wang?"

"I beg your pardon?" Miles replied, still tethered by the man's grip on his coat tail. This night was timed to the second; he didn't have a moment to waste on this idiot. Nevertheless, he couldn't make a scene.

"Wallet or wang? Portfolio or package? Dollars or dick?"

"I'm just popping into the loo," Miles explained.

Drunkie was having none of it. "Every bitch here has been eye fucking you all night. So which of yours is big? Wallet or wang."

Miles pried the man's fingers loose, leaned over, and gripped his shoulder. "Both."

Curtailing the urge to run, Miles skirted the sea of round tables and cut Kite off at the French doors.

"Lucien," Miles held out his hand.

"Henry, are you enjoying your evening?"

If Kite was upset or off his game, he gave no indication. His outward calm unsettled Miles.

"Very much. Although, before the evening gets too Dionesian, I thought we could chat. I leave for London tomorrow. I'd prefer to discuss opportunities in person."

"I understand. Unfortunately, my hosting duties are required at the moment." Kite leaned closer. "There's a little shrew inside that needs taming."

At that moment, Miles had such a clear vision of smashing his fist into Lucien Kite's face that he had to shake his head to clear it. With a tight smile, Miles bit out, "Another time then."

He waited ten seconds for Kite to move away. The band had stopped, and the orchestra was tuning up poolside to accompany Kite's famous fireworks display. As Miles turned to the house, a shriek above his head had him looking up just as something fell from the balcony into the bushes.

Miles turned the opposite way and headed for the main stairs.

Clara locked eyes with the great gray owl perched on the wall guarding her nest. She had completely forgotten Kite's mention of it. The bird screeched again, warning her away from the three owlets poking their heads out beside her. Scooting back on her butt, she stared through the low balusters to the place *Somewhere* had landed in the hedge below. Clara sagged in relief as Ren walked by, plucked the painting out of the boxwood, and stowed it beneath the white cloth on the lower shelf of his cart.

Over the comm, Ren said, "You're out of time, Clara. Toss the bag and go."

Even through the closed balcony doors, Clara heard the muffled shouting from the hall. She scrambled to her feet, unhooked the rappelling wire, and tucked it in the side pocket of her leggings. Thank god the owl was not between her and her destination. After chucking the bag, she climbed over the low wall and gracefully leapt to the neighboring balcony. Clara slipped inside Kite's bedroom as the first fireworks lit the sky in a burst of red.

The orchestra was playing the 1812 Overture as fireworks exploded in the sky.

Raphael Garza was waiting in the bedroom when Clara dove in through the balcony doors and rolled to a stop. His puppets were dancing.

Garza helped Clara to her feet, and she thanked him with a warm smile. Part of him hated doing this to her, but it was overshadowed by dollar signs in his eyes.

Clara moved to the safe without delay. He stepped back silently and let her work. Clara's reputation was well-deserved. Garza watched as she used a captured thumbprint to bypass the biometric lock, then attached a small device to decipher the combination. In seconds, she had the safe open and Kite's book in hand.

Silently, she passed the book to Garza. It was almost ridiculous how easily he had planted the idea that he should be the one to sneak the book out of the house. Clara's asshole boyfriend had actually suggested it—the gullible fool. Garza slipped the small journal into his jacket pocket and helped Clara into the new costume skirt waiting on the bed.

When she was dressed, Garza wordlessly squeezed her hand and slipped out of the room. One final thing to take care of, and then he was home free.

Sorry, Clara.

Clara stood in the doorway of Lucien Kite's bedroom and watched Raphael Garza depart.

Outside, the orchestra played a tango.

Her masked Duke bumped into Garza, muttering an apology and continuing toward her. Dramatic violin music filled the hallway as a tall party guest rounded the corner and crashed into Miles. Both men stepped back in unconscious, mirrored movements. The guest sidestepped. Miles did the same, and the men continued in opposite directions.

Clara looked past the handsome man headed her way as the other guest, Tox, hooked arms with Emily Bishop, still wearing Clara's peacock dress, and descended the stairs.

The double doors to the office flew open. Lucien Kite burst in, then stopped. The room was as he had left it, dark and quiet.

One of the door guards stepped forward. "Sir, I haven't left the door all night. No one has been in here."

In a manner befitting his kingly attire, Kite strolled over to his money throne and sat. "Maybe not yet, but she's coming."

The other man said, "We'll be right outside."

"No," Kite instructed. "Patrol the floor. Be discrete, but check the rooms and surveillance. Something's not right."

When the men left, Kite drummed his fingers on the desk. Where was she? He sat back and adjusted his wig. He hated to miss the debauchery, but if he had to stand guard over the painting to ensure The Lynx didn't steal it, so be it.

A subtle movement caught his eye. At first, Kite thought a moth had gotten into the room. He glanced at the art. *What the?* A section of the painting was bubbling and peeling. The paint was dropping in curls on the mantle below. Kite stood and walked to where *Somewhere* hung, mindful of the pressure plate he had installed to catch the thief. Before his eyes, the paint coiled and fell away. The image below was only partially exposed, but Kite could already make out what it was: the back end of a horse.

"No."

He stumbled back, looking frantically left and right. "Noooo!"

A figure appeared in the doorway.

Kite turned and sat at his desk. "You. Get in here. We have a problem."

Raphael Garza stepped into the room. "Yes, we do."

At the doorway to Kite's bedroom, Clara stood face-to-face with Miles. "All set?"

Miles seared her with a fiery look and replied, "Almost." Then he backed her into the bedroom and kissed her with a fire and desperation that left her breathless. He buried his face in her neck and said, "I've wanted to do that all night. Show everyone who even looked at you who you belong to."

His words left her dizzy and elated, but there was no time. "We have to move," she whispered.

Miles stepped back and took her hand. "Let's get out of here."

He led her down the long hall to the main stairs, looking perfectly in place—two guests exploring the house. When they reached Lucien Kite's office, Clara paused. The door was open. It took a moment to process what she was seeing.

Lucien Kite sat at his desk with a dagger in his heart and a trickle of blood running from the corner of his mouth. Clara had never seen a dead body before. Kite stared right at her. His gaze vacant yet somehow accusatory. The fireworks changed his powdered wig and the pallor of his skin from red to blue to yellow, and Clara stood transfixed by the sight.

She stood frozen in place, taking in the bloody ruffles of his blouse, the painted blush on his cheeks, the curved handle of the blade protruding from his chest.

It was the dagger that indicated her table assignment, the curved-handled knife Clara had chosen when she entered the party—the one she had gripped barehanded. She clapped a hand over her mouth to quell her rebelling stomach, willing herself not to throw up on the carpet.

Miles pulled her to his side, his body tense. It was only then that she noticed Raphael Garza standing in the shadows. He wore latex gloves and a menacing expression, looking nothing like her old friend.

"You shouldn't have come in here," Garza said in an icy voice.

"You're setting Clara up." Miles gestured to the knife and then her little tool kit on the floor by the desk. When had Garza taken it?

Garza lifted a shoulder. "It's not personal. It's just business. Someone has to take the fall. She's the logical choice."

Miles took a step forward. "You'd really ruin her for money?"

Garza looked at Miles like he was speaking gibberish. "Of course. Only now, I have to kill her and you." Garza pulled a gun and came around the desk, telling his concocted version of events. "I came in to check on Lucien and found you attacking him. In an attempt to stop you, I shot you both, but was too late to save him." He jerked the gun in a silent command for them to move to the desk. As they rotated positions, Clara saw her opportunity.

Rather than step to the right of the desk, Clara pulled Miles to the left, forcing Garza to step back. He was almost where she needed him. She brushed her hand across Kite's desk, sending a half-full glass of whiskey flying. Garza retreated to avoid the liquid.

And stepped on the newly installed pressure plate.

In an instant, a trap door in the ceiling fell open, and a cargo net dropped over Garza, pinning him down and sending the gun spinning across the floor. Leave it to Kite to plan a grand scheme to catch her.

Miles was already moving when she regained her composure. With a kick to the temple, he knocked Garza out. Then he wiped the knife handle, grabbed Clara's tool kit, and pocketed Garza's gun.

"Come on, Bluebird."

She tugged on his hand, inches from the unconscious man who had betrayed her. "The book."

"It's been handled." Miles hurried her to the door.

"What do you mean? How?"

Miles all but shoved her into the hall. "You're not the only pickpocket here, Clara."

When they stepped into the hallway, Miles peered over the banister, spotting a group of determined security guards pushing through the crowd toward the stairs.

The pressure plate Garza stepped on must have triggered an alarm. Behind them was a dead body, in front of them, trigger-happy mercenaries. Miles spoke into the comm, "Valkyrie." Then, he turned to Clara. "Plan B?"

"Always. Follow me."

Winding through the corridors, she finally stopped before a closed door that appeared to be a closet. Clara pulled it open, revealing the top of the famed spiral slide that ran from the attic to the basement.

"After you," she said.

Miles climbed over the low side rail. Then, without missing a beat, he scooped Clara up by her waist and placed her facing him on his lap. She hiked up her skirt and straddled him, wrapping her arms behind his neck.

She fit on his lap like a missing puzzle piece. Miles wrapped his arms around her and, with a push, sent them careening down the slide.

They spun and swooped down the spiral, eyes locked, holding tight. They were suspended in the moment as light and space revolved around them.

Miles slowed them with the sides of his boots, and they came to a smooth stop in a cleaning pantry. Neither of them wanted to move.

Clara pressed her lips to his. "That was dizzying."

He chuckled. "Come on, Bluebird. I'll hold you up."

They passed through the kitchen, avoiding the catering staff, who were apparently unaware of the murder that had just taken place. Seconds later, they were outside, racing across the lawn.

CHAPTER FIFTY-SIX

Lucien Kite Estate

October 31

With Clara's hand firmly in his own, Miles strode across the front lawn of the house to the hired town car. As they pulled away from the mansion, Miles hauled Clara into his lap and kissed her. They had done it.

The gentle weight of her body was a comfort he had missed for far too long. Clara Gautreau was stubborn and impulsive. She was too bright for her own good and adventurous to the point of foolhardy. In short, she was perfect in every way.

He loved her. And he would tell her as soon as they reached the safety of his loft.

The car pulled smoothly to a stop at the curb in front of Miles's building. Miles was so lost in Clara's scent and touch he noticed far too late the two armed men flanking the rear passenger doors—the same guys he and Tox had taken down in his decoy apartment. The larger man tapped Miles's window with the barrel of his gun and smiled through the glass. "Remember me?"

Sliding Clara over on the seat, Miles pushed the emergency button on the watch and exited the car.

The goon eyed his costume. "Well, good evening, your lordship."

Ignoring him, Miles stepped farther from the car, away from Clara. "What now, fellas?"

Spotting Garza's gun in his waistband, the guy flapped his fingers in a hand-it-over gesture. Miles complied.

The smaller man peered through the window behind the driver, who was cowering in his seat. "Who's this?"

Miles replied dismissively. "One of Chug's by-the-hour girls, she's nobody."

Chug's muscle knocked on the glass. "She'd be money well spent."

Miles needed to get their attention off of Clara. "What does Chug want now?"

The big man smiled. "He'd like a word, your eminence, or should I say, *Miles Buchanan*."

Miles's face fell. He was typically inscrutable; nothing fazed him, but Chug Ugentti, of all people, had cracked his alias.

"That's right," the enforcer continued, tapping the gun barrel to his own temple. "I got your number."

"Big Mike, let's move. People are starting to notice."

"All right, Your Highness, hop in. Keep your hands where I can see them. We're going to grace New Jersey with your kingly presence."

Miles complied as he walked to the side of the panel van parked in front of their town car. The other accomplice joined them and slid open the door. Miles had roughly ten seconds to pull this off. He had laid the groundwork. He stepped into the bare rear section with his hands in the air and sat on a pile of painter's tarps. When the door closed, Miles pulled out his phone and sent a text. Then he shared his location, locked the screen, and slipped the phone between the layers of canvas under his legs.

"Sit tight. We'll be there in a jiff."

"Where is there?"

The man didn't answer, but it was clear where they were headed. Miles went into survival mode. He was on his own. Miles looked down at his costume. He had been caught off guard.

Big Mike pulled out of the parking spot. "Mikey, get his cell phone. Chug will have our asses if we forget."

The smaller man, Mikey, climbed into the back and extended his hand. "Phone."

"I didn't bring it. Doesn't really go with the period." Miles indicated his costume.

"Yeah, right." Mikey patted him down, then said to his partner, "He doesn't have it."

"Check around him."

Mikey hauled Miles up, then pushed him into a pile of paint cans on the other side of the space. It didn't take him long to find the phone. "Got it."

"Toss it." Mikey followed the order and threw the phone out the passenger window.

In the back of the town car, Clara watched the kidnappers pull away. Something flew out the window as the van headed west. She'd heard the conversation and knew Ugentti's men were taking Miles to New Jersey. She squeezed the driver's shoulder.

"Follow them."

"Forget it. I've got a wife and kids. Call the cops."

"Please," she begged. "I just need you to get me close. You won't be in any danger."

"Lady, get out of my car."

Clara stood on the sidewalk as the driver peeled away. Glancing toward the corner, Clara raced over and grabbed Miles's cracked cell phone from where it had landed in the gutter.

She scanned the street for a taxi, but there was nothing. Then she remembered. Running down the alley to the back door, she tore away the cumbersome skirt and let herself into Miles's building. Clara spotted it instantly. Thirty seconds later, she was speeding after the van on the Ducati.

CHAPTER FIFTY-SEVEN

Perth Amboy, New Jersey
October 31

The two enforcers that had beaten him up the last time joined their entourage in the warehouse and shackled Miles to a chair in the center of the room.

The bald one asked, "You pat him down?"

Big Mike replied, "Took a gun and his phone. He's clean."

The sound of footsteps on metal stairs had everyone looking to the back of the room where Chug Ugentti, dressed in a too sharp suit, was coming down from his office.

Chug looked at Miles in his costume. "Well, well, if it isn't Little Lord Fuckalot. Or should I say, Miles Buchanan?"

Miles revealed nothing as he sat chained. Chug walked up to him and punched him in the face.

His head flew back, and blood ran from his nose and upper lip.

Ugentti shook out his hand and paced the gritty floor. Another man entered with a laptop under his arm and sat at a folding table opposite them.

"I gave you carrot after carrot, you stupid fuck. Now you get the stick. You see, I'm not some pinky-out, polo-playing politician who makes problems go away with a checkbook. I'm Chester fucking Ugentti. I'm a made man. I make problems go away by putting them in the foundation of construction projects. I make problems go away by chopping them in a million pieces and throwing them in the Atlantic."

Miles gave a frustrated yank to his restraints, then gathered himself. He needed to remain calm. After spitting a mouthful of blood on the floor, he said, "I'll do what you want, Chug."

Ugentti nodded to his enforcer, and the man stepped forward and rammed his fist into Miles's gut.

"You're goddamned right you will." Ugentti turned to the young man sitting behind him. "Antonio here is my sister's son. He's a real whiz on the computer. You're going to sit at that table and transfer every file on every client you've ever had. Antonio is going to watch you. If he holds up a finger, that means he doesn't like what you're doing, and I fire a bullet into your knee. Every fuck up is another bullet. So, I suggest you work clean."

The other guard unlocked his cuffs, hauled Miles to his feet, and shoved him into the folding chair in front of the laptop. Antonio stared over his shoulder as Miles accessed his client files.

Chug said, "I don't operate like the rest of your Ivy League fucks. The rules don't apply."

Miles looked at Chug over the laptop screen and said, "There's one rule that applies."

"Oh, yeah? And what's that?"

"You can't kill the daughter of Vincent Barzetti."

Clara cut the ignition and wheeled the bike to a stop beneath the rickety fire escape. She glanced up at the loose bolts and peeling paint, hoping it would hold her weight. Gingerly, she began to climb.

The roof was a minefield of cracked skylights, some tipped open, others broken out entirely. She looked through a hole and saw Miles being dragged across the cement floor to a computer. He already looked badly beaten. Clara maneuvered across the asphalt in the climbing shoes she still wore, mindful of the broken glass and loose pieces of jagged metal. She found an opening above some high shelving and stopped. She didn't have any tools or a weapon, but she did have the rappelling line from the art heist at Lucien Kite's still tucked in the side pocket of her leggings.

Clara debated the wisdom of her actions. If Miles had his way, she'd be locked in a high tower or on a plane to Timbuktu. Convinced that if their situations were reversed, he would unhesitatingly come to her aid, she prepared the line. A car passed beneath the floodlights at the gate. Clara moved to the front of the roof and peered over the edge as a Bentley rolled to a stop. Moments later, two SUVs parked behind it.

All Clara could see from this distance in the dark were the tops of heads and vicious-looking guns as the group of ten moved silently toward the building. Without a moment's hesitation, she hurried back to the rappelling line. She had no climbing gear, so Clara slid the mechanism under a pipe, secured it, and then clipped the wire to the corset laces on the front of the costume bodice. If there was one thing The Lynx could do better than anyone, it was improvise.

Slowly, Clara began lowering herself into the warehouse.

Every head in the room was focused on Miles as he spoke. She couldn't make out the words, but Miles was a strategist; he was always outthinking, outmaneuvering. This was when he was at his most compelling.

When her feet touched the top of the storage shelf, Clara knelt between two crates filled with old machine parts. She listened to what Miles was saying, waiting for an opportunity to help.

CHAPTER FIFTY-EIGHT

Detroit, Michigan

March 10

Nineteen years ago.

Miles steered the old Schwinn into the driveway, relieved both cars were gone. He had forgotten the folder with his homework sheets. The Man didn't want Miles there during normal hours; he wouldn't like Miles appearing in the middle of the day. When he inserted his key in the side door lock, nothing clicked. He turned the knob, and the door opened smoothly. It wasn't like them to forget to lock the house.

Miles stepped into the mud room. His room. The sleeping mat was rolled and stored in the corner, and his school books were arranged neatly in a cubby. After grabbing the folder he needed, Miles considered stealing a snack from the kitchen. He dismissed the idea; The Man had set a small camcorder up on a curio shelf by the door. "Don't think you're gonna sneak in here and steal my food. I'm watching you, kid." He was just about to leave when a loud clank had him turning back.

Miles peered through the paned glass door and spotted a man. He was old, maybe forty, and slim, wearing coveralls and a ball cap. Miles took a step back, and the man looked up. He opened the door and smiled at Miles. "What are you doing here, buddy?"

"I forgot some school stuff."

The man nodded his understanding. "I used to come up with some crazy excuses for why my homework wasn't done. I was a real delinquent."

"What are you doing here?" Miles asked.

"I'm with the gas company. Paulie's got a leak. I'm fixing the leak."

Miles wasn't a fool. They'd run from the mobsters chasing The Man before. Plus, The Man didn't go by Paulie. Miles had only heard his wife call him that. He was about to mention it when he spotted the gun, equidistant between them, sitting on the counter.

"Go ahead, kid. I dare you."

Miles took a step back. The repairman smiled and turned to the sink. After removing a thick pinky ring, the guy washed his hands. Miles could already smell the sweet, putrid smell of gas.

When the man turned to the paper towel roll, Miles swiped the camcorder on the curio shelf, unplugged it, and dropped it into the open backpack at his feet.

"Christ, that smell makes me woozy." He turned to the stove, gathered his tools, and dropped them into the open canvas bag. Miles slid to the sink, plucked the thick gold ring from where it sat on a sponge, and pocketed it.

The man turned and steadied himself on the counter. "You gonna go for that gun?"

"No, sir."

"You sure? You're closer than me now, and I gotta tell you, I'm a little high from the fumes."

Miles shook his head.

"Smart decision. Never play the ace up your sleeve when you have a winning hand."

"Yes, sir."

"*That's life advice right there. So get lost. Forget everything you've seen. We clear?*"

"*We're clear.*"

"*Oh, and kid?*"

"*Yeah?*"

He emptied the bullets and slid the weapon across the counter. "*Take the gun. I need to get rid of it. Shot a cop, so don't use it.*" He peeled a twenty off a wad from his pocket. "*Throw it in the river.*"

Miles felt the surge of excitement. This was wrong, but for once, he was the one profiting. He put the gun and the money into his backpack.

"*Okay.*"

"*Good. Now get back to school before you get detention or whatever the fuck they do to kids now.*"

Three hours later, Miles felt the explosion from his seat in the public library five blocks away. He knew instantly what it was. He hadn't warned The Man or his wife and felt no remorse. For three years, he had lived like an unloved dog.

When the few other people in the room had wandered to the windows to watch the smoke-filled sky, Miles scooped up his backpack and walked to the office to find Miss Anita. He hoped she would help him, but even if she didn't, being alone was better than the life he'd had.

CHAPTER FIFTY-NINE

Perth Amboy, New Jersey
October 31

Chug flew out of his chair and shouted into Miles's face. "What the fuck did you just say to me?"

"*Never play the ace up your sleeve if you have a winning hand.* I would never have known until you repeated it last week in your office. It's the exact thing you said to me twenty years ago in that house."

"You're off your rocker."

"7727 West Charger Drive. Ringing any bells, Chug?"

"The fuck?" Ugentti went deathly still.

"I was the kid, Chug. I stood there and watched you rig the gas line."

"What's he talking about, Boss?" One of Ugentti's goons asked.

Chug fastened the button on his suit jacket and smoothed his lapels. "Ancient fucking history is what he's talking about."

"I didn't realize it for years. You see, I didn't know much about the people who adopted me. I was fifteen when they died. Five or six years later, I was sitting in a coffee shop, and someone had left a newspaper on the table. It was folded open to a picture of Vincent Barzetti; he and his new wife welcomed a baby daughter. In the inset was a photo of Barzetti's oldest daughter, who'd died in a house fire. I can't tell you how long I stared at that picture. It was the woman who adopted me. You murdered two people. One of whom was the daughter of Vincent Barzetti, the most infamous crime boss on the East Coast. I have you on video, Chug. And the ring. I took your pinky ring."

When Miles mentioned Barzetti, Chug paled but quickly recovered. He let out a booming laugh. "That's a pack of lies. The Feds came nosing around twenty years ago, jackass. I have an airtight alibi for that murder. If you think I can't explain away decades-old evidence, then you must not be very good at your job. Send that fucking file to the ghosts of Eliot Ness and J. Edgar Hoover for all I care."

Ugentti pulled out a gun from inside his suit jacket. Regaining his composure, he pointed the weapon at Miles. "Finish transferring your client files. It's a bullet in the knee if it takes longer than ten seconds. Then, my nephew is going to delete the other file. You're a valuable resource, *Caleb Cain*, but if I get wind that law enforcement has new information about that house fire, you'll have a girder in your gut holding up a support beam of my latest construction project."

"I didn't send the file to the cops, Chug."

"He sent it to me."

Vincent Barzetti stepped out of the shadows.

Wearing a pin-striped double-breasted suit with a full head of graying hair and tan complexion, Barzetti looked straight out of central casting for the role of mob boss. He was composed and commanded respect. Miles could see how the man had held the reins of the New York mafia for forty years.

More of Barzetti's men filed in, blocking the exits. Chug's men surrendered instantly, dropping their guns and raising their hands.

Barzetti turned to Miles. "Your team is waiting outside at my request."

"Mr. Barzetti, I can explain." Ugentti paced frantically through the open space.

"There's no need, Chug. I always suspected it was you. You were overly fond of the gas leak back in the day."

"Vinnie, I'm a fucking United States Congressman now. Think of what I can do for you."

"I have seven Congressmen, three Senators, and a Supreme Court Justice on my payroll. I doubt there's anything you could provide that would deter me from avenging my daughter's death."

"She ran off with that rat!" Chug screamed, grasping at any straw to stop the inevitable.

"She was spoiled and reckless, that's true. She was also the light of my life."

Quicker than Miles would have thought him capable, Chug dove for the fully automatic machine pistol dropped on the ground by one of his men. In an instant, at least ten weapons were trained on him. Barzetti held up a hand. Miles assumed Barzetti had plans for Chug's demise, and it would not be a quick death.

"I'm walking out of here, you fucks. I'm Chester fucking Ugentti, a member of the United States House of Representatives. In four years, I'll be sitting in The Oval—"

The rant was interrupted by an engine part about the size of a softball hitting Ugentti square in the face. He fell backward as he pulled the trigger, sending a spray of gunfire in the air. Barzetti's men surrounded Chug and disarmed him as the Bishop Security team poured in the doors.

Miles shook Barzetti's hand. "Glad you found some closure."

Barzetti watched as his men corralled a semi-conscious Ugentti. Water from a pipe overhead dripped onto Miles's head.

Barzetti said, "Not yet, but soon. I owe you one. I'll keep you in mind if I ever need a fixer."

"Thanks, but I'm retiring." Miles jerked his head toward the team. "Joining this motley crew. I'll be running the New York office of Bishop Security."

Another splat hit Miles.

Barzetti rested a firm hand on Miles's shoulder. "Then may our paths never cross."

Miles turned to leave. He needed to get back to Clara. He needed to hold her.

Barzetti called after him. "Is your team accounted for?"

Miles scanned the room, confirming the count. "Yeah, why?"

Barzetti held up the hand that had squeezed Miles's shoulder. "Because somebody's bleeding."

Just then, Herc, the Bishop Security sniper, shouted through the transom window in the ceiling, "Man down!"

Miles's eyes ran up the storage shelves until they settled on the out-of-place image. A slender hand hanging over the edge, limp.

Tox watched from across the room as his twin realized Clara had been shot. He ran to help Miles. They located the electric lift in the corner of the room and brought Clara down. They were a perfect team working in unison without a word needed.

Tox stood to the side as Ren examined the bullet wound in Clara's shoulder.

"Looks like a through and through, but she's lost a lot of blood. Pass me my kit," Ren said. When Tox complied, Ren poured the coagulant powder on the wound and bandaged it. "We'll need to get her to a hospital for antibiotics and stitches."

Tox looked up to share his relief with his twin. Miles had backed away and was watching the scene with a distant, dazed expression.

Tox bit back a curse. Miles had come so far. If anything happened to Clara, he would lose his twin for good. Miles would never recover from another loss. Tox crossed to his brother in long strides, hauled back, and punched him in the face.

Miles staggered back, cradling his jaw. "What the fuck?"

"Snap out of it. The self-pity stops fucking now. Yes, we've lost people we love. Would you trade loving Clara for sparing yourself pain?"

Tox dared Miles to protest. If his brother couldn't see that he loved her, he was blind.

Miles rested the top of his head against Tox's chest. "I don't know if I can."

Tox wrapped his twin in a hug. "You can. Now, go take care of your girl."

CHAPTER SIXTY

New York City
November 1

Don't do this to me, Clara.
You owe me a favor now, and what I want is you.
Wake up, Bluebird.
I love you, Goddammit. I can't do this without you.

Clara awoke in a private hospital room. In her right hand, an IV port connected to a drip that must have contained some sort of painkiller because she was high as a kite. Her left hand was also attached—to Miles. He sat in a vinyl chair, his fingers gently laced with hers.

"Did you mean all those things you said?" she rasped.

Miles scrambled over. Sitting next to her on the bed, he touched her face reverently. "That depends. What did you hear?"

"You love me."

"Then, yes." He took the glass of water from the side table and placed the straw between her lips.

Clara sipped gratefully, then said, "Do you remember what you told me when I was a girl?"

At his confused expression, Clara explained, "I told you I was falling in love with you, and you said, 'Don't.'"

"Then I was a stupid, stupid man because there's nothing I want more."

"Good. Because you didn't stop it from happening." She brushed her fingertips over the scruff of his cheek. "I've always loved you, Miles Buchanan. And Caleb Cain and Duke Henry and Jake and the whole damn lot."

Miles kissed her, speaking with his lips a breath from hers. Clara breathed his air, swam in his presence. "You're my sun, Clara. For so long, I was content to be a frozen planet in your outer orbit. I should have known. Your light, your warmth, I'm alive again because of you. I love you, Clara, always, forever."

She clasped his dear face in her hands. "I really hope I'm not dreaming."

Miles ran his thumb along her jawline. "It's real, Bluebird. I'll repeat those words every day, so you know."

He laid back beside Clara, mindful of her injury. When she was nestled in that spot she loved beneath his shoulder, she slept.

CHAPTER SIXTY-ONE

Dordogne, France
November 5

Miles placed the painting on the easel Reynard had set up in his office, then returned to stand beside Clara.

"Well, we did it, Papa. You have your painting."

Reynard sat behind his desk and looked at *Somewhere*, lost in the image of the woman on the riverbank. After a long moment, he nodded to his assistant, Ahmed, who left the room.

"Actually, the painting is a gift. For Miles."

Miles looked up in surprise. "For me? Why?"

"Patience," Reynard said as he waved in Ahmed, who set up a second easel. He then placed a second covered frame on the ledge.

"Tavarro painted *Somewhere*. His only portrait. A depiction of his lost love reaching through time and space searching for him." Reynard extended his hand to the covered artwork. "What no one knew is that his pupil and soulmate, Anne, painted Tavarro."

Ahmed removed the cloth, revealing a portrait of a man standing in a dark forest. The subject's face was a mask of need as he, too, reached desperately for something in the distance.

"This one is called *Someone*. Together, they are one work of art: *Someone, Somewhere*. Do you see the marks on the frame of Tavarro's painting? It connects to the frame of its mate." Reynard nodded to Ahmed, who attached the wooden hinges and joined the two paintings.

Clara stared at the work of art. Perhaps it was the light or the angle. The woman's face seemed to change. The expression Clara had thought was pain or longing—it was rapture.

Miles stepped beside Clara and slipped his hand in hers. "Anne's has words written at the bottom, too."

Reynard spoke softly. "Read it, darling."

Clara read what Anne had written.

"My life, my breath
On the shores of my soul
Of our eternal love
Pure peace, in your arms"

"Together, they make the complete poem," Reynard said.

Miles read,

"My life, my breath, away from the world beneath the arching cliffs
On the shores of my soul, in the blood-red sage beside the river
Of our unending love, I find the riches all men seek but rarely find
Pure peace, in your arms, beneath the laden vines."

Clara swiped at a tear. "Love is the treasure."

"*Exactement, ma fille*. We have reunited the lovers. One day, I will see my Annette again. As I near the end of my life," Reynard held up a hand to quell Clara's protest. "I realize *that*," he swept his hand to the art. "Is the only thing that matters."

Wearing his rarely used prosthetic, Reynard stood, leaning heavily on his cane as he walked to Clara and tucked a lock of hair behind her ear. "You showed me that, *mon ange*. I wanted to give that to you in return."

"You're giving me the painting?" she asked.

Reynard tipped his lips in an indulgent smile as he touched Miles and Clara's clasped hands. "I wanted to give you love."

"Thank you," Miles said.

The trio stood back and admired the diptych. Two hands reaching out, touching behind the frame. Together at last for eternity.

CHAPTER SIXTY-TWO

Dordogne, France
November 5

After a quiet dinner at the kitchen table, Miles found Reynard on the terrace. Unfolding the cashmere throw, he spread it over Reynard's lap. "There's a chill tonight."

"I barely remember autumn. Now winter is here. It goes fast, my son."

Miles turned a patio chair and sat beside his old friend. "I have something to ask you."

Reynard smiled, his eyes fixed on something in the distance. "I was hoping."

"She's mine, Reynard. She always had been. I'm going to marry Clara. I'd like your blessing."

Reynard turned his wheelchair slightly and met Miles's gaze. "I've known it for so long and waited patiently for your paths to merge. You were so far apart at the beginning. Now you walk side by side."

"Yes," Miles replied. "We do."

Reynard coughed as he chuckled. "I don't know that a blessing from an old crook means much."

Miles squeezed the old man's forearm. "It means everything. To both of us."

Reynard patted his hand. "You'll protect her."

It wasn't a question, but Miles answered just the same. "With my life."

"You have my blessing and my love." Reynard turned the chair and moved to the doors. "You two are the best of me. It has truly been my honor."

Two days later, Reynard died peacefully with Clara and Miles at his bedside.

CHAPTER SIXTY-THREE

New York City
November 11

Miles and Clara stood at the fireplace mantel and admired their acquisition. *Someone, Somewhere* hung as it was meant to be, both pieces together, complete.

Suddenly, Miles felt a wave of dizziness settle over him, and he leaned on Clara for support.

"What's wrong?"

He didn't know how he knew, but Miles was sure. "Something's wrong with Tox."

Clara joined him on the couch as Miles called his brother. Tox answered on the first ring. "We're on our way to the hospital. Calliope's water broke."

Miles did the mental math. "She's five weeks early?"

Tox's strained voice broke, "Six. It's too soon, Mi."

Miles didn't realize his hands were shaking until Clara clasped his free one. He said, "It's going to be okay, Mil."

"I don't know if it is."

"Miller," Miles instructed. "Focus on your wife. Drive. Breathe. I'm on my way."

314

"Thanks, Mi."

"See you in a couple hours."

The waiting room was packed with Bishop Security people, and another crack in Miles's heart mended at the show of love and support. Nathan greeted them with a hug.

"The doctor came in about an hour ago and said it was going to be quick. Of course, quick in childbirth terms could mean anything."

"How's my brother?"

"Scared."

Chat joined them at the door. "He needs you, Miles."

Clara squeezed his hand. "Go."

Miles walked into the labor and delivery ward and headed for the nurse's station just as a door to a room opened, and two nurses pushed a contraption out of the room with his twin on their heels. Tox looked over his shoulder, saw Miles, and, after speaking to the nurse, changed direction. He jogged over and lifted Miles off his feet in a bear hug.

"She's born, Mi. She's here."

"Is she—" Miles didn't know how to ask.

"Four pounds two ounces. She's in an incubator. Doc thinks a week. They need to make sure her lungs are developed, and she's digesting food, but Doctor Webber thinks she looks good for an early arrival."

"Calliope?"

"She's a queen. I better get back in there."

Tox staggered to the wall and slid down the the floor. Miles sat beside him.

"You have a daughter."

"I've never been so scared in my fucking life."

"I know."

The twins leaned together, shoulder-to-shoulder. Tox said, "I'm so fucking glad you're here."

"You better watch the F-bombs. You're a father now."

"Our dad would have been the best grandfather," Tox said.

"Yeah. We'll have to tell her all about him—and mom, too."

Tox nodded into his chest. Together, they sat and embraced the bitter-sweet moment.

Miles squeezed his twin's shoulder. "Good thing she has about a hundred surrogate aunts and uncles."

Tox blew out a breath. "I'm okay now."

"Good."

"Let me check on Cal, and we can go down to the NICU, and you can meet her."

Miles stood and pulled his brother up. "Hey, what's my niece's name?"

"Jane."

Miles swallowed thickly. "After Mom."

"Yeah." Tox smiled.

Miles pulled his twin into a tight hug. "I love it."

EPILOGUE

The Fifth Avenue jewelry store was dark. Miles sat at the pedestal table in the center of the room and sipped his wine. He was moments away from the most important event of his life—and that was saying something after the past few months.

Lucien Kite was dead. Raphael Garza had been arrested for the murder; he escaped custody and disappeared. Despite his frustration that Garza had slipped away, Miles smiled. He could only imagine the look on Garza's face when he opened the little black book Miles had swapped out in the hallway of Kite's house. Miles had filled the pages with random numbers and, at the end, a smiley face. Nathan had turned Kite's real little black book over to the feds.

Chug Ugentti had vanished. Miles knew he would never be found. In an ironic twist, Chug had created an alibi for himself for that night at the warehouse. He had planned on killing Miles and needed to cover his tracks. So Ugentti had made a big show of checking into an Atlantic City casino for a campaign event before sneaking out to the warehouse. As a result, law enforcement had focused their investigation on the casino. Unsurprisingly, they had no leads.

Miles had closed out all of Caleb Cain's business and would begin his new job running the Bishop Security New York office in two weeks. His life was starting anew, and tonight, he planned to kick it off with a bang.

Miles checked the time, his outward calm belying his inner nerves. Where was she?

Tapping the comm device in his ear, Miles said, "Anything?"

From his position on the roof across the street, Steady replied, "Negative."

Maybe she wouldn't come. Miles had spent a month dropping breadcrumbs—a necklace taken from the Palace of Versailles during the French Revolution to be used to fund the new government. Instead, it was stolen by a traitor and smuggled out of the country. A century later, the necklace reappeared around the throat of a drug lord's mistress, only to vanish again. The jewels resurfaced last year in a collection of a British royal who had taken great pains to falsify the item's provenance.

After a brief stop at this renowned jeweler for appraisal and cleaning, the necklace would be auctioned tomorrow. Coincidentally, the store's alarms would be briefly disabled for routine maintenance.

The fictional story ticked every box to be a target for Clara. She just needed to take the bait.

His twin's voice came over the comm. "Mi, it's the walking dead out here. I don't think she fell for it."

Miles sighed. "Let's give it a few more minutes, but you're right. If she isn't here by now, she's missed the window."

At the back of the room, a lock clicked.

"She's here."

Tox whispered, "How the fuck did she get past four SEALs?"

"She's The Lynx," Miles replied.

The door to the back room opened, and a shadow moved across the black and white parquet floor. Miles had doctored an image of the storefront window where the necklace was proudly displayed. Clara moved silently in that direction.

With a tap to the comm to signal Twitch, the elegant chandeliers lit one by one. Clara froze at the side of the room, those blue eyes piercing through her mask. When she spotted Miles sitting at the table, he lifted his glass. "Care for some wine, Bluebird?"

Clara pulled off the mask with a puzzled smile. "What's going on?"

"What does the countdown timer on your watch say?"

Clara glanced at her wrist. "Three minutes and twenty-three seconds."

"Then we'd better hurry. Come. Sit."

Clara complied. "There's no necklace, is there?" She eyed the covered dish before her. "And there is definitely no food because I would have smelled it."

"Clever girl. Lift it."

Clasping the silver handle, Clara lifted the dome, revealing an open velvet box. Perched inside was a three-carat, cushion-cut diamond ring. The cloche hit the floor with a clank.

"Quiet, Bluebird. We are breaking in after all."

She plucked the ring from the box and stared at it.

"It was our mom's," Miles said.

Clara looked up at Miles in a daze.

"Clara, will you marry me?"

"What?" she asked.

Miles would have laughed if he hadn't been so nervous. "Clara, we have about ninety seconds before all hell breaks loose."

"Eighty-one," his twin said over the comm.

"You want to marry me?"

"Of course, I want to marry you. How could I not?" He clasped her hand. "Clara, you taught me how to love again. I'm never letting you go, Bluebird."

Her stunned expression faded to one filled with so much love and joy, Miles could have burst. Clara tugged off her left glove and slipped on the ring. "I love you."

"I love you too. Now, answer the question."

"Of course, I'll marry you." She leaned over the table and kissed him. After checking her watch, Clara said, "And thirty seconds should be plenty of time to escape a locked jewelry store."

Miles hauled her over the marble table and onto his lap. "Yes, Bluebird, but *I'm* walking out the front door. You need to find your own way out. Meet me at the corner of 57th and Fifth. I have a suite at the Plaza, where I plan on doing some truly appalling things to my future wife."

Her lips were still touching his when she said, "See you there."

Miles pulled open the heavy front door, hearing it latch behind him as the locks and alarms re-engaged. Glancing through the window, he spotted Clara still sitting at the table, giving him a flirty wave.

One by one, the team joined Miles as he walked up Fifth Avenue in the gray pre-dawn. Tox emerged from the passenger door of the van parked out front and fell into step beside him. Twitch and Finn hopped out the back and followed. Nathan emerged from the building next door. Ren joined the group from a side street, and Steady and Chat jogged across Fifth Avenue to complete the phalanx. They walked in matched step, quiet and smiling. The sun was just peeking through the tall buildings as they walked at an unhurried pace to the corner...

...where Clara was waiting for them, beaming.

She ran to Miles and flew into his arms. His Bluebird. Life, long dormant, bloomed inside his heart, reaching for the sunlight surrounding him.

Clara whispered in his ear, "I bet there really is a necklace like that."

"There is indeed. You can steal it on our honeymoon. It'll be my wedding gift."

"But I'd want to return it," she said.

Miles held her close. "That's the gift."

Clara slid down his body with a grin, and they continued past the Pulitzer Fountain to the Plaza.

Life would never be dull with his Bluebird. Miles held Clara close, surrounded by his new family. They were a patchwork brotherhood of honor, love, and support. He had never felt so lucky.

Miles had finally found his way home.

ACKNOWLEDGMENTS

Thank you to everyone who helped make this book an adventure-filled, romantic romp! I couldn't have done it without the help of my wonderful French sister-in-law, Marie-Pierre Baldwin, editor and translator. My husband Richard has been a rock and an amazing sounding board. I'd especially like to thank my miraculous proofreader, Angela Howard, at Proof Positive Author Services. Her input was invaluable. I am also grateful to the whole crew at Gatekeeper Press, who have done a fantastic job creating my books. In what turned out to be an incredible stroke of luck, I had to find a new cover designer this go-round; I couldn't be more thrilled with how this one turned out. Krystal Penney is a true artist, and I feel so fortunate to have found her. Finally, thank you to the readers. There are so many books by indie authors out there; I am honored that you have chosen the Bishop Security series. Your reviews, support, and positive word of mouth have meant the world!

FALL IN LOVE WITH NATHAN AND EMILY IN THE FIRST BOOK IN THE BISHOP SECURITY SERIES, FALSE FRONT!

False Front (Bishop Security #1)
By Debbie Baldwin

PROLOGUE

Two Years Ago ...

Emma Porter looked bored. No surprise there. It was her standard expression—her failsafe. She, with some effort, avoided the imposing lighted mirror in front of her and kept her gaze on the screen of her phone. Her violet eyes, masked by colored contacts that turned them an unremarkable blue, glazed. It didn't help that the stylist was working his way around her head in a hypnotic rhythm, pulling long strands of honey-colored hair through his enormous round brush. He would have put her to sleep but for the incessant chatter. Sister, do you model? How has no one approached you before? Oh, they'd approached her. She gave her standard reply.

"Nope, just in school."

She checked her phone again. A text.

We're good for Jane Hotel. I talked to my buddy. Bouncer's name is Fernand. See you at 9!

The exclamation point annoyed her. You're a guy, she thought. Guys shouldn't use exclamation points when they text. She'd probably end up dumping him over it. She'd done it for less.

"Big night tonight? It's a crazy Thursday. Are you going to that thing at Tau?"

"No. Just meeting a friend for a drink."

A friend? She guessed he was a friend. She'd met him twice—no, three times; he'd kissed her on 58th Street before she got into a cab three nights ago: hence the big date.

"A friend, huh? Sounds like a date."

"Yeah," Emma sighed, "it's kind of a date."

"So, no one special? No BF?"

"Nope. No boyfriend. Just a date."

"Well, I imagine the boys are climbing through your window, gorgeous girl."

She wanted to say the last time a boy tried to climb in my window, security guards tackled him on the front lawn as a leashed German shepherd bared his teeth at his neck while Teddy Prescott cried that he was in my seventh-grade ceramics class, and he just wanted to ask me to a school dance. Instead, she buttoned her lip and checked her phone. Again.

"No, not so much."

"Well, my work here is done. What do you think?"

He ran his fingers up her scalp from her nape and pushed the mass of hair forward over her shoulders, admiring his handiwork. She managed as much enthusiasm as she could muster.

"Looks great. Thanks."

She grabbed her bag, left the cash and a generous tip—partly for the blowout, mostly for enduring her mood—and headed out.

The walk home was a short-ish hike. While Broadway up ahead was always jam-packed, the little Tribeca side street was surprisingly desolate. Scaffolds stood sentry, and crumpled newspapers blew across the road like urban tumbleweeds. Emma's footsteps clacked on the pavement, and her shopping bags swished against her legs. In the waning daylight, the long shadows reached out. Emma moved with purpose but not haste, running through the plan for the evening in her head. Across the street, a pair of lurking teens stopped talking to watch her. The jarring slam of a Dumpster lid and the beep, beep, beep of a reversing trash truck echoed across the pavement. Near the end of the block, a homeless man in a recessed doorway muttered about a coming plague and God setting the world to rights. Emma forced herself to keep her pace even but couldn't stifle her sigh of relief as she rounded the corner and joined the hordes. A businessman let out a noise of irritation as Emma forced him to slow his pace when she merged into the foot traffic. Yes, this was better. She hurried up Broadway and headed for home.

Spring Street was insane. The stores ran the gamut from A-list designer shops to dive bars and bodegas. Beneath the display window of Alexander Woo, a ratty hipster strummed a guitar. In front of Balthazar, there was a hotdog vendor. The street was dotted with musicians and addicts and homeless and shoppers and tourists and construction crews and commuters and students. There was a French crêpe stand next to Emma's favorite Thai place that was next to an organic vegan café. It was like somebody took everything that made New York New York—the art, the diversity, the music, the food, the bustle, the noise—and jammed it all onto one street. The street Emma called home.

Outside her building, a group of guys from her Abnormal Psychology class was coming out of the corner bodega.

"Hey IQ, what's up tonight? Heading downtown?"

"Maybe."

"Martin's parents' brownstone is on Waverly. Party's on!"

"Okay, I'll try to stop by."

"Cool."

The guys in her class had started calling her "IQ" freshman year. She was flattered at first, thinking it bore some reference to her intellect. A few months in, she discovered it was short for "Ice Queen." That was fine with her too. Whatever.

Her elegant but inconspicuous building sat just down from Mother's Ruin, her favorite pub, and next to a heavily graffitied retail space for rent. She waved to her doorman, who rushed to help her with her bags. "Hey, Ms. Porter. Shopping, I see."

"Hey, Jimmy. Yeah, just a few odds and ends."

He glanced at the orange Hermes shopping bag and raised an eyebrow but didn't comment.

"You want me to take these up?"

"Yes, please, Jimmy." She handed over the bags and pushed through the heavy door to the stairs, while Jimmy summoned the elevator.

As she climbed the seven flights, Emma felt pretty calm. It was just a date. People had them all the time. Normal people had them all the time. She was normal. Well, she was getting there, and this outing tonight was proof of that. She had met a cute guy. She liked him well enough, and he was taking her out. She was excited about it; well, the progress more than the date. Another box to check on the list. She could crow about it to her therapist next week. The guy, Tom, seemed excited too, based on the aforementioned errant exclamation point. That, and the fact that she had actually heard him high-five a guy over the phone when she'd said yes.

Her bags were waiting by the door when she emerged from the seventh-floor landing. She fumbled with her key and pushed the door open with her butt as she scooped her purchases from the hallway floor. As she walked into the small but tasteful apartment—well, huge and elegant by college standards but certainly low key for Emma—she was greeted by a squeal and then the vaguely familiar strains of Rod Stewart's classic, "Tonight's the Night," so off-key it was barely recognizable.

"Jeez, Caroline, could you take it down a notch?"

"Nope. Can't. Sorry."

Caroline Fitzhugh had been Emma's best friend since before they were born. That wasn't an exaggeration. Their mothers had grown up together, had married men who were themselves best friends, and were neighbors in Georgetown as newlyweds. The women were inseparable until Emma's mother crossed the line separating "life of the party" from "addict." Their pregnancies were well-timed. It gave the two women a chance to rekindle their friendship, and it gave Emma's mother a fleeting chance at sobriety. Their moms spent their pregnancies together, nearly every day for the nine months leading up to the girls' arrival.

Well, seven months and three weeks—Caroline was always in a rush to get places. After that, Emma's family moved to Connecticut, Caroline's to Georgia, and the girls saw each other on holidays and trips. Caroline knew Emma before. Before what one of her shrinks had euphemistically referred to as "the event." Before she was Emma Porter. Before she was from a small town near Atlanta. Before. Caroline was one of a handful of people with that knowledge. She knew Emma, and she protected her with a ferocity that rivaled Emma's father. Tonight, however, was a different story. Tonight, Caroline was pushing her out of the nest. It's time, she had said.

Caroline popped a bottle of Veuve Clicquot way too expensive for pre-gaming, declaring a dispensation on Emma's father's strict alcohol ban, and poured them each a glass.

"One glass, Em, to loosen up."

Emma answered her with a sip.

"Go get dressed. The LBD awaits."

The "little black dress" to which she referred was the Versace black crepe safety pin dress. It was the sexiest thing either of them had ever seen. The sleeveless dress hit Emma mid-thigh and was accented with mismatched gold safety pins at the waist and hip. Caroline had bought it for Emma on her credit card to avoid any questions from her father. He was generous to a fault, but anything remotely provocative was frowned upon. Emma garnered enough attention as it was, and a sexy dress only upped the ante. Now the dress was laying on her bed next to a pair of strappy sky-high heels and a small box holding a pair of diamond hoops. The outfit for the virgin sacrifice. She laughed to herself, then stopped abruptly, surprised by the term her thoughts had conjured: virgin. It was a word she never used because it had no meaning for her. She hated the word because the status of one's virginity was inextricably linked to one's past, and she couldn't dwell on what she didn't know. Therapists encouraged her to embrace a term that expressed her "emotional virginity," but Emma never could think of one. Her shrink was not amused when she suggested "vaginal beginner" and "hymenal newbie," so they let it slide. She could be an actual virgin after all. The point was that it shouldn't matter, and if everything went according to plan, after tonight it wouldn't. She could pop her emotional and/ or physical cherry and move on. At this point, she just wanted to get the damn thing over with.

They had hours before she had to meet Tom. JT, her driver and body-guard, usually accompanied her out in the evening, but Caroline told him they were heading to a study group at a friend's in the same building, so he had the night off. She was on her own, and she was thrilled. Caroline pulled up the zipper on the dress and bounced around to Katy Perry, while Emma sipped tentatively on the same glass of bubbly. "Oh Jeez, Em, just drink it. One glass won't have you cross-eyed. It'll calm your nerves."

She was right. Emma was nervous. For obvious reasons.

Emma left Caroline at Mother's, their local bar, with some friends and ordered an Uber to head to the Jane Hotel. As Tom had said, the bouncer, Fernand, was expecting her. Not that she would have had any trouble getting in anyway—she never did—but that dress was like a VIP pass. The group of people waiting gave a resigned sigh almost collectively as Emma deftly moved past them and entered the elegant bar.

Tom had a table he was guarding with his life, and she made a beeline for him. When a guy at the bar grabbed her arm as she passed, not hard, just enough to stop her, Emma paused, stared at the hand on her bicep, and then slowly looked up at him with a perfected impassive glare. Ice Queen indeed. He released her without a word, and she dropped into the seat across from Tom.

"Hey, Gorgeous. You look amazing."

"Thanks."

"I didn't know what you like, so I ordered you a white wine."

She rarely drank. Well, that wasn't entirely true. She drank in one of her self-defense classes. Jay, her instructor, had insisted that she know how to do some of the moves "impaired," as he put it, so he'd fed her three beers and then had her train on the mat. She'd thrown up all over him. The wine did relax her, and they chatted effortlessly. It took Emma nearly an hour to polish off the drink, and when she returned from the ladies' room with a fresh coat of lip gloss, a second glass sat waiting.

What the hell. It was a big night.

It took her exactly four sips and ten minutes to realize what was happening.

Emma wasn't normal. Her father, in an extreme effort to get control of their world, made sure of that, and at this moment, she was thankful for it. Most girls would think the subtle blur of vision and the slight wave of nausea were due to nerves or too many drinks. But she knew exactly what was happening. She reached into her purse and texted her panic word, "lighthouse," to JT, but he was off duty. It could take him hours. She took a calming breath, keeping her heart rate as low as she could in her panic.

"I'll be right back. I think I left my lip gloss in the bathroom."

"I'll go with you. You look pale."

"No, no, I'm fine. Just dizzy from the wine, I guess. I'm a lightweight."

She forced a giggle. That appeased him. He didn't know she knew.

"Okay, I'll be waiting."

"Be right back," she repeated.

Emma took deliberate steps. When she glanced over her shoulder, she saw Tom throw some cash on the table and pull a key card from his breast pocket. She needed to focus on making her way down the hall. She couldn't get help in the bar; a stumbling, slurring girl in a bar would only bolster Tom's ruse. There was an elevator at the end, but as she made her way toward it, she stumbled and realized that it was exactly where Tom wanted her. She needed help or a hiding place, and she needed it fast. Whatever he had slipped in her drink was strong.

The symptoms were hitting her fast. She moved down to a janitor's closet. Locked. She started moving frantically hand over hand, keeping her balance on the wall, avoiding looking at the nauseating pattern of the wallpaper as it started to blur. Tom's footsteps were heavy behind her as he closed in. She got to another door, pushed it open, and stumbled into the room. A group of surprised suits looked up as she blinked at them with terrified eyes. The man at the head of the table stood.

"Jesus, are you all right?"

"No. Help."

She heard the man closest to her mutter, "she's wasted." The man at the head of the table moved like a flash. He was coming toward her, and she was losing her ability to discern whether she had put herself in more danger by stumbling into this room. He seemed to float toward her, and Emma started to shake.

"Not drunk. Drunk," she slurred. "Drugged," she amended. "Help."

"Jesus." He put his hands on her shoulders, and she instantly calmed. Emma tried to shake the fog out of her head, but it only got worse. When she looked up, she saw three of him. So, she looked straight ahead at his tie. A cornflower blue tie that hung between the open sides of his dark suit jacket. She grabbed it with both hands, crunching it in her fists. She tried to remember her training, but all that came out was a plea.

"Please."

He put his arm around her protectively and calmly spoke.

"It's okay. I've got you."

And with that soothing notion, she passed out in his arms, still clutching his cornflower blue tie.

Emma woke up nineteen hours later in a hospital room that looked like a suite at the Ritz. JT was standing at the side of the bed like a royal guard, a pissed-off royal guard. He felt responsible for her indiscretion; she could feel his anger and guilt. Her father dozed, ashen, in an upholstered leather arm-chair. The night was a bit of a blur, and she ran through a timeline in her head to catch up. She had as much of it recalled as she probably ever would. Other than the mother of all headaches, she was otherwise uninjured. When she lifted her arm, the one without the IV, to move an itchy strand of hair from her face, the final few moments before she blacked out came flooding back. There, in her hand, was the cornflower blue tie, still knotted, with the length of it dangling down her forearm. It was wrapped around her palm and knuckles. JT informed her with a perplexed smirk that the nurses gave up trying to pry it from her, and the man, who had not given anyone his name, had ended up pulling it over his head and wrapping it around her hand as they wheeled her away on a gurney. Completely unconscious, she had refused to let the thing go.

READ TOX AND CALLIOPE'S THRILLING LOVE STORY IN ILLICIT INTENT.

Illicit Intent (Bishop Security #2)

By Debbie Baldwin

CHAPTER THREE

New York City
April 16

Come on, come on, come on. Calliope Garland willed the indicator bar on the monitor displaying the percentage of download completion to move faster. *Fourteen percent, twenty-seven percent.* Then it seemed to stop at thirty-two percent as if it were deciding whether to continue. She rubbed the side of the CPU, encouraging the beast to comply. She checked the time on her phone: 10:17 p.m. The slick, suited brokers and analysts had abandoned their laptops and balance sheets for dirty martinis—and other pastimes with "dirty" as the descriptor—at a chic nearby nightspot *Stock* around the corner. The offices of Gentrify Capital Partners that occupied the top two floors of the Financial District tower were all but abandoned. The low hum of a vacuum cleaner down the hall and the faint voice of a newbie client-retention specialist trying to earn his stripes were all that remained. No one should interrupt her.

Her little undercover assignment was proceeding seamlessly. Farrell Whitaker, her boss at the news site where she worked, *The Harlem Sentry*, smelled a rat at this prosperous asset management firm, so he sent her in to investigate. She arranged to be hired as a part-time receptionist through a temp agency and had worked at the front desk for two weeks when she caught her target's eye. Calliope's editor had then arranged for the target's personal assistant to get wind of a massive federal investigation in the offing, and the woman had quit without notice. Badda bing, badda boom, Calliope was in.

Gentrify Capital Partners was housed in a soaring monolith at the bottom of Manhattan. The office was a shrine to eighties' financial corruption. From the sky-lighted two-story reception area to the interchangeable supermodel receptionists to the boys club of Ivy League analysts, the place was a throwback. It was as if the man who created it, Philip "Phipps" Van Gent, had developed his fantasy business model during the era of Ivan Boesky and Michael Miliken, and had duplicated that world without update.

Calliope had worked at *The Sentry* for nearly two years, longer than any of the other dilettante jobs she'd had over the past six years. She actually liked it, but it would soon be time to move on. Where would she go next? Maybe a nanny in London or an aid worker in Khartoum. She shook herself out of her revelry. First, she needed to make sure she didn't end her career as an investigative reporter with a literal bang.

At the moment, she was sitting at Phipps Van Gent's desk—nothing out of the ordinary. He often called her from the road to retrieve some piece of information or update a spreadsheet. Other than the late hour, there was nothing suspicious about her presence. Furthermore, the minions seldom popped in to see the boisterous CEO, on the rare occasion he was in the office. Despite the fact that half of this floor was a private apartment, and his office alone was bigger than most Manhattan studios, the eccentric man spent most of his time at his estate in Greenwich or on his yacht, currently anchored in Palm Beach. No subtle, hidden-gem locations for Phipps Van Gent; he chose the most obvious ways to display his wealth.

Fifty-eight percent. Calliope glanced around Van Gent's inner sanctum. Other than the desktop computer she was currently breaking into and his rarely-used personal laptop sitting open on the desk—a pin-dot of light at the top of the screen—one would hardly suspect this was a place of business. She wouldn't describe the office as gaudy, more like an elite hodgepodge. It was as if the decorator, or more likely Van Gent himself, had selected the most expensive item in any given category and put it in the room. Calliope guessed his tactic: if a potential client knew art, he or she would be impressed by the Rothko over the fireplace or the Hopper behind his desk. If they knew antiques, the imposing Goddard and Townsend desk would elicit a response. It was the same with the Persian rug, Tiffany lamps, and the ego wall filled with photos of Phipps with Oscar winners, heads of state, professional athletes, and so on and so on. It was the very definition of conspicuous consumption.

Ninety-one percent. She rolled her eyes. She could afford any or all of these items in her own right but preferred the sparse interior of her Brooklyn brownstone, decorated with thrift store furniture, quirky accents, and street art. The photos she displayed were of people and places that *mattered* to her: Calliope with her mother playing in the sand on a beach in Corsica, her dog, Coco, looking at the camera lens as if it were edible, her mother and stepfather looking at each other as if no one else existed.

She had conducted dozens of these surreptitious fact-finding missions. Most were as simple as watching who came and went or copying shipping records or a calendar. Computer piracy was a little out of her league, but Farrell had a bee in his bonnet about this particular story. Based on the proudly displayed photos of her publisher *Occupying Wall Street* years ago she could guess why. Nevertheless, her role had always been observer, not filcher. She should simply be telling Farrell that the files existed, not duplicating them. She shuddered at the implications of this little theft. Some people in some very high places were going to be livid.

Download complete. Just as she sighed her relief and reached to snatch the little flash drive from the port, she noticed another document on Van

Gent's desktop. It was titled "Golf Scores," but the "S" in "Scores" was a dollar sign: "Golf $cores." She clicked on it, and a password prompt appeared. She checked under the keyboard—where Phipps had told her his login information was kept—and sure enough, there, on another Post-It, was a second password. She entered it and viola. The document consisted of a single-page spreadsheet listing a series of numbered codes Calliope couldn't interpret.

Her computer genius friend immediately came to mind. *Twitch will know what this is.* Then, as if Calliope had conjured her, the disposable cell phone in her pocket buzzed.

"How did you get this number?"

"Please." Calliope could hear the mischief in her friend's voice. "How goes the wet work?"

"Nerve-racking."

"Oh, take a picture of his desk photos. Be interesting to see who's in Van Gent's inner circle. It'll take the Feds forever to get a warrant for that office."

Calliope turned back to the monitor and extended her hand to snap a picture of the cluster of framed photos on Van Gent's desk when a device mounted on the side of the screen started beeping.

"Shit. I'm setting off the cell phone detector on the monitor. I gotta go."

Calliope cut Twitch off mid-protest, pushed back in the chair to stay out of range of the device, and snapped the picture. Then she tossed the disposable phone into her purse and returned to the mysterious "Golf $cores" document.

When she tried to drag the document to her flash drive folder an ugly noise sounded and an additional password prompt appeared. She re-entered the second password, and the evil wonk sounded again. Double-checking the letters and numbers, she retried it and was denied a second time. In a final attempt, she entered the original login password. At the third failed attempt, a box appeared in the center of the monitor: *initiating security protocol.*

Now she was sweating. A countdown clock in the corner of the monitor was ticking down from five. Four...Three... At zero the screen went momentarily blank. *Was that the distant bing of the elevator's arrival?* No way was this going unnoticed. She imagined a tiny room with an IT tech sitting at a desk filled with monitors and drinking coffee from a Styrofoam cup while alarms clanged and red lights flashed, signaling the breach. Who knew? Phipps was a strange guy. At this very moment, his wall safe sat open above the credenza. She could see stacks of cash and documents. Honestly, if she took several thousand dollars and left a note on the safe door, she didn't think Phipps would care. It wasn't that money didn't matter to him, it was more like money wasn't real.

Calliope shook away the thought and returned to her task. Something bad was happening, something very, *very* bad. A progress bar appeared in the middle of the screen. Below it, commands flashed: *removing files, wiping backup server, clearing logs.* With each notification, a new progress bar would start and run up to 100%. Calliope didn't know much about computers, and she certainly didn't know if touching something would improve or exacerbate the situation, so she sat there and watched until the screen went dark and an ominous message appeared in the center of the monitor: *security protocol complete.* All the more reason to skedaddle. Just as she was reaching down to extract the flash drive, the imposing double doors to Phipps's office flew open with such force the knobs put a dent in the drywall.

Boof. Ten blocks north of Gentrify Capital, Miller "Tox" Buchanan was in the basement security room of a Chinatown office building. He was being held by two men and beaten by a third. The punch was nothing, but Tox needed to make this look good. A series of jabs and he stifled a yawn. Qi was maybe five-five, a full foot shorter than Tox, but he was well-built. Nevertheless, the blows were about the same force his buddies nailed him with when he told a bad joke. He just needed to keep these guys busy until his partner, Steady, got the cameras and bugs planted.

Their client's son had been abducted two days earlier by her estranged husband. She came directly to Bishop Security for help. The security company was an offshoot of defense contractor Knightsgrove-Bishop. Heir apparent, Nathan Bishop, had eschewed the CEO position in favor of running this humble branch. Bishop Security took a variety of national and international jobs—bodyguard to black ops—but the team's pride was The Perseus Project. Born of ghosts haunting Nathan Bishop after his childhood friend, now wife, Emily Webster Bishop, had been abducted, The Perseus Project worked to rescue victims of kidnapping. They rarely charged money, and they never received recognition.

This was exactly the type of case for which Perseus was created. The missing boy's father was a powerful man with connections to organized crime and enough money to buy silence. The good guys needed to break into his Manhattan offices, plant the cameras and bugs, put a trace on his technology, and have a quick look around; some damning evidence would be a useful deterrent to repeat attempts to abduct the child in the future.

Tox had the easy job: distract the security guys with a little poker—and a little cheating—until exactly 11 pm. To be fair, Tox didn't have to get caught cheating, but this beating was far less painful than listening to these jackasses' incessant chatter.

"You think this is funny, you fucking giant?" Qi's face was red with exertion.

Tox shrugged. He must not have been as good an actor as he thought. Qi shouted something over his shoulder in clipped Mandarin. A moment later Tox thought he felt the floor rumble. He was pretty sure he was imagining the *Jaws* theme. Then a man appeared in the doorway. The mammoth was nearly as wide as he was tall. This beating was about to take a bad turn.

"Hey, Qi, do you have the time?" Tox asked.

"Ten-forty-three. Why? You in a hurry?" The men holding Tox chuckled.

Shit. He had to kill seventeen minutes. Well, he knew he couldn't survive seventeen minutes of being beaten by this rhino. He could, however, survive seventeen minutes of being *chased* by him. In a vintage *Three Stooges* move, Tox engaged his massive biceps and pulled together the two guys holding his arms, then pushed them into Shamu. Qi pulled a Glock, but Tox quickly nailed him with a combat-booted foot to the chest, sending Qi flying back into the surveillance equipment, disrupting the feed. At least his partner could finish up undetected. *You're welcome, Steady.* A gunshot rent the air. Apparently, Gigantor realized he wouldn't be able to catch Tox if he ran. At six-five and two-thirty, Tox was by no means nimble, but his opponent had to weigh in at over four bills. The Ruger semi-automatic acted as an ersatz starter's pistol, and Tox bolted for the street.

The shout was even louder than the bang of the door, and the last vestiges of Calliope's composure dissolved. She flew to her feet, a flimsy excuse on her lips.

"Who's the luckiest bastard on the fucking planet?!!!"

Calliope didn't think Phipps Van Gent was expecting a response, and when she didn't reply, he continued.

"I am, Cathy." He hadn't bothered to learn her name. Cathy was the name of his former assistant. "I just won two hundred thousand dollars on one hand of poker." When her eyes widened, Phipps smiled with glib satisfaction. "Wanna know how?"

Calliope glanced briefly at the flash drive still sticking out of the computer and nodded.

Phipps stumbled and expelled an alcohol-tinged huff of air. He righted himself and, with the deliberate care of a drunk, tried to make the hand he used for support on the desk look casual rather than essential. "Because everyone fucking bluffs." He seemed to contemplate propping one hip on the desk, then reconsidered and flopped down on the taupe suede couch. He continued with his head on the butter-soft arm and his Gucci loafers propped up.

"I'm in a penthouse at the Wynn courting this whale. He's supposedly some totally infamous mobster, but he's worth a quarter of a billion, and he's looking for an asset manager. Money's money. It's all dirty, so what the fuck?"

He was talking to the ceiling now, and Calliope wondered if he realized she was still in the room. "I chased him around for two straight days. I finally landed him and got an invite to this high-limit poker game in his suite. The guy provided everything: coke, whores, cards, booze. Everything but sleep," he chuckled. "So the last hand, every asshole in the room wants to show how big his dick is, but I know I've got it. Not the dick stuff cause mine's nothing to write home about, but my hand of cards is something for the record books."

Calliope thought that her editor really might be onto something when he voiced his suspicion that Phipps Van Gent was a con artist running a Ponzi scheme. Phipps sounded more like a street thug than American ex-pat and the product of Cambridge and the London School of Economics that he claimed to be.

"It's hold 'em. I get dealt two fours down. The flop is a four, a four, and a nine. Right off the fucking bat, I've got four of a kind. *Four of a kind*, Cathy. Do you even get how rare that is? The odds of it…well, it's insanely rare, like Powerball rare."

He seemed satisfied he had made his point and continued the story. "The turn is a jack. I don't even remember the river because who the fuck cares? So I'm guessing someone at the table has a full boat, maybe a flush. Or they're all fucking bluffing. Doesn't matter. Lil' ol' me is sitting back and watching with four of a kind. Oh, it gets better. This other fucker, high as a kite, is out of cash, claims his credit card has some kind of travel block so he can't transfer funds, so he sends a guy to his room and comes back with this little tube and tosses it onto the table."

Phipps felt around in his carry-on bag to retrieve it, but it slipped from his grip and rolled across the rug out of reach. Calliope watched it roll. It was white and capped and only about twice as large, in both diameter and length, as the center tube in a roll of paper towels. Phipps extended his hand in a grabbing motion like a toddler asking for an out-of-reach toy, then abandoned his effort and continued. "Says what's in the tube will cover the bet."

He half-gestured toward the bar. "Pour me a scotch, Cath." Apparently, now they were on a wrong *nickname* basis rather than a wrong *first-name* basis. Calliope pushed back to stand and quickly snatched the flash drive, dropping it into her messenger bag that sat open on the floor. She fetched his drink, so nervous she didn't realize Phipps was still talking..."So I flip my hand and the guy, he shoots up from the table like a bull ready to charge. Then he drops dead.

"One of the hired goons starts doing CPR, and that's it for me. Anyway, glad I got cash from the other saps because the painting in that tube isn't worth shit."

With great effort, he sat upright, retrieved the tube with his foot, and popped off the cap. He upended it, and a small rolled canvas slid out. He unrolled it on the coffee table and weighted the edges with magazines. "It's a reproduction of a Titian called *The Thief's Redemption*. It's the schmuck on the cross next to Jesus. The original is in Barcelona. I Googled it. This isn't even the right size."

He reclined again, yawned, and closed his eyes. "Certainly a fitting title, because I got robbed." He chortled. "*The Thief's Redemption*." The scotch, perched precariously on the ridge of his gut, splashed in the glass. "Have my gal look at it on Monday. Could be it's something else, but I doubt it. Maybe I'll frame it and hang it at home. A memento of the one time Phipps Van Gent got taken."

He tossed the plastic tube that held the painting in the direction of the small trash can and yawned. "I don't mind losing money, but I do mind losing," he grumbled. She started to ask if he even wanted her to have the painting examined, but he was already snoring softly.

Calliope plucked the tube off the floor. With the intention of putting it in the recycling bin, she shoved it into her bag and headed for the door. She glanced over her shoulder at Phipps passed out on the couch—one hand in his pants, one still holding his scotch—and bolted for the elevator. She almost laughed at the fact that she hadn't uttered one word the entire time Phipps was there.

The ding of the elevator's arrival before she had summoned it surprised her. She thought about ducking around the corner into a vacant conference room but decided against it. She had every reason to be here and nothing to hide—well, stolen files aside. When the doors parted, Calliope studied the occupant. A late-night client meeting was par for the course at Gentrify; Phipps would meet a prospective client any time, anywhere—as evidenced by his recent junket.

The elevator doors slid open. The man in the car was handsome if non-descript. He reminded her of one of those spit-polished stars from the fifties movies her mom loved to watch. Although with his dark eyes, black hair graying at the temples, trimmed beard, and smartly tailored suit, this guy would be the villain. He brushed by her without so much as a glance, his Aquatalia boots silent on the terrazzo. As she entered the elevator and hit the button for the lobby, she noticed him pause, like an animal catching a scent, and while the doors closed she briefly glimpsed him resume his pace. *That will be a short client meeting.* She rolled her eyes and imagined that pristine man trying to rouse a passed-out Phipps.

Just as the car began its swift descent, a deafening blast met her ears, then a second, quieter with the distance the elevator car had gained. *Were those gunshots?* Surely not. There was no one on her floor except for a comatose Phipps and the suited man she had just seen standing in the middle of the expansive office floor. Unless he was shooting computer terminals with some hidden cannon, he couldn't have been the source. She was in that weird, paranoid panic mode, and the reminder of the late-night client and Phipps kept her blood racing. Once at the lobby, Calliope sprinted toward the security door. The guard watched her swipe her security pass to release the lock, then returned his gaze to the Islanders game playing on one of the monitors. She sprinted out into the New York night. And ran smack into a brick wall.

Tox looked over his shoulder and chuckled at the lug huffing and puffing behind him. He rounded a corner and barely broke stride when a black-haired butterfly of a girl smacked into him and landed on her bum on the sidewalk, the contents of her messenger bag scattering everywhere. Tox was about to sidestep her to fend for herself—man with a gun in pursuit and all—when he saw her sky-blue eyes and startled face. Her stunning, startled face.

"Calliope?"

"Tox?"

"No time. Let's go."

In her irrational panic, Calliope grabbed her bag from the bottom, upending it further. Her work phone smacked the pavement and shattered. She scrambled for the flash drive, the cylinder, the ruined phone, and the various odds and ends littering the sidewalk while Tox grabbed her around the waist and heaved her toward the open rear door of the black SUV that had screeched to a stop at the curb next to them.

"Need a lift?" Steady smiled from the passenger seat.

Tox grinned. "We could probably walk. That fucker's big as a glacier and twice as slow."

"Not his bullets, dipshit. Let's move."

As if to prove Steady's point, a bullet pinged off the armored tailgate. Calliope glanced over her shoulder to see an absolute elephant of a man with a gun. The man put his hands on his knees and heaved for air as their car rounded a corner and sped to safety.

Calliope had met Miller "Tox" Buchanan twice. The first time was on a street corner in SoHo when he gave her her dog. He had been bigger then. She remembered wondering if he was an NFL player or a bodyguard. It wasn't his size that struck her, though; it was his energy. He was this odd combination of arrogant asshole and teddy bear. Despite his obvious disinterest when he looked at her, she felt inexplicably drawn to him—like she could slip into the space under his arm and they could continue on down the sidewalk. She was hit with this overwhelming desire to peel the onion to discover what made Tox Buchanan tick. She'd also realized she had an overwhelming desire to peel the layers of his clothes off, so she quickly diverted her attention to the dog at his side before she started acting on any of those urges. She had scratched behind the pup's ears and rubbed her back, all the while repeating to herself, *don't gawk at the beautiful man, do not gawk at the beautiful man.*

And so, in an effort to ignore the gorgeous animal at one end of the leash, she had adopted the gorgeous animal on the other, Coco. Well, when Tox was fostering her, the dog's name had been Fraidy, short for Fraidy Cat. The rottweiler had been "fired" from her job guarding a warehouse because she was too friendly; she had actually been painted with graffiti by vandals as they defaced the building. When Calliope took the beautiful dog off his hands, her first order of business had been to change her name to something less demeaning: Coco Chanel.

Coco rarely left Calliope's side. She came to work with her at *The Harlem Sentry*, accompanied her on errands, and followed her around her cavernous Brooklyn Heights brownstone like she couldn't bear to have Calliope out of her sight. Her unwavering loyalty and undemanding presence were a balm in her chaotic life.

The second time Calliope had seen Tox was at the beachfront wedding of her coworker and friend, Emily Bishop. Calliope had brought her other work friend, Terrence, as her date. She needed the emotional support, and he wanted to ogle the mouthwatering military man meat—his words—who worked with Emily's new husband, Nathan Bishop. When the guys had invited Terrence to join them to "sugar cookie" a buddy, he hadn't asked questions, he had simply spun Calliope into the arms of Tox and scrambled off the dance floor after the men. Turned out, much to Terrence's dismay, that "sugar cookie-ing" someone simply meant throwing them in the ocean then rolling them around on the beach, coating them with sand. SEALs or not, boys will be boys.

Calliope was tall, nearly six feet in her four-inch heels, but when Terrence had twirled her into Tox, her forehead bumped his chin. She had struggled to find her footing as Tox steadied her. When she finally met his gaze, she saw something intriguing. He was smirking at first, like the cocksure jackass she assumed him to be, but then, as he held her gaze, the smirk had morphed into a sweet, almost vulnerable, crooked half-smile bracketed by dimples that melted her heart. His eyes reminded her of a dog's eyes, brown and glassy and longing. The attraction she felt wasn't sudden or jolting, like a spark or a zing; it was something indistinct and yet profound, like the force of the tide easing a ship into port. They'd stood still on the dance floor for a solid minute. Then, they both went stiff as boards and danced with the formality of middle-schoolers at a mandatory lesson. The phantom pain of the severed connection lingered, the sudden awareness of an ever-present absence, but Calliope refused to dwell on it.

Tox had revealed nothing about himself that day, and the reporter in her had been brimming with frustration, paradoxically adding to both his allure and his repulsion.

"Why do they call you Tox?"

"Long story."

"So, you were in the Navy with Nathan?"

"I work for him."

"Where are you from?"

"West of here." (They were on Nantucket. *Everywhere* in the U.S. was *west of here*.)

"Do you have family in the area?"

"So, Emily said you were from Greece or something?"

She had corrected him and then, for the rest of their dance, talked about herself in the same vague terms. When he thanked her and turned to reconvene with his friends at the bar, she stood on the dance floor with balled fists, feeling quite certain she had been, not manipulated per se, but maneuvered. When he glanced over his shoulder to meet her gaze, he winked, confirming her suspicions. She had refused to talk to him again the entire evening. And while her mouth was in full agreement, her eyes made no such promise. Calliope had to repeatedly scold herself for tracking his movements throughout the tent; she allowed herself a little leeway by rationalizing that he was so big, statistically, the chances that he would be in her line of sight were high. Right. Nevertheless, she had done what she could to ignore him.

Tonight she felt no such compunction.

Tox sat behind the driver, eyes forward. He was this remarkable combination of relaxed and focused, his body calm yet coiled. He had lost some muscle mass in the past year; he'd gone from "linebacker" to "running back," still strong and massive, but less…beefy. He also had been bald when she had danced with him that first time, but his dark hair was now a very short buzz cut; it was exactly the same length as the heavy stubble that covered his jaw.

Everything about him flipped her switch. He wasn't the kind of handsome that starred in movies or appeared in cologne ads; he had the kind of face an artist might sketch, *Primal Man* or *Man Restrained*; the portrait would definitely have "man" in the title.

His sable gaze met hers and startled her from her uncharacteristic musings. He didn't smile, didn't cock a brow. He simply looked at her, placid. A scar on his forehead bisected his right eyebrow, giving his kind face an edge. Maybe she should give him a month.

Calliope had never had a relationship that lasted longer than a month. It wasn't a hard and fast rule; it was just that she never seemed to stick around long enough to entertain the notion of permanence. *Tox though...* As quickly as she conjured the thought, she dismissed it. If the parts of his body she couldn't see were as compelling as the parts she could, she would have a problem—not necessarily leaving him, but finding the next guy to fill his battered boots. He'd be a hard act to follow. And if she understood on some level that she was rejecting the idea of involvement with him because he might be the guy to make her rethink things, she didn't acknowledge it.

"So, how's your day?" Tox asked the question with genuine interest as if he had just picked her up from a nine-to-five.

"Um, good?" Calliope had a million questions, but her reporter instincts had fled.

"Good. Mine too."

"What...I mean why...I mean, what was that all about?"

"Just a little dust-up over a poker game. All good."

"A little dust-up?" Calliope thought about the poker game from which Phipps had just come; probably not the same stakes.

The driver, a striking African American man they called Chat, stifled a chuckle. The guy in the passenger seat—she couldn't recall his name—checked GPS coordinates as they flew across the Brooklyn Bridge. A phone rang, echoing through the Bluetooth. Chat answered.

"Go Twitch. You're on speaker. Steady and Tox are here, and we picked up a passenger."

Steady. His name was Steady. Twitch was going to have a field day with this. For someone who saw the world in ones and zeros, she was shockingly romantic. Calliope could practically picture her sighing with her hands clasped under her chin. Having girlfriends was something of a foreign concept to Calliope. She was never in one place long enough to bond. Twitch and Emily Bishop had somehow wormed their way into Calliope's heart. At the moment, she was regretting the friendship.

"Hey, Twitch. It's Calliope. Tox bumped into me on the street, and the guys are giving me a ride."

Tox quirked a brow, pointing to himself and then her while mouthing, *I bumped into you?* Calliope ignored him.

The incessant click-clacking on Twitch's keyboard paused. "Interesting."

"Not interesting. The opposite of interesting. Mundane, in fact." *Stop talking.*

"Okay." Twitch resumed her typing with the trademark twinkle in her voice.

Twitch already knew most of it, but Calliope explained for the benefit of the men in the car.

"Farrell Whitaker, my crazy editor, has me pulling the threads on another of his conspiracy theories. He thinks Phipps Van Gent, the hedge fund billionaire, is up to something."

"Crazy like a fox," Twitch responded. "The Feds are on him like chrome on a bumper. Lots of chatter. I'd like to take a peek at what you discovered tonight."

Steady saved her from having to explain the computer nightmare.

"First things first, Twitch," he admonished.

"Right. Sorry. Got distracted. This one was almost too easy. No fun at all. The client's ex-husband has a nanny cam routed to his phone and laptop. The little boy is at the father's country house. Already got the location. Nathan's in town for a board meeting, so he's handling the extraction with Ren."

Calliope fingered the flash drive in the bottom of her now nearly empty messenger bag. Most of her makeup and sundries were scattered on Broad Street. A wave of dread washed over her. She felt her keys, but not her wallet. The conversation in the car faded as her ears started to buzz.

"What's wrong?" Tox laid a hand on her shoulder, sensing her distress.

"My wallet. It fell out of my bag when I dropped it."

Steady chimed in. "Forget it. It's gone by now. Do you have your bank's app? You can block your cards right now."

"Yeah, I'll do it when I get home. This work phone had a fight with the sidewalk and lost." She held up the shattered phone with two fingers.

Tox squeezed the shoulder he was still touching. His hand was so big his fingers touched her spine. "It's just a thing, Cal. Things can be replaced." He spoke like a man who had lost something that could not.

Calliope loved her name. She always corrected people when they shortened it or mispronounced it, but the endearment coming from this fierce giant warmed her as much as that big paw on her back. God, that hand felt good. She sighed.

"I know. It's just another inconvenience in a very inconvenient night."

Tox retrieved the cylinder that had once again rolled out of her bag and flipped it over one-handed. "Let me guess. A map to the secret vault where Phipps Van Gent has hidden billions in gold and the nuclear launch codes."

"No motherfucker named *Phipps* has nuclear launch codes," Steady grumbled. Chat chuckled. He was proving the irony of his nickname tonight. Other than answering Twitch's call, he had not uttered a word so far.

"Nothing even remotely that exciting," Calliope clarified as she took the tube. "Phipps got scammed in a poker game. He won what he thought was a valuable painting but turned out to be nothing." Calliope handed the cylinder back to Tox. "This is trash. I meant to put it in the recycling, but I got distracted."

Tox turned the tube over in his hand, then banged it on his thigh. "Mind if I take this? I have a leaky pipe in my kitchen and this might just do the trick."

"Sure thing. Glad to assist with your pipes."

Steady coughed into his closed fist. Tox gave her a look that nearly ignited her thong.

As they pulled up to her home, Chat spoke to her for the first time. "Calliope, do you have a security system?"

"Yes, of course."

"Make sure it's armed."

"Okay."

Tox gave her shoulder another comforting squeeze—although Calliope was beginning to think *comforting* wasn't quite the right word—and lifted his other hand in a motionless wave.

"Thanks for the ride guys." She addressed all of them but locked eyes with Tox.

Their black SUV idled at the curb until Calliope had climbed her exterior stairs, let herself inside, and waved through the glass sidelight.

Inside, Calliope turned to see her rottweiler, Coco, engaging in her wake up stretches: butt up, paws out, followed by back legs out behind her in a sploot. Coco produced a squeaky yawn and followed Calliope to the back of the house. Calliope lifted one foot in front of the other, suddenly overcome by profound fatigue. She aimed for the checkerboard porcelain tile floor of the kitchen. Depositing her cumbersome bag on the island she grabbed a bottle of water and headed for the stairs, the clittering of Coco's nails on the hardwood reassuring, the old stairs creaking as she mounted them.

Coco stopped on the landing and growled. Calliope noticed a strange, flickering light at the end of the upstairs hall. She stepped carefully, quietly, making her way toward the second-floor window overlooking the street. She finally breathed an inaudible sigh when she saw that a plastic grocery bag had hooked the neck of a streetlight, disrupting the beam each time the wind kicked up. She scratched Coco behind the ears as her trusty pet braced her front paws on the sill and gave a stern warning bark to the grocery bag.

"Come on, puppy. Let's get to bed."

Coco tossed another bark back at the offending bag and trotted into Calliope's bedroom. She was a docile, good-natured dog. She had once inadvertently caught a car thief when the perpetrator had misconstrued Coco's enthusiasm for a car ride as an attack. Coco's uninterrupted barking and pawing at the car door had delayed and distracted the man and caused such a ruckus, the car's owner came out to investigate. She napped in the sun, begged for belly rubs, and greeted visitors with a happy spin and a wet lick. But woe betide anyone who threatened Calliope while Coco was around. She may have been a sweet dog, but when it came to Calliope she could be a werewolf.